A Concise Introduction
to Music Listening

A Concise Introduction to Music Listening

Third Edition

Charles R. Hoffer
Indiana University

Wadsworth Publishing Company
A Division of Wadsworth, Inc.
Belmont, California

To the Armers: Bob, Clarice, Andy, and Erica

Available from your bookstore:

Record Album (a five-disc set prepared by Columbia Special Products, CBS Records, a Division of CBS Inc.)

Study Guide and Scores

Guide to Live Performances

Music Editor: Sheryl Fullerton
Production Editor: Patricia Brewer
Designer: Paula Shuhert
Cover Photograph: Roger Allyn Lee

Library of Congress Cataloging in Publication Data

Hoffer, Charles R.
  A concise introduction to music listening.

  Includes index.
  1. Music appreciation. I. Title.
MT6.H565C6 1984   780'.1'5   83-10262

ISBN 0-534-02947-7

Printed in the United States of America
1 2 3 4 5 6 7 8 9 10—88 87 86 85 84

Brief Contents

Detailed Contents

Preface

The third edition of *A Concise Introduction to Music Listening* retains the focus of its two predecessors. The book is still *concise*, which means it doesn't overburden students with detail; yet it surveys the entire world of music. Still an *introductory* book, it assumes students know little, if anything, about music. And it continues to emphasize *listening*, that elusive skill students need to become perceptive and interested listeners to any type of music—past, present, and future; simple and complex; Western and non-Western. This third edition capitalizes on these strengths and takes them a step further.

Content and Coverage

The third edition has been thoroughly reviewed and revised to make sure that it is accurate, timely, and balanced in coverage. The length of the book has been kept the same so that it will be just as manageable, economical, and useful for students and professors. While most of the chapters remain essentially unchanged, the third edition includes:

1. Revised and reorganized chapters on the materials of music, a portion of the course that is typically difficult and boring for many students. In this edition the various aspects of pitch are combined in one chapter, and rhythm, dynamics, and timbre are covered in another. The new arrangement presents the information more clearly and efficiently.

2. A new chapter on form, which explores more deeply how sounds are organized into musical works. Pachelbel's Kanon in D serves as the culminating example for the chapter.

3. A new, carefully constructed Chapter 1, which gives the students better insight into what they will be studying and why.

4. Several changes in the musical repertoire, thus offering better coverage. For example, a movement of Vivaldi's *The Four Seasons* now serves as an example of Baroque concertos, Mozart's Horn Concerto No. 3 fulfills the same role for concertos of the Classical period, and Puccini's *La Bohème* has become the representative of Romantic opera.

5. A greatly enlarged glossary of musical terms, each with a page reference to its appearance in the text.

Approach to the Subject

A Concise Introduction to Music Listening, Third Edition, approaches the subject of music by answering four basic questions:

What is music?

What is music made of?

What forms does music take?

What kinds of music have been created at various times and places?

After the opening chapters on the nature of music and on listening, the book's first major section presents the basic elements of music. The second major section examines music's various forms—songs, symphonies, keyboard works, and so on. The final section covers the stylistic periods of music and explores some significant types of music, including folk, jazz, and American music.

The organization of the book is basically nonchronological. However, the concluding section is devoted to style periods, an arrangement that offers students the opportunity to review, augment, and synthesize the information covered previously. This pattern of concept-to-history has been very helpful to students, as the success of the earlier editions has demonstrated. Those professors who prefer a chronological approach will find the new edition adaptable to their courses by incorporating the music in Section II into the appropriate style eras of Section III.

Listening

The core of the third edition remains its active, practical approach to teaching listening skill. All music appreciation texts urge their readers to listen better, but few do much to help students achieve that goal. Those few texts that require the use of a specially created set of recordings, which are useful but ultimately rigid and limiting, usually fail to provide enough information for the students to understand adequately what they hear. This third edition promotes the development of listening skill through:

1. Twenty "Listening Guides". These detailed, timed outlines "walk" students through the music, moment by moment. The guides not only point out important features to listen for, but also help the students to avoid becoming lost or confused as they listen.

2. A chapter on listening. Chapter 2 orients students to the process of listening and gives them eight suggestions for improving this skill.

3. *Record Album*. The five-disc set includes every work covered by a Listening Guide or contained in the supplementary *Study Guide and Scores* and is carefully keyed into the text.

4. *Study Guide and Scores*. This supplementary volume has listening practice exercises, one-line scores for six works, and a libretto for half an act from an opera, all of

which are covered in the text. These simple scores, which include information on form and translations of terms, give students something to follow as they listen so that they keep their attention on the music and its features.

5. *Guide to Live Performances.* This 20-page pamphlet (free to all students upon adoption) answers the most frequently asked questions by first-time concertgoers and provides them with a glossary of terms.

Acknowledgments

I would like to thank the following professors for their reviews of the manuscript: Ann Anderson, University of Minnesota; Charles Buffham, Grand Rapids Junior College; David Champion, California State University at Dominguez Hills; Richard C. Cole, Virginia Polytechnic Institute and State University; Robert Forman, San Diego State University; Aubrey S. Garlington, University of North Carolina at Greensboro; Robert B. Gregg, North Texas State University; Wynne Harrell, Southwest Missouri State University; Marie Henderson, University of Florida; Sara McFerrin, Fullerton College; Melvin N. Miles, Jr., Morgan State University; Larry M. Timm, California State University at Fullerton.

CHARLES R. HOFFER

A Concise Introduction
to Music Listening

1

Learning About Music

Almost all your life you have been hearing music. Probably as a youngster you sang songs, and in school you may have played an instrument or sung in a choral group. The chances are that you like music, at least some kinds of music. Now you are taking a course that has as one of its goals helping you to listen to music more fully and to like it better. Why? Do people need to be taught how to listen to music? Do they need to take a course to learn to enjoy it?

These questions are logical ones to ponder as you begin a music course. Not only are they logical, they also touch some basic points about music and people. They are worth exploring further.

Why Learn More About Music?

It is possible to know a little about music through casual contact with it, without ever having had any formal instruction. You can learn a few songs, listen superficially to music on the radio, and be familiar with one or two types of music. Although that limited understanding is better than nothing, it is only a small fraction of the potential enjoyment and enrichment a fuller experience with music can provide. It is something like the foreigner who assumes that a visit to one city in the United States is a rather complete involvement with America and its people. In short, people should learn more about music because there is a whole world of music that no one should miss out on.

What's so bad about missing out on some music? That question is best answered by imagining that you had to live in another culture. Suppose, for example, that you moved to India. Like most Americans, you would find Indian music difficult to understand and appreciate. However, if you have to live there, you should learn something about its music, because if you don't, you will be even more an outsider in Indian life. You will find your existence in India a little duller, shallower, and less satisfying. Although an ignorance of music does not ruin one's life, it does reduce its quality.

What Should Be Learned in Music?

If you and other college students who are not music majors should become better informed about music, what do you need to learn in a music appreciation course? Three things. First, you should learn to listen to music intelligently and perceptively; you need to be able to hear what is happening in a musical work. Second, you should learn some basic information about music—its styles, forms, terminology, and other information that contributes to a fundamental knowledge of the subject. Third, you should develop positive attitudes toward music.

Each of these three areas of learning—listening skill, basic information, and positive attitudes—is vital. The information presented in a book or course is rather useless if you are unable to hear what is happening in the music; you can't appreciate what you don't hear. Listening skill by itself is of limited value, however, if you have no idea where the piece fits into the world of music, what the techniques used in it are, what their effects are, and what music as a fine art is all about. That is why some information is needed. The third goal of positive attitudes is equally important, because information and listening skills are largely wasted if you end up disliking music and avoiding it whenever possible.

Therefore, in this course you can expect to gain information that will help you understand music better and to work at improving your ability to hear various aspects of music. As you acquire greater knowledge and listening skill, your feelings about music will become more positive. A cycle will be started in which greater feelings of competency about music lead to more positive attitudes, which in turn lead to greater competency, and so on.

What Is Art Music?

The word *music* refers to a wide variety of pieces that have been created for many different reasons. Many of the different uses of music are already familiar to you. In a motion picture the background music contributes to the mood of the scenes. Religious ceremonies are made more effective through the use of music. Certain pieces of music may be used to promote unity in a group or nation; the song "We Shall Overcome" sung by the civil rights workers in the 1960s is but one of many instances of music being employed in this way. People sometimes use music (or clothing or hair styles) to help identify themselves with a certain social group. Teenagers who learn certain pieces of music because other teenagers know and like those pieces are examples of this use of music. People use music to vent deep feelings; black spirituals are examples of such music. At other times people enjoy music merely as recreation and diversion; singing "Ninety-Nine Bottles of Beer on the Wall" while riding on a school bus is an example of recreational music. Many Americans use music as "sonic background" to activities such as driving a car, studying, and jogging. Although not common in America, in many parts of the world people use music to accompany physical work such as paddling a canoe or harvesting crops. All these uses of music have one thing in common: Music is being used to promote or accompany something else; it is secondary to some other purpose.

One type of music differs from those just

Copyright © 1958 by United Feature Syndicate, Inc.
Used by permission.

mentioned in that it exists *only* for the intellectual and psychological satisfaction it provides. This is music intended for careful listening—period. Such music is called *art music*, although it is more often called "classical" music by nonmusicians. People listen to art music simply for the satisfaction and enjoyment of doing so. They value the experience of hearing interesting organizations of sounds; they have no practical reason or purpose beyond listening to it. It exists only for what it is, a point that Schroeder can't seem to get across to Lucy in the "Peanuts" cartoon above.

Like Lucy, many people find it difficult to understand that music can be important in and of itself. How can something have value if it doesn't do anything for us? It is true that most things are created because we have some practical use for them. But art music and the other *fine arts* are different. Painting, sculpture, ballet, poetry, literature, and music exist only for the interest and fascination people find in them. They have psychological—not functional—importance.

Why do people create nonfunctional objects whose value lies solely in intellectual and psychological satisfaction? No one knows for sure, although there are a number of interesting speculative theories. One thing is known, however: Such creations are a distinctly human activity. The valuing of objects for their artistic satisfaction seems to call for a higher form of mental activity than animals possess. As far as can be determined, animals have no sonnets, sonatas, or sculptures.

A basic difference between humans and animals is represented by the difference between the words *exist* and *live*. People want to do more than exist. They don't want only to survive in a cave and grub roots for food; they want a richer and more satisfying life than that. They notice sights and sounds and have feelings about them, and they find life more interesting because of these feelings.

The arts are not human beings' only attempt to live rather than exist. Recreation—playing tennis or cards, for example—is also an attempt to enjoy life. The difference between recreation and contemplation of the arts is that the arts involve a type of thinking. They call for an approach of mentally standing back and carefully considering an object for the qualities it possesses, something that is not an aspect of recreation.

Why is the word *fine* coupled with the term *arts*? To answer that question, think back to your elementary school days when you decorated a paper plate or carved a figure on a potato for block printing. Would you consider these efforts to be fine works of art? Probably not. Why? Weren't they sincere human creations? Well, yes, but they weren't really *that* good. Most people can do as well. The arts-craft project didn't represent unusual skill, devotion, or talent, at least not enough to be considered "fine" or to be valued as something above and beyond the ordinary. If nearly everyone can do something, it may be art, but it is not fine art. Epic poems, symphonies, and marble sculptures, when skillfully created, are of value partly because very few people have the talent and energy to create them.

Why Learn About Art Music?

The information presented in a music appreciation course about melody, rhythm, and form is useful for almost all types of music. In a sense, music is music, and when you learn something about one kind of music it often can be applied to other types.

As you may have suspected, however, the greater share of this course will involve learning about and listening to works of art music. Why? One reason has to do with the various uses of music, a topic discussed earlier in this chapter. When a piece of music is secondary to some other purpose (group solidarity, sonic background, and so on), the quality of the music is not so important. It is not usually considered carefully in terms of its sound qualities. A piece of art music, however, lives or dies solely on its musical qualities. For this reason the composer and performer pour their best efforts into the sounds that make up the work. They know that careful attention will be paid to them.

Because a piece of art music must stand on its own, it is usually somewhat more complex and requires more careful and thoughtful listening than other music, which brings us to the second reason for studying art music. Such music requires some knowledge and listening skill in order to understand and appreciate it. In a sense, an appreciation of art music is a "cultivated taste," something like a fine gourmet dinner or a beautiful, ancient Greek vase. Most works of art music do not reach out and "grab" the uninitiated listener; instead they require some education and a little getting used to.

There is a third reason for studying art music. Because its works are created only to be listened to, they tend to provide greater listening satisfaction and interest than pieces created for some other purpose. More things happen to sounds in them, which makes them more interesting and challenging to hear.

"I Know What I Like"

Does gaining new knowledge and listening skill mean that you should discard the music you now prefer, which may not be the type studied in this course? Not at all. The course will probably result in an expansion of the types of music you know and like, but no one will urge you to give up any kind of music. Instead, the goal is to broaden your musical horizons, which will offer you more and richer musical choices.

It's a fact: People generally like what they know and avoid what they don't know. If there be truth in the phrase "I know what I like," there is also truth in the phrase "I like what I know." This is partly because people don't hear unfamiliar types of music accurately or fully; they simply miss a lot the unfamiliar music has to offer. Another reason people prefer what they know is that they feel more comfortable and competent with it. An unfamiliar type of music may make you somewhat uncomfortable because you can't make much sense of it, and that encourages self-doubt about your capabilities in handling it.

To demonstrate how a familiar style affects your reaction to music, the *Record Album* that supplements this book contains two versions of "Jesu, Joy of Man's Desiring" by J. S. Bach (Record 1,A). Bach's version has no accompanying rhythmic backup, while the contemporary one (which is called "Joy") does. Also, you are probably accustomed to the electric guitar and piano heard in "Joy," which is the shorter and simpler of the two. Listen to these works and then compare your reactions to them. Chances are you will prefer the version that is more familiar in style. But don't cross off Bach's version yet. More will be said about it in Chapter 17.

The fact that knowledge and preference are two sides of the same coin has some important implications for students in a music course. First, you should know something about a type of music before deciding whether or not you like it. Be a student first and a judge only after you are well informed about the type of music being heard. Next, remember that there are no inherently inferior types of music, only types that are unfamiliar to you. (Individual pieces within a certain type may be inferior to others in quality, however.) Third, keep in mind the purpose or role of the music you are hearing, because that knowledge should affect how you listen to it. Folk songs should not be judged in terms of concert music, and vice versa.

This chapter has presented the view that music is more than just a pleasant diversion or a background for other activities. In a way that no one fully understands, skillfully organized sounds are important to human beings. Such music exists for its artistic qualities, and it is often profound and complex. Learning to listen to and understand this music will be a challenge. Fortunately, the effort is well worth making. Music is one of mankind's great accomplishments, and it offers people who listen to and understand it much richness and enjoyment.

2

Learning to Listen

While in college I had the good fortune to take an art appreciation course. One day the instructor projected a Rembrandt painting on the wall and proceeded to point out Rembrandt's genius in his treatment of light and shadow, the overall design, the brushwork for the hands of one of the figures, and similar features. After 15 or 20 minutes I was struck by the fact that every feature of the painting was there when I had first looked at it. They were there before his explanation, but I hadn't been aware of them; I had looked but not really seen. I realized then that I needed to be taught to see all that a fine painting has to offer.

It is similar with music. Most people need to be educated to hear what a fine piece of music has to offer in terms of listening satisfaction. The purpose of this chapter is to provide such help.

Attitude

It may seem strange to make attitude the first requirement for appreciation of an art. But it is essential. You are the only person who can make yourself pay attention, who can center your listening on one part of the music, who can make yourself remember a musical pattern. No book or instructor can do this for you.

What makes up the attitude necessary for increased musical understanding? One part of it is the willingness to make an effort. It requires effort to move beyond a superficial acquaintance with music and to understand what it has to offer. Diligence and concentration are necessary while learning.

A second aspect of attitude is the acknowledgment that you are dealing with something subtle and complex. If a musical work is too simple, too obvious, it won't be successful as art music. Certainly an art that reaches to the very roots of people's psychological nature isn't going to be understood all at once.

Another feature of proper attitude is tolerance toward all music. Much of the music discussed in this book may be new to you and some of it may seem strange. But if you are open-minded, if you assume the integrity of the creative artist and give yourself a chance to understand the work, your chances of learning to like the music are greatly increased.

Perhaps the most fundamental feature of attitude is a basic interest in hearing and understanding what composers do with sound. How do they organize it? What are they trying to do with it? Factual knowledge may help you answer these questions, but it can't replace careful listening.

Learning to listen is a matter more of wanting to understand the music than learning the techniques for understanding music. Without the desire and effort no amount of technique will succeed.

Types of Listening

There are three somewhat interrelated types of listening. The first can be termed *sensuous*. This delicious word means "of or appealing to the senses." In music it refers to the purely physical effect that music has on its listeners—the chill running up the spine, the tapping of the foot, the sheer pleasure of a beautiful sound.

Hearing is an action involving a sense organ and sounds are physical in nature. So the sensuous pleasures of music are not intellectually profound. They are not to be downgraded, however. There is real pleasure to be gained from listening to even a single long tone on a violin or a French horn, just as there is pleasure in looking at a beautiful blue color in a picture. Sensuous pleasures are one of music's attractions, and the more you are aware of them the more you will enjoy music.

It is a mistake to think that sensuous effects are the main thing in music. An emphasis only on sensuous qualities eliminates from consideration many musical works of much merit. What's worse, a dependence on sensuous effects leads to a dead end. The listener grows accustomed to one effect and so searches for another piece with even greater physical impact.

This cycle leads finally to music that is simply orgiastic. When music reaches this point, it has lost most of its artistic quality. Music of lasting value is more than an aural roller-coaster ride or cold shower.

The second type of listening involves feeling or mood. It is sometimes called *expressive*. There can be little doubt that music has expressive power. Music frequently can relate to something the listener thinks or feels. A particular phrase may evoke a psychological reaction similar to the reaction to some event in life. But music is limited in its ability to designate specific thoughts that can be put into words. For example, music may give an impression of sadness, but it cannot describe what is causing the feeling. Nor can it define objects. For most people, one sound does not represent *clouds*, another *bread*, and another *wheel*. Music can provide general moods but not specific thoughts.

The indefiniteness of music is to its advantage. One musical work may be heard by a thousand people, but each will hear it in a slightly different way, depending on the individual's inclinations. But even more important, music can break through the limitations of words. Words are too brittle, too inflexible, too conventional to allow for full expression. Between the words *anger* and *rage*, for example, there are infinite shades of meaning. Also, anger is usually coupled with frustration or sadness, or both. As a feeling becomes more complex, it is harder to describe. When a loved one dies, a person feels emptiness, grief, remorse, powerlessness, and much more. But these feelings cannot be fully communicated to someone else, no matter how many words are used or how carefully the words are chosen.

The third type of listening involves concentrating on what happens in the music—what notes are being played, at what speed, in combination with what other notes, on what instruments in what range, and so on. This type is often called *musical*, and it is in this type of listening that the more musical values are realized. Here the listener reaches the most sophisticated type of musical experience, a type in which understanding of the sounds and their characteristics is unhampered by physical response or a search for expressive meaning.

Achievement of this type of listening requires more education, but it also offers greater rewards. So this book concentrates primarily on making it possible for you to listen to music in this way.

Improving Listening Skill

There are several things you can do to increase your listening ability. The suggestions here are general, and they are not presented in order of importance.

1. *Improve your memory for music.* Memory is absolutely necessary for the comprehension of music. At any particular instant all that can be heard is one sound. This may be a single tone or several tones occurring simultaneously. In any case, it can be perceived only briefly, for time moves on and other sounds are heard in succeeding moments. The only way to make sense out of these brief and apparently isolated aural impressions is to use the phenomena of memory and anticipation. Even anticipation is a memory activity in that it involves a prediction of what will happen in the future based on what has been presented in the past.

Visual experiences do not rely basically on the element of time. The graphic arts, for example, aren't involved in time. An entire picture can be seen in a moment. (Closer analysis and full appreciation requires a longer period of viewing, of course.) But suppose that memory and anticipation are made an integral part of looking at a painting. It might be done as follows: Assume you are to see an unfamiliar picture that is entirely covered except for a thin slit running vertically. Then the slit is drawn slowly across the picture. Your knowledge of the picture will have to be derived solely from (1) your memory of what you have seen, (2) the slit-sized portion you are presently viewing, and (3) your guess as to what will be revealed in succeeding moments. Difficult? Yes. But that's the way music is perceived. That is why memory is so necessary in understanding it.

As a general rule, the more frequently you engage in an activity involving memory, the better your skill at recall will become. Think again of the picture analogy. The fifth time the slit is drawn across the picture, you will have a much clearer idea of what the picture is like. The same is true of music. The more you hear a piece, the better you will remember it and the more fully you will understand it. Repeated hearings of a musical work are about the surest way to gain greater understanding of it. In fact, with many musically interesting works, repeated hearings are necessary in order to reach a satisfactory degree of understanding.

Sometime when you are listening to a recording by yourself, select a short portion and listen to it several times. This practice is especially useful in places that sound like a jumble of sound to you. Between playings attempt to run through the portion in your mind. Shut your eyes and try to rehear in your own mind what you previously heard. Repeat this process of actual and imagined hearings until your mental rendition of the portion is accurate.

2. *Concentrate on main themes and the important musical ideas.* When listening to a work that is new to you, especially if you are not particularly experienced at listening to art music, don't try to comprehend everything the first time. Learning to listen is like learning to drive a car. When you first learn to drive, your total attention is directed toward executing a few basic actions; your primary goal is to keep the car on the road and avoid hitting other cars or pedestrians. With increased experience, however, you find you can safely do other things— glance at the scenery or carry on a conversation with a passenger. Had you tried to do all this too early in your training, a catastrophe might have occurred!

How can you distinguish the important features of a piece before hearing it? In this book the main themes and sections are indicated for you. A "roadmap" or "guided tour" of the composition is provided in 20 Listening Guides. If you are listening at a concert or to a recording of a work not covered here, you can read the notes on the concert program or record jacket. Such commentary can be quite helpful, if it is well written.

3. *Hear as much detail as possible.* Although following single aspects of the music is helpful, don't stop there. Musical works written for artistic reasons have many inflections, many subtleties. And as in other phases of life, it is often the little things that make the difference. A slightly changed chord, a brief interruption of the rhythmic pattern, a new combination of instruments, the sounding of a fragment of the theme—such apparently insignificant techniques can spell the difference between an ordinary piece and an exceptional one.

The overriding reason for hearing as much as possible in a musical work is that the com-

Listening Guide

Copland: *Rodeo*, "Hoe-Down"   *Record 1,A*

0:00	Orchestra begins at loud dynamic level and fast tempo; repeats the following figure several times:

0:04	Trumpets and violins exchange a short figure.
0:14	Orchestra plays opening figure again at loud dynamic level.
0:18	Piano and strings play plucked note patterns that emphasize note off the beat and simple chord changes; woodblock heard.
0:40	First phrase of first theme (*A*) played by upper strings, clarinets, and xylophone; theme includes opening figure:

0:48	Violins begin a "square-dance"–like phrase of the melody; brasses and low strings sound chords in off-beat pattern:

0:56	First phrase of theme returns, played by upper strings and xylophone.

poser intends for *everything* to be heard.

4. Encourage your reactions to music. This suggestion should *not* be taken to mean that you should emote or talk to yourself when hearing a piece. Rather, be aware of your feelings about

what you hear and let them be active. Consciously notice your responses while listening.

To notice your own reactions to sounds, try this experiment. In a quiet place play on a piano or guitar a series of three or four sounds. Listen for about 3 seconds between groups of sounds to allow you to contemplate what you

1:04   Second phrase of theme played by violins; followed by oboe and then orchestra; chords off the beat are also heard in brasses and low strings.

1:20   First phrase played again by upper strings, clarinets, and xylophone.

1:36   Opening figure played several times by orchestra.

1:40   Trumpet solo, answered by upper strings, is new theme (*B*):

1:48   Oboe, violin, and clarinet solos continue the *B* theme, followed by trumpet and violins.

2:04   Winds play off-beat figure; answered by violins, idea repeated three more times.

2:13   Violins, oboes, and clarinets begin a second "square-dance" tune; music increases in intensity leading to a sudden break.

2:26   Piano and plucked strings play short section heard very early in the work; music grows softer, slower, and descends in pitch.

2:51   A theme, first phrase, returns in violins, xylophone, and clarinets; loud dynamic level.

2:59   Second phrase of theme *A* played at loud level by strings and oboe; brasses and low strings sound chords in off-beat pattern.

3:12   First phrase of *A* theme played again by upper strings; followed by off-beat notes for low strings and French horns and xylophone, and then by even notes for strings and trumpet.

3:29   Closes with same note sounded rapidly and loudly three times.

heard. You probably won't be able to describe exactly what you feel about the sounds, but you will have some response. Experiencing your reactions when you listen is one of music's appealing activities. In musical compositions, of course, the sounds come at you rapidly, with few silent spots in which to analyze your reactions. Single sounds heard in a gapped series soon become boring.

5. Do not attempt to visualize specific scenes or fantasize. Sometimes students in elementary school are given listening lessons dealing almost exclusively with "program" music—music in which the composer consciously attempts to associate the work with a particular story or scene. This type of music is in many ways well suited to the requirements of guided listening experiences in the early grades. Unfortunately, however, students sometimes begin to assume that for every piece there must be a picture or story. They conclude that music is incomplete or inadequate if it exists alone.

As was pointed out earlier, the best music is most fascinating in terms of its sounds. Trying to conjure a tender love scene or the image of a ship plowing through the waves only distracts the listener's attention from the sound of the music itself. Instead of listening, the mind is engaged in creating fantasies. Pictorial association can also easily become an invitation to daydream. Only keen concentration on the music itself will lead to an understanding of it.

6. Acquire some different listening habits and expectations. By the time they are 18 or so, most people have become very good at *not* listening carefully to music. Music is around us everywhere—in supermarkets, airports, our cars; even the home or dormitory is not without the radio or record player going as dishes are washed or studying attempted. The trouble is that we learn not to pay attention to all that music and sound; we would be mentally exhausted if we tried.

People also have acquired expectations about what music is like. It contains a steady background rhythm, is quite loud, lasts about 2 minutes and 30 seconds, states its musical ideas right off and does not attempt to develop or vary them to any extent. However, many works of music, especially art music, violate all these expectations. Musical ideas are strung out over many minutes, as if the music were progressing in slow motion. The music is often soft and subtle. Musical ideas are not stated obviously, and they are often subjected to all sorts of manipulation and variation. Therefore, if you are going to listen to art music more effectively in the future, it will be necessary to shake off some of the habits and expectations that you have acquired about music over the past 15 or more years.

7. Apply the knowledge you acquire about music to the music you hear. Information about musical forms, styles, compositional devices, and the like can help you listen more effectively to music. Knowledge *and* listening skill are both needed.

Information about music will also help you avoid the disappointment of listening for qualities in a musical work that were not intended in the first place. For example, Mozart wrote music that is tasteful, well designed, and beautiful. He lived in an age that esteemed the tasteful, the well designed, and the beautiful; big, powerful effects were not in style. So if you listen to his music expecting to be overwhelmed by lush harmonies and sensuous melodies, you will be disappointed.

8. Practice learning to listen to music more effectively. If you have decided that you want to improve your skill in listening to music (the matter of attitude mentioned earlier in the chapter), you need to practice listening just as you would practice tennis if you wanted to improve your game. This book offers two ways to practice listening. The 20 Listening Guides that appear at various places in the book provide an outline of the main features of a work, such as changes of melody, prominent solos, and so on. On the left-hand side of the guide appears the time at which the feature will appear in the recording in the supplementary *Record Album*.* Other recordings will have similar but not identical timings. The times offer an idea of how soon something in the music will happen. The numbers can also serve as a way for instructors in class to identify a place in the work. Whether or not you keep track of the times as you listen is a matter of personal preference.

Listen to the recording while following the Listening Guide as many times as you need to be able to follow along without losing your place. When you can listen and hear most of the points listed in the guide, you can be reasonably sure that you are hearing the main features of the work, although the more subtle aspects may remain to be uncovered by later listening efforts. Probably it is not wise to listen to any work more than twice in one day; spread the listening practice out over a number of days by doing a little bit each day rather than "cramming" immediately before examinations.

The first Listening Guide, on pages 10–11, is for Aaron Copland's "Hoe-Down" from his ballet *Rodeo*. That work will be discussed in more detail in Chapter 14, but you can begin listening practice now with this work.

The second way this book helps you practice listening is through the simplified line scores that appear in the supplementary *Study Guide and Scores*. These scores take the 20 or more lines of an orchestral score and reduce them to one or sometimes two lines that present the most noticeable and significant aspect of the music at that point. Also, they indicate the instruments heard most clearly and describe the form and other features. While you may not be able to read music, you will probably be able to follow a line score as you listen. As with the Listening Guides, it is suggested that you listen

as many times as needed until you can follow the music without getting lost.

Tests of Good Listening

How can you tell if you are hearing a piece of music fully and accurately? There is no easy answer, but you can ask yourself these practical questions:

Does the music seem sensible in its own way?

Does it move along without seeming dead and stagnant?

Am I hearing specific details of form, rhythm, and melody?

Have I kept my attention focused on the music all the time?

Do I get some reactions or feelings from the music as I hear it?

Do I like to listen to the music? Do I enjoy it? Does it seem interesting?

Do I want to hear the work again?

If your answer to all these questions is yes, there can be little doubt that you are listening to the music rather fully. Composers intend their music to be enjoyed, to be found interesting and meaningful. They mean for their skill at handling music to be appreciated, and they want to produce something that will have lasting attraction. In most cases they realize that music will cause reactions in the listener. When you hear the music fully and with feeling, you are understanding it.

---

*Time notations are given in minutes and seconds. For example, 2:30 means 2 minutes, 30 seconds.

I
SECTION ONE
The Ingredients of Music

The question of what music is made of is a logical place to begin a study of the subject. Since you already know something about music, you might try this short quiz about the elements that are combined to form music. Decide whether the following statements are true or false.

1. A musical work must include high and low notes. *T   F*

2. All music proceeds through a period of time. *T   F*

3. All musical works tell a story or describe something in everyday life. *T   F*

4. Every sound has some level of loudness. *T   F*

5. In order to be considered "music," sounds must be written down in notation. *T   F*

6. All sounds have some type of tone quality. *T   F*

7. Musical sounds must be organized. *T   F*

8. Music must have a pulse or throb that you can tap your foot to. *T   F*

9. A change in any element of music (speed, tone quality, loudness, etc.) affects the overall impression of the music. *T   F*

10. Because the physical properties of sound can be measured scientifically, music can be judged scientifically. *T   F*

Five of the statements are true and five are false. Each one will be answered at an appropriate place in the next three chapters. What is significant here is that each item relates to what is necessary for music. An understanding of each musical element aids in knowing more about music. So the first section of this book discusses each element in some detail.

Christ in the Storm on the Lake of Galilee *by Rembrandt van Ryn. (Isabella Stewart Gardner Museum, Boston.)*

3

The Materials of Music: Melody, Harmony, and Texture

Music is one form of sound. Quite a lot is known about sound. A stimulus acts to set in motion the molecules in the air. The molecules bump into one another, something like billiard balls on a table, each setting the next in motion. This chain reaction continues until the molecules strike the eardrum, where the nervous system picks up the impulses and transmits them to the brain. But not all sounds are music. So merely exploring the physical nature of sound is not going to answer the question of what is necessary for music.

Pitch and Melody

Music usually (but not always) contains sounds of different *pitch*. Pitch in music refers to the quality of highness or lowness of sound. It depends on the frequency of the molecular vibrations. The faster the motion of the molecules, the higher the pitch is.

A *melody* is a cohesive series or line of pitches. These pitches must "hang together" if the melody is to be any good. Not any series of pitches will do. Whether a series of pitches seems cohesive or not depends on the perception and mental ability of the individual hearing the sounds, not on some law in nature. Since no one understands the processes of the brain precisely, it is impossible to determine scientifically if a series of pitches forms a melody. So statement 10 on page 14 is false. Music has physical properties that can be measured scientifically, but it's much more than that.

Although most music involves different pitches and some type of melody, these elements aren't necessary in every musical work. Some sounds of indefinite pitch have been placed on tape as musical compositions. Also, some musical instruments, such as snare drums, have no definite pitch, as is mentioned in Chapter 6, yet they can play solos of considerable complexity and interest. So the first statement on page 14 is false. Most compositions have higher and lower notes, but they are not always necessary.

Intervals. The word *interval* refers to the distance between two pitches. If the two notes are on the same line or space on the music, the interval is a prime or unison. If the two are on an adjoining line and space, an interval of a second exists. The interval from one line to the next or from one space to the next, either above or below, is a third, and so on. The designation of intervals is further refined by labels of *major* and *minor*, plus some othe terms, but this additional designation is of little value to the nonmusician.

Scales. A *scale* is a series of pitches that proceeds upward or downward according to a prescribed pattern of intervals. It is the underlying pattern or "skeleton" of pitches on which the music is built. A scale can be extracted from the music, but it seldom appears intact in a melody. (One exeption is "Joy to the World.") The most prominent note in a scale—step 1 in most scales—is the key center.

Some pieces are known by the name of their key—Prelude in F Sharp Minor, for example. This is a means of identification, and it indicates the importance with which keys were regarded at one time in the history of music. The ability to play scales well is an important part of an instrumentalist's development as a performer. (That's why instrumentalists practice scales so much.) Although the listener doesn't need a detailed knowledge of scales, some information about them does aid in understanding music.

Theoretically, thousands of scales are possible, but only a few are prevalent today. The basis of these standard scales is the *octave*. An octave is the distance between two pitches, one

being either double or half the number of vibrations of the other pitch. Not only do the notes of an octave sound similar, they also bear the same letter name. This is why only seven letters of the alphabet are needed for note names. The eighth note in an eight-tone scale must match the first in sound and name, no matter what note the scale begins. An octave can be split up into any number of pitches, but in the music of Western civilization the division of an octave into 12 equal parts or half steps has been standard for the last several hundred years.

A scale composed of all 12 tones is called a *chromatic* scale. None of its notes is more important than another. Because it conveys no feeling of tonic or "home," the chromatic scale is never the basis for an entire piece of music. (Some styles make use of all 12 tones equally, but they are not built on the chromatic scale, and they have no tonic.)

The two scales most common in Western countries today each involve all seven letters of the musical alphabet in some form. The differences among scales result from adjustments in the pattern of these seven notes. The most frequent pattern is called *major*. It can be played on the piano by sounding consecutively all the white keys from C to C. If you look at the keyboard on page 282, you will see that the white keys E–F and B–C are not separated by a black key. This means they are closer together in pitch than the other white keys. The placement of these *half steps* or *semitones* determines the type of scale. In a major scale the half steps occur between the third and fourth notes and the seventh and eighth notes.

Every *minor* scale has a half step occurring between the second and third notes, rather than between the third and fourth notes. The basic form of a minor scale can be duplicated on the piano by playing on the white keys consecutively from one A to another A. This pattern of whole and half steps is called *natural* minor. There are other types of minor scales involving alterations of the sixth and seventh steps of the scale.

Other types of scale patterns using the same seven notes within the octave are heard in Western music. These patterns are called *modes*. Until about 1600 they were more common than major and minor, but they fell into disuse until the twentieth century. Today they are heard about as often as major and minor, and in popular songs they have regained the lead. The various modes can be played on the piano by sounding the white keys from D to D, E to E, F to F, and G to G. (The mode from B to B is almost never used. Play it and you will hear why.)

Any scale or mode can be moved or *transposed* to notes other than the ones mentioned above as long as the pattern is retained. This requires adding one or more black keys and omitting one or more white keys.

Melodies

For some pieces—especially pieces known as songs, including popular songs—the melody is synonymous with the piece itself. It *is* the piece. So the quality of the melody and the quality of the music are often virtually the same thing. If the melody isn't attractive or can't be remembered, the piece simply does not make it as music. In art music this is less likely to be true. Art music composers are frequently more interested in the overall musical effect than in the quality of the melody; they are seeking to do something more than create a catchy tune. They see the melody as important not only for its own qualities but also for its potential manipulation.

A melody can be a unifying thread in a long musical work. Such a melody is often called a *theme*, to indicate its place as a central musical idea for a piece. A theme may or may not be a highly attractive series of pitches. The world of music contains many examples of average tunes that have become the central idea for great works. In other words, a theme is good not so much because of *what it is* but because of *how it is developed and what it becomes*.

Melodies are affected by a number of musical factors. First, melodies are played on an instrument or sung. The features of the voice or instrument—its tone quality and adaptability to the requirements of the melody—contribute to or detract from the effect of the melody itself. Second, since melodies must exist in a dimension of time, they all have rhythm. Third, most melodies tend to center around one particular pitch. There is a sense in which music moves away from and returns to a "home" pitch. More will be said about this important fact in the discussion of harmony later in this chapter. Fourth, other music usually precedes and follows the melody, and this musical context influences the listener's impression of the melody. Fifth, almost all melodies have other pitches sounded with them. The kind of accompaniment or the nature of melodies occurring at the same time can make a big difference in the musical results. So statement 9 on page 14 is true.

Melodies have several aspects that make them intriguing in themselves.

Range. The term *range* refers to the upper and lower pitch limits of a melody. Two extremes of range can be demonstrated by the two melodies in the first movement* of Igor Stravinsky's *Symphony of Psalms*, which is included in the *Record Album* (Record 5,A). The first melody in this work begins in the singers' parts about 34 seconds into the music. (A fragment of it is heard earlier in the orchestra.) Its two different pitches are only a half step apart. The second theme also appears in the singers' parts about 1:41 from the beginning. It opens with a leap of an octave and soon moves down nearly an octave. This is a wide range for a vocal melody, although "The Star-Spangled Banner" is even more extreme, with a range of 1½ octaves. Most songs stay within a range of an octave.

Register. The term *register* refers to the general pitch level of the melody. Some are in a low

---

*A movement is a large independent section of a musical work.

register, while others are in a high register. And of course, the same melody may appear in different registers at different times. This depends on the wishes of the composer-arranger. Some melodies seem more suited to one register than to another. A masculine melody seems out of character when played high, and a birdlike song seems inappropriate in a low register.

Length. Melodies come in all sorts of lengths. Some are short, like the first theme from Stravinsky's *Symphony of Psalms.* The first theme from Brahms' Second Piano Concerto is longer. Some works have a melody that seems nearly continuous, yet it never quite repeats itself.

Contour. Contour is the shape of a melody in terms of pitch. The contour of the first theme from the first movement of Brahms' Second Piano Concerto is (see page 90):

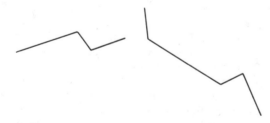

The contour for the first theme from the first movement of Stravinsky's *Symphony of Psalms* is:

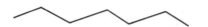

As you can see from the contour drawings of these works, there is no one shape for a melody. Some are rough in contour, some are smooth. Some start high and end low, while others do just the opposite. Some don't move much at all, while others jump around.

Steps and leaps. Melodies exhibit wide variety in their movement to other pitches. Some move

largely to adjacent notes. Stravinsky's first theme from the *Symphony of Psalms* moves only by half steps. The second theme from that work demonstrates some wide leaps.

Prominence of melody. There is also variance in the prominence given the melody in different musical works. Sometimes the melody is clearly heard while the accompaniment stays very much in the background. At other times the melody is just part of a total fabric of sound.

Fragments and motives. Some melodies seem to be made up of several small segments that have been combined to form a larger melody. As the music progresses, the composer takes one of the fragments and uses it as a unifying element in the composition. When a fragment is so treated, it is called a *motive.* To be musically effective, the motive needs to have a characteristic interval or rhythmic pattern that helps the listener to remember it. Many art music composers are gifted at pulling motives from melodies and unifying long pieces of music with them.

Embellishment. Some melodies are as solid and basic as a rock. Other melodies are laced with filigree and decoration. In some types of music the composer adds special symbols that call for decorative figures. The Sarabande from *English Suite* No. 2 by J. S. Bach presents two versions of the same melody, one rather plain and the other much more decorated (see page 105).

Chord outline. Chords are generally formed by combining the pitches of every other letter in the musical alphabet—A C E, D F A, E G B, and so on. Because this every-other pattern is such an integral aspect of music, it appears in melodies as well as in chords. Of course, in melodies the pitches are sounded one after another. Not all such melodies exhibit a chord outline so clearly as "The Star-Spangled Banner" or "The Blue Danube Waltz," but chords are sometimes rather strongly implied.

Style of performance. The impression you get of a melody is affected a great deal by how it is performed. The opening solo in Brahms' Second Piano Concerto gives the impression of a flowing, songlike melody. But when the orchestra takes up the same theme after the piano solo, the music has a marchlike character. This change can be clearly heard in the recording in the *Record Album* at about 1:27 into the work. Brahms makes this change of style to achieve variety in his music.

The opening theme of Brahms' Second Piano Concerto can serve as a summary of the points presented about melodies. The scale, which in this case is B flat, is not fully present, but it is strongly implied. All notes except two, A and G, are there. The half step occurs between the third and fourth steps (D and E flat in the key of B flat), so the music is in major.

The range is one octave, and the opening solo is in the middle register of the piano. The melody contains two phrases, with the second serving somewhat as an answer to the first. The first phrase ascends; the second descends. Each phrase has the same rhythmic pattern. The melody is beautifully designed, with the two halves balancing each other and providing a symmetry in sound. The melody is of moderate length. Most of its movement is to adjacent notes except the leaps at the end of the first phrase and the opening and ending of the second. It is very prominent in the piece; in fact, it is the only thing going on for a while. Later in the work Brahms extracts a motive of the first three notes, the same three that begin the song "Do-Re-Mi." The melody doesn't outline a chord, but the notes that make up the tonic chord are strongly present. They are marked with an X in the example.

There is, however, something about a melody that defies analysis, something that goes beyond range, phrase design, and contour. A good melody contains just the right combina-

tion of rhythmic patterns, pitches, and all the other aspects. And on this last indefinable quality Brahms' melody scores easily as a musical entity of interest and substance.

Counterpoint

Pitches are frequently sounded together in music. One way in which this happens is for two melodies to be sounded at the same time, or for the same melody to be sounded at two slightly different times, as in *rounds* such as "Row, Row, Row Your Boat" and "Are You Sleeping?" The term for such simultaneous sounding of two or more melodies is *counterpoint. Counter* implies contrary or contrasting, and *point* is a carryover from hundreds of years ago when musical notes were called points. The adjective form of counterpoint is *contrapuntal.*

Counterpoint involves the combining of independent lines of music. Usually it is not as clear-cut as the appearance of two well-known songs at the same time. Sometimes one of the lines is harder to remember than the other. Sometimes the contrasting line is not a full-fledged melody but rather a repeated figure—an ostinato; this is true of Stravinsky's *Symphony of Psalms.* When the first melody begins, the bassoons (the instruments playing the lowest notes during this portion of the music) repeat the figure five times in succession, and then return to it several more times before the first theme closes.

Often a line of counterpoint is added to a melody. The additional line contrasts with the main melody. If the notes of the melody are slow, the line of counterpoint often has faster moving notes; if the melody is plain and simple, the added contrapuntal line is more decorative.

Harmony

The other way to sound pitches together is to create *harmony*. Harmony is somewhat like the scenery on a stage. It adds to the total effect, but your main attention isn't centered on it. Most of the melodies we hear are *harmonized*—given a backdrop of other pitches to make the music sound more complete. Harmony does not mean that the combination of pitches sounds pleasing. So the use of the word in music differs from its use in everyday life. Instead, harmony refers only to the combination of pitches at any given instant, while counterpoint implies attention to lines as they progress at the same time. In both harmony and counterpoint pitches sound at the same instant, and yet they also progress in terms of time. The difference between them is one of viewpoint.

If musical sounds give the listener an impression of repose, equilibrium, or agreement, they are called *consonant*. If they are given an impression of harshness, tension, or disequilibrium, they are called *dissonant*. But words are inadequate to describe these two concepts. They must be heard in actual combinations of sounds, and even then there is no clear-cut distinction between consonance and dissonance. Since any judgment of these elements must be subjective, involving individual impressions and reactions, it is more accurate to speak of degrees of consonance and dissonance.

Dissonance is not necessarily unpleasant and to be avoided. Because contrast is needed if music is to be interesting, both consonance and dissonance are vital. The composer considers the amount of dissonance contained in the various combinations of sounds and then balances these with more conventional sounds to get the desired effect.

Chords. Most harmony consists of *chords*— three or more pitches sounded together. These pitches are usually selected according to a definite pattern. The most common pattern involves every other note above a basic sound, somewhat in the manner of the black and red squares on a checkerboard. If you go to a piano and play every other white key, the first three sounds you play will form a chord of some type. In music notation chords take on a line-line-line or space-space-space appearance, although this pattern is partly disguised many times by the particular chord note that is the lowest at that point in the music. The basic sound or effect is not changed when a chord has its pitches rearranged in terms of which one is lowest.

The two main types of chords found in music over the past couple of hundred years are *major* and *minor*. These terms refer to the placement of the middle note in a three-note chord. The major triad can be heard by playing C E G on a piano. It can be made into a minor chord simply by moving the middle note, E, to the black key immediately to the left, E flat. This change gives the chord a different quality. Several other types of chords are possible, of course. Quite often chords consist of more than just three notes. Generally the every-other pattern is followed in doing this, and the addition of other notes does not change the essential character of the chord.

Although most chords are constructed in *thirds* (the every-other pattern), that is not always so. In the twentieth century composers have used some different chord structures. The notes of a chord can be placed two, four, or five notes apart. Sometimes they are only clusters of sounds and follow no particular pattern.

Seldom does a composer merely write basic chords to harmonize a melody. Basic chords without some elaboration are not very interesting. Usually chords are treated in a variety of ways to give the harmonizing part more appeal. So when you look at a piece of music, you may have some difficulty finding the basic chords, although you probably sense them when you hear the music performed.

To compare how chords are used in musical works, listen to the songs by Aaron Copland ("Simple Gifts") and Charles Ives ("Autumn"), and the third movement of the *Pathétique* Sonata by Ludwig van Beethoven, all of which are present in the *Record Album*. Copland's accompanying music to the melody (presented on page 54) is designed to further the idea of simplicity that is central to the words of the song. The chords appear in about as basic a manner as they ever do in music. Also, the rate at which they change is quite slow. The first half of "Autumn" (page 58) also presents very simple chords. Most of the interest is achieved by having them occur off the beat. As the song gains in intensity, however, the chords are repeated more often, and sometimes the notes are not all sounded at the same time. Beethoven's piano sonata (page 112) presents some chords with notes sounded one after the other in "harp style" (the musical term is *arpeggio*, pronounced with soft *g*'s) instead of simultaneously. The chords change more rapidly and frequently in the Beethoven sonata then they do in either of the songs. This is partly true because its tempo is faster.

Tonality. Most music in Western civilization (Europe and America) starts from and returns to a tonal center, which is called the *tonic*. The tonic is something like the home office of a business concern. There may be branch offices at other places, but the activity of the company is centered at the home office. In music the identity of the tonic, and the activity going to and from it, create the feeling of *tonality* or *key*. Tonality is the framework within which harmonic movement takes place, and it is what makes a chord seem logical or illogical.

Through the skillful choice of chords the composer or arranger can "punctuate" the music—that is, suggest varying degrees of tension and repose comparable to clauses and sentences in language. One of the ways this is done is by the use of patterns of two chords called *cadences*. (The word as used in harmony has little to do with a cadence in marching.) Cadences appear at the ends of phrases, and they contribute much to the feeling that the music should either move or stop, depending on the chords in the cadence. The type of cadence that gives a sense of stopping can be compared to a period on the printed page, and the kind that gives a feeling that the music should move on can be compared to a comma. One cadence that may be familiar is the "Amen" conclusion of hymns in Protestant churches. Cadences are not usually so obvious, however.

"Simple Gifts" is an easy piece of music in which to hear the effect of cadences. The chord for the words "... gift to be simple ..." is the home chord for the song. The chords work away from it but return briefly on the words "... when we find ourselves...." Although there is a held note on "right," which might be expected to be a good place to conclude, the chord does not give the impression that the music will end—and it doesn't. The end of the phrase comes with the words "... love and delight." At that point the second portion or half of the song begins. Another cadence is clearly presented in the final chords of the song.

The tonality can change during the course of a piece of music. The term for a change of tonality or key is *modulation*. If handled properly, changes of key make the music more interesting and "fresh." The continuous use of one tonal center becomes tiring, a problem apparent in Scottish bagpipe music because the instrument cannot play in more than one key. Modulation should not be confused with changes of chords. Chords change often within a key; a modulation occurs only when there is a definite movement to another tonal center.

Not all music must be in a key. At one time composers always established a tonality, but over the years composers have become more free in their treatment of it. The idea of tonal center was gradually weakened over the years, and by the beginning of this century some music was created that is *atonal*—without tonality.

Chords move to other chords during successive moments of time. In doing so, the harmonies convey a sense of progression, just as do other aspects of music. The logic of harmonic progressions is probably culturally learned, although it may be based partly on the physical laws of sound. No one really knows whether nature or nurture is more important in this matter.

Chords can be built on any degree of a scale, and the *tonic chord* is the name for the chord built on the home note. It can also be designated by the Roman numeral I. Other chords can be designated accordingly. The next most important chord is the *dominant chord*, which is built on the fifth note of a scale. Traditionally the dominant chord generally led to the tonic chord, and there are other tendencies in the pattern of chord progressions. Some of the past traditions have changed, and so today their logic is not as prevalent as it was a hundred years ago.

Harmony is both an interesting and complex topic, but it is also an aspect of music that listeners are not particularly conscious of. It affects music very much, but like a good supporting actor in a drama does not draw attention to itself very often.

Texture

As the word is used in music, *texture* refers to whether a piece of music is conceived more in a linear sense of melodic lines or in a vertical sense of simultaneous sounds or chords. In music, texture does not refer to the perceived roughness or smoothness of the music; there are other terms for that. There is a special term for each type of texture. A melody alone is called *monophonic* and could be pictured in this way:

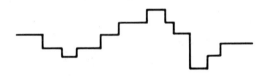

The texture of a melody with accompaniment is called *homophonic*. It might be represented in this way:

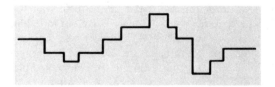

The existence of two or more melodic lines at the same time results in a texture that is called *polyphonic*. It could be represented in this way:

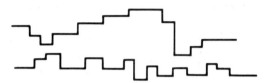

Polyphony is the result of writing counterpoint, and often sections of music that contain much line-against-line writing are called contrapuntal rather than polyphonic. Many people use both terms interchangeably, although there may be a slight difference in emphasis between them. Keep in mind that the lines in polyphonic or contrapuntal music must have a character of their own and not just be accompaniment.

It is much more effective to hear texture in music than to describe it graphically or verbally. Monophonic texture is not heard a great deal today; Gregorian chant and unaccompanied singing of folk songs are two examples. Bach's Fugue in C Major (Record 3, B) is a good example of polyphonic texture, and Ives' "Autumn" (Record 1, A) is about as homophonic as a piece can be.

Both polyphonic and homophonic textures are somewhat relative terms. A polyphonic work may have some moments that are quite homophonic, and a homophonic work may contain places in which two or more melodic lines are heard simultaneously.

Melody, harmony, counterpoint, and texture are all aspects of music that involve the use of pitches, a fundamental material of music. As important as pitch and its manipulation are in music, there are other equally important materials. They are the topic of the next chapter.

4

The Materials of Music: Rhythm, Dynamics, and Timbre

Music has been described as a "time art." That is, it exists in a span of time, not in physical space as do arts such as painting and sculpture. Therefore, statement 2 on page 14 is true. All musical works move through a period of time.

Rhythm

The word that refers to the flow of music in terms of time is *rhythm*. It does not refer only to a recurrent pattern, orderly movement, or a repeated situation, as it sometimes does in everyday usage. The word rhythm in music is a broad term that has several aspects.

Beat. One such aspect is *beat*, which many people incorrectly consider a synonym for rhythm. The beat is the recurrent throb or pulse that makes you want to move along with the music. The beat is more strongly felt in some pieces than in others, but it is present most of the time. In fact, if by some mechanical means "Hoe-Down" were to be produced without a feeling of beat, the listener would tend to put one there. If you have any trouble feeling the beat in music, play the opening of "Hoe-Down" again and tap along with your finger or foot.

Beats can be fast, slow, or moderate. The musical term for the speed of the beat (not the speed of the notes) is *tempo*. The word in Italian literally means time. The composer suggests the desired tempo, but the performer can interpret it somewhat differently. For example, some pieces can be thought of in a pattern of two slow beats, or four fast beats. In either case the music consumes the same amount of time. The listener's impression of the music is changed slightly, however.

Most beats in music are steady for relatively long periods of time (a minute or more). There are changes from section to section and some gradual changes in the music, but certainly the beat is not erratic, with frequent starting and stopping. In only a few styles is much irregularity allowed, and even there its use is limited. Erratic changes in tempo sound disorganized and are annoying.

The beat is the unit of measurement by which the duration of a musical tone is judged. In music a tone is not designated as lasting for 3 seconds or one-half minute. It is thought of as lasting for several beats, one beat, or a fraction of a beat.

Meter. In most music, beats are organized into patterns called *meter.* There is a natural human tendency to organize sounds into patterns. The sound of a clock becomes "tick-tock" in our minds, even when all the sounds are the same. Meters are created by emphasizing certain beats: "ONE-two, ONE-two" gives the listener a two-beat pattern; "ONE-two-three, ONE-two-three" gives a three-beat feeling, and so on. Poetry often reveals patterns (called iambic, trochaic, etc.). Here is an example from Edgar Allan Poe's "Annabel Lee":

> It was many and many a year ago,
> In a kingdom by the sea,
> That a maiden there lived whom you may know
> By the name of Annabel Lee;—
> And this maiden she lived with no other
> thought
> Than to love and be loved by me.

Each metrical pattern in music is called a *measure,* with the emphasized beat being the first of each measure. Short pieces may have 16 measures or fewer, while longer pieces have hundreds of measures.

Not all pieces of music need to have a beat or meter. Therefore, statement 8 on page 14 is false. Pieces for tape recorders often have no beat. Neither does some folk music, especially that from the Orient. And there are several types of music in our culture that have no regular beat.

Beats and notes. The speed of the beats and the speed of the notes are not the same thing. They are related, of course. A fast tempo usually has more notes in a given span of time, but not always. Even though a piece may have a rapid tempo, the sounds may be in long note values, giving an impression of slowness. And the opposite can happen: A phrase of music with a slow tempo may have short note values and appear to be quite fast. Other things being equal, a note will last longer at a slow tempo than at a fast tempo.

In most music the sounding of the notes themselves provides the only clue as to where the beats occur. A drum doesn't need to tap out the beat so that the listener can feel the pulse of the music. Most of the time the note patterns fit the underlying metrical pattern. If this doesn't happen, the music has been incorrectly written. Putting the measure lines in the wrong place is like putting the periods and commas in the wrong place when writing a paragraph. Imagine reading: "The music of Bach is. Very interesting to, hear it makes much. Use of. . . ."

But if a piece of music always follows a predictable pattern, it doesn't have much rhythmic interest. In such music the composer must make sure there is enough that is interesting in the harmony and melody so that people will want to hear it. Therefore, how composers and performers create deviations in the regular rhythmic patterns to make the music more exciting and fascinating to hear is a topic worth studying.

Syncopation. Sometimes a composer or performer deliberately misplaces the rhythmic emphasis and puts emphasis—called *accent* in music—where it's not expected or removes it where it is expected. This alteration of the accents is termed *syncopation*. It appears in most types of music to some extent, but it is especially prominent in jazz and twentieth-century music. In the song "When the Saints Go Marching In" there is syncopation on the word *number*. If you sing the word *number* so that the second syllable occurs exactly on the second beat, it will be a duller piece of music.

Many popular songs contain a kind of syncopation. The normal pattern for accented and unaccented beats in two- and four-beat meter is $\underline{1}$ 2 $\underline{3}$ 4, or $\underline{1}$ and $\underline{2}$ and. However, many popular songs have those beats performed 1 $\underline{2}$ 3 $\underline{4}$, or 1 *and* 2 *and*. The first theme in the first movement of Beethoven's *Pathétique* Sonata (page 110) contains syncopation when the second note in the third measure occurs off the beat.

Alterations in regular meter. Sometimes composers choose not to follow a regular metrical pattern. To achieve rhythmic interest, they establish a somewhat regular pattern, then change it just enough to make the music more interesting. Not all music that maintains a regular beat is dull; not by any means. But something different is nice once in a while, too.

It is possible to combine two or more melodies that have different patterns of accents. When two rhythmic patterns are combined without any consistent change of meter, the result is called *polyrhythm*. If the meter is changed for several measures, it is called *polymeter*. The difference between the two terms is slight. For example, the melody of a piece may not follow

the same metrical pattern as the accompanying chords. They might be in a steady four-beat pattern, while the melody is in a three-beat pattern or changes meter every so often. The effect of polyrhythm or polymeter can be quite exciting. And it's a challenge for a pianist when one meter is played in the right hand and another meter in the left.

Almost no single musical work includes all the different aspects of rhythm discussed in this chapter, but Leonard Bernstein's two dances from *West Side Story* are excellent examples with which to summarize a discussion of rhythm. Both "Mambo" and "Cha-Cha" are Latin American dance patterns, and both are incorporated in the original Broadway version of the musical in a dance sequence called "The Dance at the Gym."

"Mambo" certainly demonstrates the excitement that rhythm can create. It achieves this partly through a rather fast tempo, although that is not the main reason for the tremendous energy of the music. The more important causes are the simultaneous appearance of more than one rhythmic pattern and the frequent and rapid use of syncopation. The color provided by the trumpets, voices, and percussion also contributes to the overall sense of excitement.

"Mambo" is filled with examples of interesting rhythmic writing, but perhaps the best one appears at about 1:11 into the recording in the *Record Album* (Record 1, A). In this example the notes are placed so that the progression of sound at any point can be seen from the pattern of sixteenth notes at the top (see the music at the bottom of the page). These fly by at the rate of *four* in *less* than *half a second!* (The chevron-shaped mark indicates an accented note.)

The "Cha-Cha" is the opposite of "Mambo." It contains a little syncopation, but it is quite subtle. The four-beat meter is followed regularly. Actually, much of the rhythmic interest of "Cha-Cha" lies in the rests, in which finger snapping takes place on the recording in the *Record Album*. The melody, by the way, is a version of the song "Maria," which appears a little later in the musical.

Dynamics

All sounds have some degree of loudness and softness. Statement 4 on page 14 is true. The musical term for the levels of loudness and softness is *dynamics*. In most music the level of dynamics is constantly changing, something like the surface of the ocean. The term for a gradual buildup of sound is *crescendo*, and its opposite is *decrescendo*. These are Italian words that mean simply to get louder and to get softer.

A work that makes especially good use of dynamics is Wagner's *Siegfried's Rhine Journey* (Record 3,B). Listen to how it begins softly and slowly builds to a loud level.

Dynamics is an important aspect of *phrasing*. The term *phrasing* refers to the way that musical segments, called *phrases*, are presented by a performer. The phrases in music are somewhat comparable to the phrases and clauses in language. By skillful gradation of dynamics, by emphasizing some notes more than others, and by subtle changes of speed in music, the performer can give a more meaningful performance of the music.

Timbre

Every sound has a distinctive quality to it, which makes statement 6 on page 14 also true. In musical terminology the word for tone quality is *timbre* (pronounced *tam*-ber or *tim*-ber). Each voice and each type of musical instrument has its own unique tone "color." Three people singing the same note in the same way will each produce a different quality. The same is true when different types of musical instruments sound an identical pitch.

Timbre is an important musical element. Often the most significant difference among types of music is not the rhythm or the melody but in the timbre. In recent years composers have become even more intrigued with timbre. They are exploring sounds other than those made on conventional musical instruments, which already offer a myriad of possibilities. Different qualities of sound can form the basis of entire pieces of music that contain little else except tone colors produced in a planned order and span of time. Although such pieces may seem strange the first time you hear them, they demonstrate the inventiveness of the human mind and the vast possibilities available through the use of tone color.

Although many of the works in the book make effective use of timbre, one that is especially interesting is *Until Spring* by Subotnick (Record 4,B). The timbre of some of the pitches slowly changes as the sound is sustained. Furthermore, all its sounds are electronically produced.

Although dynamics and timbre are more easily explained than harmony and rhythm, they are no less important in terms of the musical results achieved. Each aspect of sound plays an important role in music. However, important as they are, the materials that go into a musical work must be brought together in an effective way, just as the bricks, wood, and metal that go into a building must be properly organized. That crucial factor is organization, and it is the topic of the next chapter.

5

Form In Music

In 1962 the British Broadcasting Company played a deliberate trick on its listeners. It announced that it would play a work by an unknown Polish composer named Zak. The trick was that no composer named Zak ever existed. For some minutes the technicians walked around the studio banging and rattling whatever they could find. Fortunately for their professional reputations, the music critics wrote that the work by Zak was awful. Why weren't the sounds concocted by the technicians really music? They had no structure, no plan, no organization, no form.

A group of sounds may have pitch, rhythm, timbre, and dynamic levels, but that does not make them music. To become music, sounds must be pulled together and related to each other in a way that sounds meaningful to people who listen to them. Being able to learn and comprehend what creators of music do with sounds is, therefore, the very heart of understanding music; it's the "ballgame," especially in art music.

Nonmusicians (and even some musicians) have difficulty realizing the importance of perceiving what happens to sounds in works of music. When short, uncomplicated pieces of music are treated as an accompaniment or background for something like studying or shopping, paying attention to the music is unnecessary. However, in music intended for careful listening, noticing what is happening to melodies and rhythmic patterns is essential. A listener who fails to do this is like someone who attends a basketball game and pays attention only to the cheerleaders, crowd, and players' uniforms but doesn't know the score or notice what happens in the game. Therefore, the most important single suggestion for students in music appreciation classes is to be aware of and pay attention to what happens to sounds in a piece of music. Unless you do this, much of what is studied in the course will be of little value.

Ways of Organizing Sounds

Because the organization of sounds in music is so important, you should know some of the ways in which composers, and to some extent performers who improvise music, achieve a sense of organization. The manner in which sounds are organized into a meaningful piece of music is referred to as *form*, as in "forming a piece of music." Actually, the word form is used in three different ways in music. One use refers to how the sounds are organized, while another refers to the patterns of lines in a song or short piece. The third use refers to the plan or scheme for a large independent section of music or an entire musical work. The last two uses of the word—those involving patterns or plans—are presented in greater detail in subsequent chapters. This chapter concentrates on the ways in which pieces of music are organized.

Sectional Forms

The basic idea of sectional forms is easy to understand: It is music that has been constructed out of somewhat distinct sections. For example, one of the most common forms in music involves an opening melody or section of music, which is followed by a contrasting melody or section of music, which in turn is followed by a return to the original melody or musical material. Such a pattern is usually designated by the letters *A B A*; it is clearly sectional. The sections may be rather brief or quite lengthy; length does not change the sectional nature of a work.

A good example of *A B A*, or three-part sectional form, is Copland's "Hoe-Down" from *Rodeo*, which was presented in a Listening Guide in Chapter 2. The opening *A* section has a couple of short subsections, as does the *B* section. The final section of the music is a return (although not a literal repeat) of the music heard in the opening section. A number of other works utilizing the sectional idea of organizing music will be presented in later chapters. Among them is the third movement of Beethoven's *Pathétique* Sonata, which follows a sectional plan called *rondo*. This form is presented in more detail in Chapter 10.

Variation Forms

The principle of variation forms is just what the word variation implies: making changes or alterations of a melody or other musical material for an entire work. While some varying of musical material is found in most music, in works built on the process of variation it consumes the entire work or at least a sizable portion of it.

The most frequently encountered type of work using the variation principle is *theme and variations*. The second movement of Haydn's Op. 76 No. 3 Quartet, which is presented in Chapter 11, is typical of this form. An easily remembered theme is presented, which is then followed by four variations of that theme. The theme can be heard throughout the movement. A simplified score is included in the *Study Guide and Scores*.

Less familiar to listeners today is the idea of creating a piece of music over a short, persistent melody in the bass or lowest part. One such form is called a *basso ostinato*, Italian words that literally mean "obstinate bass." This chapter concludes with a presentation of Kanon in D by Johann Pachelbel (*Pahk*-hel-ble; 1653–1706); a recording of the work is included in the *Record Album* (Record 4,B). In this work a two-measure bass pattern is repeated 28 times. Although 28 appearances of the same short melody may sound like a dreadful bore (and in one sense it is for the players on that part), as used in Kanon in D it provides a strong sense of unity while variations on the pattern are played in imitation in the upper string parts.

Two other forms utilizing the process of variation are the *passacaglia* (pah-sah-*cahl*-yah) and *chaconne* (*shah*-cone). The passacaglia is a melodic basso ostinato repeated for an entire work of some length. Usually it is rather dignified in character and has three beats per measure. The chaconne is also slow and in three-beat meter. However, a pattern of chords, not a melody, is repeated throughout the work.

The idea of variation is not confined to art music. One of the principle features of jazz is its nearly continuous variation over the chord progressions of the song being varied. In the case of jazz, however, the variations are made up on the spot by the performers and are played in a jazz style.

Contrapuntal Forms

Contrapuntal forms are different from sectional and variation forms in that two or more lines possessing melodic character are sounded at the same time. In a sense, contrapuntal forms are not so much formal patterns as they are works built on the process of composing counterpoint. These forms are especially challenging for listeners because, like a three-ring circus, they offer more than one thing to pay attention to at the same time.

Counterpoint can be achieved in one of two ways. In the first, two or more contrasting melodic lines are sounded simultaneously. In the other, the same melody is sounded in different parts one after the other. Short songs that do this are called *rounds*; a longer piece in which one line imitates another exactly is called a *canon*. Originally the word canon meant "according to the rules," but in music it has come to mean a composition built on strict imitation. Pachelbel's Kanon in D (the German spelling of canon), mentioned earlier in conjunction with variation form, contains three violin parts that are played in strict imitation above the *basso continuo*.

The *fugue* (fewg) is probably the best known contrapuntal form. One example of a fugue appears in the next chapter as the last portion of Britten's *The Young Person's Guide to the Orchestra*. While it is an interesting and enjoyable fugue, it is not as typical of the form as Bach's C Major Fugue, which is presented in Chapter 12.

Another form that uses much counterpoint is the *concerto grosso*, which literally means "grand or large concerto." This type of concerto is represented by Vivaldi's *The Four Seasons*, which appears in Chapter 10.

Madrigals and *motets*, discussed in Chapter 8, are also contrapuntal forms. These vocal works contain portions that are in strict imitation and other portions in which line-against-line writing is emphasized, plus portions that are not contrapuntal.

Sonata Form

Sonata form is a particular scheme or plan that allows considerable use of the process of developing themes. Because both sonata form and the concept of theme development are best learned by studying them in musical works, their presentation is reserved for Chapter 9.

The term *sonata* is used in two ways in music. One is to designate a particular form. The other use is for a work containing three or four movements for piano alone or for piano and another instrument. Usually the first movement of a sonata is in sonata form (which has a certain logic about it), but other movements may be as well. The form is found as the first movement of most symphonies, concertos, and string quartets, all of which are presented in the next section of this book. Further complicating the distinction between sonatas and sonata form is the fact that some composers around the time of Bach wrote works they called sonatas that have no movements in sonata form.

Free Forms

In a sense, few works of music are truly free of form in terms of not being organized. However, a number of musical works do not follow any of the four basic formal processes just mentioned. Additionally, composers are free in their use of the basic forms. No two movements in sonata form, for example, are exactly alike; each contains features that make it somewhat different from any other movement in sonata form.

One sizable group of musical works following no particular form consists of the short instrumental pieces with names such as *fantasie, impromptu, prelude, étude,* and so on. A fantasie is supposed to sound imaginative and free, and an impromptu is intended to sound as though it is an inspiration of the moment. Such information, however, tells you little about the form of the work, other than it is a piece of instrumental music.

The other type of music that is especially free in its use of form is *program music.* Such works are usually instrumental and associated with some nonmusical idea. The composer does not try to have the music relate a "story," but rather uses the nonmusical association as a stimulus or springboard. That idea helps to provide a structure of sorts for the music, but it is not usually a traditional formal plan such as those covered earlier. Two works of program music are presented in Chapter 20, *Les Préludes* by Liszt and *Don Juan* by Richard Strauss.

Some vocal works utilize the forms discussed earlier in this chapter, but most do not. Like program works, they are developed around a nonmusical idea. In the case of vocal music, however, the message is contained specifically in the words being sung. For this reason there is usually a close association between the message of the words and the expressive qualities of the music.

Unity and Variety

If all there were to composing music was the filling out of a form, it would indeed be a rather easy thing to do. As you may have suspected, however, composing music that people want to listen to more than once is very difficult. The choice of form by a composer might be compared to the choice of subject matter by a painter. Deciding whether he or she will paint a still life, a portrait, or a landscape is only the first step in a long and difficult journey.

One thing that both composers and painters must accomplish is the creation of something that seems to hold together as a unit and yet at the same time is interesting and fresh. Often these contrasting qualities are described by the words *unity* and *variety,* although several other words such as *cohesion* and *novelty* could be used equally well. Just as an interesting painting cannot be only a plain blue surface, a musical composition that anyone would want to listen to cannot be only one melody played over and over. Nor can a worthwhile painting *normally* be created accidently by merely throwing colors on a canvas, anymore than music is created when a cat walks around on the keys of a piano.

Yet, when you think about it, unity and variety are contradictory requirements; they are opposites. The problem for any creative artist is to strike the right balance between them. Too much unity leads to a dull work, while too much variety leads to confusion and meaninglessness. To see how one composer handles this need for unity and variety in one musical work, let's examine more closely Johann Pachelbel's Kanon in D.

Pachelbel's Kanon in D

Two reasons have already been given for using Pachelbel's Kanon in D as an example of how sounds are organized into musical compositions: (1) It shows the principle of variation through the use of a *basso ostinato,* and (2) it exemplifies contrapuntal writing through its use of strict imitation. In addition, there are at least three more reasons for studying this work: (1) It demonstrates a balance between unity and variety by using the same two-measure phrase over and over, but each time with different music in other parts; (2) it is slow, so it is easier to hear what is happening in the music than when the tempo is fast; and (3) it is a gorgeous piece of music. For some reason the work was largely overlooked for a couple of hundred years, but in the last decade it has catapulted into great favor. It was the theme music for the Academy Award–winning motion picture *Ordinary People* and has been used as background music for television commercials that seek to project a "classy" image, as well as being made into a popular work by several performers.

The continuous bass part played slowly by the low strings and harpsichord consists of only eight notes, all of equal length, which are heard alone at the beginning of the work.

Before the Kanon in D ends five minutes later, the pattern is repeated 28 times. Clearly this amount of repetition provides a strong sense of unity in the work.

The melodies that the violins play above the *basso continuo*, which is also a *basso ostinato*, all fit with the eight-note melody and are variations of it. These melodies tend to be grouped so that they span 16 beats. The first violin part is imitated exactly eight beats later by the second violin part, which in turn is imitated exactly eight beats later by the third part. The strict imitation continues throughout the work until the last few measures, when the music is brought to a conclusion. Although one violin part imitates another exactly, the combination of sounds (which is what the listener hears) in each measure is different. Obviously this fact contributes to the sense of variety in the work.

Pachelbel also exhibits a sense of design, or form, although the work does not follow a standard pattern. After the opening measures with the bass melody heard alone, the violins begin playing their melody, which has the same slow, steady beats and notes as the bass part. After eight beats, that melody changes to two notes

on each beat. Then it doubles so that there are four notes in each beat, and then doubles again to many beats in which eight notes are sounded. The effect on the listener of this doubling of note speed with each new melodic variation is one of increasing momentum. Then the amount of activity is reduced for a bit, only to change again to two notes per beat, then to four, and then eight on some beats. As the music moves toward its conclusion, the violin melodies become more like they were at the beginning, which gives the work a sense of balance.

The complete first violin part is presented on the opposite page. To those of you who read music, it may look like it contains many rapidly moving notes. It has some, but because of its slow tempo it is not as formidable as it looks. The numbers above the staff, which usually appear every eight measures, indicate the elapsed time for the recording in the *Record Album*. At a few places it may be difficult to distinguish the first violin part from the other two; one such place is at about 2:13 in the work. That does not last for more than about eight measures at any one place, however.

Johann Pachelbel really did a lot with sounds in his Kanon in D. He employed two types of formal structure (variation and contrapuntal) and achieved a balance between unity and variety. But he did even more than that. He demonstrated the truth of the maxim of Gestalt psychology that the whole is greater than the sum of its parts. Although each element that he incorporated in the music is important, even when added up individually they cannot equal their effect when combined.

Kanon

Johann Pachelbel

6

Musical Instruments

There are hundreds of different kinds of instruments in the world, and they can be grouped in a variety of ways. One way is to discuss them according to the type of music they perform; this chapter is so organized.

Orchestral Instruments

The instruments of the symphony orchestra can be divided into "families" on the basis of similar design and principles of sound production. There are four families: strings, woodwinds, brasses, and percussion.

Strings. The strings are the backbone of the orchestra. They constitute about half its membership. The violin, viola (vee-*o*-la), cello (*chel*-lo; officially the violoncello), and the bass viol have essentially the same design. The main difference among them is one of size and consequently the general pitch level at which they play. The player produces tone by plucking the strings with the finger or, most often, by drawing a horsehair bow across the strings. When the hair of the bow is examined under a microscope, tiny depressions can be seen. The uneven surface catches on the string to set it vibrating. The player also applies rosin to the bow to help it sound the string.

The body of the instrument is largely hollow. The wooden bridge visible on the top of the instrument props up the strings and transmits their vibrations to the body, which amplifies the sound and provides the distinctive tone quality of the instrument.

Extending out from the body of the stringed instrument is the neck, on which is glued the black fingerboard. The player presses the string down firmly on the fingerboard to change the pitch. The shorter the string—that is, the smaller the distance between bridge and finger—the higher the pitch. The four strings are of differ-

Violins.

Cellos.

ent materials, thicknesses, and tension. Tension is regulated by the pegs at the scroll end of the instrument. When the player tunes, a tightening of the string produces a higher pitch; loosening the tension causes a lowering of pitch. The instruments are tuned so that there is an interval of a fifth between the pitch of each string and the one adjacent to it; on the bass viol the interval is a fourth.

It is possible to play two or even three notes at one time, a technique called *double* (or *triple*) *stops*. In this instance the bow is drawn across adjacent strings in a single stroke so that they vibrate simultaneously.

While pitch is controlled by the fingers of the player's left hand, volume and phrasing are

manipulated by the bow held in the right hand. The more pressure applied to the bow, and the faster it is drawn over the strings, the louder the tone will be. The player can bow smoothly or can separate the strokes to produce a variety of styles.

All good string players vibrate the left hand in a slight, rapid motion when playing. This motion creates *vibrato,* which adds warmth to the tone by causing rapid but small changes of pitch. The tone can be made softer and more mellow by the use of a *mute*—a wood or plastic device that is fitted over the bridge.

The violin is the smallest and highest pitched of the four instruments. Its range covers well over four octaves from its lowest note,

Bass viols.

which is G below middle C. There are two sections of violins in the orchestra: first and second. There is no difference in the instruments themselves; the distinction lies in the way the music is written for them. The first violin part is generally higher, more difficult, and more easily heard in the total orchestral sound.

The viola is somewhat larger than the violin, but it is also held under the chin. Its general range is about five notes lower than the violin's.

The cello rests on the floor and is supported lightly between the player's knees. It is pitched an octave below the viola. In general, its range is comparable to that of a baritone singer, so it is especially well suited for warm, melodious passages.

The bass viol is known by several other names: contrabass, double bass, and string bass.

When playing, the performer either stands or partially rests on a high stool. The bass viol is seldom heard alone, although its tone is not unpleasant in the slightest. The instrument contributes substantially to the important low sounds of the orchestra.

The harp is also a member of the string family. Its sounds are made by plucking the strings with the hands. There are only about half as many strings on a harp as there are keys on a piano. But the harp compensates by means of a pedal mechanism, which can change the length of the strings almost instantaneously to provide any necessary pitches.

Woodwinds. As their family name implies, these instruments use wind to produce the tone and are (or were) made of wood. Their strong point is the varied timbres they provide. Usually two flutes and a piccolo, two oboes and an English horn, two clarinets and a bass clarinet, and two bassoons and a contrabassoon are found in a symphony orchestra. Saxophones seldom appear in a symphony orchestra.

All woodwinds are alike in that their bodies are hollow tubes. Holes along the length of the tube are opened and closed either by the fingers or by small pads attached to *key* mechanisms. As the holes are opened closer toward the source of air, the pitch gets higher because the tube is being "shortened." At a certain point a key is opened to permit the instrument to move into a still higher range, and the holes and keys can be used for a new set of pitches. Tones are started and stopped by the player's tongue, and each instrument can usually produce only one note at a time.

The flute changed its wooden body early in the twentieth century in favor of a metal one, which is usually of a silver-nickel alloy. The metal construction gives the instrument a more brilliant tone. The flute and its diminutive version, the piccolo, are unique in that they produce sound on the stopped-pipe principle. Many a youngster has made a sound by blowing across an empty pop bottle; the flute operates in a similar way. The air going into the pipe collides with the air returning from the stopped end, and a sound results. The flute's

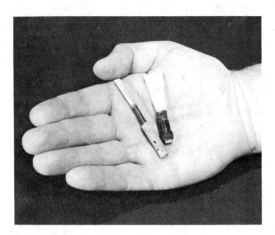

Oboe and bassoon reeds.

Bassoons and clarinets.

range is from middle C up about three octaves, and the piccolo's range is higher.

The oboe is made of wood that, like the wood in the clarinet and the bassoon, has been carefully treated to prevent warping and cracking. The distinctive tone of the oboe is produced by a double reed. The reed is similar to bamboo cane. It is shaved, and the two small reeds are wired together. The instrument does not have a wide range; it extends only a little over two octaves. Its best notes lie around an octave above middle C, where they can be easily heard. The English horn is neither horn nor English. It is basically a large oboe with a bulb-shaped bell.

The bassoon is also a double-reed instrument. It can play from more than two octaves below middle C to at least one octave above it. Its tone is highly distinctive but not powerful. The range of the contrabassoon is an octave lower; its lowest pitch reaches almost to the lowest note on the piano.

The clarinet has the most varied timbre in its more than three-octave range. Its low notes have a quality quite different from its high notes. It has only one reed, which is placed on a mouthpiece. Clarinets come in a variety of sizes, but only three are found regularly in the symphony orchestra: the B flat and A soprano, and the B flat bass, which looks like a black wooden saxophone.

The saxophone is the newest instrument in the woodwind family. There are eight different-sized saxophones. The saxophone is used only occasionally in orchestral music but is a regular member of concert and jazz bands.

Brasses. The sound on brass instruments is produced by a "buzzing," or vibrating, of the lip membranes on a cup-shaped mouthpiece. This buzzing sound is then amplified through a metal tube with a flared bell at the end. Today all brass instruments have curves in them so that they can be held more easily. Also, all the orchestral brasses have some means of changing the length of the tube.

A bugle is not an orchestral instrument, but it can illustrate an important principle of brass playing. The bugle has no valves, so all its different pitches must be produced solely by changes of tension in the player's lips. This limitation means that the bugle can produce only a certain series of pitches, the familiar ones heard in bugle calls. All brass instruments achieve these different pitches by lip manipulation, but if pitches outside the series are desired, the

French horns.

Trumpets with trombones in back.

Six-valve F tuba and C tuba held by Abe Torchinsky. (The Getzer Company, Elkhorn, Wisconsin.)

length of the tube must be changed so that a new series is possible—one that contains the desired pitch. This is the function of the valves on most orchestral brasses: By pushing down various combinations of valves, the player opens or closes different portions of tubing so that the air column can be made the desired length for a new series.

Like the woodwind instruments, the brasses are articulated by the player's tongue.

Generally an orchestra uses three trumpets, four French horns, two tenor trombones, one bass trombone, and one tuba.

The trumpet is the highest pitched brass instrument. It has three piston valves, which, when activated, change the tube length in varying amounts. Its range is not extremely wide, extending from a few notes below middle C up somewhat over two octaves. What the instrument lacks in range, however, it makes up in power. The cornet is similar to the trumpet except for the conical tapering of its tube, or bore. (The trumpet bore is more cylindrical.) Differences in the shape of the bore account for

the mellower sound of the cornet. A mute for cornet or trumpet can be inserted into the bell to soften the tone and make it sound more pinched. The most common is a fiber mute, although there are other materials and several variations of the basic mute.

Extreme accuracy of lip tension is required

(Left to right) Trumpet, French horn, trombone, and tuba mouthpieces.

Timpani. The pedal for each drum is at the side of the instrument.

in order to produce the desired note on the French horn. It can sound more than an octave lower than the trumpet, and its overall range is wider. Its valves, operated by the player's left hand, are of a rotary type. The valve mechanism turns to open up lengths of tubing. The player inserts the right hand into the bell to control the tone somewhat. A mute is occasionally used.

The trombone is an octave lower than the trumpet. It is unique in that it has a slide to regulate the length of its tubing. The trombone has great power. The bass trombone is somewhat larger than the usual tenor trombone and plays a few notes lower.

The tuba is comparable to the bass viol in its musical function. It seldom gets to play a solo.

Percussion. All percussion instruments produce sound by being struck or rattled. They may be further grouped into those that play definite pitches and those that don't. First to be considered are those that can produce definite pitch.

Timpani are large copper bowls over each of which is stretched a calfskin head. Around the rim of each drum is a ring that regulates the tension of the head when the small protruding handles are adjusted: the tighter the drumhead, the higher the pitch. The problem with this procedure is that it takes a minute or two, which means the performer must stop playing

for that period of time. Until the middle of the last century, composers had to consider the inconvenience of retuning when they wrote for the instrument. Today there is a pedal mechanism that regulates pitch very quickly. The sticks have padded, rounded heads on the end. To permit a variety of tone qualities, the player has available several pairs, each having a different firmness.

Timpani do not appear singly. A minimum of two is required, and more are often used, each of a different size and tuned to a different pitch. The timpanist positions the instruments in semicircular fashion for ease of playing.

The glockenspiel, xylophone, marimba, and vibraphone are similar. All have tuned bars arranged to resemble a piano keyboard, and the player strikes them with mallets. The glockenspiel is highest in pitch and has metal bars that produce a light, tinkling sound. The xylophone has wooden bars and produces a dry, brittle tone. The marimba also has wooden bars, but below them hang hollow metal tubes that permit the sound to resonate for a few moments

Glockenspiel and snare drum.

after a bar is struck. The vibraphone also has tubes but has, in addition, an electrically powered device that produces a vibrato in the tone.

The piano and celesta are keyboard instruments. The piano tone is produced when a felt hammer, activated when the player pushes a key, strikes the strings. Because of this striking action, the piano is mentioned among the percussion instruments despite the fact that its tones are produced by the vibration of strings. The celesta looks like a small spinet piano, but it is essentially a glockenspiel operated from a keyboard. Its steel plates are struck by hammers.

The chimes also produce definite pitches. The player hits near the top of a hollow metal tube with a wooden hammer.

Percussion instruments of indefinite pitch are many in number. Most important is the snare drum. It is hollow, with calfskin or plastic heads stretched over both top and bottom. On the underside are several strands of wire that rattle against the lower head when they are tightened sufficiently to touch it. These are the snares, and they give the drum its characteristic crisp sound. The snare drum is played with a pair of wooden sticks.

The bass drum is the largest non-keyboard percussion instrument; it is placed upright on its side for playing. It is struck with a single stick, or "beater," with a rounded head. When hit hard, the bass drum has tremendous power.

The cymbals are large metal discs that are often struck together as a pair. A cymbal also can be suspended from its center and struck with a stick. A gong is a large metal disc of thicker metal than a cymbal. It is suspended from one edge and struck with a beater.

The triangle is a three-sided metal frame suspended from one corner. A small metal beater activates the sound. The player can produce single strokes on one of the sides or can produce a more sustained effect by placing the beater inside one of the angles and moving it rapidly back and forth between the two adjacent sides.

The tambourine has a calfskin head stretching over a wood or metal rim, around which are placed small metal discs that rattle. The player shakes the instrument or taps it against the hand. Castanets are hollow pieces of wood or plastic that are clicked against each other.

Percussion players are assigned many unusual instruments. They hit the woodblock, crack a whip (which consists of two large, flat wood pieces that are slapped together), shake maracas (hollow, dry gourds in which metal pellets have been placed), and even get to blow on whistles.

Britten's *The Young Person's Guide to the Orchestra*

To become acquainted with the sounds of the various musical instruments that make up the orchestra, there is no better work than *The Young Person's Guide to the Orchestra* by Benjamin Britten, a twentieth-century English composer. In spite of its title, the work is *not* juvenile in any sense. For the theme of this work Britten chose a melody by the most esteemed English composer of the seventeenth century, Henry Purcell.

The first section of the work is a set of variations on Purcell's theme. Britten makes it especially easy to follow the instruments because he first introduces the full orchestra, then the woodwinds, then the brasses, then the strings, and finally the percussion. He closes this section with the full orchestra again. Having presented the full orchestra and each family of instruments, he proceeds through each section from the highest pitched instrument to the lowest.

The last section of *The Young Person's Guide to the Orchestra* is a fugue. The fugue form will be discussed in greater detail in Chapter 12, but remember from Chapter 5 that a fugue is a contrapuntal form. The main theme (called the *subject*) is presented, then other instruments enter in imitation of that main theme. In the fugue Britten presents each section and instrument in the same order in which he featured them in the variations, which means that the subject is introduced by the piccolo. The music closes with the full orchestra sounding Purcell's theme.

A Listening Guide for *The Young Person's Guide to the Orchestra* appears on pages 42–43.

Band Instruments

Band instrumentation is far less standardized than orchestral instrumentation. Several instruments have been tried out in bands at various places and times and have been dropped from the organization—the flügelhorn, the saxhorn, the bass saxophone, and others. Bands vary tremendously in size. Some are as small as 30 players, while others run well over 100 players. Arrangers and composers cannot be sure of what kind or size group will play their band arrangements or compositions.

Although the wind band has a long tradition running from the courts of kings to the touring band of John Philip Sousa, most people tended to think of bands in "town band" terms, that is, a small but noisy group that existed primarily to give concerts on hot summer nights in a park. Nobody took the group very seriously. Following World War I and on into the 1940s, the band took on a new dimension. It became a

much larger organization and played a heavy diet of transcriptions of orchestral music. When the band was good, the effect was something like the sound of a mighty pipe organ. Since World War II another idea has appeared in bands and band music. Often called a *wind ensemble*, this concept strongly favors original compositions and a much smaller group. Gone are the romantic sounds of yesteryear, replaced by a more intellectual and detached kind of music.

Until well into the twentieth century, the band suffered from a serious lack of quality music written for it. Very few of the great "name" composers wrote much music for a group of wind and percussion instruments. And of the few works that were available, none were considered major contributions of the composer. Some improvement is evident in the last 50 years, however. Several outstanding contemporary composers have been commissioned to write works for wind band, and a few are making it their primary medium of musical expression.

The concert band is largely an American institution. Very few bands are found in schools and colleges in the rest of the world. Most bands in Europe and Asia are adjuncts of military organizations. There are very few permanent professional bands in any country, except for the armed services bands. There is no "New York Philharmonic Band" or anything of that quality or permanence in any city of the United States or the world.

The main difference between the instrumentation of the band and the orchestra is that the band includes no violins, violas, or cellos. Larger concert bands often use one or two bass viols. Bands use a greater variety of some of the instrument types: There are often cornets in addition to the usual trumpets, and tenor and baritone saxophones in addition to the alto saxophone. There is the regular clarinet, an alto clarinet, a bass clarinet, and sometimes even a contrabass clarinet. Bands are likely to include a baritone horn, which is almost never found in an orchestra. The baritone horn is in the same range as the trombone, but it has a slightly different bore and piston valves. Because tubas are extremely difficult to carry while marching, an

Listening Guide

Britten: *The Young Person's Guide to the Orchestra, Op. 34,*
"Variations and Fugue on a Theme by Purcell"   *Record 1,B*

Theme and Variations

0:00   Theme presented at loud dynamic level by orchestra; a stately, solid melody

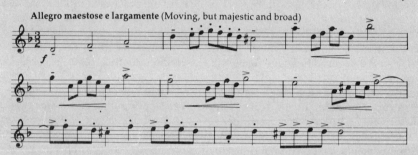

Allegro maestoso e largamente (Moving, but majestic and broad)

0:28   Theme played by woodwinds.

0:54   Theme played by brasses.

1:17   Theme played by strings.

1:38   Theme played by percussion, especially timpani.

1:57   Theme repeated by entire orchestra.

2:20   Variation 1—flutes and piccolo; playful, with many notes.

2:53   Variation 2—oboes; plaintive, songlike melody.

3:50   Variation 3—clarinets; many arpeggios and runs.

4:30   Variation 4—bassoons; marchlike, with a little songlike melody.

5:24   Variation 5—violins; rhythmic accompaniment and dancelike melody.

5:59   Variation 6—violas; songlike melody with a wide range.

7:01   Variation 7—cellos; rich, flowing melody.

8:14   Variation 8—bass viols; melody in which the three-note pattern ascends one note with each appearance; after the middle it basically descends one note each time.

9:13   Variation 9—harp; presents the theme upside down (inversion).

10:00   Variation 10—French horns; variation built around chords.

10:53   Variation 11—trumpets; marchlike figures.

11:23   Variation 12—trombones and tuba; heavy and majestic.

12:40   Variation 13—percussion; timpani opens with portion of theme; followed by bass drum and cymbal, tambourine, triangle, snare drum, Chinese blocks, xylophone, castanets, gong, and finally the whip.

Fugue

14:32   Subject played by piccolo:

14:38   Subject played by flutes.

14:47   Subject played by oboes.

14:52   Subject played by clarinets.

15:03   Subject played by bassoons.

15:13   Subject played by first violins.

15:15   Subject played by second violins.

15:23   Subject played by violas.

15:29   Subject played by cellos.

15:33   Subject played by bass viols.

15:45   Subject played by harp.

15:57   Subject played by French horns.

16:03   Subject played by trumpets.

16:11   Subject played by trombones and tuba.

16:17   Subject played by percussion.

16:27   Purcell's theme played loudly in long notes by brasses; upper strings and woodwinds continue contrasting material based on fugue.

16:57   Percussion enters loudly.

17:16   Closes with long, full-sounding chord.

Suggestions for Listening to Orchestral Instruments

Flute
Bach, Sonatas for Flute and Harpsichord (any of seven)
Griffes, *Poem for Flute and Orchestra*
Mozart, Concertos for Flute (K. 313 or K. 314)

Oboe
Handel, Concertos for Oboe (any of three)
Mozart, Concerto in C Major for Oboe, K. 314
Poulenc, Sonata for Oboe and Piano

Clarinet
Brahms, Sonatas for Clarinet and Piano, Opus 120, Nos. 1 and 2*
Debussy, *Première Rapsodie for Clarinet and Piano*
Mozart, Concerto in A Major for Clarinet, K. 622

Bassoon
Hindemith, Sonata for Bassoon and Piano
Mozart, Concerto in B Flat Major for Bassoon, K. 191
Vivaldi, Concertos for Bassoon and Orchestra (any of several)

Saxophone
Debussy, *Rapsodie for Saxophone and Orchestra*
Glazounov, Concerto for Saxophone
Ibert, *Concertino da Camera, for Saxophone and Chamber Orchestra*

Trumpet
Haydn, Concerto in E Flat Major for Trumpet and Orchestra
Hindemith, Sonata for Trumpet and Piano
Purcell, Sonata for Trumpet and Strings

French Horn
Hindemith, Sonata for Four Horns
Mozart, Concertos for Horn (K. 412, K. 417,

K. 447, or K. 495)
Strauss, Concertos for Horn (either of two)

Trombone
Hindemith, Sonata for Trombone and Piano
Poulenc, Sonata for Trumpet, Trombone, and French Horn

Tuba
Vaughan Williams, Concerto for Bass Tuba and Orchestra

Percussion
Chavez, *Toccata for Percussion*
Harrison, *Canticle No. 3 for Percussion*
Milhaud, Concerto for Percussion and Small Orchestra

Harp
Handel, Concertos for Harp, Op. 4, Nos. 5 and 6
Hindemith, Sonata for Harp
Ravel, *Introduction and Allegro for Harp, Flute, Clarinet, and String Quartet*

Violin
Beethoven, Concerto in D Major for Violin, Op. 61
Chausson, *Poème for Violin and Orchestra*, Op. 25
Prokofiev, Concerto No. 2 in G Minor for Violin, Op. 63

Viola
Bartók, Concerto for Viola and Orchestra
Berlioz, *Harold in Italy*, Op. 16
Hindemith, *Trauermusik for Viola and Strings*

Cello
Block, *Schelomo*, Rhapsody for Cello and Orchestra
Haydn, Concerto in D Major for Cello, Op. 101
Schumann, Concerto for Cello

Bass Viol
Dittersdorf, Concerto in E for Double Bass
Koussevitzky, Concerto for Double Bass

---

*The word *opus*, meaning *work*, is put on compositions by the composer (or publisher) to indicate the general order in which works were written. The practice began early in the seventeenth century, but only since the mid-nineteenth century have opus numbers been applied consistently to new compositions.

instrument of a comparable range and sound was developed in the band of John Philip Sousa and appropriately named the sousaphone. The sousaphone is coiled over the player's shoulder and can be carried far more easily than the tuba. Sousaphones are the horns most evident in marching bands, and they are often used by school bands in concert as well.

Keyboard Instruments

Keyboard instruments that produce sounds with strings can be divided into two types. One produces the tone by means of a quill that plucks the string when the key is depressed. The other type produces sound when a key causes a hammer covered with felt to strike against the string.

Harpsichord. The harpsichord and virginal both operate on the principle of the plucked string. The main difference between these two instruments is that the virginal is a smaller, simpler instrument. It looks somewhat like a box that sits on a table. It was probably intended to be an instrument befitting a young lady, due to its rather delicate tone. The first piece of virginal music was published in England, and the cover featured a young lady playing the instrument.

The harpsichord looks somewhat like a grand piano. The case, or body, is much the same, and the keyboard is composed of the usual black and white keys (sometimes with the colors reversed) in the same arrangement. Later harpsichords, built in the seventeenth century, had two keyboards plus stop knobs. These knobs allowed other notes to sound with those the player was performing and permitted the strings of the two keyboards to sound together.

Neither the harpsichord nor the virginal mechanism allows the player to alter the volume by the finger pressure applied to the keys. The only way to change the dynamic level is for the harpsichordist to play on the second keyboard or, on the more complicated harpsichords, to engage a knob that doubles the tones an octave higher or lower. In either case the change is abrupt because no gradual dynamic shadings are possible.

Clavichord. The clavichord is basically a simple piano. It consists of a shallow box with strings running from left to right. The strings are secured on the left by pins in a block of wood and are sounded by brass tangents that strike the strings when depressed. The clavichord has a weak tone, but the player has some control of the musical expression.

Piano. The piano came on the musical scene relatively late. It was first constructed in about 1709, and the early models were not very impressive. The piano did not gain prominence until the last half of the eighteenth century.

If you don't know how a piano works, you may wish to lift up the top of one and take a look at its mechanism. Basically, the piano has a flat table of wood called the soundboard, the purpose of which is to amplify the sound from the strings. The strings themselves are strung over a cast iron frame. The cast iron frame is absolutely rigid, enabling the strings to stay in tune for relatively long periods of time. The strings are tuned by means of pins that are sunk in a block of wood. The tuner merely twists the pin with a wrench to raise or lower the pitch. The keyboard mechanism itself is more complicated than it appears to be, with about 27 pieces of metal and wood for each key. The most critical phase of the key's action is the movement of the hammer, which must leave the string immediately after striking it so that the string can vibrate freely.

The piano has two advantages over the other keyboard instruments mentioned previously. It has a much more powerful tone, and the player can make gradations in the dynamic level by the force with which the keys are struck. One pedal on the piano allows the sounds to ring even after the fingers have left the keys. Another pedal allows only certain strings to ring—those whose keys are depressed at the moment the pedal is activated. A third pedal moves the entire keyboard mechanism slightly so that the hammer cannot strike all the strings for each note, so a somewhat softer sound is produced. On upright pianos this pedal moves the hammers closer to the strings, which weakens the hammers' strokes.

Pianos come in two types. The grand piano is long and flat, like a large table. Because of its large size, its sound is superior to the upright. The upright piano has its strings mounted vertically, and the low strings are shortened in order to fit into a smaller space. Therefore, it has a less powerful tone and is a little more difficult to keep in tune. Concert music is always performed publicly on a grand piano. Throughout history keyboards have been constructed with differing numbers of notes. The modern piano is standardized at 88 black and white keys.

The console of an organ. (Rogers Organ Company.)

Organ. The sound of the organ is made when air is blown into pipes. Even a small change in the design of a pipe will cause a change of tone quality. Each timbre must have its own set, or rank, of pipes, one pipe for each pitch in the rank. A large organ can have as many as 100 ranks; medium-sized organs have 40 to 60. Each rank is brought into play by pulling a knob. Various knob combinations can be activated by pushing a button with the hand or foot. In the picture above, the knobs are on both sides of the keyboards, and the buttons are below the keys and on both sides of the center pedals. So even when the organist depresses only one key, 50 or more pipes could be sounded, depending on which knobs have been activated.

Several keyboards are visible. An organ usually has at least two keyboards, called *manuals.* Each manual has 61 keys, which is less than the piano's 88. The different manuals facilitate the use of different ranks of pipes. There isn't time during the playing of a piece for the organist to adjust the knobs for each of the manuals; this work must be done ahead of time.

The organist's feet are nearly as important as the hands. On the floor are black and blond wooden slats, which form another keyboard, the pedal board; it is played with the feet. Most tones sounded by the pedals are low in pitch. Playing music with the feet is not easy, but good organists can perform remarkably fast passages on the pedals.

Organ music utilizes three staves simultaneously: one in treble clef and two in bass clef. Generally, the organist plays the treble-clef part with the right hand, the upper bass-clef part with the left hand, and the lowest line with the feet on the pedals.

The twentieth century has brought forth many inventions, among them the electronic organ. Many pipe organists object strenuously to the electronic version. Their objection is based on the fact that the synthetic tones simply do not sound like an organ as it is traditionally conceived. It is generally conceded, however, that a *good* electronic organ usually has a better sound than a *poor* pipe organ. In any case, the tone quality of most electronic models is a far cry from the instrument of Bach. The organ of Bach's time is considered the standard for organs built today; modern quality pipe organs have copied it in nearly every detail. They are custom-made and extremely expensive.

Folk Instruments

Folk instruments can be grouped into four large categories. One is composed of those that are played with the breath. The most common instruments of this type are flutes. Some flutes are played sideways; others are played straight out from the player's mouth and are held like a recorder. The nose flute, a type of flute played by the natives of Oceania and Hawaii, is literally blown with the nose. There are double-reed instruments similar to the oboe and single-reed instruments similar to the clarinet. The *pungi* played by the snake charmers in India is another example in the reed category. A few simple brass folk instruments also exist.

A second classification involves percussion instruments other than drums. Included in it are bells, chimes, xylophones, rattles, and the Jew's harp, which is a flexible metal strip attached to a small horsehoe-shaped frame. Its name originally may have been *jaw's harp*.

A third group includes all kinds of drums, which involve a stretched membrane of some kind. Drums are constructed from many materials, including wood, metal, coconut, and gourd, and they come in shapes ranging from the hourglass drums of the Cameroons to friction drums, on which sound is made when a piece of hide is rubbed across the drum skin.

The fourth classification includes all the string instruments. Most of these are plucked—zithers, lyres, and harps, for example—but some are struck with mallets, and a few are bowed like a violin.

The instruments of a culture are usually constructed of materials readily available in that culture's area—animal horns or bones, skins, wood gourds, and so on. The availability and complexity of instruments also depend on the knowledge of such crafts as smelting metals and shaping wood. Some folk instruments are unreliable and have a weak tone.

Popular Instruments

Guitar. The ancestry of the guitar can probably be traced back to the Near East. The instrument was popular in France by the 1500s, and soon it became well known in Italy and Spain. Early guitars had only four strings, but today six is standard. Except for acoustical improvements the modern guitar has not changed much in the last several hundred years. The guitar has two somewhat different relatives. One is the ukulele, which is basically a small guitar. The other is the banjo, which has a parchment skin stretched over a hoop and no

back. The banjo has a much more brilliant sound than the guitar. It may have come to America with the slaves from Africa, but its ancestry is probably Arabic.

Electric guitar. The electric guitar predominates in current popular music. Its timbre is the "sound" of rock. The electric guitar is only distantly related to the traditional acoustic guitar just described. Instead of having a hollow sound box that amplifies the sound, it has an artificial box that serves more for decoration and as a site for mounting the control knobs. The sound of the strumming is picked up and amplified by electronic means. By turning knobs the player can adjust the volume level, change the the timbre of the sounds, and produce a vibrato. The electric guitar comes in basically two sizes. Like the acoustic guitar, the electric guitar has metal strips that cross the fingerboard. These strips are called *frets*, and they help the player find where to place a finger to achieve a certain pitch.

Drums. The percussion used in pop groups usually consists of a drum set played by one player. The set includes one or two cymbals that are placed on top of a stand. They are activated by striking them with a stick or a brush. Often there are three or four drums, usually without snares. The absence of snares gives the drum a more "tubby" sound. The largest drum in the set is a small bass drum that the player hits by pressing a pedal mechanism with the foot. Often this drum has a felt pad braced against one side to muffle the sound and cut down the reverberation. Much showmanship is involved in such drumming.

Accordion. The accordion has enjoyed several waves of popularity in the United States, and it is still quite popular in some European countries. The accordion is constructed somewhat on the principle of the organ, in that air is squeezed through the instrument to activate metal reeds. The accordion has a short keyboard for playing the melody. The accompanying chords are produced by pushing buttons that sound entire chords; there is one button for each type of chord in each key. In addition, when playing on a quality instrument, the accordionist may achieve different timbres by pushing different buttons. In a small way the varied timbres of the organ can be emulated.

The Voice

It may seem odd to think of the voice as an instrument, but in many ways it is. The voice is a device composed of several parts that function together to make musical sounds. We may not think of the voice as we do other instruments because we are born with it and learn to use it to some extent without formal training, something usually needed on the violin or trombone.

The voice operates when air is drawn into and forced out of the lungs by the up-down motion of the diaphragm, which is a "floor" of muscle under the lungs. As air is forced up it passes through the vocal cords, causing them to vibrate. The speed of the vibration, and therefore the pitch, changes according to the length and tension of the vocal cords. The tone quality is affected by the body and the chest, but even more by the resonating cavities in the head, including the sinuses. The tongue formation and cheeks also affect the timbre, including forming the particular vowel sound that is being sustained.

The difference between men's and women's voices lies largely in the length and thickness of the vocal cords. A man's vocal cords are normally about twice as long as a woman's, and they are also thicker, which contributes to a heavier timbre. The longer vocal cords of the male require a larger voice box, or larynx, which results in the more prominent Adam's apple in the adult male.

The vocal instrument is similar to other instruments in one other way. Using it to its fullest capacity in making music usually requires special training (although not for everyone who succeeds as a singer of art music), because singing difficult music demands both a great deal of muscle development and sensitive coordination of the various parts of the body.

Morton Subotnick and the "Electric Music Box"—one version of a synthesizer. (California Institute of the Arts.)

Instruments of the Future

The most important new instrument is not an instrument at all in the usual sense of the word. It is the tone synthesizer—an electronic instrument that can produce all sorts of sounds and timbres and is sometimes used in conjunction with a tape recorder. The player-composer does not actually interpret a work while the audience listens. Instead, a piece is prepared on the synthesizer and recorded onto a tape. Then the composer works with the tape to produce the composition.

Synthesizers are extremely complex, as the picture above indicates. One almost has to be an electrical engineer and acoustician to develop music for it. Synthesizer and tape compositions are usually "solo" endeavors. That is, they are seldom combined in an ensemble, as one might combine a violin and a piano.

Sometimes a computer is used in conjunction with electronic music. Computers direct the equipment according to a particular program, and they are useful in analyzing music.

Like the synthesizer, the tape recorder is not an instrument in the usual sense of the word. It can only reproduce sounds that are fed into it. The composer's job is, of course, to decide which sounds should be recorded. One of the chief sources of sound for the tape recorder in contemporary music—in addition to the tone synthesizer—is the world of commonplace, everyday sound: the cry of a baby, the chirp of a bird, the drip of a faucet. Sounds from conventional instruments are also used. The performer-composer then manipulates the tape by increasing or slowing down the speed, by splicing the tape, by rerecording sounds on top of one another. The composer experiments freely to create radically different sounds. This type of music has been called *musique concrète*. It alters natural sounds by means of the tape recorder itself.

Minor improvements in instruments will continue to be made, of course. Different materials will be tried and other refinements will be made.

II
SECTION TWO
Musical Forms and Media

The elements of music discussed in Section I can be sounded in a variety of ways. One way is the voice. It is the first musical medium presented in this section. Following the presentation of music for solo voice comes the discussion of choral music—music for a number of singers.

Another means of musical expression is through instruments. One chapter is devoted to symphonic music, another to concertos, and another to music for small instrumental groups. Yet another chapter is devoted to keyboard music.

Some types of music are related to other fine arts. A chapter is devoted to opera, which is a unification of music and drama. The section concludes with a discussion of ballet, the bringing together of dance and music.

Scene from La Bohème. *(Indiana University School of Music.)*

7

Songs and Singing

It is hard for contemporary Americans to realize the importance with which singing is regarded in many parts of the world and to appreciate the place it held in our society in the past. Most of the folk and ethnic music to be cited in Chapter 15 is vocal music, not instrumental. Much of it is sung by nearly everyone in the society. Until about 60 years ago singing was a more common means of expression than it is today.

One reason singing seems to be less vital today is the advent of recordings and other means of producing music. In the past if you wanted to hear music, you or someone you knew had to make it. Every performance was a live performance. People often sang at square dances because they had to; without the singing there would have been only a little fiddle music. People heard little music that they or their acquaintances didn't produce.* Today it is very nearly the opposite; we hear only a small amount of music that we or our acquaintances produce.

The type of work we do today also discourages singing. The automobile assembly plant is hardly conducive to singing, and neither is an office filled with typewriters and computers. If you were to sing on the subway or bus on your way home from work, fellow passengers would suspect either your sanity or your sobriety. And the romantic notion that a young man sings to his loved one seems as quaint as the custom of bringing her a box of candy and

---

*Sometime before World War I my grandfather was the first in his area to buy a phonograph, a wind-up model with a long horn that played cylindrical records with what today we would consider poor fidelity. Nearly every evening for several winters, one or more of the neighboring families would drive through the cold Minnesota nights and call at his home to listen to the wonderful new machine that played music.

some flowers when calling on her in the parlor.

Singing is not going to pass from the face of the earth, however, because the use of voices to make music is too basic a means of expression. Nearly everyone has a voice, and through talking and singing people express themselves. Every so often there is a revival of interest in folk songs, and guitars to accompany them are sold by the thousands. These facts indicate that singing is by no means obsolete.

Folk Songs

Chapter 15 will present various types of folk music from around the world; this chapter deals with some of the types found in Western cultures.

Work songs. Work was a more integral part of life a few generations ago because many more hours of labor were required to maintain oneself and one's family. The sea chantey (pronounced *shantey*) "Haul Away Joe" is an example of a song to accompany work. Clearly, the words are of little importance.

> *Louis was the King of France before the*
> *Revolution,*
> *'Way, haul away, we'll haul away Joe.*
> *King Louis got his head cut off which spoiled*
> *his constitution,*
> *'Way, haul away, we'll haul away Joe.*

Dancing and recreation. A second type of folk song was intended to accompany dancing. In America this frequently meant square dancing. Again, the words were of little importance; some, in fact, were added just to fill out a phrase. A well-known example is "Turkey in the Straw," in which one verse is:

> *As I went out to milk, and I didn't know how;*
> *I milked a goat instead of a cow.*
> *A monkey sittin' on a pile of straw,*
> *A-winkin' his eye at his mother-in-law.*
> *Turkey in the hay, turkey in the straw,*
> *The ole gray mare won't gee nor haw;*
> *Roll 'em up and twist 'em up a high tuck-a-*
> *haw,*
> *And hit 'em up a tune called Turkey in the*
> *Straw.*

Some "fun" songs were not for dancing. "The Deacon Went Down to the Cellar to Pray" is one example. Its next line is: "He found a jug and stayed all day."

Storytelling. Many English and American folk songs tell a story. "Careless Love" has a story of woe that concludes:

> *Love, oh love, oh careless love,*
> *See what careless love has done to me.*
>
> *When my apron strings were long,*
> *You passed my window with a song.*
>
> *Now my apron strings won't tie,*
> *You pass my cabin door right by.*

Expression of feeling. Many songs, both folk and art, exist primarily to express feelings. The white spiritual is one example. The words to "The Wayfaring Stranger" are:

> *I'm just a poor, wayfaring stranger,*
> *A-trav'ling through this world of woe,*
> *Yet there's no sickness, no toil, no danger,*
> *In that fair land to which I go.*
>
> *I'm goin' there to see my mother,*
> *I'm goin' there no more to roam,*

I'm goin' over to Jordan,
I'm just a-goin' over home.

Sometimes composers find songs that they consider worth arranging for concert or recital hall performance. They leave the original melody largely intact and devise an accompaniment for piano or orchestra. Aaron Copland did this with the Shaker song "Simple Gifts," which appears on Record 1, A. The song originates from the period between 1837 and 1847, and the text expresses the Shaker ideal of the simple, orderly life.

'Tis the gift to be simple, 'tis the gift to be free,
'Tis the gift to come down where you ought to
*   be,*
And when we find ourselves in the place just
*   right,*
'Twill be in the valley of love and delight.

When true simplicity is gained,
To bow and to bend we shan't be ashamed,
To turn, turn will be our delight
'Till by turning, turning we come round right.

As pointed out in Chapter 3, the setting of the melody for "Simple Gifts" is in keeping with the text and melody by being very open and uncluttered. There are only very brief introductory measures based on the melody for each half of the song. Sometimes the chords are sounded off the beat in a subtle syncopation, but generally everything is understated and plain.

Strophic Songs

Most of the songs we know consist of a melody and several verses of words. This type of music is called *strophic*. Church hymns, popular songs, and most folk and community songs are strophic, including our national anthem. The melody existed long before Francis Scott Key wrote his poem. If you have ever tried singing the second and third verses, you probably discovered that they do not fit the music too well at some points.

Strophic songs are made up of rather distinct units or phrases. Phrases can be compared to clauses and sentences in language. The "punctuation" in music is done by shaping the melody, dynamics, and chord patterns. Try singing "When Johnny Comes Marching Home" to yourself. Notice that each of the four phrases seems self-contained, like a rather complete musical statement, and yet only the last phrase suggests conclusion.

When Johnny comes marching home again,
*   hurrah, hurrah!*
We'll give him the hearty welcome then,
*   hurrah, hurrah!*
The men will cheer, the boys will shout, the
*   ladies they will all turn out,*
And we'll all feel gay when Johnny comes
*   marching home!*

Different sets of words can often be sung to the same melody. Most church hymnals contain an index that groups hymns according to meter. (The numbers in the index—8. 6. 8. 6., for example—refer to the number of syllables in each line.) All hymns grouped under a particular meter may exchange words or music. Words of nonsacred songs have been exchanged also ("America" and "God Save the King"), and *Mad* magazine regularly makes up humorous lyrics to familiar songs.

Many strophic songs include a refrain—a section of music with a single set of words—although the verses have changing words.

Strophic songs often display an overall musical design, one of the uses of the word *form* mentioned in Chapter 5. Take, for example, "Deck the Halls": The first line is:

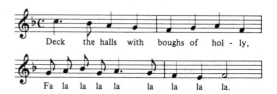

Let's label this line *a*. (If it were a long section, it would be identified by a capital *A*.) The second line is:

It is exactly like the first line, so it can also be labeled *a*. The third line is different:

Since it is different, it can be labeled *b*. The fourth line is like the first, except that it is altered somewhat toward the end.

It is best marked by *a'*. The prime mark (') denotes a slight alteration but not enough to warrant a different letter. The form of "Deck the Halls," then, is *a a b a'*. This pattern is one of the most frequent in music. It seems to contain the best balance between familiar and contrasting material. The two basic song forms are *a b*, which is called *binary*, and *a b a*, which is called *ternary*. "Simple Gifts" is in binary form and "Deck the Halls" in a modified ternary form.

Chant and Recitative

Chant is a style of singing that usually has no regular meter and its range is narrow, to suggest the inflections of speech. Frequently it is not very tuneful. Once it was quite important, but it is not common in the United States today. The style goes back at least to the ancient Greek poet Homer (about 850 B.C.), who recited his epic tales in a singsong fashion as he plucked out notes on an ancient guitarlike instrument. The word *psalm* means song, and the biblical psalms were probably often recited in a singsong fashion, too. Chant is still a part of Judaic worship. The style was adapted by the early Christian church and is heard today in some Roman Catholic churches and briefly in some Protestant worship services. A portion of a "Credo" from a Mass (the central worship service of the Roman Catholic Church) is shown at the bottom of the page. The words are the creed of the Christian church: "I believe in God the Father Almighty," and so on.

The reciting style is also heard in many vocal works such as operas (see Chapter 13). The term for this kind of singing is *recitative*. It is especially suitable for telling the listener a lot in a short period of time. Long-flowing solos or choruses, on the other hand, usually cover only a small amount of text; the words are often repeated throughout the number. Another feature of recitative is that it can be very expressive. The composer of the music and the singer who performs it can adjust the melodic line to fit the mood suggested by the words. Recitative looks on a page of music as though it would be performed quite regularly. Tradition, however, permits the singer considerable freedom. The accompaniment is kept simple to allow the singer greater latitude of expression. An example of a recitative from *Messiah* by George Frideric Handel is given on the next page. This recitative is included in the *Record Album* (1, B). Notice its simple accompaniment and the many repeated tones in the voice part.

The voice of him that cri-eth in the wil-der-ness, Pre-pare ye the way of the Lord, make straight in the des-ert a high-way for our God.

Chant and recitative are types of singing, but they are not songs as we know them. The style has a certain haunting charm, and it is strangely effective in projecting the message of words.

Music Written for One Set of Words

When composers want to give maximum expression to a set of words, they do not try to write a catchy tune. Rather, they design the music for one particular text so that each supports the impact of the other. No substitution of words is desirable; if it were done, it would probably not be musically effective.

The ability of music to enhance words was mentioned earlier, in the explanation of recitative. Handel wrote certain notes and rhythms for the singing of the words "Fear not" because he thought that they best expressed the feeling of those words in sound. A strophic song cannot do this. The same notes and rhythms are not equally suitable for words as varied as "He's going," "You villain!" or "I love you."

Another example of unity in words and music is the *art song*, which is primarily a nineteenth-century German development. In fact,

this type of composition is often called a *lied* (plural *lieder*), the German word for song. It is usually written for one singer and piano accompaniment. The song is created mainly to express the idea of the words in music and only secondarily to provide a memorable melody. The accompaniment also contributes to the mood of the music and is nearly as important as the singer's part. The result is maximum musical expression of the words.

Some art songs are strophic to a degree, but many are *through-composed*; that is, there is no literal repeating of lines of music. One of the best known examples of an art song is "*Gretchen am Spinnrade*" ("Margaret at the Spinning Wheel") by the Austrian composer Franz Schubert (1797–1828). The text is by the great German poet Goethe, who lived from 1749 to 1832. In the song Gretchen has lost her love, and her heart aches for him, and how she longs to have his arms around her again and be kissed! The mood is one of pained anxiety, and the music is set in a minor key. The piano bolsters the words by supplying the motion of the spinning wheel with continuous moving notes.

As you listen to the recording (Record 1, A), notice that the music for "All my rest is gone . . ." is repeated each time the words occur in the poem. The vocal line on the word *Ruh*

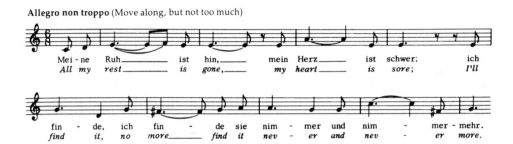

Allegro non troppo (Move along, but not too much)

Mei - ne Ruh____ ist hin,____ mein Herz____ ist schwer; ich
All my rest____ is gone,____ my heart____ is sore; I'll

fin - de, ich fin - de sie nim - mer und nim - mer - mehr.
find it, no more____ find it nev - er and nev - er more.

(rest) has a sighing sound that adds to the pained character of the music. The song builds to a point of excitement beginning with the words *Mein Busen drängt.* The contour of the line moves up by half steps until it reaches a high point on the word *küssen*, thereby emphasizing the idea of excitement and eagerness. Again, Schubert has worked out the music to amplify the thought of the text.

Because words and music are so closely related in the art song, translations from the original language are difficult. It is hard to retain the original meaning of the words and also make the emphasis of the translated words and the music coincide. Usually the songs are sung in the original language. Here is one translation:

Meine Ruh' ist hin,
Mein Herz ist schwer;
Ich finde, ich finde sie
Nimmer und nimmermehr.
Wo ich ihn nicht hab',
Ist mir das Grab,
Die ganze Welt ist mir vergällt.

Mein armer Kopf ist mir verrückt,
Mein armer Sinn ist mir zerstückt.

Meine Ruh' ist hin,
Mein Herz ist schwer;
Ich finde, ich finde sie
Nimmer und nimmermehr.
Nach ihm nur schau' ich
Zum Fenster hinaus,
Nach ihm nur geh' ich
Aus dem Haus.

Sein hoher Gang, sein' edle Gestalt,
Seines Mundes Lächeln,
Seiner Augen Gewalt,
Und seiner Rede Zauberfluss,
Sein Händedruck, und ach, sein Kuss!

Meine Ruh' ist hin,
Mein Herz ist schwer;
Ich finde, ich finde sie

All my rest is gone,
My heart is sore,
I'll find it no more,
Find it never and nevermore.
If he is not near,

My grave is here,
The world is stress and bitterness.
My poor, weak head is tempest-tossed,
My poor weak senses seem quite lost.

All my rest is gone,
My heart is sore,
I'll find it no more,
Find it never and nevermore.
'Tis he alone
From the window I seek,
'Tis he I leave the house
To meet.

His noble form, his bearing so high,
And his mouth so smiling
And his powerful eye,
His magic words which bring such bliss,
His hand, his clasp, and O! his kiss!

All my rest is gone,
My heart is sore,
I'll find it no more,

Nimmer und nimmermehr.	*Find it never and nevermore.*
Mein Busen drängt sich nach ihm hin.	*My bosom strains to meet his clasp,*
Ach, dürft ich fassen und halten ihn!	*O! might I seize him with eager grasp!*
Und küssen ihn so wie ich wollt',	*And kissing him as I would kiss,*
An seinen Küssen vergehen sollt',	*In his embraces I'd die with bliss!*
O könnt ich ihn küssen,	*Ah! could I but kiss him*
So wie ich wollt',	*As I would kiss,*
An seinen Küssen vergehen sollt'!	*In his embraces I'd die with bliss!*
(last line repeated)	
Meine Ruh' ist hin,	*All my rest is gone,*
Mein Herz ist schwer!	*My heart is sore!*

A more contemporary example of an art song is "Autumn" by the American Charles Ives, who wrote 114 songs. Written in 1908, this song is the setting of a short poem by Harmony Twichell Ives, the composer's wife. The text is:

Earth rests!
Her work is done, her fields lie bare,
and 'ere the night of winter comes
to hush her song and close her tired eyes,
She turns her face for the sun to smile upon
and radiantly, radiantly
thro' Falls' bright glow,
he smiles,
and brings the Peace of God!*

The music casts a feeling of calm and rest. As can be heard on the recording in the *Record Album* (Record 1, A), the lower notes in the piano part throb smoothly off the beat in syncopated style for almost all the 23 measures of the song. The upper notes of the piano part present a contrasting melodic line that sounds many of the same melodic figures either before or after the singer. The word "radiantly" is an example of how a text is given a "customized" treatment by an art song composer. The music does seem to radiate, especially the second time at which point the first note is raised a half step and the accompanying chord changed to major. The word "smiles" is given the highest pitch and loudest dynamic level in the singer's part. "The Peace of God" is written to be sung in a calm, slow, and reassuring manner.

Nineteenth-century art songs sometimes reveal an uneven quality of text, and they seem a trifle dated today. But such music has melodic appeal, and the accompaniment enhances the mood of the music in a beautiful and effective way. When a Schubert or Ives combines text, vocal line, and accompaniment, something of artistic worth is created. That "something" is not duplicated elsewhere in the world of music. Folk songs and songs from operas do not achieve the same kind of expression; they have other virtues. The art song is a high point in the expression of specific thoughts in music.

Singing Styles

Each type of song—folk, popular, art—is associated with a style of singing that seems most suitable for it. For example, to sing a popular song in the manner of an art song is as inappropriate as wearing a tuxedo at a picnic. And vice versa; singing an art song in a pop style is ineffective and out of place. Several factors make up a singing style—fluctuations of pitch, speed and size of vibrato, and the manner in which words are pronounced. But the most significant aspect of vocal style is timbre. Some styles call for a nasal quality, others for a light timbre, and others for a virile, powerful sound.

When you first listen to it, the singing style evident in art music may seem unnatural and a little contrived. It is not as natural as the style associated with folk songs. It is more trained, and it exhibits greater power, range, and tech-

---

* © Copyright 1956 by Peer International Corporation. Used by permission.

nical skill. Very few pop or folk singers can even perform the notes called for in many works of art music, to say nothing of sounding good while doing so.

As for being contrived, almost all singing implies drama, which is a type of artificial situation. Certainly much singing in jazz, rock, and art songs sheds "crocodile tears" over lost loves and expresses exuberant joy over found ones (although for some reason there seem to be more songs about unhappy events than happy ones).

But contrived or not, natural or trained, folk, popular, or art—singing has an expressiveness about it that is fascinating. It is a very human activity.

Franz Schubert

Franz Schubert (1797–1828) was born into the family of a schoolteacher in a Vienna suburb. Young Schubert's creative talent was evident while he was still a boy. After completing school, he tried to follow in his father's footsteps, but he couldn't accept the routine involved in teaching. He preferred to spend his time writing music.

Schubert didn't adjust well to adult life. He never held a real position of employment; in fact, he made only halfhearted attempts to find one. He had a small circle of friends who appreciated his talents. They housed and fed him when he was in need, which was his normal condition. Schubert was incompetent in dealing with publishers, who made good profits on his music. He sold some pieces, later worth thousands of dollars, for the price of a meal.

As the years passed, he became lonelier and more discouraged. He was even unlucky in love. But his output of compositions never dwindled. He died of typhus at the age of 31, leaving the world his clothing, his bedding, some manuscripts valued at 10 florins—and a vast store of beautiful music.

Schubert was a versatile composer. He wrote piano works, chamber music, and symphonies. Popular legend has falsely assumed that the familiar Symphony No. 8 (*Unfinished*) was left incomplete because of his death or because of his despair over a lost love. The real reason is less dramatic. The work was probably left unfinished because Schubert never got around to completing it. He went on to compose and complete another long symphony.

In his instrumental works Schubert tended to be less subjective than in his vocal works. His vocal music, which included seven Masses and about 15 operas, was thoroughly Romantic. His 600 songs did much to assure his posthumous success and immortality.

Song Composers Presented Elsewhere

Charles Ives, page 261
Aaron Copland, page 139

8

Choral Music

Not all vocal music is intended to be sung by only one person at a time. Many vocal works are created for groups of singers, and such music is called *choral* music. This chapter explores the most important types of choral music. Some large choral works contain sections for soloists, but because these works require a number of singers performing together they are considered choral music. Let's begin by looking at the oratorio.

Oratorio

An oratorio is a long work for chorus, soloists, and orchestra, and it usually deals with a religious topic. It is generally performed in a concert hall without scenery, costumes, or actions. It is not written as part of a worship service but more as a concert. The text of an oratorio is dramatic (often taken from the Old Testament), and each soloist represents a specific character.

The man who developed the oratorio as it is known today was George Frideric Handel. Handel was born in Germany, and as a young man he moved to England to write Italian operas. (Things weren't always logical in the eighteenth century, either.) When Italian operas went out of style in England, he developed a type of opera without staging, costumes, or actions. His new compositions were called *oratorios* and were very successful; some of them are still performed today, more than 200 years after they were composed.

Handel's *Messiah*

The oratorio *Messiah* is musically rather typical. It differs from other oratorios chiefly in that its text is taken entirely from the Bible and has no part for a narrator, who through singing describes the events of a story. *Messiah* is primarily a contemplation on Christian belief starting with a section on prophecy and Christ's birth, followed by His suffering and death, and concluding with the resurrection and redemption. Handel wrote its nearly three hours of music in the unbelievably short time of 24 days. As he wrote, he was aware that he was creating a great work. Afraid that if he stopped he might lose his momentum, he hardly slept, ate, or left his house for three weeks.

Messiah was well received by critics and the public at its first performance in Dublin. At the first performance in London on March 23, 1743, King George II was so awed by the "Hallelujah Chorus" that he rose and stood at his seat. And in those days, when the king stood, everyone stood. So the king's spontaneous action became a tradition that is still followed today.

Like other oratorios, *Messiah* contains many individual musical numbers—53 in all. Each number is one of three types: recitative, aria, or chorus.

Aria. An aria (pronounced *ar*-eeah) is a vocal solo of some length and complexity. It is not just a tune like "America" or "When Johnny Comes Marching Home." Like the art song, it is intended to be musically expressive, although often it doesn't cover as much text. The aria makes sizable demands on the performer's singing technique, with frequent passages of rapidly moving notes and a wide range. Arias are often *virtuoso* music, music that requires a highly skilled performer. They are generally longer than art songs, and they are intended to be sung with orchestral accompaniment.

One of the first arias in *Messiah* is "Every Valley Shall Be Exalted." It is sung by the tenor soloist. A Listening Guide for this aria appears on pages 62–63.

The soloist often has to sing rapidly moving notes or perform long phrases on a single word or syllable. The long runs on the word "exalt-ed" illustrate the virtuoso singing that is found in many arias.

When arias were first written in oratorios and operas, they were intended to be pleasing and expressive solo songs. But soon the soloists began to add flashy runs and decorative notes. The custom snowballed until the composer's music became just a skeleton that the singers fleshed out as they wished. Astounding singing resulted, but musical expressiveness and quality suffered. Some reform had taken place by Handel's time, but audiences still liked to hear virtuoso singing and expected some of it in arias.

In "Every Valley," the runs do more than show off the singer's skill. Handel cleverly integrates them into the entire musical fabric so that they enhance the effect of the piece. For example, it is easy to imagine that the singer's runs are an instrument adding a countermelody. Handel uses the runs to bring out the idea of the words. In this aria the word "exalted" is treated to the long runs. *Exalted*, meaning raised or lifted up in a spiritual sense, is the word that most appropriately expresses the main thought of the text. The low places will be raised up spiritually, says the poet in Isaiah 40:4. Not only does "exalted" have a crucial meaning within the text; it has an especially good vowel on which to sustain the singing: the *awe* or broad *a*.

Virtuoso passages are sometimes baffling and disturbing to nonmusicians. They cannot understand why a syllable is stretched out over 40 or more notes. Of course, "exalted" can be sung with just three notes, and these can even occur on a single pitch level. But the musical interest would be diminished. It is impressive to hear a skilled singer execute the long runs, and it is even more rewarding to hear the line fit into the music and to sense the emphasis given certain words. In everyday practical terms it's silly to use 40 notes to sing one word, but in terms of music it makes much sense.

The chorus. The word *chorus* has a double meaning in music. It can refer to a group that sings choral music or to the choral sections of an oratorio or opera. So a chorus sings a chorus.

In many ways the chorus portion of the music is similar to the aria. It is a rather lengthy section. It involves about the same amount of text and has frequent repetition of words. Metrical rhythmic patterns are followed strictly, and lines of music calling for considerable singing ability are found. The accompaniment may be heard alone in certain passages.

There is one fundamental difference between the chorus and aria, however. If you study the music for the "Hallelujah Chorus," you will observe that the parts are sometimes contrapuntal. This imitation tends to occur when a new section of text begins.

A Listening Guide for the "Hallelujah Chorus" appears on pages 64–65. As you listen to the "Hallelujah Chorus," notice how skillfully Handel has placed the words in regard to rhythmic accent. The word "Hallelujah" is written as one would say it when excited. In phrases such as "and He shall reign forever and ever," the important words of the phrase land on the important beats and parts of the beat in the rhythmic pattern. It is interesting that Handel combined words and music so well in a language that he himself never learned to speak very well.

Walton's *Belshazzar's Feast*

William Walton (1902–1983) was born in England. Unlike Handel, Walton spent two years composing his oratorio *Belshazzar's Feast*, completing it in 1931. Like Handel, he uses a chorus, orchestra, soloist, and biblical text (selected and arranged by Osbert Sitwell), but no costumes, scenery, or acting. Walton's forces are significantly larger. The chorus is a double chorus (eight voice parts instead of the usual four), piano, organ, large percussion section, and two brass bands located at the sides of the hall to give a stereo effect. Two additional choirs are called for from the sides of the hall.

The music is not divided into separate movements but does fall into three broad sections. The first section describes the sorrows and suffering of the Jewish captives in Babylon. The chorus sings: "By the waters of Babylon, there

Listening Guide

Handel: *Messiah*, Tenor Aria: "Every Valley Shall be Exalted"   *Record 1, B*

Form: *A B A B*

0:00   Orchestral ritornelli (refrain) playing main melodic ideas from both main portions of aria.

0:23   Solo tenor sings "Every valley shall be exalted" (*A*); short responses by orchestra:

0:38   First long run on "exalted."

0:54   Second long run on "exalted."

we sat down, yea, we wept. . . . How shall we sing the Lord's song in a strange land!"

The second section tells about the pagan worship of the false gods. "Babylon was a great city, her merchandise was of gold and silver . . . and the souls of men." Belshazzar orders a feast "to a thousand of his lords," and wine is brought forth in gold and silver stolen from the temple in Jerusalem by his father, Nebuchadnezzar. The king praises the god of gold and the gods of silver, iron, wood, stone, and brass. With harp and timbrel the guests extoll the king.

Then in the hour of revelry there is a chilling silent pause. The soloist grimly tells about the handwriting on the wall:

And in that same hour as they feasted came forth the fingers of a man's hand, and the king saw the part of the hand that wrote. And this was the writing that was written: "Mene,

mene, tekei upharsin." "Thou are weighed in the balance and found wanting."
In that night was Belshazzar the King slain, and his Kingdom divided.

As the words about the handwriting on the wall are sung, the cymbal shakes, the gong sounds, the strings play dissonant clusters of notes, and the piccolo emits a high trill to give the music a spooky quality. The translation of the words by the chorus is preceded by a short, forceful fanfare figure from the trombones. After the words "slain" and "divided" the chorus or orchestra punches notes out of the silence almost as though they were kicking the body of Belshazzar. This portion of the oratorio is included in the *Record Album* (Record 1, A).

The third section of the oratorio (below) presents the rejoicing of the Israelites over the fall of Babylon. The text is on the next page.

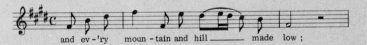

1:02   Melodic and text ideas "and every mountain and hill made low," etc.; enter *B*:

1:54   Repeat of first melodic material, with some changes, and text *A*.

2:35   Repeat of second melodic ideas, with some changes, and text *B*.

3:12   Tempo slows much for last repeat of text and music, "and the rough places plain."

3:29   Orchestra repeats its opening nine measures exactly.

3:54   Conclusion.

Then sing aloud to God our strength; make a joyful noise unto the God of Jacob. Take a psalm, bring hither the timbrel, blow up the trumpet in the new moon. Blow up the trumpet in Zion, for Babylon the Great is fallen. Alleluia!

After a while the text expresses some sympathy for the silent and dark Babylon. The oratorio concludes with words of praise to "the God of Jacob. Alleluia!"

Motet, Madrigal, and Cantata

Three other types of choral music are the motet, the madrigal, and the cantata. Because they are associated closely with a particular musical style, they are presented in Chapters 16 and 17

Listening Guide

Handel: *Messiah*, Chorus: "Hallelujah"   *Record 1, B*

0:00	Short orchestral introduction.
0:07	Chorus sings together the word "Hallelujah" five times and then five times more.
0:27	Chorus sings together "for the Lord God Omnipotent reigneth"; followed by four "Hallelujahs":

0:39	Altos, tenors, and basses repeat "for the Lord God . . ." phrase; followed by four "Hallelujahs."
0:52	Sopranos sing "for the Lord God . . ." phrase, with rest of chorus singing "Hallelujahs" forming counterpoint.
0:59	Tenors and basses take up "for the Lord God . . ." phrase, while sopranos and altos sing contrasting "Hallelujahs."
1:09	Altos and tenors sing "for the Lord God . . ." phrase, while sopranos and basses sing contrapuntal "Hallelujahs."
1:20	Chorus sings together with no counterpoint "The kingdom of this world is become the Kingdom of our Lord and of His Christ."
1:42	Basses begin new melody and text, "and He shall reign forever and ever":

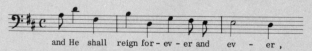

in conjunction with the Renaissance and Baroque periods. Both the madrigal and the motet are short, usually unaccompanied pieces for a small group of voices. Both contain much counterpoint. The main difference between the two vocal forms is that the motet is a religious work sung in Latin, while the madrigal is a nonreligious work in a language such as Italian, German, or English. The madrigal is also somewhat more liberal in its harmonies, texts, and rhythms.

The cantata is quite similar to the oratorio. The main difference is length; the cantata is much shorter. It often requires fewer performers and was composed for use in the worship service. Often cantatas use a church hymn tune (chorale) as a theme. A cantata is presented in Chapter 17.

1:47	Tenors sing "and He shall reign . . ."; basses sing free contrapuntal material.
1:53	Altos sing "and He shall reign . . ."; tenors and basses continue contrasting lines.
1:59	Sopranos sing "and He shall reign . . ."; other three parts continue in counterpoint.
2:06	Sopranos and altos sing "King of Kings," with second "Kings" held; basses and tenors sing "forever and ever, Hallelujah," and alternate with "Lord of Lords."
2:17	Same basic idea is repeated four more times, each time at a higher pitch level.
2:45	Sopranos reach highest pitch level for "and Lord of Lords"; are joined by other sections of chorus.
2:50	Basses begin "and He shall reign . . ." melody again; other sections sing contrasting imitative material.
2:56	Sopranos sing "and He shall reign . . ."; other sections sing contrasting imitative material.
3:03	Tenors sing "King of Kings"; other sections respond with "forever and ever" and "Hallelujah."
3:13	Chorus sings together (basses on melody) "and He shall reign . . ."; followed by "King of Kings." Same basic idea repeated, except sopranos sing "King of Kings."
3:56	Closes after four "Hallelujahs" and one long "Hallelujah."

George Frideric Handel

(Painting by Philip Mercier, formerly in Halle. New York Public Library.)

Handel was born in 1685 in the city of Halle in Saxony, which is a part of Germany today. His father was a well-to-do barber-surgeon who didn't think music was a good career for his son, so he discouraged young George in music study. But the boy showed much ability in composing, and he played the harpsichord and organ well. He also studied oboe and violin. After a year in college, he went to Hamburg, where he took a job playing violin in the orchestra. Italian opera was extremely popular throughout Europe, and Handel quickly learned its style. By the age of 20 he had written his first opera.

Italy was the center of the musical world at that time, and Handel lived there for several years. He learned much, made many friends, and continued writing operas.

In 1710 he returned to Germany to be musical director of the Court at Hanover. During his two years there he managed to take two leaves of absence to go to London. His second visit was made on the condition that he return to Hanover "within a reasonable time." But he was still in London two years later when his employer, the Elector of Hanover, was proclaimed King George I of England. Just how Handel handled this embarrassing situation isn't known. One story has it that he composed a group of pieces to be played while the king sailed on the Thames River; thus the title for the *Water Music*.

From 1720 to 1728 Handel held an influential position in the musical life of London. His efforts during this time were spent in writing and presenting Italian operas. By 1728 this type of opera began to lose favor because of something called *The Beggar's Opera*, a satirical play with songs inserted. Stubborn and unrelenting, Handel kept on writing Italian operas, investing and losing money in the process. At the age of 52 his health broke, and he left the country to recover.

And recover he did. He tried opera again, without success, and then turned to a new form. Years before, he had written one or two works in operatic style but without scenery, costumes, or acting. Handel began writing oratorios again, and within a few years he was back on top of the English musical world. During the 1740s and 1750s he wrote an amazing number of oratorios, including *Messiah, Samson, Semele, Joseph and His Brethren, Hercules, Belshazzar, Judas Maccabaeus, Joshua, Susanna, Solomon, Jeptha*—more than 26 in all.

In 1759 Handel collapsed after participating in a performance of *Messiah*. He died a few days later and was buried with state honors in Westminster Abbey in London.

William Walton

Walton was born in 1902 in Oldham, Lancashire, England. His father was a music teacher, and as a child Walton showed exceptional talent. He attended school at Christ Church in Oxford and later went to college there. Partly self-taught, he began publishing works when he was just past 20 years old. His earliest successful work was *Facade*, a recitation with music. *Belshazzar's Feast* was completed about five years later. Later he composed a viola concerto, a violin concerto, a number of sizable works for orchestra, chamber music, choral music, and songs. Twice he composed works for the coronation of British monarchs; *Crown Imperial* in 1937 for King George VI and *Orb and Scepter* in 1953 for Queen Elizabeth II. He also composed a number of works for plays, films, and radio broadcasts. He was knighted by the king in 1951. He died in 1983.

9

Symphonies

A *symphony* is a work for full orchestra. Usually it is rather long and divided into *movements*, which are large, independent sections of instrumental compositions. From about 1790 to 1920 symphonies were to musicians as novels were to writers: the largest and most significant creative effort in their art. A composer who brought forth a symphony was in effect saying, "This is an important creative effort." Johannes Brahms, one of the great composers of the nineteenth century, fussed and fumed over his first symphony and did not bring it out until he was past 40 years of age.

In the last half of the eighteenth century, Haydn (the so-called father of the symphony) wrote 104 symphonies, of which only the last 16 or so are played with any frequency today. From that point on the numerical output declined. Mozart, who was 24 years younger than Haydn, composed about 50 symphonies, but only 10 are played much today. In the next generation Beethoven composed 9, all of which are standard works in the current orchestral repertoire. Two generations later Brahms wrote only 4, and they too are all heard frequently today. Haydn's and Mozart's symphonies are shorter and lighter, while Beethoven and later composers regarded their symphonies as long and serious efforts.

A logical place to start an examination of the symphony is with a work of Mozart. He did not originate the form, but his symphonies are some of the earliest examples to be maintained in the standard orchestral repertoire today.

Mozart's Symphony No. 40

Mozart's Symphony No. 40 in G Minor, K. 550, was written in the summer of 1788, along with two other symphonies, Symphony No. 39 and Symphony No. 41, the *Jupiter*. Little is known about the circumstances that encouraged the writing of these symphonies, but it is likely that Mozart never heard them performed. The instruments called for in Symphony No. 40 are violins, violas, cellos and bass viols (separate parts were not yet written for the two instruments), a flute, two oboes, two bassoons, and two French horns. Mozart later added parts for two clarinets.

First movement—sonata form. The first movement of this symphony is in the usual form for first movements in the eighteenth century: It is called a *first-movement* or *sonata-allegro* or, more commonly, *sonata* form. As can be heard on Record 2,A, with no introduction, the music opens at a moderately fast tempo with the theme at the bottom of the page.

Several things should be pointed out about these nine measures. First, the theme is divided into two equal parts, the second being nearly identical to the first but one note lower. Each half is further divided in half, the first part being on the order of a melodic statement and the second a sort of musical answer. So the melody is symmetrical in both its larger and smaller sections. The melody is not particularly singable, which indicates that it is designed for instruments. Also, and this is significant in the music of the eighteenth century, the melody is in a sense a collection of several melodic fragments. It is not sweeping, flowing, or overarching; it is neat and precise. Not only is this type

of melody appropriate for the artistic goal of Mozart's times, it also subjects itself well to development, an important feature of sonata form to be mentioned shortly.

After a few closing chords, the theme begins to be repeated, but this time, halfway through, the music shifts to some firm chords and rapid running scales—a *transition* of 15 measures. The transition acts as a bridge to the second theme and a new key. It might seem that a transition doesn't need to have much musical interest in itself if its function is merely to join one theme to another. But a good composer can make a transition musically quite interesting. Later, composers in the nineteenth century became much more subtle in their handling of transitions, but Mozart wrote in such a way that the parts of sonata form are clearly delineated. In fact, the end of the transition is easily identified by its two closing chords followed by a measure of silence.

One function of a transition is to allow for modulation. If the first theme is in a major key, the second theme in sonata form will usually be in a key five notes higher, the *dominant* key. If the original key is in minor, as it is in the case of Symphony No. 40, the second theme is usually in the relative major (the major key that shares the same key signature but whose center is one and a half steps higher). The pattern of keys was quite significant to eighteenth-century musicians, but by the middle of the nineteenth century, keys were treated more freely. Today the effect of key arrangements in long works is

Allegro molto

		EXPOSITION		
First theme (in tonic key)	Transition	Second theme (in dominant key or relative major)	Transition	Codetta (in dominant key)

negligible. Another function of a transition is to allow time for the listener to absorb the first melody and get ready for the second. If one theme follows immediately upon another, this seems too obvious to be artistically desirable.

In this particular movement the second theme is played between the violins and woodwinds:

Even if you don't read music very well, you can see that the second theme doesn't look like the first. The second has longer note values, and it doesn't have the repeated rhythmic pattern. There are only a few skips up and down to other notes. The theme is also more difficult to remember than the first. In fact, it comes dangerously close to being insipid. But the two themes in sonata form are seldon similar in mood or style; one usually contrasts with the other.

After the second theme a transitionlike passage appears. Interspersed in it are fragments of the first theme. At this place in sonata form, composers have some options. Sometimes they introduce a third theme, at other times they engage in an extended transition, and occasional-

ly they manipulate a fragment of one of the preceding themes, which is what Mozart does here.

The transitional section following the second theme concludes with a *codetta*. The term is derived from the word *coda*, meaning tail. The suffix is a diminutive ending suggesting shortness, so the codetta is simply a short wrap-up section, a concluding series of scales and chords. Often it has a brief melody associated with it.

Exposition. So far only a third of the movement has been accounted for. The musical ideas of the composer for the movement have been presented, exposed. The section to this point, therefore, is called the *exposition.* A diagram of the pattern of the movement to this point is shown at the top of the page.

Normally a composer writing in this form indicated a repeat of the entire exposition. In performances today this sign is frequently ignored, and the music moves right into the next section, the development.

Development. In music, *development* means manipulation of the themes. It demonstrates the composer's ability to present the themes in different and musically satisfying ways.

What does Mozart do in the development section of the first movement of his Symphony No. 40? Basically, he subjects the first theme to three kinds of treatment:

1. He has the first half of the theme played three times, each time in a new key. Musical interest is achieved by shortening the theme and frequent key changes.

EXPOSITION					DEVELOPMENT	RECAPITULATION				
First theme (tonic)	Trans.	Second theme (dominant . . . . (or relative major)	Trans.	Codetta	Working over of musical ideas. Rarely are new melodies introduced	First theme (tonic	Trans.	Second theme	Trans.	Coda)

2. He adds counterpoint. While the lower strings play the first theme in a new key, the violins begin a countermelody of rapidly moving notes (music at the bottom of page 70). When the lower strings finish the first half of the first theme, they pick up the countermelody, while the violins play the theme in yet another key. A similar exchange occurs two more times, with each key center a note lower than its predecessor.

3. He further fragments the theme. The first few notes are tossed back and forth between the flute, clarinet, and violins. Again new keys are utilized, but the section is quiet compared to the busy, vigorous exchange that preceded it. Soon the answer in the woodwinds is shortened further to include only the first three notes of the first theme. Several times the direction of the first two notes is inverted, so that they ascend in pitch rather than descend as in the original theme:

Theme fragmentation is so complete throughout this section that the first two descending eighth notes appear, at various pitches and in various instruments, in *all but the first two measures* of the development section. Fragmentation is also apparent in the transition leading from the development into the next main section of the sonata form.

In this particular development section Mozart works with only the first theme. He fragments it, uses frequent modulation, adds countermelodies, and inverts the direction of melodic intervals. These devices are typical of development sections in sonata form. He could have done more. He could have developed the second theme or introduced an entirely new one. He might have altered the rhythm of the original theme, written different chords to harmonize it, or combined the two themes in a contrapuntal manner. The means of development are infinite.

Recapitulation. The term for the third section of sonata form, *recapitulation*, means literally return to the top. And sure enough, Mozart comes back to the same theme that began the movement. It is played by exactly the same instruments, with exactly the same accompaniment, and it involves exactly the same notes. This exact repetition is quite brief, however.

As the music moves into the transition heading toward the second theme, some changes occur. The transition is longer than it was in the exposition. The second theme is not in a new key. It stays in the tonic. If the second theme were in a different key, the composer would find himself caught off base, away from the home key and near the end of the movement. He would need to get back to the tonic in a hurry and make the key change sound convincing—a difficult thing to do. Following the second theme the transitional music is similar to that found at the same place in the exposition.

The movement ends with a *coda.* The coda is like the codetta except that it is longer and provides the movement with a convincing conclusion. In the coda to this movement, Mozart again utilizes a fragment from the first theme, passing it to the violins, then to the violas, and finally to the woodwinds. Concluding chords alternate between dominant and tonic. So ends one movement of one symphony.

No two movements in sonata form are exactly alike. Each contains some small deviations from the form. In general, however, sonata form can be diagrammed as shown at the top of the page.

An excellent way to understand sonata form better and also improve listening skill is to follow the simplified score of the first movement of Mozart's Symphony No. 40 that appears at the back of the *Study Guide and Scores* for this book. All the parts of the form are labeled and instruments identified.

Second movement. The second movement of a symphony is usually slow and melodious, and so its theme is not as easy to develop. So the presence of sonata form in this movement is somewhat unusual. This explains why the development section is very much abridged. The first theme starts with six equal soundings of the same pitch—hardly a melodious beginning.

But Mozart achieves interest by having the theme reenter in another instrument, and to balance the evenly spaced unison notes he concludes the theme with a gentle rocking melody.

The second theme, in good sonata-form tradition, contrasts with the first:

Notice that this theme is also symmetrical in design. Each short phrase in the first two mea-

sures is played twice; then the entire theme is played again. When the theme appears the second time, the third measure is embellished, but this version is easily heard as being related to the first.

Third movement. For the third movement of the work, Mozart composed the traditional *minuet and trio.* (It appears on Record 2, A of the *Record Album.*) The movement begins at a moderately fast speed with this melody in the minor key of the symphony:

Next, a 13-measure section occurs that is quite similar to the first, but it is in the relative major key, B flat. The low strings and woodwinds play a two-measure segment much like the first while the violins and bassoon play a downward pattern outlining the tonic chord, B flat major.

On its reappearance the theme is treated somewhat in imitation. In this music one violin section enters, then the other.

The trio section derives its name from the fact that traditionally it contained only three instrumental parts: the bass or continuo plus two other instruments. As a result the sound was quieter than the preceding minuet. By the time Mozart wrote this symphony, custom no longer required such sparse instrumentation for the trio, but the change to a quieter mood was retained. The trio contrasts with the minuet not only in style but also in key; it is in G major. The first theme of the trio is:

The section is repeated. The second melody of the trio also outlines basic chords. In fact, it is so common a pattern that it is hardly distinguishable as melody. Then the first theme is heard again, with one change: Two French horns are added for contrast. This second section of the trio is repeated. The minuet is then played through again exactly, but without repeats.

The third movement is based on a strict formal structure:

Minuet	Trio	Minuet
A	B	A
aa ba' ba'	aa ba' ba'	a b a'

Like the first movement of this symphony, the third movement has been included in a simplified score in the *Study Guide and Scores*.

Fourth movement. As is typical of symphonies in this period, the last movement of Mozart's Symphony No. 40 is lively and brilliant. It moves at a rapid rate and provides an exhilarating finish to the work. In fact, Mozart marked the movement with the word *finale* (fee-nahl-ee) in addition to a tempo marking. When composers want a dashing conclusion to a symphony, they do not pour their most profound musical efforts into it. Instead, they tend to fall back on simpler ideas, common patterns, and technical brilliance. That's what Mozart did in this movement.

Final movements come in several forms, some of which will be presented later. Mozart on this occasion uses—you guessed it—sonata form. The first theme is based on the notes of the G minor chord. The theme itself was not

completely original with Mozart. Many composers of his time used a similar pattern; so many, in fact, that the theme has acquired a nickname—"the Mannheim rocket." (Mannheim, a city in southern Germany, had a famous symphony orchestra.) Like the first theme in the first movement, the melody again follows a symmetrical statement-answer scheme:

The transition that follows is longer and more interesting than the transitions found in the other movements of the symphony. Again, the end of the transition is easily heard because of the clearly marked cadence followed by a rest.

The second theme, like its counterpart in the first movement, contains many notes a half step apart and makes more use of the woodwinds. It is in the relative major key, B flat:

A melodic fragment from the first theme occurs frequently in the codetta that concludes the exposition.

The development is built around the first theme. It begins with harmonies that sound unsettled. Soon the "rocket" is passed back and forth between the violins and bassoon. Then the strings treat the theme in a manner that resembles a round. The appearances of the theme in the various string parts are not identical, but they are similar enough to suggest the theme strongly. The music modulates many times.

The recapitulation is conventional and faithful to the pattern of the form. The development and recapitulation are marked to be repeated—a direction that is somewhat unusual. The coda is almost identical to the codetta except for being slightly expanded.

Beethoven's Symphony No. 5

Beethoven's Fifth Symphony is probably the best known symphony ever written. It was composed in 1805, only about 15 years after Mozart's Symphony No. 40. How different Beethoven's music is!

The outline of the first movement and its sonata form is provided in the Listening Guide on pages 76–77. Therefore, the discussion here will concern the characteristics of Beethoven's music. One feature is the extreme contrast he achieves. At times he erupts from a very soft section with a loud, accented chord (often indicated by a *sforzando* sign *sfz*). Or the music may suddenly shift from a rough, combative style to something very tender and lyrical.

A second characteristic is his fondness for and ability at developing themes. The first movement of the Fifth Symphony uses one of the least promising melodic ideas ever to grace a page of music; and yet what Beethoven makes of that little idea is sheer genius. This example indicates how the same idea is repeated many times, each time at a different pitch level and all the time leading up to a climactic point in the music. Toward the end of this example he also turns the figure upside down, using what is termed *inversion*:

The love of developing musical material led to another Beethoven characteristic: an extended coda section. The coda grows from being a closing section to a second development section as long and as important as the exposition, development, or recapitulation sections.

A fourth characteristic is the sense of drive that can be sensed in many of Beethoven's musical works. At times he reaches the point of almost hammering notes with repeated blows. He makes much use of accent signs to tell the players to accent certain notes. The sense of drive can be seen in the preceding music example in the repeated notes and the way the music builds—three phrases each leading to a fuller chord, and each phrase leading to a yet more powerful phrase.

Second movement. The second movement shows another side of Beethoven's creative abilities—his skill at writing serene and lovely melodies. The movement is a theme with variations built on two melodic ideas. The first melody is:

It is played first by the violas and cellos. The second theme is:

As the movement progresses, Beethoven achieves variety in the themes by changing the melody and ornamenting it and by altering the harmony, rhythm, dynamics, tempo, registration, key, and type of accompaniment.

Third movement. The third movement is quite a change from the traditional minuet and trio of Haydn and Mozart. In its place Beethoven writes what he calls a *scherzo*, which in Italian means joke. No longer is the music refined and polished; it becomes more rollicking and dramatic. The initial theme is the "Mannheim rocket." This time, however, it is very smooth and pitched in the low strings so that it sounds more appropriate for Halloween than for the courts of nineteenth-century Austria.

The middle section of the scherzo is still called the trio, but it assumes a much more significant role in the movement. The opening figure is a lusty motive of running eighth notes played by the cellos and basses. In turn, the theme is played by the violas, second violins, and first violins.

The opening motive of the trio is treated to repetition at different pitch levels. The form of the minuet is retained as the original opening section, the *A* portion, returns in a modified version but with different orchestration. It is followed by a transitional passage that develops out of the scherzo theme and rhythm and is sounded by the timpani. The transition slowly accumulates power until it surges without a break into the fourth movement.

Fourth movement. The fourth movement is in sonata form and is of massive proportions, a characteristic that lasted for the rest of the nineteenth century among symphony writers. The movement is in sonata form and built around two themes.

The development section is marked by active rhythm and frequent changes of key. In it Beethoven does something rather unusual for his time—he brings back the initial motive from the first movement of the symphony. When themes from one movement are found in other movements, the treatment is referred to as *cyclical.* The recapitulation is followed by an extensive coda, which at times sounds as if Beethoven is having trouble deciding when to stop. The final result, though, is a monumental piece of music.

Shostakovich's Symphony No. 5

Dimitri Shostakovich, a twentieth-century Russian composer, finished his Fifth Symphony in 1937. Although over a century later than Beethoven's Fifth Symphony, it stands in the same tradition, just as Walton's *Belshazzar's Feast* follows in the tradition of Handel's oratorios.

First movement. The first movement is in sonata form and begins with a violent-sounding theme that is treated in imitation:

A second portion of the first theme soon appears:

Listening Guide

Beethoven: Symphony No. 5 in C Minor, Op. 67, First Movement   *Record 2, A*

Sonata Form

Exposition

0:00   First theme (form *A* of theme), with fourth note held, played by strings; loud:

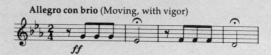

0:06   First theme played quietly and repeatedly by strings; leads to held note by violins.

0:20   First theme played loudly by full orchestra; fourth note held.

0:22   Transition beginning with repeated playings of first theme; grows in volume and rises in pitch.

0:44   Vigorous short French horn solo based on first theme (form *B* of theme):

0:47   Second theme, in major key, played softly by violins; followed by other instruments; motive of first theme played softly every fourth measure by cellos and basses:

1:08   Codetta starts as violins take up chord outlines in pattern of first theme; leads to playing of motive loudly by orchestra.

1:18   First theme idea reappears.

Development

1:27   First theme sounded loudly by French horns and then strings; fourth note held; followed by first theme, sometimes inverted, passed among sections of orchestra at soft dynamic level; music slowly increases in volume.

1:56   Full-sounding chords in winds; repeated notes and first theme in strings; followed by silent places.

2:04   Strings sound B form of first theme; first theme fragments passed among the woodwinds.

2:14   Two-note motive (circled in example) derived from B form of first theme predominates; later reduced to only one note exchanged between winds and strings.

2:37   Vigorous, loud sounding of B form of first theme, contrasted with softly played single notes.

2:46   Sudden loud appearance of first theme, form A.

Recapitulation

2:52   First theme played loudly by full orchestra; fourth note held.

3:11   Short oboe cadenza.

3:25   Transition growing out of first theme; music increases in volume and pitch.

3:47   French horns play the B form of the first theme.

3:51   Second theme, in tonic minor key, played softly by violins; transition based on portion of second theme; first theme sounded occasionally by lower strings.

4:16   Coda begins as smooth phrases of second theme end, and violins take up chord outlines in pattern of first theme.

4:34   Rhythmic pattern of first theme alternated between winds and strings; much repeating of notes; silent places follow.

4:49 B form of first theme played by low strings; two-note motive expanded and extended.

5:05   Four-note melodic idea, sometimes inverted, derived from second theme is played in ascending sequence by violins.

5:16   Woodwinds and strings alternately play four-note idea; fragmented to two notes as music progresses.

5:35   First theme pattern played loudly again by orchestra, leading twice to held notes.

5:51   Quiet appearances of first theme, then suddenly loud.

6:05   Closes with series of brusque chords.

The next theme has a wide range and is presented over a throbbing rhythmic background:

Throughout the movement these themes are varied and combined with each other. The first movement is long by contemporary standards.

Second movement. Shostakovich follows Beethoven's scherzo idea in the second movement, which is filled with humor and occasional satire. The cellos and bass viols begin it in waltz tempo, but what they play is too jovial, too fat to be a waltz in the graceful Viennese tradition. It reminds one of music for a dancing bear in a circus. The tiny E flat clarinet wheezes out a little tune as though it were trying to take itself seriously. The bassoons burp out notes of the shortest possible length, and the solo violinist slides around on a glissando. A peculiar march starts up in the horns; instead of conventional two-beat meter, however, there is an extra beat in each measure, so that the music hobbles along with an uneven gait. At the very end, when the heavy chords suggest that something important is about to happen, a meek and plaintive oboe is heard, sounding as though it were apologizing for being there. The whole movement is filled with ideas, instrumentation, and rhythms that are incongruous when combined.

Third movement. The third movement is impressive. It begins slowly with warm, romantic sounds from the strings. The themes have a chantlike quality about them:

The third theme is introduced by the oboe:

Throughout this portion of the music, the extremely transparent nature of Shostakovich's writing is evident. At times only one instrument is playing. After a while the first two themes are heard from the strings. The music then winds up to a tremendous climax of intensity, and the strings move higher and higher with an excited tremolo. At the climactic point the second part of the first theme is heard coming through the orchestra, its notes doubled by the xylophone. The cellos come in full force on the third theme. The movement closes with the same music that began it.

Fourth movement. In this movement Shostakovich follows in the symphonic tradition of Beethoven with extensive manipulation of melodic and rhythmic motives. The music of Shostakovich sounds different, as could be expected of music composed 132 years later. But there is a similar sense of "drive" and a superb ability in handling musical ideas. To assist you in hearing Shostakovich's music better, a simplified score for this movement is provided in the *Study Guide and Scores* book (and the movement appears on Record 3,A of the *Record Album*). Themes, instruments, and compositional devices are indicated in that score.

The opening two pitches played repeatedly by the timpani are the opening interval of the first theme. The first four notes of that theme become the main motive for the movement; sometimes only its rhythmic pattern is used.

It is followed by an excited, energetic melody:

From this theme (also present in the first theme) Shostakovich takes another four-note figure that is used as a motive, especially for transitions:

On first hearing, the music may sound like a random jumble of sounds, as though just about any notes would make as much sense. Actually, just the opposite is true; the music is extremely well organized, so much so that one must know it very well before appreciating all the interrelationships it contains.

Shostakovich not only demonstrates a great ability to develop themes and motives, he also gives an overarching design to the movement in terms of intensity. The first portion is vibrant and vital. The middle section is more contemplative and quiet and lyric. The third portion brings a return of the themes from the first section and a return of its power and drive. The transition from the calmer middle portion to the third portion gradually leads up to a climactic point. Shostakovich's fondness for continuing one pitch (doubled here in several octaves) can be heard in the powerful coda section. A number of higher pitched instruments in the strings and woodwinds repeat one pitch as the brasses sound the motive from the first theme in major (which sounds similar to the musical phrase "How dry I am").

Other Notable Symphonies

This chapter has discussed three well-known symphonies but only scratched the surface of the quantity of great works that carry the title. To acquaint you with some outstanding symphonies, the following list is offered:

Beethoven, Ludwig van
  All nine symphonies

Borodin, Alexander
  Symphony No. 2 in D Minor

Brahms, Johannes
  All four symphonies

Bruchner, Anton
  Symphony No. 4, *Romantic*

Dvořák, Antonin
  Symphony No. 8, Op. 88
  Symphony No. 9, Op. 95, *New World*

Franck, César
  Symphony in D Minor

Hanson, Howard
  Symphony No. 2, *Romantic*

Haydn, Franz Joseph
  Symphonies No. 94 through 104

Mahler, Gustav
  Symphony No. 4 in G Major

Mendelssohn, Felix
  Symphony No. 3, Op. 56, *Scotch*
  Symphony No. 4, Op. 90, *Italian*

Mozart, Wolfgang Amadeus
  Symphony No. 35, K. 385, *Haffner*
  Symphony No. 36, K. 425, *Linz*
  Symphony No. 38, K. 504, *Prague*
  Symphony No. 39, K. 543
  Symphony No. 41, K. 551, *Jupiter*

Prokofiev, Sergei
  Symphony No. 5, Op. 100

Schubert, Franz
  Symphony No. 8 in B Minor, *Unfinished*
  Symphony No. 9 in C Major, *The Great*

Schumann, Robert
  Symphony No. 1, Op. 38, *Spring*

Sibelius, Jean
  Symphony No. 1 in E Minor, Op. 39
  Symphony No. 2 in D Major, Op. 43
  Symphony No. 5 in E Flat Major, Op. 82

Tchaikovsky, Peter
  Symphony No. 4 in F Minor, Op. 36
  Symphony No. 5 in E Minor, Op. 64
  Symphony No. 6, Op. 74, *Pathétique*

Wolfgang Amadeus Mozart

An unfinished painting of Mozart by Joseph Lange, his brother-in-law. (International Foundation Mozarteum, Salzburg.)

Mozart was born in 1756 in Salzburg, Austria. His father, Leopold, was a recognized violinist and composer in the court of the archbishop. The elder Mozart was quick to realize that his son had extraordinary talents and to capitalize on them. Under his father's tutelage young Mozart showed remarkable mastery of the piano and, to a lesser extent, the violin. By the time he was five he had composed his first pieces, and at six he performed at the court of the Empress Maria Theresa. When he was seven, Mozart and his sister, who was four years older, went on a grand tour of Europe that included Paris, London, and Munich. By the age of 13 he had written concertos, symphonies, and a comic opera; at 14 he was knighted by the Pope.

The most phenomenal aspect of Mozart's musical talent was his memory for music and his ability to work out whole pieces in his mind. He once wrote, "Though it be long, the work is complete and finished in my mind. I take out of the bag of my memory what has previously been collected into it. For this reason the committing to paper is done quickly enough. For everything is already finished, and it rarely differs on paper from what it was in my imagination."

Mozart never experienced the stability of a good appointment as a composer to a patron. For a while he worked for the Prince-Archbishop of Salzburg. The archbishop was a difficult man, and the high-spirited Mozart resented the restrictions of the patronage system. (He wrote his father, "The two valets sit at the head of the table. I at least have the honor of sitting above the cooks.") He quarreled with the archbishop and was dismissed. At the age of 25 he left Salzburg to pursue a career as a free musician in Vienna.

A year later he married Constanze Weber. Since Mozart didn't fare well under the patronage system, he spent the next—the last—ten years of his life, as he put it, "hovering between hope and anxiety." Due in part to his impractical and overgenerous nature in financial affairs, his only recourse was to eke out an existence by teaching, giving concerts, composing, and borrowing from friends.

In 1791, at the age of 35, Mozart died of uremic poisoning. Because he was so deeply in debt, he was given the cheapest funeral and buried in a pauper's grave.

Despite his short life and the disappointments that plagued him, Mozart composed over 600 complete works. He never used opus numbers, although some were added later by publishers. His works were catalogued by a Viennese botanist and amateur musician named Köchel (*Keh*-shul), who assigned each composition a number on a generally chronological basis. So today every Mozart work is identified by a number (up to 626), preceded by the initial K, for Köchel. A few Köchel numbers have been corrected on the basis of later musicological research.

Ludwig van Beethoven

An 1819 painting of Beethoven by Josef Stieler. (Art Reference Bureau.)

Beethoven was born in 1770 into the family of a ne'er-do-well musician in Bonn, Germany. His father, a drunkard, observed the boy's talent and nourished dreams that he might have sired a prodigy who, like the young Mozart, would bring in a good income from his performances. So Ludwig was pushed into music study, especially piano, viola, and organ. He also sang in the chapel choir at Bonn. Although talented, he never became the prodigy his father had hoped for. At the age of 22 Beethoven set off for Vienna to make his fortune in the world of music.

Beethoven had little formal academic schooling. He studied composition with several teachers, including Haydn, and made a name for himself as a pianist. He won friends and admirers among the aristocracy of Vienna, and within a decade he had established himself as a leading composer and performer whose services were in demand.

The musical training he received was steeped in the careful, formal style of the time, which made a lasting impression on him. But there were other influences. One was the revolutionary spirit that was awakening in Europe. The spirit of independence was burning not only in Beethoven's music but in the works of other artists as well.

Then there was Beethoven's own personality. Were he alive today, he would probably identify himself with humanitarian causes and social protest groups. Two events give support to this view of the man. His Symphony No. 3, entitled *Eroica* (the "heroic" symphony), was originally dedicated to Napoleon. When Beethoven heard that Napoleon had declared himself emperor, he was disappointed to learn that his idol was just another ambitious soldier-politician, and he angrily tore up the dedication. In its place he wrote: "To the memory of a great man." Another example of Beethoven's belief concerns his Ninth Symphony. As early as 1792 he had thought of setting Schiller's *Ode to Joy* to music. The ethical ideals of the poem—the universal brotherhood of mankind and its basis in the love of a heavenly Father—had strong appeal to Beethoven.

Beethoven is probably the first composer in history to be considered a "personality." Beethoven's mature works sound like no one else's music. And his personal life reflected this same desire for independence. He took orders from no one. He was successful enough at selling his music that he could remain free from worry about deadlines or patrons.

In appearance he was described as "a short, stout man with a very red face, small piercing eyes, and bushy eyebrows, dressed in a long overcoat which reached nearly to his ankles. . . . Notwithstanding the high color of his cheeks and his general untidiness, there was in those small piercing eyes an expression which no painter could render. It was a feeling of sublimity and melancholy combined."*

*From a description by Sir Julius Benedict (1823), quoted in Alexander Wheelock Thayer, *Life of Beethoven* (Princeton, N.J.: Princeton University Press, 1964), p. 873.

Beethoven's personality was also affected by a hearing loss that eventually led to complete deafness. The condition was evident by the time he was 28, and it became progressively worse.

His deafness caused him to lose contact with others and to withdraw into himself, becoming more irritable, morose, and suspicious of people. His final compositions were products of this period of his life. They tend to be more personal, meditative, and abstract. His output of new works during the last 15 years of his life was not large.

You may wonder how it was possible for the deaf Beethoven to write entire symphonies. The process becomes understandable when you look within your own experience. You can recall melodies and the sounds of people's voices in your memory, even though physically you hear nothing. Trained people can "think out" a sizable amount of music in their minds. And Beethoven was obviously a well-trained musician with more than average abilities.

There is a second reason for his success despite his disability. It has to do with the way he composed. It was his custom to write down themes in a sketchbook. Then he would work over the themes, revising and rewriting them, making slight alterations and trying them out to determine their suitability for the piece he had in mind. This trial-and-error process might be resumed intermittently over a period of years. So the thematic material for many of his later compositions had been worked out when he was still able to hear fairly well.

Beethoven poured strenuous effort into each measure of his music, for he was not the "natural" composer that Mozart was. Beethoven is reported to have compared the writing of a particular work, his opera *Fidelio,* with the bearing of a child. And with good reason. His manuscripts look "like a bloody record of a tremendous inner battle."*

He died in 1827 of jaundice and cholera. That his death occurred during a hailstorm was a coincidence that seems appropriate to the man and his life.

*From *The Joy of Music* by Leonard Bernstein (New York: Simon and Schuster, 1954), p. 81.

Dimitri Shostakovich

(Novosti Press Agency.)

Dimitri Shostakovich (1906–1975) received all his musical training in Russia, and he spent very little time outside the country. He was born in St. Petersburg (Leningrad), and his mother was a well-trained pianist. At 13 he entered the Conservatory at St. Petersburg. In 1925, at the age of 19, he finished his First Symphony, which is a mature work that has become a part of the repertoire of most symphony orchestras. His career was off to an auspicious start.

In 1934 he ran into trouble with the Communist Party over an opera entitled *Lady Macbeth of Mzensk*. It was accused of being "formalistic," a vague charge meaning that the music was not sufficiently political or that it was too much like music of the Western world. He publicly promised to do better in the future. In 1937 he brought out his Fifth Symphony.

During World War II Shostakovich was not permitted to serve in the armed forces because he was considered so valuable a citizen. He spent the war years in Leningrad, where he remained even through the long siege of that city, writing his Seventh Symphony and serving as a volunteer fireman. He had another falling out with the Communist Party in 1948 when he was again accused of "musical formalism." A public apology and a new opera extricated him from the predicament. He came to be revered in his native land. His symphonies number 15, making him the first important composer since Beethoven to write more than nine.

10

Concertos

A concerto (con-*chair*-toh) exhibits some of the same features as symphonies and sonatas. It is a composition for instruments, usually consisting of several movements and utilizing traditional forms. The principle of a concerto is the contrast between groups of different size or instruments of different types.

Concerto Grosso

The *concerto grosso* was the first type of concerto to predominate in music history.* It achieves contrast by pitting a small group against a larger one. There is little difference in instrumentation or in the music that each group performs. There is no attempt to have the small group "show off," as is true in later concertos. The small group remains seated and often plays along with the large group. Usually concerti grossi are composed for strings, with a harpsichord helping out on the harmonies. A few wind instruments are sometimes included in the small group. For example, four of the six frequently heard *Brandenburg Concertos* by Bach contain solo parts for winds.

The same or similar instruments playing the same music sometimes makes it difficult to distinguish which group is playing. The orchestra of Bach's day was small, so the larger group was not large by today's standards. Also, three or four good string players can produce a healthy, vigorous sound. Recordings tend to make the groups less distinguishable by taking away most of the physical distance that is present in live performances.

Concerto grosso means "grand concerto" in Italian; there is no implication of ugliness in the term.

Vivaldi's *The Four Seasons*

Antonio Vivaldi's *The Four Seasons*, Op. 8 Nos. 1–4, is a quartet of four concertos, one for each season. In many ways it is a typical concerto grosso of the seventeenth and eighteenth centuries. It contrasts three violin parts (the small group) against the orchestra (the *tutti*). The bass line is doubled by a harpsichord. The portions of the music for each group are easily distinguishable. In fact, some themes are given only to the small group or the orchestra. Each concerto consists of three movements set in a fast-slow-fast arrangement of tempos.

Two features make *The Four Seasons* a bit different. One is the special opportunities given the principal violinist. This music is more demanding than the other two solo violin parts or those given the orchestral players. Therefore, at some places the music is a solo concerto.

The second feature is the nonmusical ideas that Vivaldi strongly associated with the music. A sonnet about each season appears in the score for each concerto. In addition, phrases from the sonnet appear among the lines of the music, as well as letters referring to each line of the poem.

The text for the "Spring" sonnet expresses the joys of spring with its singing birds, babbling brooks, and gentle breezes, but also includes a brief thundershower. It is not necessary, however, to know the nonmusical associations to enjoy the music; the music can stand on its own.

The movement repeats short melodic and rhythmic ideas that are typical of Vivaldi's music, as is a sense of momentum that seems to propel the music forward. The movement also displays the type of form found in the other movements of the four concertos that make up *The Four Seasons* and in most concerti grossi: Short sections contrast with a main theme that appears several times. The first movement also

contains a number of other features of Baroque music that are discussed in Chapter 17. See the Listening Guide on pages 86–87.

The Solo Concerto

Gradually the concerto grosso lost favor, and by 1750 it was replaced by the solo concerto. The newer form became so prevalent that the word *concerto* is understood today to mean a solo concerto. The part that the soloist plays in the solo concerto is intended for a virtuoso performer. It is much more difficult and showy than the parts assigned to the orchestra players. The orchestra serves largely as accompaniment.

Although three instruments have been especially favored by composers—piano, violin, and cello—a concerto can be written for any instrument. A concerto for French horn will be examined first.

Mozart's Concerto for Horn and Orchestra

Mozart composed the third of his four horn concertos (K. 447) in about 1783. It is for a natural French horn—one with no valves; valves were not added until about 1815. On a natural horn the player can sound only the notes of the overtone series (the same ones a bugle plays) without altering the way he places his hand in the instrument's bell. The results of this technique are not very successful by today's standards. The sound is somewhat muffled and the pitch only approximately correct.

As was true of several of his concertos for other instruments, Mozart composed this one for a particular performer, Ignaz Leutgeb. Like Mozart, he was from Salzburg and later in life settled in Vienna. According to a number of accounts, he was an excellent performer.

First movement. The focus of this discussion is on the techniques involved in writing for a soloist and orchestra, so the characteristics of sonata form will not be repeated here. Before the solo horn enters, the orchestra presents a shortened version of the exposition. The first and main theme is:

The second theme is heard soon after the first. It is short and serves as a counterbalance to the first theme.

After both themes have been presented, the exposition is heard again, but this time featuring the solo French horn. This *double exposition* is typical of concertos composed in the eighteenth and nineteenth centuries. Except for the double exposition, the movement proceeds through the normal sonata form. The development section is shorter and simpler than was its counterpart in the G Minor Symphony. The concerto was written when neither Mozart nor sonata form had reached full musical maturity. The development section is more like the addition of different musical ideas than a true development.

There is another feature of the concerto that is not found in symphonies. Shortly before the end of the movement, the orchestra comes to a stop, and the soloist begins playing a freely constructed and often technically difficult paraphrase of the preceding musical material. Many stops and starts are made, holds and altered tempos appear freely, and the rhythm is entirely flexible. This portion of a concerto is called a *cadenza.* It is usually found in one of three movements and permits the soloist to show off in terms of both playing and improvising.

Listening Guide

Vivaldi: *The Four Seasons,* "Spring," First Movement   *Record 3, A*

0:00   Movement begins with main theme played forte by the entire orchestra.

0:33   The three solo violins play a section that gives the effect of birds singing.

1:11   The main theme returns, played by the entire orchestra.

1:19   The music changes to a section that attempts to portray the gentle breezes of spring.

Originally the cadenzas played were supposed to be the performer's improvisation, although one suspects that the performers must have thought out well in advance what to play for the cadenza. Therefore, Mozart indicated only where the cadenzas were to be inserted in his music; he did not write them out for the performer.

Second movement. As in a symphony, the second movement is slow and melodious. The solo horn plays the melody before the violins take it up. The main melody appears several times, twice with contrasting material inserted between its appearances. There is no cadenza in this movement.

Third movement—rondo form. For the final movement of the concerto Mozart chose *rondo* form. The basis of the rondo idea is a melody that returns several times, with other musical material interspersed among its various appearances. Symbolically it can be represented *A B A C A D A* and so on. Theoretically there is no limit to the number of sections possible in a rondo, but a minimum of five is customary. Normally the main theme of a rondo is a distinctive, easily remembered melody; the subordinate themes are less memorable. This characteristic holds true in the case of Mozart's rondo. One can easily miss the *B* theme and even more easily miss the *C*. In effect, they are as much contrasting material to the main theme as they are additional melodies.

A Listening Guide for this movement is provided on pages 88–89.

1:45	The main theme returns, played by the entire orchestra.
1:53	A new section giving the musical impression of a spring thunderstorm is played by the full orchestra alternating with flashing passages by the solo violin.
2:22	The main theme returns, played by the entire orchestra.
2:31	Music representing a return of the birds' singing is performed by the three solo violins.
2:40	The main theme returns, played by the entire orchestra.
3:00	Principal violin and cello play a short duet.
3:14	The main theme returns, played forte by the entire orchestra.
3:35	The movement ends with the main theme played softly.

Brahms' Piano Concerto No. 2

The first theme of the first movement of Brahms' Second Piano Concerto was presented in Chapter 3 as an example of good melodic writing. Finished in 1881, the concerto is of monumental size; it actually is more like a symphony, with four movements instead of the usual three. The first movement is about 17 minutes long. The music has a sweeping, rolling, robust quality. Even the chords the pianist must play are big (Brahms apparently had large hands), and the full range of the keyboard is exploited from one end to the other.

The music has a quality that is hard to put into words—optimistic, positive, and healthy come as close as any. There is an unabashed love of beautiful harmony and melody, and a quality that seems to say all will work out right in the end.

Brahms wrote this concerto when he was well established as a composer. It is typical of his well-conceived and careful approach to writing music. Brahms worked with most of the same forms that Haydn and Mozart had

employed. By the time Brahms composed his music, however, such forms had become passé, and he was considered hopelessly conservative by many of his contemporaries.

By nature Brahms was, in fact, conservative. But the combination of his rational approach to music and the emphasis on emotion and personal feelings that marked the nineteenth century produced just the right mixture for some enduring and beautiful music. Depending on your inclinations, you can listen to Brahms' music in one of two ways: You can simply enjoy the lush sounds and beautiful melodies, or you can admire his skill in manipulating themes and forms. The best way, of course, is to do both at the same time.

Brahms typically took fragments from a melody and then manipulated and developed them throughout an entire movement. As a result, most of the time you are hearing a theme or fragment of a theme. The music sounds familiar, but it does not repeat itself literally. Brahms also blurred the changes from one part of the form to another so that the "seams" between the parts are difficult to detect.

Listening Guide

Mozart: Horn Concerto No. 3 in E Flat, K. 447, Third Movement   *Record 2, A*

Rondo

0:00   Main theme (*A*) played by French horn at rather fast tempo.

0:07   *A* theme repeated and extended by orchestra, ending in a clear cadence, followed by a rest.

0:31   Solo horn begins *B* theme.

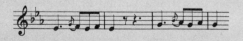

First movement. A Listening Guide for the first movement appears on pages 90–91. Notice that the time dimensions for the movement are longer than for much of the music presented earlier in this book. Also, the movement contains a first theme with two distinct portions, a second theme, plus two other themes that appear as the music progresses. There is also a double exposition, as there is in the first movement of Mozart's Horn Concerto. In short, it is a massive and masterful musical work.

Second movement. The second movement is in a lusty $\frac{3}{4}$ meter. It is a sturdy-sounding scherzo. The opening theme is:

The second theme reminds one of a Viennese waltz:

The third theme enters well along in the movement:

It is given a varied rhythmic treatment, with an occasional meter of $\frac{2}{4}$ $\frac{3}{4}$.

0:39	Violins repeat and extend *B* theme.
1:10	Solo horn plays *A* theme again.
1:17	*A* theme repeated and extended by violins.
1:29	*C* theme (the same theme featured in the second movement) introduced by solo horn; followed by a developmentlike section with interplay between the horn and orchestra.
2:24	*A* theme returns, played by the solo French horn.
2:31	Violins follow horn in playing the *A* theme.
2:39	Coda begins with violins playing figure heard earlier in the movement.
3:14	Movement closes with three solid-sounding chords.

Listening Guide

Brahms: Piano Concerto No. 2 in B Flat, Op. 83, First Movement   *Record 2, B*

Sonata Form

Exposition I

0:00   First theme, first portion, played by French horn; piano answers the two phrases of the theme:

0:22   First theme, second portion, played by the woodwinds:

0:34   Cadenza for piano.

1:27   First portion of first theme played by orchestra; leads into transition; loud dynamic level.

2:16   Second theme, in minor key, played rather softly by violins:

2:38   Transition based on dotted-note figure; marchlike.

2:50   Codetta begins with loud statement of first theme; is followed by descending chromatic passages by strings and winds.

Exposition II

3:08   Piano begins with free-sounding solo but soon takes up first portion of first theme.

4:01   First theme, second portion, played smoothly by violins.

4:42   Transition containing free material for piano; fragments of first theme played by orchestra.

5:24   New theme introduced in transition section by French horns; is repeated several times by other instruments:

6:01   Two-note motive (circled in example) is repeated many times by orchestra and then piano.

6:34   Second theme played in rhapsodic style by piano alone.

6:56   Transition with dotted-note figure and marchlike melody played by piano.

7:46   Codetta begins with first part of first theme played loudly by orchestra; is followed soon by a portion of second theme played by violins and flutes; concluded with descending chromatic passages in violins and clarinets.

Development

8:24   French horn softly plays opening measures of first theme; is soon answered with the second measure from woodwinds.

8:58   Dotted-note figure is played by violins with rapidly outlined chords played by piano: tempo increases.

9:22   Piano plays chords off the beat as dotted-note figure continues in orchestra.

9:36   Episode: Marchlike melody based on dotted-note figure begins in piano; similar material is heard four more times, each time somewhat varied, and each time with runs by piano interspersed between the appearances:

10:35   Opening notes of first theme sounded loudly by orchestra; free cadenzalike material for piano.

10:52   Opening three notes sounded loudly by orchestra again; three-note fragment of first theme, second portion, begins to appear in orchestra; piano has free material.

11:30   Calm, quiet chords held by orchestra, with alternating notes played by piano.

Recapitulation

11:42   French horn plays first theme, first portion, rather quietly.

12:04   Second portion of first theme played by woodwinds.

12:37   Theme from transition in second exposition played by woodwinds and used as transition.

13:13   Two-note motive from transition theme played by piano and later taken up by woodwinds.

13:47   Second theme played rhapsodically by piano alone.

14:10   Transition using dotted-note marchlike material; is developed somewhat.

15:03   Coda begins with playing of first theme, first portion, by French horn; piano continues free-sounding lines; music becomes calm.

15:28   First three notes of first theme played loudly by orchestra.

16:00   First theme, second portion, played by piano; other instruments take up this theme.

16:37   Suddenly music gets loud; second phrases of first portion of theme played by orchestra.

17:01   Closes with full-sounding chord.

Third movement. The third movement is the slow and melodious one in this concerto. It is built on one theme that is introduced by a cello solo:

Fourth movement. The fourth movement is marked *Allegro grazioso* (allegro, gracefully). The opening theme is playful:

The second theme seems to be straight out of Vienna:

Two more themes are heard before the movement ends.

Brahms' Piano Concerto No. 2 is especially significant because he was one of the master composers of the nineteenth century and also because that era is referred to as "the Golden Age of the piano." The peak period for the writing of piano concertos extended from the time of Mozart until about the beginning of the twentieth century.

Johannes Brahms

Brahms when a young man. (New York Public Library.)

Johannes Brahms (1833–1897) was the son of a musician, a somewhat shiftless bass viol player in Hamburg, Germany. Young Brahms got his start by playing piano in the dance halls in the poorer sections of town. He demonstrated considerable talent, and by the age of 20 he was serving as piano accompanist to one of the better violinists of the day. He showed talent in composition as well and soon went to study with Robert Schumann. The Schumanns took the shy young man into their home. Schumann also published a magazine on music in which he praised Brahms' music, and before long Brahms was known throughout the musical world. He was a great help to the family when Schumann suffered a mental collapse and had to be hospitalized.

At first Brahms admired and then grew to love Clara Schumann, who was 14 years older than he and the mother of seven children. Because he had the highest regard for her husband, his ailing benefactor, the situation caused him much conflict. After Schumann died, Brahms should have felt free to follow through on his love for Clara and marry her; she was no longer the unattainable ideal. But somehow he could not bring himself to take a step that would have obligated him and limited his freedom. Later in life Brahms fell in love with other women, but he chose never to marry.

Brahms reacted in a similar way to employment. He never accepted a position that made heavy demands on him. The one position Brahms coveted—conductorship of the orchestra in his native Hamburg—eluded him throughout his life. Apparently the directors of the orchestra couldn't forget that he started out as a waterfront musician. Most of his adult life, therefore, was spent in Vienna, where for short periods of time he directed various choral groups and a music society. Most of his income came from the sale of his compositions and from conducting.

Brahms was aware that he had extraordinary talent as a composer, and this was partially the reason for his wanting to be as free as possible. Unlike Beethoven, he left no rejected versions of his music for posterity. He wanted the world to know only his best work, so his rough sketches were carefully destroyed. It is said that he burned as many of his compositions as he allowed to be published.

Brahms composed almost every type of music—symphonies, concertos, chamber music, piano works, songs, and choral music—and wrote with consistently high quality. One of his greatest compositions, *A German Requiem*, was written early in his career. This work for chorus, orchestra, and soprano and baritone soloists is one of the most profound in all music literature.

In spite of his demonstrated skill in writing for both the choral and strictly instrumental idioms, Brahms was not attracted to either opera or tone poems, and therefore he attempted neither. His coolness toward opera may have been partly due to the excessive competition raging between the followers of Brahms and those of the German opera composer Richard Wagner. In the second half of the nineteenth century, music lovers evidently felt obliged to choose sides between the two men. The division concerned the artistic role of music as much as it did personalities. The Wagnerites held that music was a medium for the expression of emotions and ideas. Brahms promoted the idea that music was an end in itself. Since there is truth in both views, the dispute has never been resolved. Brahms handled the matter sensibly: He ignored it as best he could and went about his composing.

Antonio Vivaldi

Vivaldi, popularly known in his day as the "red priest," was born about 1678. The appellation "red priest" resulted not from his political beliefs but from his red hair and the fact that he was an ordained priest. Actually, Vivaldi spent very little time serving as a priest; most of his career he taught music in Venice, Italy, at the Pieta Conservatory, an orphanage for girls. Although he started out teaching only music lessons, he gradually took on the direction of an orchestra and choir and the responsibility for weekly concerts. Vivaldi composed an enormous amount of music, much of it for performances at the conservatory. Of some 550 instrumental pieces, 300 are concertos for the violin, a preference that may have stemmed from his lessons on the instrument from his violinist father. However, in addition to the violin, he composed concertos for cello, viola d'amore, lute, guitar, mandolin, flute, recorder, oboe, bassoon, trumpet, and even one for piccolo.

Vivaldi's music was rather well received during his lifetime, but interest in it had waned by the end of his life. After 35 years he left the school in 1740 and seemed to disappear. Only years later was it discovered that he had died in Vienna in 1741 and been buried in a pauper's grave—a parallel to Mozart's fate 50 years later.

11

Chamber Music

Chamber music is distinguished by the fact that each part is performed by only one player. For instance, even though a string quartet contains two violins, in addition to a viola and a cello, each violin part is different. As long as each part is different, there could be ten violin parts and the result would still be chamber music (but not a quartet).

Because chamber music requires few instruments, it is more suitable for performance in a room than in a concert hall. (The word *chamber* comes from the French for room.) Musicians value chamber music because it permits a refinement and intimacy of expression that cannot be derived from a large group. An orchestra has power and color, while a string quartet provides a sense of involvement and clarity. One medium can be as effective as the other in the hands of a skilled composer.

Chamber music is an instrumental medium, although a few works also include voices. Chamber works usually contain several movements, employing sonata form, rondo, and other formal schemes. A few string quartets are almost as long as symphonies.

Chamber music has been written for almost every conceivable combination of instruments. Certain groups are more frequently found, however. The most common are the sonata and the string quartet. Another likely string group involves two violins, two violas, and one or two cellos. The woodwind quintet is made up of a clarinet, oboe, bassoon, flute, and French horn. Although the French horn is a brass instrument, its timbre blends well with woodwinds, so composers have included it in this woodwind group. Brass ensembles have the least standardized instrumentation. Perhaps the quintet (two trumpets, French horn, trombone, and tuba) has most frequently drawn the attention of composers.

It is not unusual to find one nonstring instrument added to a string quartet. For example, a work for clarinet and string quartet is called a *clarinet quintet*, though only one clarinet is present. If a piano plus a string quartet is called for, the work is a *piano quintet*. A *piano trio* is a piano plus violin and cello. Apparently the presence of strings is taken for granted, so the unusual instrument is designated in naming the group.

Haydn's "Emperor Quartet"

Franz Joseph Haydn's String Quartet Op. 76 No. 3 was composed in 1797, which was late in his long career. The first movement is in sonata form, which is rapidly becoming familiar to you now. Although a movement well worth study, the quartet is known mostly for its second movement, which is on Record 3,A in the *Record Album*. A line score for the movement is included in the *Study Guide and Scores*. For its theme Haydn revised a melody he had given to

Austria as a national anthem. It is still the melody for the Austrian national anthem, and it is also sung in many churches under the title "Glorious Things of Thee Are Spoken." The quartet is sometimes called the "Emperor Quartet" because the original title resembles the English "God Save the King." The melody (below) does have a hymnlike quality, as well as a sense of symmetry in its contrasting sets of repeated phrases.

The movement is a *theme and variation*, which was mentioned in Chapter 5. Especially helpful to the listener in this movement, Haydn has one of the instruments continue to play the melody while a variation is introduced. Variation I presents the melody in the second violin, while the first violin plays a contrapuntal line that embellishes the melody. In the second variation the melody is in the cello, supported by the second violin. While this is happening, the first violin plays a countermelody that is quite rhythmic. The third varia-

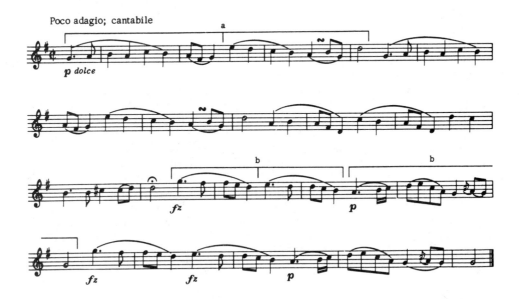

tion presents the melody in the viola, with the other instruments playing contrasting parts.

Variation IV finds the first violin again playing the melody, sometimes an octave higher than before. The other three instruments play a more intricate, chordal accompaniment (top of the page). Notice that several accidentals appear in the accompaniment. As you can probably hear, the harmony has been changed; other chords were used in the original presentation of the theme. A four-measure concluding section is added to this final variation.

Most examples of theme-and-variation form are not so easy for the listener to follow. Not often does the composer keep the melody intact and sounding in some part. Indeed, later composers wrote variations that were so remotely related to the original theme that no discernible relationship was left. Haydn, however, treats the theme imaginatively without obscuring it. He employs two devices in doing this: He adds contrapuntal parts and he changes the harmony. He might also have varied the rhythm or the pitches of the melody itself. (This latter technique is extremely common, and a delightful example of its use can be found in Mozart's variations—K. 265—on "Twinkle, Twinkle, Little Star," which he knew as the French folk song "Ah! Vous dirai-je, Maman.") Although in this movement Haydn chose not to exploit every possible means of altering the theme, all

four variation techniques—melody, harmony, counterpoint, and rhythm—are used frequently and effectively by composers, often in combination.

The final two movements of this quartet maintain the standard of excellence found in the first two movements. Typically, the third movement is a minuet and trio, and the fourth movement is a fast finale.

The Sonata

Early eighteenth-century musicians did not use the word *sonata* consistently. Originally the word meant any piece for instruments. But a distinction was drawn between a *sonata da camera*, or chamber sonata, which was usually based on dances, and a *sonata da chiesa*, or church sonata, which was more serious and complex. Actually the two types of sonatas overlapped, and after 1750 the distinction was dropped altogether.

Many seventeenth- and eighteenth-century sonatas were for small ensembles, often four players. Frequently the music was written for three instruments plus keyboard, and it acquired the name *trio sonata*, even though more than three players usually performed the piece.

Solo *sonatas* were composed for only one instrument. Domenico Scarlatti (1685-1757), an

Italian who spent much of his adult life in Spain, wrote over 500 solo keyboard pieces that he called sonatas. Bach wrote a number of solo sonatas for cello, flute, and violin, and more recent composers have also written solo sonatas. The instrument most commonly used in a solo sonata is the piano. More will be said about the piano sonata in Chapter 12.

Early sonatas have short movements that alternate in tempo. Since the time of Mozart, the sonata (not to be confused with sonata form) has been a sizable work in three or four movements. The movements correspond to those found in the symphony, except that the minuet or third movement is often omitted. In tempo, form, and key relationships, each movement of the sonata tends to resemble its symphonic counterpart.

A sonata is usually a composition for two instruments: a piano and one other instrument. The two parts are considered to be of *equal* importance; in no sense is the piano simply accompanying the other instrument. In fact, the piano part often contains the more important musical idea, while the other instrument accompanies. Since the presence of the piano is assumed, the sonata is called by the name of the other instrument. So a violin sonata is for violin and piano.

Because the sonata is ensemble music, the players perform with the music before them. The custom of memorizing has come to be associated with solo playing, as when a soloist performs a difficult concerto. In chamber music, however, the individual must be subordinate to the ensemble, so memorizing is inappropriate. Furthermore, the complexity of the various lines and the number of players involved (two people for a sonata, more in other ensembles) make the memorized performance more susceptible to error. An exception is the solo sonata, which is usually played from memory.

Franck's Violin Sonata

One of the best known sonatas for violin and piano is César Franck's Violin Sonata in A Ma-

jor. Franck lived and wrote in the latter half of the nineteenth century, and his music is full of rich harmonies and luscious melodies. Franck himself was an organist, and his music shows an advanced knowledge of harmony.

The first movement of the sonata is in moderate tempo and presents two themes. The first theme has no distinct ending. Franck keeps the elements of a thematic idea going for quite a while and in so doing transforms them into transitional material. He gives the impression of a brief development shortly after each presentation:

The second theme appears almost exclusively in the piano part. The movement is in a loose sonata form, but there is little actual development.

The second movement is a dazzling allegro. A difficult and dynamic piano solo opens the movement. The piano is soon joined by the violin:

The second theme is far more lyric and smooth:

Again the music is in a loose sonata form.

The third movement is marked *Recitativo-Fantasia*. The word *recitative* should be familiar to you from Chapter 7. It is a free declamatory style that is featured in sections of operas and oratorios. Here Franck adapts that style for the solo violin. *Fantasia* indicates a free piece with no particular form. The second theme that appears in the fantasy is of interest because it appears again in the fourth movement:

For the final movement Franck combines a flowing melody with one of the oldest techniques in music, a canon, which was discussed in Chapter 5.

The piano opens the movement and is followed in strict imitation by the violin, four counts later:

The movement is dominated by the main melody, but the appearance of the theme from the third movement provides the sonata with some cyclical writing, a favorite technique of Franck.

Dvořák's String Quartet No. 6

This quartet, Op. 96 of Antonin Dvořák, is often referred to as the "American" Quartet. The reason for this name is the fact that Dvořák composed it during the summer of 1893 in the little town of Spillville, Iowa. Dvořák was for three years Director of the Conservatory of Music in New York. He missed his native Bohemia very much, so he spent his summers living among the Czech-Bohemian people in Spillville. The music is largely Bohemian in character, not American. It has about it some of the qualities of Brahms' music—good cheer, enjoyment, optimism. It is not as complex as Brahms' music, however, although it may be just as enjoyable.

The first movement is presented in the Listening Guide on pages 102–103. As the guide indicates, the movement is in sonata form.

Second movement. This movement is in a large three-part form. It presents flowing, sentimental melodies. The melody for the *A* portion is shown at the bottom of the page. The middle section of the movement is also melodic, with the first and second violins playing some of the time three notes apart. The gradual nursing of the music up to climactic points can be clearly heard. The movement closes with the cello restating the opening theme.

Third movement. This movement contains some of the scherzo character found in Beethoven's Fifth Symphony; however, the pattern is extended to five sections: *A B A B A*. There is also some variation on the theme during the

Second movement, A theme.

Third movement, A theme.

Fourth movement.

movement. The *A* theme begins in the cello. Like several other themes in the quartet, the *A* theme (top of the page) is basically pentatonic—based on a five-note scale.

Fourth movement. The fourth movement is a rondo with a pattern of *A B A C A B A*. It is very lively and ends in a flourish of sound. The main theme is shown above.

Franz Joseph Haydn

Portrait of Haydn by Thomas Hardy. (Royal College of Music, London.)

One man who had much to do with the development of orchestral music was Franz Joseph Haydn (1732–1809). He was born in the same year as George Washington, in the town of Rohrau in eastern Austria. Unlike Mozart, he didn't have the advantage of early musical training. An uncle, with whom Haydn went to live at the age of six, gave him his first musical instruction. At eight he became a choirboy at the Cathedral of St. Stephen in Vienna, where he gained musical experience but little theoretical instruction. When his voice changed, he was dismissed. For the next few years he lived a precarious existence, doing odd jobs and teaching as well as studying music theory on his own initiative. In 1761, at the age of 29, Haydn was taken into the service of Prince Paul Anton Esterházy (*Ester-hahzy*), head of one of the richest and most powerful noble families in Hungary.

The next year Nicholas Esterházy succeeded his brother Paul Anton. Nicholas, besides being rich and powerful, was also a connoisseur of music. Most of the time he lived at a country estate at Eisenstadt, the sumptuousness of which rivaled the French court at Versailles. On the estate were two beautiful concert halls and two theaters, one for opera and one for marionette plays.

Haydn both composed and conducted the performances, trained the musicians, and kept the instruments in repair. He had 25 good instrumentalists and a dozen or so fine singers.

Haydn's contract was typical, It required him "to produce at once any composition called for" and to smooth out all difficulties among the musicians. He was expected to present himself twice daily in the antechamber to await orders.

For the most part, Haydn's experience with the Esterházy family represented the patronage system at its best. Haydn liked them and they him.

After Haydn had been with the Esterházys for 30 years, Prince Nicholas died. Haydn subsequently made two visits to London in the 1790s. For each trip he composed six symphonies, which collectively are known as the London symphonies, numbers 92 to 104. They represent Haydn at his orchestral best. After the London trips he returned to work for a while for Nicholas Esterházy II, who was not as interested in music as his father had been. Haydn then wrote mainly vocal works, including two oratorios, *The Creation* and *The Seasons*. He gradually retired from composing and died in 1809.

Haydn was recognized during his lifetime as a great composer by the public and by other musicians. He admired, and was in turn admired by, Mozart. The two learned from each other's music, a fact especially evident in Haydn's string quartets written after 1781. Beethoven also regarded Haydn with esteem.

Haydn is sometimes referred to as the "father" of the symphony, the string quartet, the modern orchestra, and instrumental music in general. Although such claims are exaggerated, they give some indication of his significance. What Haydn did was to work out a better balance for the new forms. For example, he developed the finale of the symphony. Prior to Haydn, the fourth movement had been only a frothy little section. Haydn expanded it into a movement with a definite form.

César Franck

Franck was born at Liege, Belgium, in 1822, and died in Paris in 1890. His father was a banker who had a keen love of music. He gave his two sons, Joseph and César, a good musical education. To make sure it was adequate, the family moved to Paris so that the boys could finish study at the conservatory there. César won a number of prizes for his music abilities. He was a quiet, unassuming man who spent most of his adult life as the organist at St. Clotilde. At the age of 50 he was appointed organ professor at the conservatory, but his music was little understood by his colleagues. His compositions received only modest acclaim during his lifetime. What success and recognition he did achieve came in the last few years of his life, and his best compositions were written after the age of 57: a piano quintet, a string quartet, his only symphony (which is performed frequently today), a set of variations for piano and orchestra, and the Violin Sonata discussed in this chapter.

Most of his music consists of compositions for organ and sacred choral works. Several of his techniques influenced later composers, especially Debussy.

Antonin Dvořák

Dvořák was born in 1841 into the family of a Bohemian innkeeper and amateur musician. Antonin grew up listening to the folk music of his native land. After several years of conflict between his music teacher, who wanted his talented pupil to go to Prague to study, and his father, who wanted him to become an innkeeper, an uncle provided Antonin the necessary funds for a year of music study in Prague. When the money ran out, Dvořák earned his living for the next 15 years by playing in café bands and the National Opera orchestra.

As he grew older, Dvořák became less satisfied with the prevailing German style and more determined to write Bohemian music. When he was about age 40, his fortunes changed. He submitted a composition to the Austrian Commission. Although the prize he won was small in monetary value, it gained him the devoted friendship and unsparing help of committee member Johannes Brahms. Brahms opened many doors to publishers, performers, and conductors for Dvořák, who was humble and grateful. He once wrote Brahms, ". . . all my life [I] owe you the deepest gratitude for your good and noble intentions toward me, which are worthy of a truly great artist and man."*

By 1885 Dvořák was esteemed throughout the world. A few years later he accepted the directorship of the National Conservatory of Music in New York at a salary over 20 times what he was earning in Prague. During his summer stays in Spillville, Iowa, he wrote some of his best works, including the New World Symphony (formerly numbered 5 but more recently designated as No. 9) and the Cello Concerto. He was introduced to Afro-American music by Harry T. Burleigh, who was a pupil of his. He also became acquainted with the music of the American Indian. He was the first composer, native- or foreign-born, to recognize these great musical resources.

After three years in the United States, Dvořák returned to Bohemia, where he became director of the Prague Conservatory. In 1904 he collapsed and died of a stroke; in his honor a national day of mourning was declared.

---

*Milton Cross and David Ewen, *Encyclopedia of the Great Composers and Their Music,* vol. 1 (Garden City, N.Y.: Doubleday, 1953), p. 234.

Listening Guide

Dvořák: String Quartet in F Major, "American," Op. 96, First Movement   *Record 2,B*

Sonata Form

Exposition

0:03   First theme played by viola:

Allegro ma non troppo (Move along, but not too much)

0:12   First theme repeated by first violin.

0:20   Transition based on fourth measure of first theme; exchanged among other instruments.

1:32   Second theme, in new key, played softly by first violin:

2:00   First three notes of second theme used to work into transition.

2:28   Codetta containing measures 1 and 2 of first theme; soft.

Development

2:38   First theme, somewhat changed, played by viola.

2:48   Measure 1 of first theme played by first violin.

2:56	Measure 3 of first theme played loudly by first violin.
3:15	Viola plays out melody based on measure 3 of first theme.
3:36	Cello plays out with measures 3 and 4 of first theme; is followed by first violin.
3:48	New melodic idea introduced; is imitated in fugal style starting with second violin, then first violin, viola, and cello:

Recapitulation

4:22	First theme played by viola.
4:31	First theme repeated by violin.
4:40	Transition based on measure 4 of first theme; music modulates and transition is longer than in exposition.
4:45	Brief cello countermelody.
5:59	Second theme, in tonic key, played by first violin.
6:12	Second theme repeated by cello, dynamic level increases.
6:30	Climactic point; full dynamic level; music turns to softer and slower material.
6:55	Coda; measures 3 and 4 of first theme are played.
7:09	Closes on loud chords.

12

Keyboard Music

As was pointed out in Chapter 6, there are several types of keyboard instruments, the most important being the harpsichord, organ, and piano. The piano was the last to arrive on the musical scene, and when it did, it surpassed the organ and supplanted the harpsichord in popularity. Before about 1750 composers did not specify which keyboard instrument should play a work. The work *clavier* meant any keyboard instrument and was considered a sufficient designation.

Because keyboard instruments can sound several pitches at the same time, certain types of music are especially suitable for them. This chapter examines some of the more important types of keyboard music.

Suite

A *suite* (pronounced sweet) is a composition for keyboard or a group of instruments. The word *suite* simply means a collection or group of items that belong together. So we speak of a suite of rooms or a suite of furniture. In the time of Bach suite referred to a collection of dances that were intended for performance as a unified series.

The dances were *stylized;* that is, they were "dressed up" to make them attractive pieces for listening. The composer wrote original music for them, but in meter, tempo, and other characteristics, their similarity to known dance types was apparent. A composer today might do the same thing by selecting a popular dance of a generation ago, say, the fox trot or the Charleston, and writing similar music with more interesting melodies and harmonies while retaining the essential rhythm and style of the original dance. This is what Bach and other composers of his time did. They selected several contrasting dances that were no longer in vogue, then applied their skills as composers to stylizing them. The resulting music was for listening, not dancing.

Many different dances were incorporated into suites. In the early 1700s the four most commonly found were the allemande, sarabande, courante, and gigue. The *allemande* (*ahla-mahnd*), which means *German* in French, probably came from Germany. It has a moderate tempo and a rather continuous movement of eighth or sixteenth notes. The *courante* (*koo-rahnt*) was French in origin. It moves a little more rapidly than the allemande. The *sarabande* (*sara-bahnd*) is a slow dance. It was probably imported by the Spaniards from Mexico. The *gigue* (zheeg) originated in Britain, where it was called *jig*. It is lively and is appropriately placed as the final dance in a suite. It also tends to be more contrapuntal in character than most dance types.

Other dances less frequently encountered in the eighteenth-century suite are the bourrée, minuet, gavotte, louré, polonaise, and passapied. Often a composer wrote a *double*—a variation of the dance preceding it. Many times a suite was prefaced by a prelude or an overture. It was customary for all the dances in a suite to be written in the same key. The composer achieved variety by arranging the movements in a suite so that the faster dances contrasted with slower ones. Most dances were in two-part form, with each part repeated, although when they are played today, the performer sometimes omits the repeats and attaches the *double* to form a single piece.

Bach's Suite No. 2 of the *English Suites* is for solo keyboard instrument. Since the most prominent keyboard instrument of Bach's day was the harpsichord, the music is most authentically rendered on that instrument. The harpsichord has a light, brilliant sound and a mechanism conducive to playing rapid decorative notes. Therefore, composers often wrote highly decorative versions of a melody. The example shows the unadorned and decorated versions of the same two measures of a sarabande from Bach's suite:

In the bourrée (boo-*ray*), a lively dance with two beats per measure, Bach employs a running accompaniment in the left-hand, or lower, part (Record 3,B). Instead of simple block chords, he takes the pitches of the chords and spreads them out. The broken chord is a different way to sound the harmony. The opening portion of Bourrée I is shown at the bottom of the page.

Bourrée II is similar in style to Bourrée I, but the key and manner of presenting the chords are different, as shown in the music at the top of the page. The other movements of the suite include a prelude, an allemande, a courante, and a gigue.

Some suites are for orchestra. One of the best known is Bach's Suite No. 3 for Orchestra, with its famous "Air," which is often heard alone under the title "Air for the G String." Other well-known orchestral suites are Handel's *Water Music*, composed for the king as he sailed down the Thames, and Handel's *Music for the Royal Fireworks*. The latter was written for a victory celebration, which went awry when the fireworks ignited the wooden pavilion and caused widespread panic.

Suites composed in the nineteenth and twentieth centuries departed from the eighteenth-century model of stylized dances. These later suites consist largely of a collection of orchestral pieces from an opera or ballet.

Fugue

A most important type of keyboard music in Bach's day was the *fugue*. The fugue, like most musical forms, did not appear full-blown. It evolved from less complex types of keyboard music. The fugue and its predecessors have in common their contrapuntal conception, with lines of music imitating one another.

J. S. Bach's Fugue in C Major is one third of a longer work that includes a toccata and an ada-

gio. A Listening Guide containing the themes for the fugue appears on pages 108–109.

For the first nine measures only one melody is played. Although it is a single melody, it is divided into four distinct phrases, with rests between each phrase. Those rests may seem to interrupt the flow of the music, but Bach soon fills them with other music. This melody serves as the main theme for the fugue and is called the *subject*. At the tenth measure the subject begins in a second line. In fugues these lines are called *voices*, even though they are to be played, not sung.

While the second voice is sounding the subject in a key different from the first appearance, the first voice continues with a line of counterpoint. This line is somewhat of a melody but is not as distinctive and easily remembered as the subject. Logically, it is called the *countersubject*. Notice that it is active at points where the subject has the rests, and vice versa.

At measure 19 the third voice enters, sounding the subject in the original key, while the second voice continues into the countersubject. The first voice begins free contrapuntal material. In this fugue the contrapuntal material actually is parallel with the subject, sounding two octaves and a third lower.

At measure 28 the fourth voice enters in the pedal part. The first and second voices continue in the free contrapuntal material, with the first voice somewhat parallel to the countersubject (which is in the third voice at this point) and the second voice parallel to the subject in the fourth voice.

EXPOSITION					DEVELOPMENT	
Voice I	S	CS	FM		Return	Close
Voice II		S	CS	FM	and	with
Voice III			S	CS	development	subject
Voice IV				S	of	
					subject	
					and countersubject	

S = subject   CS = countersubject   FM = free contrapuntal material

The fourth voice completes the subject at the beginning of measure 37, marking the end of the *exposition*—the rather standard beginning section of a fugue. From that point until the end of the fugue, the subject appears in different keys and voices, free contrapuntal sections are included, and the subject and countersubject are combined in different ways. In this fugue Bach brings back the subject seven more times, sometimes with the countersubject. The final appearance of the subject is an especially healthy one in the pedals.

The basic design for the Fugue in C Major is diagrammed at the top of the page.

This fugue has four voices. It could have had two, three, or five; more than five is not common. The order in which the voices enter is a matter of choice for the composer. Composers often vary the structure slightly to suit their desires for the piece.

What is necessary to understand a fugue? Certainly knowing the plan of the exposition helps. More valuable is the ability to listen and think in linear, contrapuntal terms.

Remember that the subject is the unifying element of the fugue. The plan of the exposition makes it likely that you will recognize the subject when you hear it again. The interlacing of counterpoint around a central subject (with its contrasting countersubject added for interest) reminds one of a complicated mathematical formula working itself out to a beautifully correct conclusion.

Other Keyboard Forms

The fugue is not the only form that is well suited to the organ. Two others are based on the chorale. The plain, sturdy melody of a chorale makes it especially suitable as a theme for other works. One type of adaptation is called *chorale variation*. The other form is called a *chorale prelude*—a contrapuntal piece built around a chorale melody.

A third type of music well adapted to organ is the passacaglia. It begins with a statement of the theme, usually in the bass and without accompaniment. The melody is likely to stay in the bass throughout. (The pedals are ideal for maintaining the rather slow-moving melody, leaving the hands free to play the faster, higher pitched lines of music.) The continuous repetition in the bass, combined with continuous variation in the upper parts, can build to a mighty climax. One of Bach's finest organ works is his *Passacaglia in C Minor.*

Some types of pieces that were common for the harpsichord were also written for organ. One such type is the *toccata*, a flashy work with many rapid scale passages. The *prelude* is another type. In the eighteenth century, it simply meant a short piece of instrumental music. A *fantasia* is supposed to give the impression of improvisation, with abrupt changes of mood and sound. An *invention* is a short contrapuntal piece for a keyboard instrument. Bach wrote several famous inventions to help his wife and children learn to play the harpsichord. Piano teachers use them often today. *Sinfonias* are *not* symphonies. Rather, they are overtures, or introductory movements to longer works. In a few cases the term is a synonym for invention.

Piano Music

The piano is credited to Bartolomeo Cristofori (1655-1731) of Florence, Italy, who produced such instruments in the early 1700s. It did not become popular until after 1770, when its key action was improved. Even then the piano did not sound like today's instrument. The tone was softer, lighter, and a bit duller. A significant improvement was made about 1820, with the addition of the cast iron frame, which allowed the strings to be given more tension and enabled them to produce a bigger sound. Also during the nineteenth century the action was improved, and pedals were added to sustain tone and alter dynamic level.

Today the piano is the most frequently played instrument. More than 18 million Americans play it, compared to 15 million who play guitar, the next most popular instrument in the United States. The piano has had a huge

Listening Guide

Bach: Toccata, Adagio, and Fugue in C Major, BWV 564, Fugue   *Record 3,B*

Exposition

0:00   Subject, in four distinct phrases, is presented in first voice alone, at moderately high pitch level.

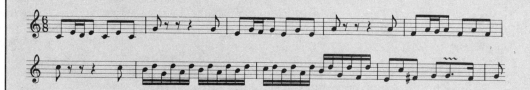

0:18   Subject presented in second voice (four notes lower than first voice); countersubject begins in first voice and appears largely between the phrases of subject:

0:36   Subject presented in third voice (five notes lower than second voice); second voice takes up countersubject; first voice begins free material, which in this fugue parallels subject at a higher pitch level.

0:54   Subject starts in fourth voice (four notes lower than third voice), played on pedalboard; third voice presents countersubject; second voice parallels subject, and first voice somewhat parallels countersubject at higher pitch levels.

amount of music written for it, ranging from short simple pieces to long works of terrifying complexity. Virtually every significant composer since 1770 has written piano music. The remainder of this chapter is devoted to examining three works that represent the main trends of nineteenth-century piano music.

Beethoven's *Pathétique* Sonata

The Piano Sonata in C Minor, Op. 13 (No. 8) was named *Pathétique* by Beethoven himself. The *No. 8* comes from its order among the 32 piano sonatas Beethoven composed. It is a relatively early sonata, dating from 1799.

End of Exposition

1:12 Episode begins with upper voice sounding fast-moving notes in sequence by raising the pitch level one step with each appearance.

1:24 Subject played in middle pitch range in third voice; countersubject in first voice.

1:45 Subject played in fourth voice (pedals); countersubject played in third voice.

2:04 Subject played in first voice at high pitch level; new contrapuntal material in third and fourth voices.

2:25 Episode similar to first episode, with third voice sounding rapidly moving notes sequentially.

2:38 Subject played in second voice; first voice has running notes derived from countersubject.

2:56 Subject played in third voice (in minor key); second voice partially imitates subject one measure later; first voice continues running notes in sequence.

3:15 Episode uses figures in sequence, outlining chords similar to free material appearing earlier with subject, except that patterns basically ascend instead of descend.

3:22 Subject returns in fourth voice (pedals) at rather loud dynamic level; countersubject in third voice.

3:40 Episode begins in first voice, with fast notes in sequence; very similar to initial episode; followed by sequence that descends.

4:09 Subject makes final appearance in fourth voice, doubled with low pitch level at loud dynamic level; other three voices sound free material.

4:27 Free material containing a figure repeated in sequence; long, low tone sustained until nearly the conclusion.

4:56 Closes with a rather low pitched chord.

First movement. It was probably the introduction to the first movement that suggested the idea of *Pathétique.* It is marked *Grave* (solemn), and sounds like a brooding fantasy. Each measure begins on a loud chord and is followed by a dotted rhythm at a soft dynamic level (see the music at the top of the page). Contrary motion can be seen and heard between the treble and bass parts.

The sonata-form portion of the movement is marked to be played fast and vigorously:

Typically, the second theme is in contrast to the first:

It is in E flat minor, the relative major key to C minor. There is a third theme and a codetta. The introduction returns just prior to the development section. In the development Beethoven combines the first theme with the theme from the introduction. Before the end of the movement, the slow introduction appears once more, adding a sense of drama to the entire movement.

Second movement. The second movement is songlike. Its main melody opens on middle C and is heard over a typical accompaniment figure of the eighteenth century. The melody is repeated one octave higher, and then contrasting sections are heard:

The overall form is *A B A C A,* which gives it the form but not the spirit of a rondo. The C section is especially dramatic, with sudden changes of dynamics.

Third movement. The third movement is the final one, thus following the classical pattern for a sonata. Also typical is its rondo form. Although in minor, the theme is not as somber as the minor theme in the first movement. The form for the entire movement is *A B A C A B A.* This arrangement shows the eighteenth-century fondness for symmetry. There is a codetta after the first *B* section and a coda at the end of the movement, producing a form that combines rondo and sonata—logically called rondo-sonata by some musicians.

A Listening Guide for the third movement appears on pages 112–113.

Chopin's *Fantasie-Impromptu,* Op. 66

Chopin was the leader of the "intimate-sensitive" school of piano music and performance. He was not fond of the concert hall; he preferred to play for his friends in the more informal atmosphere of a parlor. He treated rhythm more freely than did other pianists. He was sometimes criticized for doing this, and one contemporary of his even complained that

Chopin couldn't keep time. Undoubtedly he could, but he chose not to.

The *Fantasie-Impromptu* is typical of the free-form *character piece* of the nineteenth century. Although it bears the name *Impromptu*, it is not actually improvised. Chopin and other nineteenth-century composers worked very hard at sounding casual.

The first large section of the work (top of the page) has the left-hand, bass-clef line confined entirely to broken chords. The right-hand, treble-clef part contains a rippling melody made up exclusively of sixteenth notes. Many notes are altered by sharps and flats, indicating harmonic changes. Of interest also is the extensive use of three notes in the left hand against four in the right. The combination of patterns tends to blur the rhythmic effect of each.

The notation frequently includes the symbol *Ped.* This mark tells the pianist to depress the sustaining pedal, thereby lifting the dampers and allowing the strings to ring freely. The effect adds richness to the music by prolonging the sounds, which would otherwise be immediately curtailed by the dampers. Proper pedaling also contributes to smooth and lyrical phrasing. The composer and/or performer must plan carefully for the use of the pedal, since unwanted notes that are allowed to ring have a blurring effect.

The middle section of the piece changes character by becoming much more lyrical. In fact, the melody is so singable that it was made into a successful popular song entitled "I'm Always Chasing Rainbows." Chopin confines his ornamentation of the melody to a few five-note turns and *trills* (rapid alternation between two adjacent pitches):

Again the pedal is employed as an integral part of the music. Chopin indicates that the melody should be played *sotto voce* (so-toh vo-chay), literally "under the voice," or in a subdued manner.

The first section is repeated, this time with an extended coda at the end. The ending seems to fade away. Nineteenth-century composers favored one of two endings, both of which tend to be "effects." One is the glorious, full-blown climax of sound. The other is its opposite: the quiet fade-out.

Bach, Handel, Mozart, Haydn, Beethoven, and Schubert were all extremely versatile composers. They wrote successfully in nearly every medium, vocal and instrumental, solo and ensemble. Chopin was different. He was one of the first of the "specialist" composers, who tended to limit their writing to one or two areas. Although Chopin attempted a few other media, the bulk of his effort was directed to-

Listening Guide

Beethoven: Piano Sonata, Op. 13, No. 8, *Pathétique*, Third Movement   *Record 3,B*

Rondo—*A B A C A B A*

0:00   Main theme (*A*) in major played in the upper notes at soft dynamic level:

0:17   Extension of main theme begins after short silence following two decisive chords.

0:34   Transition using triplet patterns takes over in rapidly moving notes.

0:45   First subordinate theme (*B*) in new major key; a return of the triplet figures follows:

1:03   Main theme (*A*) starts again at soft dynamic level in the same key as its first appearance.

ward his piano works, and through them he earned his reputation as a composer.

Liszt's *Mephisto Waltz*

Franz Liszt was the opposite of Chopin in many respects. Liszt was fond of the concert hall and was the outstanding piano virtuoso of his day. He succeeded in dazzling his audiences with his piano-playing ability.

Mephisto Waltz is program music—music written to be associated with a nonmusical idea. The story for this work was suggested by an excerpt from Nikolaus Lenau's poem *Faust*. Faust is the man who makes a bargain with the devil, Mephistopheles, thus the name *Mephisto*. In this section of the poem, called "The dance at the village inn," Mephistopheles and Faust wander through the countryside looking for pleasure. They come upon a dance at a local inn. Faust is attracted to one of the girls but is afraid to ask her to dance. Mephistopheles scornfully seizes a violin and plays so beautifully that no one there is able to resist the music. Faust and the girl dance together and then disappear into the night.

A Listening Guide for *Mephisto Waltz* appears on pages 114–115.

Mephisto Waltz is not a polished and proper waltz, such as Johann Strauss, composer of "The Blue Danube" and other waltzes, might

1:21 Second subordinate theme (C) begins in new major key and is repeated a number of times, some of the time in imitation:

1:51 Transition of rapidly moving notes that become triplets used for earlier transition.

2:05 Main theme (A) starts again after long, loud chord followed by a short silence.

2:28 Transition containing the rapidly moving notes in triplets.

2:39 Second subordinate theme (B) returns in different major key; modulates several times.

2:58 Main theme (A) returns at soft dynamic level in original major key.

3:10 Coda begins with triplet figures leading up to short "punched out" chords; music increases in intensity; key changes to minor.

3:33 First portion of main theme appears at soft dynamic level after long, loud chord.

3:44 Closes with a series of rapidly moving notes and a short chord.

Listening Guide

Liszt: *Mephisto Waltz* *Record 4, A*

0:00   Rapid, low, repeated notes; more notes appear as music progresses; short figure soon added in upper notes.

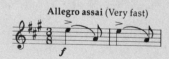

0:14   After a short silence, four quick figures are played, leading into opening repeated-note material.

0:31   After another short silence and four quick figures, the pitch level ascends as the intensity of music increases.

0:42   More repeated chords and notes; music grows louder and heavier.

0:55   First theme (*A*) is played at rather low pitch level:

1:08   Section sounding somewhat like scherzo begins; opening figure played several times in lower notes.

1:44   After a very rapid ascending scale and repeated notes, *A* theme is played in lower notes.

1:57   Scherzolike material returns.

2:17   Rapid and loud sounding of chords, two to the beat instead of usual three; noticeable key changes.

2:31   *A* theme returns in upper notes; music gradually grows softer and calmer.

2:56   Second theme (*B*) appears; music is slower and calmer. Motive (circled in the example) sounding somewhat like a sigh is used extensively as music progresses:

3:09   *B* theme repeated one note higher.

3:39   Motive and phrases from *B* theme appear as music slowly grows louder and more passionate.

4:21   After a silent place playful theme (*C*) appears; played rather softly at high pitch level:

4:34   After a short silence, phrase from *B* theme is played in upper notes over runs in lower notes; music grows slowly more intense and louder.

5:05   *C* theme is played softly.

5:23   After two silences and ascending run, *B* theme is played rather smoothly and somewhat softly in high repeated notes.

6:05   Descending phrases repeated and phrases from *B* theme heard again in repeated notes.

6:19   *A* theme returns at low pitch level; rather soft.

6:34   After a long descending run of notes, portion of *B* theme is played in lower notes below dazzling chord outlines in upper notes.

6:52   "Sigh" motive from *B* theme played in upper notes; loud repeated chords and increasing tempo lead to silent measure.

7:12   Very fast, loud section; alternates notes between player's hands; some of *B* theme and "sigh" motive used.

7:30   Scherzolike section, softer and lighter, with certain chords accented; phrase from *B* theme in middle notes.

7:52   "Sigh" motive appears below very fast runs in higher notes.

8:13   Free, cadenzalike runs.

8:25   *C* theme played softly in upper notes.

8:45   Portion of *B* theme played slowly and softly; free rhythm as in a cadenza.

9:49   Coda starts softly and builds quickly to climactic point; repeated notes and rapid alternation between hands.

10:13   Closes with two short chords.

have written. In fact, some sections of *Mephisto Waltz* are in $\frac{3}{4}$ meter. This music is intended for listening, not dancing.

One purpose of the piece is to show off the virtuoso technique of the pianist who plays it. Liszt wrote most of his piano music for his own performances, and he surely gave himself plenty of opportunities to show off. *Mephisto Waltz* is filled with rapidly repeated notes and chords, passages with hands crossing at great speed, extremely rapid scales and arpeggios (chords outlined with consecutive notes), many decorative trills and other figures, and the full range of the piano employed from the lowest to the highest notes. It is the type of piece that only a very accomplished pianist can undertake.

Since the nineteenth century, composers have certainly not stopped writing for piano, but piano music did seem to reach the high point of its development during that time. For range, power, and musical versatility, the piano is almost unexcelled as a solo instrument.

Johann Sebastian Bach

Mezzotint of Bach by E. G. Haussmann. (Library of Congress.)

Johann Sebastian Bach (1685–1750) lived an uneventful life, one not very different from that of many successful musicians of his time. The most notable feature about him was his lineage—he was one of a gifted musical family. Over a period of about six generations, from 1580 to 1845, more than 60 Bachs were musicians of some sort, and at least 38 of these attained eminence. Included among the latter were several of J. S. Bach's own sons.

Bach, the son of a town musician, was born in Eisenach, Germany, in 1685. When the boy was ten, his father died. Johann's musical training was taken over by his older brother, who was an organist. During his lifetime Bach was known more as an organ virtuoso than as a composer. After two short-lived positions as organist, Bach, at the age of 23, was appointed to his first significant post—court organist and chamber musician to the Duke of Weimar (*Vy*-mar). He stayed nine years. It was during his Weimar years that he concentrated on the organ, as both performer and composer.

When the duke failed to advance him, Bach accepted another position at Cöthen. The prince at Cöthen was interested in chamber music, so the versatile Bach turned from writing church and organ music to composing primarily for instruments other than the organ. It was during this time that he wrote the famous *Brandenburg Concertos*. After the death of his wife, Maria Barbara, he remarried. He immortalized his second wife, Anna Magdalena, by writing a book of keyboard music for her.

The last third of Bach's life began with his appointment in 1723 as cantor of St. Thomas Church in Leipzig. It was one of the more important musical posts in Germany, but it demanded that he teach the choirboys music and nonmusical subjects (and "in case they do not wish to obey, chastise them with moderation"). He was required to "so manage the music that it shall not last too long, and shall be of such a nature as not to make an operatic impression, but rather incite the listeners to devotion."

Bach was not the first choice for the position. A member of the town council is reported to have said, "Since the best man could not be obtained, lesser ones will have to be accepted." The Leipzig position required the writing and direction of church music, so Bach again complied by changing the emphasis of his composing. Not only were the Leipzig city fathers unaware of his genius, they were stingy. They paid him a poor salary and provided him with a choir of about 30 singers, few of whom were competent musicians.

In spite of the annoyances of the position at Leipzig and tragedy in his personal life (six of his eight children born in Leipzig died), Bach continued his endless stream of compositions. Late in life he suffered a stroke and became blind. In 1750 he died, with his greatness as a composer still unrecognized. His music went largely unnoticed until 1829, when young Felix Mendelssohn rediscovered the *St. Matthew Passion*.

Except for brief journeys in Germany, Bach knew little of the world outside his native country. He was neither well read nor well educated. He created no new musical forms and instituted no new techniques of composing. His music was seldom heard outside of Leipzig during his lifetime, and even there it was probably not performed well.

Why is it that Bach is so dominating a figure in music? Simply because he wrote with such effectiveness and skill. Words are not adequate to describe his genius. Perhaps the late Dag Hammarskjöld, Secretary General of the United Nations, expressed it best. In speaking of Bach and Vivaldi, he said, "Both have a beautiful way of creating order in the brain."

All of Bach's music is catalogued with the letters BWV, an abbreviation of the German title of the thematic list of Bach's music edited in the twentieth century by Wolfgang Schmieder.

Franz Liszt

Early daguerreotype of Liszt.

Franz Liszt (1811–1886) was a varied and complex man. The son of servants of the Esterházy family in Hungary, he was sent to Paris to study under a scholarship arrangement. While there he attended a concert by the spectacular Italian violinist Niccolo Paganini. The 19-year-old Liszt was so impressed by the performance that he became determined to do for the piano what Paganini had done for the violin. He spent hours practicing flashy techniques. He even imitated Paganini's dramatic appearance and mannerisms: the black, tight-fitting clothes and tossing hair. Liszt became a dazzling performer, and he wrote pieces to demonstrate his ability. He was one of the first soloists to turn the piano to one side so that the audience could see the performer's hands. Before this soloists had played with their backs to the audience.

Liszt loved life and people and was a man of generous disposition. He had great admiration for Beethoven and tried to promote his music. He helped many musicians get their works performed, including Wagner and Berlioz. His career was a success in every way, and he wrote some fine piano music. In the last years of his life he took minor orders in the church and was known as Abbé Liszt.

Frédéric Chopin

Frédéric Chopin (*Show*-pan; 1810–1849) was the son of a French father and Polish mother. He showed considerable talent at an early age and received his musical education at the conservatory in Warsaw. Before he was 20, he set out to make his way in the world. Shortly after his departure from Poland, the Poles revolted against the Russians and their tsar. In time the Russians crushed the revolt, an event that caused Chopin much anguish.

He traveled extensively and then reached Paris, the city that was to become his adopted home. His skill as a pianist and composer made him a sought-after musician. Soon he began to move in a circle of artistic friends, through whom he met Mme. Aurore Dudevant, who wrote novels under the pen name of George Sand. She had an unusual personality and a penchant for smoking cigars and wearing masculine clothing. She was considerably older than Chopin. They lived together for several years, and her domineering personality seemed to suit Chopin's need to be governed. The years were productive ones for him.

In time his health began to fail, and the relationship with Mme. Dudevant became strained. Finally they parted in bitterness, and with this event his creative energy seemed to weaken. At the age of 39 Chopin died of tuberculosis. Symbolically, his heart was returned to Poland, and the rest of his body was buried in Paris.

13

Opera

Opera includes several artistic elements in addition to music. Opera takes place on a stage, so it is a form of theater, requiring eye appeal and action. The success of opera depends to some extent on its staging—the scenery, costumes, and actors' movements. As drama, it must present a story and delineate and project the feelings of various characters. Frequently dancing is integrated into the production. Opera, then, involves many things: literature, drama, vocal and instrumental music, staging, and dancing. It is the great union of the arts. For that very reason opera presents the composer and performer with the greatest opportunities and the most difficulties of any type of music.

The Elements of Opera

Believability is hard to achieve because, although the stage action attempts to duplicate the realism of human life, the participants communicate through singing rather than through speech. Normally a phrase such as "The class begins at ten o'clock" would be spoken. Singing it would probably cause people to wonder! But suppose the sentence about the starting time of the class is in an opera. If the singer sings the words with a minimum of musical expressiveness, the music won't be very interesting. The drama may have been preserved, but at the expense of the music. On the other hand, if the composer writes a beautiful melody to these words, then realism and believability have been sacrificed.

Time is also a factor. Stage action can proceed normally if "The class begins at ten o'clock" is spoken in the routine manner of real life. But if an aria is developed from these words, the forward motion of the plot will have to be suspended for its duration. If interesting music is to be included, therefore, the drama must be abbreviated to accommodate the pressures of time, and it will have to be interrupted occasionally to allow for artistic balance between drama and music.

The impression of realism has been further hampered by the singing style that has evolved, of necessity, within the operatic tradition. This style was developed in the centuries before recordings and mechanical amplification were available. Above all, a singer had to be heard—clearly—all the way to the last row of the balcony. If the style was somewhat unnatural, it was at least powerful.

The drama-music dilemma has a bearing on the appearance and acting ability of the opera singer. Some outstanding singers of the past were neither interested nor talented in acting. Because of the great vocal demands of opera, it is difficult to find people who can both sing and act with skill. The lengthy roles are difficult to learn, and years of experience are required to do them justice. Fortunately, opera companies today are aware of the need for a more natural vocal sound and appropriate appearance and acting ability, and they cast accordingly.

Another distracting problem in opera is understanding the words. Even when sung in English, the words may not be easily comprehended. The problem is magnified when the opera is written in a foreign language. Operas can be translated and sung in English, but should they be? Although translation is difficult, involving correct numbers of syllables, natural accents, shades of meaning, and rhyme schemes, the answer is probably yes.

It must also be admitted that some opera plots are hardly fascinating. Many of the stories make no attempt to be believable, or they try to be realistic and fail. Others are dated and quaint.

Opera companies, if they want to remain solvent, must attract an audience, which means that certain favorite operas are performed year after year, often to the exclusion of new operas. The cost of producing an opera is very high, and for this reason few opera company managers wish to undertake the risk and expense of trying a new work.

Appreciating Opera

Despite the obstacles to creating a successful opera, this musical medium often achieves a tremendous artistic impact. The drama provides the composer with situations ripe for musical expression. Some operatic "I-love-yous" encourage a sensuous reaction best described as "goose-pimply." There is also pageantry and action, as well as both vocal and instrumental music.

An appreciation of opera can be increased by accepting the same limitations on realism that are accepted for a play. For example, in a play interior scenes are designed to suggest four-walled rooms, even though one wall must be missing so the audience can watch. People accept that time in a play or movie is not measured in absolute terms. Months or years are presumed to have elapsed during a ten-minute intermission. To such limitations accepted for dramas add two more for opera: the singing of the lines and the shortened attention to plot and character development.

As with any type of music, the more you know about opera, the greater are the chances you will like it.

Early Opera

Opera began in Florence, Italy, shortly before 1600. It was an attempt to re-create ancient Greek drama. At first it was almost entirely recitative, but opera composers soon became more concerned with melody and less with dramatic declamation. By the time the first public opera house opened in Venice in 1637, the artistic ideals of reestablishing Greek drama had been largely forgotten. The stories were burdened by the addition of irrelevant incidents, spectacular scenes, and incongruous comedy episodes. But other changes were more constructive. Arias, duets, and ensembles evolved, and the orchestra took on more prominence.

As opera spread throughout Europe, its dramatic element became less and less important. The singer reigned supreme. In their desire to hold center stage, soloists added all kinds of embellishments to the melody to show off their virtuosity. The situation deteriorated so much that Christoph Willibald von Gluck (1714–1787) felt compelled to lead a reform movement. Gluck had written many operas himself, so he knew the field and was undeniably right when he said that opera was in need of correction. He tried to bring back its dramatic integrity by making the music serve the text. Everything in the opera, including ballet, was to be an integral part of the drama. Gluck wrote several operas that demonstrated his reforms.

In the decades following the opening of the opera house in Venice, opera evolved into two rather distinct styles. *Opera seria* was of a serious nature, approximating the original dramatic purpose of the first operas. *Opera buffa* (boofa) was lighter opera of a comic nature. Mozart wrote both kinds of opera, but his greatest public successes were of the *buffa* type.

Mozart's *Don Giovanni*

The title of the work *Don Giovanni* (Don Juan) reveals its language to be Italian, although Mozart's native language was German. Mozart had made several journeys to Italy and knew the language, but the *libretto* (opera text) was written by the Italian Lorenzo da Ponte, the best librettist of his day. The selection of an Italian text was a happy choice for the additional reason that opera was a thoroughly Italian product, and Vienna audiences were more accustomed to hearing opera in Italian than in their own language.

Basically, *Don Giovanni* is *opera seria*. It contains some humorous moments, but it has a serious outlook. Because of the opera's length, the discussion here is limited mainly to its last portion. The plot is intricate, so the opera should be listened to with libretto in hand.

The opera opens with a typical overture. (It's claimed that Mozart composed the overture one day before the first performance.) The stage action starts as Don Giovanni begins his adventures with Ottavio's fiancée, Donna Anna. She refuses his advances, and her father, the Commendatore (the Commander), is killed by Don Giovanni in a duel while defending the honor of his daughter. At a village wedding Don Giovanni attempts to seduce Zerlina, the bride of the peasant Masetto. Act I ends with a ball given for the peasants by Don Giovanni, during which he makes a more obvious attempt on Zerlina's virtue.

Later he plays a cruel trick on Donna Elvira, whom he had seduced long ago and deserted. She pursues Don Giovanni to Seville, and he

disguises his servant Leporello in his own clothes so that he can pretend to be in love with her and thus get her out of the way for a while. In the meantime, Don Giovanni pursues other adventures and pleasures. During one of his escapades he takes refuge in a cemetery, where he discovers the statue of the Commendatore and mockingly invites it to dinner. The statue nods its head in acceptance.

The final scene is set in the banquet hall in Don Giovanni's palace. The gay and bouncy music tells us immediately that the Don isn't worried. In fact, he seems to have forgotten all about the graveyard and the statue. He commands his private orchestra to play some dinner music. A wind ensemble plays a song from a popular opera of the day:

Leporello serves the table and looks hungrily at the food. "What a greedy appetite," he complains as he watches Don Giovanni down one mouthful after another.

A second piece is heard from the wind ensemble:

Leporello pours the Don some wine, and thinking that he won't be seen, he stuffs some food into his mouth. As the third number begins—"Non piu andrai"

from Mozart's *The Marriage of Figaro*—Leporello helps himself to more food. The Don, realizing that Leporello's mouth is full, asks him to whistle along with the selection from *Figaro*. Poor Leporello is forced to admit that he has been snitching. The whole scene bubbles along like champagne.

Donna Elvira breaks the spell as she rushes in and throws herself at Don Giovanni's feet.

She begs her former lover to give up his evil ways. Leporello is moved, but not Don Giovanni. He mocks Donna Elvira by proposing a toast to her ("Long live women and good wine!"). Angered and humiliated, she turns from him and runs out the door. Just as she leaves, she emits a piercing scream. "Go and see what's the matter," the Don orders his servant. Leporello does as he's told, only to shriek in terror himself and slam the door shut. "For God's sake, don't go out there," he implores Don Giovanni. Leporello has seen the stone guest advancing to keep his dinner appointment. Terrified, Leporello even tries to imitate the sound of the statue's footsteps. "You're crazy," the Don scoffs. But suddenly the orchestra drowns out the sound of a stone fist striking the door. "Open the door!" Don Giovanni shouts to Leporello, who refuses. "I'll go myself," sneers the Don, and he opens the door.

Two huge chords are heard from the orchestra, and the great white statue of the slain Commendatore enters the room. The whole scene suggests inevitable doom. The statue speaks: "Don Giovanni! You invited me to dine with you. And I am here."

For the first time, Don Giovanni seems shaken. His words are brave, but the music from the orchestra reveals his fear. Brazenly he orders Leporello to set another place. The statue declines "mortal food"; he has come for another reason. A brief trio begins. Mozart keeps each part distinct, according to what the character feels. Leporello sings a quick patter that gives evidence of his terror and his desire to make himself invisible. Don Giovanni's lines are brief, patient, and defiant. The stone guest sings most of his words on a few unyielding tones:

The orchestra music becomes more chilling, and the statue invites Don Giovanni to return the courtesy and dine with him. Leporello pleads with his master to say no. The Don hesitates a moment, then with true bravado says, "I'll come!" The statue offers his hand to seal

the agreement. When Don Giovanni grasps it, he cries out in pain. The stone hand is as crushing and cold as death itself. Again and again the statue calls on him to repent ("Pentiti"). Each time Don Giovanni refuses. Finally he pulls his hand away. "Your time has run out," the statue tells him. Then all hell breaks loose; flames leap up, flashes of light are seen, and the orchestra plays rapidly moving notes as Don Giovanni writhes in agony. Slowly he sinks to his death as an offstage chorus sings.

Abruptly the mood changes from tragedy to comedy. Donna Anna, Donna Elvira, and Zerlina rush in, followed by Ottavio and Masetto. They find Leporello crawling about on the floor and demand to know what has happened. Leporello stammers out the tale of what he has just witnessed. The music is again filled with wit and sparkle. Don Giovanni is already just a memory. In a brief duet Donna Anna and Ottavio tell of their plan to marry after her year of mourning for her father is over. Donna Elvira pledges to end her days in a cloister. Zerlina and Masetto are impatient to be off so they can have dinner. And Leporello sets about finding himself a new master. As the six singers face the audience, they deliver the moral of the opera. The whole scene is so mischievous that one wonders whether Mozart was not really attempting to have the last laugh in the moralizing. The sextet sings:

> *Such is the end*
> *Of those who do evil.*
> *The death of the wicked*
> *Always matches their life.*

Interestingly, the last scene—the moralizing by the sextet—has often been omitted from the opera. In the nineteenth century it was felt that adding such a finale after the damnation scene was inappropriate. Mozart himself approved its deletion the second time it was staged. In this century, however, the last scene has been reinstated.

The music in Mozart's operas represents the eighteenth-century style, which exhibits good taste and a control of emotions. True, the librettos of his comic operas are sometimes spiced with *double entendres,* and the singers' emotions

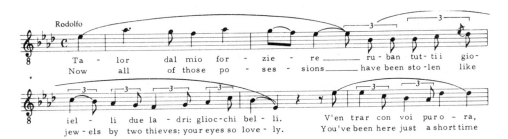

Rodolfo

Ta - lor dal mio for - zie - re ru - ban tut-ti i gio-
Now all of those po - ses - sions have been sto -len like

iel - li due la - dri: gliocchi bel - li. V'en trar con voi puro - ra,
jew-els by two thieves: your eyes so love - ly. You've been here just a short time

are exaggerated for comic effect. The situations in his serious operas often suggest strong emotions and drama. But the music is handled with a restraint that contrasts nicely with any incongruities of text or action. Even in serious moments he does not allow the music to become bombastic or sentimental. There is about his operatic writing a "light touch," an awareness that music can be worth listening to even when conceived as entertainment.

Puccini's *La Bohème*

La Bohème (The Bohemians) is a story of hippie life on the Left Bank of the Seine in Paris. The setting provides the composer with ample opportunities to inject emotion into the music.

The curtain rises on the ramshackle garret in which live four young bohemians: the poet Rodolfo, the painter Marcello, the philosopher Colline, and the musician Schaunard. Rodolfo and Marcello try to work but can think of little except the bitter cold. It is Christmas Eve, and they can't afford fuel for a decent fire. Colline and Schaunard come home shortly and flourish some of that rare item—money. The landlord, evidently aware of their good fortune, soon comes asking for the rent. By the use of a little

chicanery, they are able to get rid of him. They decide to celebrate at the Café Momus, so they leave in high spirits—all except Rodolfo, who is finishing some writing and plans to join them shortly.

There is a knock at the door. It is Mimi, who at the time has not met Rodolfo. Her candle has gone out, and she can't see to get up the stairs to her apartment. She is also weak and out of breath, so Rodolfo gives her a little wine and offers her a chair. As he helps her search for the key she has dropped on the floor, a draft of wind blows out their candles. They grope in the dark for her key. He finds it and, thinking quickly, slips it into his pocket without telling her. As they continue feeling along the floor, Rodolfo's hand meets hers and he exclaims, *"Che gelida manina!"* ("How cold your little hand is!") Then begins one of those glorious arias and a duet that exemplify Romantic opera at its best. (This portion of Act I is included in the *Study Guide and Scores.*) First, Rodolfo tells Mimi about himself and his lonely life as a poet. In the aria he joins with the orchestra in a luscious Puccini melody (top of the page).

Mimi responds with an equally beautiful aria, *"Mi chiamano Mimi"* ("I'm always called Mimi"). In it she describes her simple life and her flower embroidery (bottom of the page).

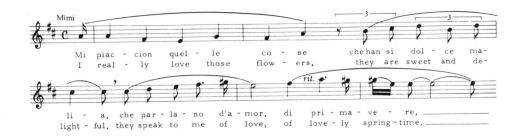

Mimi

Mi piac - cion quel - le co - se che han si dol - ce ma-
I real - ly love those flow - ers, they are sweet and de-

li - a, che par - la - no d'a - mor, di pri - ma - ve - re,
light - ful, they speak to me of love, of love - ly spring-time,

ma quan-do vien lo sge-lo il pri-mo so-lee mi-o, __
but when the frost is o-ver, sun-shine's first rays are mine, _____

il pri-mo ba-cio del-l'a-pri-le e mi-o! _____
then comes the first sweet kiss of Ap-ril, to me! _____

The aria continues with another lovely melody, some of which appears later in the opera (top of the page).

Rodolfo's friends return to the courtyard outside, urging him to hurry. He goes to the window and tells them to return to Momus and reserve a table. As the friends leave, Mimi and Rodolfo break into a duet in which they speak of the new love that binds them together. Some of the melodies previously introduced in the arias are heard again. The curtain falls with Mimi and Rodolfo embracing as they sing "Amor."

The realism problem mentioned earlier in this chapter is always present. Rodolfo and Mimi tell about themselves briefly, they are interrupted for a few moments, and then—suddenly—they are proclaiming their love for each other. Musically, the course of events is well conceived: an aria by the tenor, an aria by the soprano, a short break, and a duet in which they join forces. The scene would not be good opera if the love between the two were allowed to grow more naturally over several hours.

The scene between Rodolfo and Mimi also illustrates the smooth transition between recitative and aria. No longer is there a clear demarcation, particularly now that the recitative has assumed melodic and expressive interest.

For a small, frail girl dying of tuberculosis, Mimi engages in some rather robust singing. Again there is a break with reality that listeners must accept if they are to enjoy the opera. The full, vibrant singing style associated with opera is a musical necessity. The characters in most operas, including Puccini's, react to their environment and emotions on a grand scale. Their responses are exaggerated. Although ordinary persons are reluctant to make declarations of love, especially to people they don't know well, the characters in an opera proclaim their feel-

ings promptly and with magnified intensity. Such a telescoping of emotions and actions is good theater.

To convey the necessary power and intensity of expression, the singer must produce an "operatic" tone. Anything less will leave listeners unmoved. The vocal style of popular-song artists, even good ones, is inappropriate and inadequate for opera. Many of the currently popular singers lack tonal power, a fact usually covered up by amplification systems and recording devices. Then there is the matter of sheer singing ability. Opera singers outclass most popular singers when it comes to breath control and endurance, wide pitch range, richness of tone, control of dynamic level, and technical know-how. If a popular singer were to attempt Rodolfo's role, it might be compared to putting an amateur into the starting lineup of a professional football team.

Opera has acquired some traditions regarding the type of voice and the character to be portrayed. The heroine is almost always a soprano. In most stories she is young and beautiful, so the higher, lighter voice is more suitable. The leading male role is usually sung by a tenor. He is young and frequently sings duets with the soprano, often doubling her pitches one octave lower. This puts his pitches near the top of the male range, which gives the voice quality greater intensity. If there are older people or villains in the plot, the female parts are usually written for mezzo-sopranos or contraltos, the male roles for baritones or basses. Often they are supposed to sound ugly; Madame Flora in *The Medium*, the next opera presented in this chapter, is an example of this.

The rest of *La Bohème* is equally beautiful and not long. The second act is a delightful scene at the Café Momus in which Musetta, Marcello's former love and notorious flirt, sings

a bewitching waltz. In Act III, Mimi and Rodolfo have broken apart. There is a hint of impending doom because of Mimi's worsening tubercular condition.

In Act IV the setting is again the garret, and there are several musical and dramatic parallels to the first act. This time Musetta enters, saying that Mimi is downstairs, too weak to climb them—an ironic parallel to events of the earlier act. Mimi is helped into the room, and the

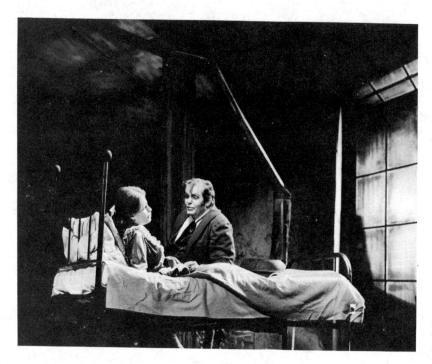

Rodolfo consoles Mimi shortly before she dies. (Indiana University School of Music.)

friends leave quickly to get medicine and a doctor. Rodolfo and Mimi recall their first meeting. The old themes are heard, but the music is no longer robust. It is pathetic and shattered. The friends return. They talk quietly among themselves, hoping Mimi can sleep. Suddenly they realize she is dead. "Mimi! Mimi!" Rodolfo cries. The orchestra strikes the same chords heard in the love music of the first act. This time the music is weighted with grief. The curtain falls.

German Romantic Opera

In the nineteenth century, opera tended to divide into a German type and an Italian type, both of which differed from their eighteenth century predecessors. In 1821 Carl Maria von Weber (*Vay*-ber; 1786–1826) wrote *Der Frei-schutz* (The Free-Shooter), an opera based on German folklore. The story concerns a marksman who receives from the black huntsman (that is, the devil) seven magic bullets; six of them do as he wills, but the seventh does as the devil wills. The devil also gets the soul of the

one who receives the bullets. Besides mysticism, the opera features peasants, rustic scenes, and hunting horns. Weber completed two more operas before his early death. Although they are seldom performed today, they exerted a significant influence on Richard Wagner (*Ree-*kard *Vahg*-ner, 1813–1883), one of the musical giants of the nineteenth century.

Wagner's Music Dramas

It is hard to know where to begin or end in discussing the music of Wagner. Entire books have been written on one or another of his operas. In fact, each of his operas has a score the size of a large book. His music is awe-inspiring, profound and pompous, fantastic and forceful. He was a complex musician and a complex personality, with one of history's more massive egos.

More than any previous opera composer, Wagner consciously tackled the dilemma of balance between music and drama. In his lengthy philosophical discourses he often indicated his belief that poetry and music should be one. To meet his artistic goals, he created a different kind of opera, one that he called *music drama* instead of opera.

Music drama required a new and different approach to the concept of libretto, so Wagner wrote his own texts. The topics were mythological because he felt that such stories best appealed to the emotions.

Wagner's favorite libretto themes were not only mythological, they were also rich with philosophical overtones—the struggle between good and evil, the contest between the physical and spiritual, and the idea of redemption through love. Because these overarching themes are present, the characters in the music dramas are not personalities but more nearly symbols or pawns being pushed about by irresistible forces. In this respect, Wagner approaches the drama of the ancient Greeks.

Wagner refined a technique that Weber had used and that Richard Strauss was later to utilize in *Don Juan.* The technique is to associate a musical motive with a particular character, emotion, or idea; the concept is called *leitmotiv,* or leading motive. As soon as various motives are established, Wagner weaves them in and out of the music at appropriate times to enhance the intrigue of the plot and to provide unity. Such use of motives also permits the orchestra to assume a more vital role in the music drama, since it can expand on people and ideas referred to in the text.

Since the division of music into recitatives, arias, and choruses interrupts the forward motion of the drama, Wagner eliminates these forms as independent sections. Instead he creates a flowing, melodious line to serve as an unending melody. The vocal line emphasizes the expression of the words being sung. With its continuous interweaving of motives, the orchestra contributes to the impression of never-ending motion. It's incorrect to say that there are no arias in Wagner's music dramas; there are, but they are woven into the continuously flowing music.

To heighten the impression that a musical work is "seamless," Wagner emphasizes chromatic harmony. That is, by making half-step alterations of chords, he weakens the "magnetic pull" of chords toward a tonic. The absence of a strong tonic means that the music seldom arrives at a cadence point or musical "stopping place," so the feeling of key is nebulous.

Wagner does not treat the orchestra as mere accompaniment for the singers on stage. The importance of the orchestra in his works equals, perhaps exceeds, that of the singers. In a real sense his orchestra is symphonic, both in its size and in its ability to stand almost without the vocal parts. In fact, many portions of his operas are performed today as concert pieces without singers. Probably Wagner's greatest genius was his ability to exploit the full resources of the orchestra. He made it produce effects that had previously not been done.

Wagner's most ambitious achievement was a cycle of four complete operas entitled *Der Ring des Nibelungen* (The Ring of the Nibelung). The four operas in the cycle are *Das Rheingold* (The Gold of the Rhine), *Die Walküre* (The Valkyries), *Siegfried,* and *Götterdämmerung* (The Twilight of the Gods).

The story of the cycle of operas is built around some gold supposedly guarded by the Rhine maidens in the Rhine River. The gold is stolen and a curse put on it. (In nineteenth-century operas the direction of events often hinges on curses and magic potions.) The curse states that if the possessor will renounce love, he will rule the world. The result is a chain of misfortunes affecting all the characters in the drama.

Because in many ways Richard Wagner and his music are the epitome of nineteenth-century romanticism, his *Siegfried's Rhine Journey* is presented in Chapter 19, which discusses that period and style.

Italian Romantic Opera

At the beginning of the nineteenth century, Italian Opera was in the style of Mozart. Gioacchino Rossini (1792–1868) even based his opera *The Barber of Seville* on the same characters found in Mozart's opera *The Marriage of Figaro.* With Vincenzo Bellini (1801–1835) Italian opera reached a high point of interest in melody. The arias in his operas, such as *Norma,* emphasize beautiful singing (*bel canto* in Italian) through technically demanding melodic lines, cadenzas, and ornamentation. Gaetano Donizetti (1797–1848) also contributed to the *bel can-*

to style of opera. Although these early operas often lack convincing dramatic qualities, the brilliance of the soloists' lines and the beauty of the melodies make for very enjoyable listening.

The most important Italian opera composers in the latter half of the nineteenth century were Giuseppe Verdi and Giacomo Puccini. Both greatly improved the dramatic quality of opera. Verdi insisted on having a good libretto and used the finest literature—Schiller, Victor Hugo, Dumas, Shakespeare. Both Verdi and Puccini contributed more realism to opera. Their characters were neither stock roles, as had often been the case in the preceding century, nor symbols, which they tended to be in Wagner's operas. They tended to be more like real people interacting with people and events. Also the recitatives stopped being just filler that provided a great deal of text. Instead they became more melodious and expressive. Finally, both Verdi and Puccini utilized the orchestra very effectively to back up the singing and actions on stage. The titles of Verdi's and Puccini's better known operas are cited in their biographies on pages 131 and 132.

Menotti's *The Medium*

The Medium by Gian-Carlo Menotti was first performed in 1946 in New York. It was commissioned by and premiered at Columbia University.

Menotti was born in 1911 in Italy, but he has lived in the United States since the age of 16. His many successful operas include *The Old Maid and the Thief, The Telephone* (a short comic opera that is often coupled with *The Medium* on the same program), *The Consul, The Saint of Bleeker Street,* and *Amahl and the Night Visitors,* which was commissioned for television. He writes the librettos as well as the music for his operas.

The cast of *The Medium* is small. There are only six characters, one of whom is mute, and three have rather minor roles. There is no chorus. The presentation, then, contrasts sharply with the large casts and choruses found in most nineteenth-century operas. Other differences can be observed. Only one stage setting is required for the opera's two acts. Furthermore,

the entire opera takes less than one hour to perform. The shortness is a distinct reversal of nineteenth-century tendencies; three or more hours is not an unusual length for an opera of that century.

Menotti's orchestra is also much smaller, and the piano is given a prominent part in the accompaniment. Gone are the lush sounds of the nineteenth century, although the orchestra does provide coloristic effects to augment the meaning of the singer's words. For instance, at one point in this opera, Madame Flora is sick with fear. As she wails out the word "afraid," the strings sound rapidly repeating notes as though to suggest trembling.

The story, which takes place in New York, is about a devious old lady (Madame Flora, known to her family as Baba) who dupes bereaved people into thinking that she can serve as a medium between themselves and the dead. She is assisted in this hoax by her daughter Monica, a sheltered girl of 17, and by a mute orphan, Toby, whom she once picked off the streets of Budapest.

The curtain opens on Madame Flora's weird and shabby parlor. The apartment's arrangement is shown in the stage sketch on page 129. Monica sings to Toby as they indulge in one of their fantasy games, in which he is an oriental king. Madame Flora enters, irked that nothing is ready for the evening séance. Quickly all is made ready—the wires that move the table, the lights, and the curtain behind which Monica imitates the voices of the dead loved ones. Mr. and Mrs. Gobineau enter; they have been attending séances for two years. Soon Mrs. Nolan arrives. It's her first experience with Madame Flora, and she is understandably nervous. The Gobineaus and Mrs. Nolan exchange information about the tragedies that have brought them there.

Finally the séance begins (Record 4,B). The lights are dimmed, and an eerie wailing is evident. Soon a haunting motive ("Mother, Mother, are you there?") is heard coming from behind the screen, where Monica is impersonating Mrs. Nolan's daughter:

Moth - er, moth - er,   are you there?

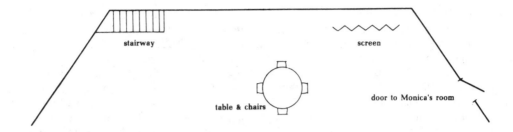

Monica and Mrs. Nolan converse for a while, and Monica sings some wonderfully warm, reassuring melodies:

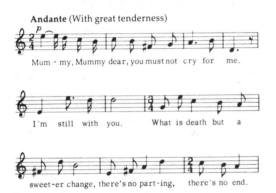

Andante (With great tenderness)

Mum - my, Mummy dear, you must not cry for me.

I'm still with you. What is death but a

sweet-er change, there's no part-ing, there's no end.

She encourages Mrs. Nolan to give away her daughter's personal effects, no doubt mostly to Madame Flora. She mentions a locket. "I have no locket," says Mrs. Nolan. Suddenly the image behind the curtain begins to disappear, and Mrs. Nolan runs to the screen. She is stopped and calmed down.

Next it is the Gobineaus' turn. They talk with their dead two-year-old son and take comfort from his happy laughter. Suddenly Madame Flora screams. A cold hand has touched her throat! But who or what? The persons involved in the séance were touching hands at all times. Toby and Monica were behind the screen. Madame Flora abruptly ends the séance and rudely dismisses the customers. As they slowly climb the stairs, bewildered and accusing, they sing a chantlike melody to her: "Why be afraid of our dead?" As the act closes, Monica is trying to calm her mother by singing an old gypsy ballad. Madame Flora, terribly shaken, mumbles superstitiously and whispers her rosary in a distracted manner.

The actions in Act II parallel the events of the first; so does some of the music. A week has passed. Monica sings a song, actually an aria, and improvises a dance for Toby. Suddenly the game is no longer childlike. Monica asks, "Toby, what is it you want to tell me?" Toby, the mute, doesn't need a tongue; the orchestra answers for him with intense, impassioned chords that can only mean love. As Monica's aria continues, she sings both Toby's role and her own. Throughout the scene, much tenderness is added by Monica's gentle caressing of Toby's head. Her lines end, "Why, Toby! You're not crying, are you? Toby, I want you to know that you have the most beautiful voice in the world!"

The mood changes abruptly when Madame Flora enters, disheveled and carrying a bottle; she is obviously still tormented by the memory of the hand that touched her throat at the séance. She pulls every known trick—emotional blackmail, bribes, threats, and love—to get Toby to admit that he was responsible. Toby's inability to answer only frustrates her further. Madame Flora sings "Toby, you know that I love you," but the orchestral accompaniment is tense and dissonant. It seems to reveal the falseness of her words. Before she is through with Toby, she loses her temper and begins hitting him.

The doorbell rings. Still breathless, Madame Flora answers. It's the Gobineaus and Mrs. Nolan arriving for their weekly séance. To ease her conscience, she offers to return their money and explains how she tricked them, but they refuse to believe her. Mrs. Nolan has even found the locket! They plead for another séance, but in a rage Madame Flora orders them out. Then, despite Monica's pleadings to the contrary, her mother orders Toby to leave and sends Monica to her room and locks her in.

Madame Flora seats herself at the table. The haunting "Mother, Mother" motive is heard. Her shouting can't seem to stop it. She tries to reassure herself; she has seen many horrors in her lifetime, and *they* have never bothered her. She prays. She laughs at her fears. She prays again. Finally, she becomes drowsy and lays her head on the table.

Silently Toby reenters the apartment. He tries Monica's door, but it's locked. He opens a trunk but the lid drops, making a sharp noise. Madame Flora wakens as Toby scampers behind the screen. "Who's there?" she cries. "Speak out or I'll shoot!" Toby can't answer, of course. Madame Flora pulls out a gun she has been carrying and fires at the screen. Silence follows, then blood begins running down the white curtain. Finally Toby's body falls headlong into the room. Madame Flora unlocks Monica's door, exclaiming, "I've killed the ghost!" Monica, horrified, sees what has happened. She cries for help and then runs out into the night. Madame Flora kneels over Toby's body, still questioning, "Was it you? Was it you?"

Here the opera ends, with its situations unresolved. The audience has looked on the tangled emotions of people under stress. As in other twentieth-century operas, considerable psychological depth is imparted to the charac-ters. People are complex mixtures of fear, gullibility, tenderness, guilt, and childishness. No longer are their emotions simple ones. Their feelings are sometimes mixed and their motives uncertain. Freudian thinking has, in effect, moved onto the opera stage. *The Medium* might be described as a "psychological opera." Madame Flora, it might be said, is suffering from hallucinations caused by extreme feelings of guilt. Menotti treats her tortured existence with insight.

Menotti and several other twentieth-century opera composers have faced the economic realities of opera production. Their operas are small in scope, the staging simpler. These composers know that there is little chance for a new opera with a huge cast and extensive scenery to be produced; it's just too expensive. Opera companies can hardly make ends meet even when they confine themselves to the standard repertoire. Besides, most modern opera composers are not at all sure that the grandiose opera is what they want to write or what the public wants to hear. They think that perhaps opera comes across best in a more intimate situation. Although a few operas on a large scale are still being written and produced, with varying degrees of success, there does seem to be a trend toward the smaller, more down-to-earth opera.

Richard Wagner

(New York Public Library.)

Richard Wagner (1813–1883) is an artistic phenomenon. Born in Leipzig, he was the son of a minor police official who died when Richard was still an infant. His mother married a talented actor and playwright, who encouraged his stepson along similar lines. For most of his career Wagner was largely self-taught. At 20 he obtained a post as chorus master in a small opera house in Leipzig and produced his first operas.

Success was slow, and for the next ten years it looked as though Wagner would spend his life hovering on the edge of poverty. His first successful opera was *Rienzi*, which earned him a position as conductor for the king of Saxony. Other successful operas followed in the 1840s: *The Flying Dutchman*, *Tannhauser*, and *Lohengrin*.

In 1848 Wagner became associated with the political uprisings that were taking place in Europe. He even published two articles in a magazine that advocated anarchy. A revolution broke out in Dresden in 1849, and the king and his court fled. Wagner was forced to escape to the home of his friend

Franz Liszt at Weimar. Since there was a warrant out for his arrest, Wagner soon fled on over the border into Switzerland. At that point he seemed a ruined man. But he was helped by some willing patrons, and the years in Switzerland were some of his most productive. It was during this time that he began work on *The Ring of the Nibelung*.

In the 1850s he composed *Tristan and Isolde*, and in the early 1860s *The Meistersingers of Nurenberg*. Wagner became estranged from his wife, who had grown unsympathetic to his artistic aims and desires. He became involved with a succession of married women. In 1864 again all seemed lost.

At this point fate seemed to step in. A 19-year-old who was an admirer of Wagner's music ascended to the throne in Bavaria. He was Ludwig II, known as "Mad Ludwig." He summoned Wagner to Munich, where Wagner resumed work on *The Ring of the Nibelung*. In time he married Cosima, the daughter of Franz Liszt.

By 1876 Wagner had reached the top of the artistic world. It was during that year that he opened his first Bayreuth (*By*-royt) festival. Later he built an opera house there, and the Bayreuth festivals continue today. It is the only theater in the world devoted exclusively to the music of one person. His last opera was *Parsifal*, which is a legend based on the Holy Grail. It was finished shortly before he died. He is buried at Bayreuth, which in a sense is his monument.

Giuseppe Verdi

Verdi was born in 1813 in a small town in northern Italy. His father was a poor innkeeper. Giuseppe probably wouldn't have had a musical education had it not been for the support of a prosperous merchant who paid for two years' study in Milan. When Giuseppe returned, he fell in love with the wealthy merchant's daughter. The marriage was a happy one, but misfortune began to plague the family. His two children and his young wife died within a three-year span.

Although his first opera had been a moderate success, the next one was not. That failure, coupled with the tragedies in his family, caused him to give up composing for about a year. Finally the manager of the La Scala Opera in Milan persuaded him to write an opera on Nebuchadnezzar which Verdi shortened to *Nabucco*. It was an immediate success, and it launched him on a long and outstanding career as an opera composer.

In the late 1840s the Italians were having trouble with the Austrians. Verdi associated himself with Italian nationalism, and some of his operas were thinly veiled protests against the Austrian monarchy. Cries of "Viva Verdi" rang out in Italian opera houses, symbolizing both admiration for the man and his music and love for Italy. To many patriots the letters of his name represented "*Victor Emmanuel, Rex d' Italia.*"

In spite of his fame, Verdi remained a simple man who preferred the quiet of his farm to the pressures of society. His second wife was a sensitive and intelligent woman who encouraged his work. After Italian independence he wrote many successful operas: *Macbeth, La Traviata, Un Ballo in Maschera* (A Masked Ball), *La Forza del Destino* (The Force of Destiny), *Aida*, and—after the age of 70—*Otello* and *Falstaff*. He died in 1901.

Giacomo Puccini

Giacomo Puccini (1858–1924) was not as sophisticated a composer as Verdi. He did possess, however, a wonderful gift of melody and an instinct for what would be successful on stage. His operas are as popular as Verdi's.

Puccini belonged to a group of opera composers who stressed *verismo* (realism). He drew material from everyday life, rejecting heroic or exalted themes from mythology and history. He was fond of parallel chord movement and selected chords for their particular sound as well as for their harmonic function.

Puccini's best known operas include *La Bohème* (1896); *Tosca* (1900); *Madame Butterfly* (1904), which is a story about the marriage of an American naval lieutenant and a Japanese girl; and *Turandot* (1926), which was completed by a friend after Puccini's death.

14

Ballet and Ballet Music

Like opera, dance involves both visual and aural aspects; it is a combination of arts. Appropriate music contributes to a good ballet, and in turn dancing has inspired the creation of some fascinating music. Although dancing is nearly universal, the discussion here is of ballet and the modern dance as they exist in Western civilization.

Classical ballet began in the courts of Europe, especially France, about three hundred years ago. Its main goal was grace and courtliness. Deportment and etiquette were supreme virtues among the aristocracy. In the court of Louis XIV, for example, *everyone* took dancing lessons. What did people learn in these lessons? One thing was proper ballet posture; another was a balance of footwork and elevation—the ability to rise on the toes and to leap gracefully. They learned a posture that was based on a straight and quiet spine, a stiffened, straight knee, and a level hip line—the hips were not to lift, thrust out, or rotate. The shoulders were not to ripple.

From such instruction there developed a systemized set of positions and steps that are basic in classical ballet. From these positions a *choreographer* (designer of dances) plans routines and sequences for a complete scene.

The art of ballet remained relatively unchanged until the twentieth century. It was (and is) a beautiful art, but it was also artificial. The first revolt against these artificialities occurred at about the turn of the twentieth century, when Isadora Duncan threw off her corset and shoes and danced barefoot throughout Europe. She believed that dancing should be harmonious and simple, with no ornaments. Although she devised no new techniques, she gave ballet a more natural look. Her ideas were adapted by Michael Fokine, Ruth St. Dennis, Martha Graham, Agnes De Mille, and others.

This chapter discusses the music of two well-known ballets: *Swan Lake*, which is in the classical ballet tradition, and *Rodeo*, which is more modern in concept.

Tchaikovsky's *Swan Lake*

Swan Lake was given its premier performance at the Bolshoi Theater in Moscow in March 1877. Tchaikovsky's interest in the story began in 1871, when he was visiting his sister's children in the country. He composed for them some pieces based on a legend from *A Thousand and One Nights*. The tale involves a woman who magically becomes a bird. Four years later Tchaikovsky was commissioned to create a ballet on the story. Its initial reception was rather discouraging. The merits of the ballet were not fully appreciated until the production was presented in St. Petersburg in 1895. Since that time it has remained one of the most beloved ballets in the repertoire. George Balanchine, one of the great choreographers of ballet of this century, has written: "To succeed in *Swan Lake* is to become overnight a ballerina. All leading dancers want to dance *Swan Lake* at least once in their careers."

The story is pure magic. Prince Siegfried is approaching his twenty-first birthday. His mother plans to hold a great ball at which he will select the most pleasing young woman to be his bride. On the day before the ball the prince and some of his friends go into the country to hunt swans. They come upon these glorious white birds, and the prince notices one that is obviously their Queen. (In the ballet she usually wears a diamondlike crown.) She is a ravishing creature, but is she a swan or a woman? Siegfried finally soothes the creature into telling him that a sorcerer named von Rothbart has transformed her into Odette, Queen of the Swans, and that she must remain that way forever—except between midnight and dawn. The spell can be broken only by a man who loves her, marries her, and never loves another. Siegfried immediately wants Odette to come to tomorrow's ball.

The third act of the ballet takes place at the ball. Siegfried is melancholy because he is afraid he has lost Odette. Six of the most beautiful young women in the kingdom dance for Siegfried, and he mimes that he can't marry any of them because he loves another. Soon the lights dim and a dark beauty is led forward by the Knight of the Black Swan. She is Odile, but Siegfried knows only that she is the image of Odette. Odile's dancing enchants Siegfried and she leads him into the garden. In the meantime the guests are honored by dances from foreign lands—Spain, Hungary, Poland. Odile reappears to do the final dance. With the Prince she performs the brilliant Black Swan Pas de deux. Siegfried is so taken with her that he swears eternal faithfulness to her, still believing her to be Odette. Now the spell cannot be broken; von Rothbart has tricked Siegfried.

In the fourth act the Queen of the Swans appears, sobbing and insisting that she must die. The Prince arrives, swears his eternal love, and embraces her. She believes him but tells him that only death will break the dreadful spell. Odette and Siegfried, wishing to drown, fling themselves into the lake. Love triumphs, von Rothbart dies, and the spell is broken. Odette and Siegfried glide on a jeweled ship into the ever-after.

Tchaikovsky arranged a suite from the music that he composed for *Swan Lake*. He did the same with his other well-known ballets, *The Nutcracker* and *The Sleeping Beauty*. The music in the suite does not appear in the same order as in the ballet because in the suite Tchaikovsky does not need to follow the story line. Also, the suite contains only a portion of the music that appears in the ballet. The first movement of the suite contains the most prominent theme from the ballet. It appears at various times in both major and minor.

The second movement is built around the waltz:

The third movement contains the theme for the dance of the swans:

The fourth movement features a harp cadenza followed by a violin solo. A Hungarian dance called the czardas (*char*-dash) appears in the fifth movement. The czardas has a slow beginning, followed by furiously paced music. Traditionally the dancers move as fast as possible. The two themes associated with this movement are:

A sixth movement provides a brilliant ending to the suite.

Tchaikovsky's style of music is especially well suited to ballet. His music has a lilting quality that seems to inspire graceful movement.

Copland's *Rodeo*

Rodeo was first presented by Agnes de Mille and the Ballet Russe de Monte Carlo in 1942, and it soon became a standard work in the repertoire of ballet companies. The music is most often heard in a suite with these four parts: "Buckaroo Holiday," "Corral Nocturne," "Saturday Night Waltz," and "Hoe-Down."

The ballet tells the story of the young Cowgirl who has been a tomboy. Suddenly she becomes aware of men and romance. She tries to impress the Head Wrangler (her favorite) and the Champion Roper with her ability as a rider. The Cowgirl is in the corral with the men, but they pay little attention, concentrating instead on their own work and riding. They finally gallop off without even noticing her, and she in turn rides away in anger and tears. The section opens with this spirited theme:

Later two American folk tunes are heard: "If He Be a Buckaroo by His Trade" and "Sis Joe."

"Buckaroo Holiday" employs several rhythmic figures that suggest dances associated with the old American West.

The music for "Corral Nocturne" contains no folk tunes. City girls wearing pretty dresses instead of jeans have come to visit the Rancher's Daughter and to enjoy the Saturday night dance. Once more the Cowgirl is ignored. She simply can't compete with feminine frills. A tranquil, somewhat sad mood is set by this melody:

The couples move off, eager for the dance, and the Cowgirl is left behind again.

Saturday night at the ranch is a time for dancing. The Cowgirl, still in jeans and boots, sits alone watching the festivities. The Roper and the Wrangler take pity on her and ask her to dance. She is too shy and misses the opportunity. As the "Saturday Night Waltz" begins—it contains the song "Old Paint"—the Roper insists that the Cowgirl dance. She wants to but then sees the Wrangler dancing with the Rancher's Daughter. Jealous and confused, she stands motionless among the dancers. Annoyed, the Roper turns and leaves, and the Cowgirl runs from the floor.

The dancing reaches a climax in the riotous "Hoe-Down," which is based partly on the folk melody "Bonyparte." (The Listening Guide for "Hoe-Down" appears on pages 10–11.) The Cowgirl reappears, this time wearing a party dress. She is vivacious and pretty, and she soon becomes the center of attention. The Roper again asks her to dance. Though she would rather have the Wrangler, she accepts the Roper and joins the others in the wild dancing as the ballet ends.

As you can tell, *Rodeo* is quite different from *Swan Lake*. No longer does the plot rely on magical events, and no longer is the main goal etiquette and courtliness. The dancing is natural, and the story is realistic. The music often draws on folk sources, and the choreography is also

Scenes from Swan Lake, performed at Indiana University. (Photographs by Richard Pflum. Bloomington, Indiana.)

based on folk dancing, especially the "Hoe-Down."

Both *Swan Lake* and *Rodeo* are fascinating ballets with attractive music. Their diversity shows the wide spectrum of styles that can be encompassed by artistic dancing.

Peter Ilich Tchaikovsky

(Library of Congress.)

Until early adulthood, Tchaikovsky (Chy-*kuff*-skee, 1840–1893) seemed destined to follow in his father's footsteps by working in a governmental position. At the age of 23, however, he decided to become a musician, so he resigned his job and entered the newly founded Conservatory of St. Petersburg (now Leningrad). He did well, and in three years he had finished his course and was recommended for a teaching position in the new Conservatory of Moscow. He taught harmony there for 12 years.

Throughout his life, Tchaikovsky was plagued by the fact that he was a homosexual. He once described his existence as "regretting the past, hoping for the future, without ever being satisfied with the present." He married a conservatory student, a rather unstable girl who was madly in love with him. The marriage was a disaster. Finally, on the verge of a complete mental breakdown, he went to live with his brothers in St. Petersburg.

At this point in his life entered Nadezhda von Meck, a wealthy widow who, though a recluse, successfully ran her inherited business empire and the lives of her 11 children. She was impressed by the beauty of Tchaikovsky's music and decided to support him financially. There was, however, one unusual twist to the arrangement. So that she could be sure she was supporting a composer and not a personal friend, she stipulated that they should never meet. And so it was. For 13 years Mme. von Meck and Tchaikovsky carried on intense and devoted contact—all by letter.

In 1891 he accepted an invitation to America, where he participated in the opening of Carnegie Hall in New York. According to his letters, he liked Americans and was gratified by their appreciation of his music. In 1893, while in St. Petersburg to conduct his Sixth Symphony, he contracted cholera and died at the age of 53.

Aaron Copland

(Photo by CBS, courtesy of Boosey & Hawkes.)

Aaron Copland was born in Brooklyn in 1900 of Russian-Jewish immigrant parents. He attended the New York City public schools, worked in his father's department store, and took his first piano lessons from his older sister. After graduation from high school, he studied piano and harmony in New York and spent much time studying scores at the public library. In 1921 he went to the American School of Music at Fontainebleau in France. The teacher there was a remarkable woman named Mlle. Nadia Boulanger (Boo-lahn-*zhay*). Copland became the first of a long list of young American composers to study with her. When she was invited to give some concerts in the United States, she asked Copland to compose a work for performance on her tour. The work he provided was the *Symphony for Organ and Orchestra*. It was first performed in New York in 1925.

Copland became interested in jazz in the late 1920s, and several of his compositions show the jazz influence. *Music for the Theater* and *Symphonic Ode* are from this period. His works in the early 1930s tend to be more abstract, as is revealed in his *Piano Variations* and *Short Symphony*. In the late 1930s he composed two works for performance by school groups: *The Second Hurricane* and *Outdoor Overture*. *A Lincoln Portrait* is a tremendously exciting work. It includes a part for a narrator and is centered on the quotations of Abraham Lincoln. *El Salón México* is a rhythmic rhapsody on Mexican tunes.

In three of his works, all ballets, Copland exploits American folk music: *Billy the Kid* (1938), *Rodeo* (1942), and *Appalachian Spring* (1943–1944). In them he reaches a happy medium between retaining the interest and respect of the trained musician and at the same time pleasing the public. Few twentieth-century composers have been able to attain this balance.

Since the late 1940s his music has become a bit more intellectual. With Roger Sessions, another able American composer, Copland organized a series of concerts to promote new music in America. He is the author of several interesting books for the musical layman. He has lectured at many universities and has written several film scores.

III
SECTION THREE
Musical Types and Styles

Section III considers the various types of music created around the world over the course of history. Chapter 15 surveys folk-ethnic music, and Chapter 16 traces the development of music in Western civilization through the Renaissance.

The rest of Section III is concerned with musical styles. When several composers organize sounds in a similar way, they are writing in the same *style*. Style refers mainly to musical qualities, not to a period of time or a geographical place. Even after a style has passed the peak of its popularity, composers occasionally return to it, sometimes centuries later. And elements of one style can appear in music of other styles.

Although not confined to a particular time and place, a style of music is named for the historical period in which it was most prominent. The designation of periods requires historical perspective, and the dates of a period can never be stated precisely; they must always be approximate.

Despite its limitations, a concept of style is useful in learning music. It helps you organize your thinking about what you hear. When you understand what constitutes musical style, you are learning the very stuff of music. An understanding of style helps you listen for the right things. Knowing that the Renaissance ideal was purity and restraint of sound, you won't be surprised by the lack of volume and flashing brilliance in Renaissance music. You will be able to listen with more realistic expectations and greater reward.

Chapters 17 to 25 discuss significant musical styles—Baroque, Classical, Neo-Classical, and so on. Chapter 26 presents some thoughts on contemporary music. The last two chapters are devoted to American music.

The Lovers *by Pablo Picasso. (Chester Dale Collection, National Gallery of Art, Washington, D.C.)*

15

Music Throughout the World

Music is found in every part of the world. It is universal among human beings. No one knows how much folk music there is, but the amount must be tremendous. The forms and styles of the music people produce are as varied as their languages and ways of life. Folk music is a fascinating and significant portion of the world of music.

What Is Folk Music?

The words *folk* and *ethnic* are not synonymous. *Ethnic* refers to music identified with a particular race or group of people. *Folk* refers only to music actually adopted by the common people. A Hungarian peasant song about harvesting hay is a folk song. And because it is characteristic of that country, it is also ethnic music. The *raga* of India is not folk music; it is not the music of the common people but rather of a highly trained musical elite. It is characteristic of India, though, so it is ethnic music. All folk music is ethnic, but not all ethnic music is folk music.

Folk-ethnic music is not created "by committee"—by a group of people sitting around a campfire or marching into battle. Individuals create ethnic music, just as individuals compose art music; but there the similarity ends. The creator of ethnic music is almost always unknown. In fact, the individual might not admit to the accomplishment even if he or she could be located. In many areas of the world, songs are considered gifts from the gods revealed in dreams or visions or created on "orders" from a supernatural being. Besides, in most cultures people neither care nor remember who was first responsible for providing a song.

Once created, the music is perpetuated through *oral tradition*, whereby individuals hear the music, remember it, and perform it for others. If no one except the originator likes the song, it passes into oblivion. This tradition ensures the survival of only those songs that are liked by the particular culture. Oral tradition also means that the music is subject to many changes.

Nonliterate societies have no system of musical notation. Even in the advanced societies of ancient India and China, only a system of visual cues was developed. Without a system of notation or recordings, music cannot be preserved accurately. For this reason folk music is always changing, which may be one of its strengths. It is both traditional and contemporary; it represents the heritage of the people and their current tastes.

A thorough study of ethnic and folk music is an enormous undertaking. The musical aspects are only the beginning. The total culture must be included—language, customs, thought forms, and so on. Ethnic music cannot be separated from the culture in which it exists.

Most of the folk-ethnic music of the world is less complex than art music. Why? First, most of it is confined to short works, usually songs. True, some African rituals last for hours, but the same music tends to be repeated over and over, with only slight variations. The Indian *raga* is also long, but it is an exceptional kind of music. Without a system of notation, musical works are usually rather short, because most people cannot remember long complex works accurately. The short length allows for little formal or thematic development, something that is important to art music.

When ethnic music does display complexity, such as the rhythm of African music, it tends to do so with only one aspect of the music, leaving the other aspects relatively undeveloped. By contrast, art music, especially in the twentieth century, displays involved combinations of pitch, harmony, rhythm, timbre, dynamics, and form.

Listening to Folk Music

Several suggestions beyond those made in Chapter 2 can be made for listening to folk-ethnic music. Listen to examples of the more significant types—African, Arabian, Latin American, and so on. Learn to identify each from listening in terms of its overall quality. Compare and contrast the timbres, rhythmic structures, instruments, singing style, melodic patterns, and other aspects of the music. While listening, keep in mind the cultural setting of the music in terms of its purpose in that society.

Characteristics of Non-Western Music

What makes much of the ethnic music found throughout the world different from most of the music familiar to us? Let's start with rhythm.

Rhythm. As pointed out in Chapter 4, most rhythms in the music of Western civilization have regular patterns of accented and unaccented beats. Measure is linked to measure, something like beads on a string. But much of the world's music exhibits unequal rhythmic patterns. Sometimes the rhythm is very free. Frequently it conforms to natural speech patterns, so that the text is not adapted to a given metrical pattern, as is usually true of the music we know.

Melodic structure. Two important differences exist between most Western music and other types of music. One concerns the exact tuning of pitches. The octave has a solid basis in the physical laws of sound, and it appears throughout the world. The higher of the two pitches is produced by twice as many vibrations as the pitch an octave lower. All other intervals in Western music are adjusted to approximate the present system of keyboard tuning. Even the splitting of the octave into 12 equal parts is an arbitrary decision by Western musicians. Non-Western music generally does not divide the octave into 12 equal half steps. *Microtones,* which are pitches less than a half step apart, are found in the Near East and Far East and, to some extent, in Africa. The octave is divided into 22 parts in India; in the Moslem world it has been variously divided into 25, 17 and 15 parts. To a listener unaccustomed to them, microtones can sound hauntingly expressive or just plain out of tune.

The other difference is the type of scale on which the music is based. A scale is a series of ascending and descending tones that follow a specific pattern of intervals. Usually the top and bottom notes are one octave apart. A scale with all its pitches sounded in order seldom appears in a melody. A scale is the underlying "formula" for the pitches appearing in a particular section of music. The major and minor scale patterns are predominant in Western music today, although other seven-note scales called modes are favored in folk and popular songs. A common scale in non-Western folk music is the *pentatonic* scale, a five-note pattern that duplicates the pitches of the black keys on the piano keyboard (*penta* means five). Many other scales are found throughout the world.

Add to the variable tuning of notes and the wide diversity of scales the fact that, in some musical systems, certain notes can be altered or ornamented by the performer, and you can see why genuine ethnic music sounds different to our ears.

Harmony. Most of the world's music contains very little harmony. Some melodies are never intended to have other sounds occurring with them. When harmony is found, it is usually in one of two forms. One is a *drone,* a single continuous sound lasting throughout a piece. The Scottish bagpipe produces one of the few examples of a drone in Western music. The other type of harmony is produced by adding a du-

plicate melodic line that moves along strictly parallel to the original melody. This harmony part is often a fourth or fifth above or below the melody. Sometimes it is a third, which is the usual interval in Western harmony.

Form. Most ethnic songs are too brief to allow for much formal development, but short sections are often arranged in various patterns. One type is the leader-response found in African music. The result is a game of "musical tennis," in which lines of music alternate between a soloist and the group. In many parts of the world, music is subjected to a simple variation treatment in which the basic melody is varied slightly and repeated many times.

Improvisation. Almost all art music is written out. The performer's main task is to re-create the notes on the page and follow the composer's intent. Not so with most ethnic music. No accurate system of notation exists outside the West, and most composers of ethnic music are unknown, so the performer is encouraged to make up new music while playing or singing. This art of performing music spontaneously, without the aid of notes, is called *improvisation.* The performer does not often improvise "out of thin air"—that is, without any guidelines at all. Melodic or rhythmic patterns and performance customs act as guidelines.

In contrast to art music, in which the ideas of the composer prevail, most ethnic music is geared to the performer. Improvised performances are never quite the same twice. They reflect the inspiration of the moment.

Instruments. Folk instruments were described in Chapter 6.

Some Significant Types of Ethnic Music

The topic of ethnic music is so vast that it could occupy many volumes. To keep the chapter within reasonable limits, it is necessary to leave out music from many areas of the world.

Europe. As might be expected, the folk music of Europe resembles Western art music more closely than does other ethnic music. Wide differences can be found within the European continent, however, especially in isolated rural areas.

One characteristic of European folk music is the singing of different lines of words, each time to the same melody. Some pentatonic scales are encountered, especially in Hungary and eastern Europe, but major and minor scales and modes predominate. The rhythm is metrical, with somewhat more freedom of meter in eastern European music.

The topics found in European folk songs include a greater percentage of epic-narrative tales and love sentiments than do the songs of other cultures. There are some folk hymns and songs about turning points in a person's life, such as birth or marriage.

India. Probably the most sophisticated music outside of Western civilization is found in India. The music described here is not folk music but an ethnic music that requires much training for both performer and listener.

Indian music is very much intertwined with religious belief and practice. It began at least a thousand years B.C., and it continues today. Despite pressures from the Near East, invasions by the Muslims a thousand years ago, and British occupation in the nineteenth and twentieth centuries, it is believed that the music has not changed much since its inception.

At the heart of Indian music is the *raga*, a melodic formula resembling a scale. But it also embraces important Indian religious concepts. The performers believe that its vibrations must be in tune with the universe, and that other arts such as poetry and painting must fit with music into the great cosmic scheme. For example,

Musical instruments of India. (Front to back) Sarod, tabla (smaller drum) and bayan (larger drum), and tambura.

there are *ragas* that should be performed only in the morning, others only in the evening, others only in the rainy season, and so on. Theoretically, thousands of *ragas* exist, but only about 50 are used frequently. *Ragas* vary in length, averaging about 20 to 25 notes. Two tones tend to stand out in each *raga*, one being a fourth or fifth higher than the other.

The next significant element in Indian music is its rhythm, which is built around the *tala*. Each *tala* is a rhythmic cycle of from 3 to 128 beats; most are from 5 to 8 beats long. Each *tala* is divided into smaller groups. A *tala* is not a measure, as was described in Chapter 4; it's a pattern. For example, a seven-beat *tala* might be made up of 3 beats + 2 beats + 2 beats. If an Indian musician taps his foot as he plays, it is not a steady tapping but an indication of the unequal divisions of the *tala*. Furthermore, the first beat in a *tala* should not be accented more heavily than the other beats. Like each *raga*, each *tala* is named.

With the *raga* and *tala* as their guides, the performers improvise as they sing a religious narrative poem from one of the holy books. Because the musical system is so complicated, they have a dazzling array of melodic and rhythmic possibilities—enough to last a lifetime. The pleasure for the listener lies in hearing performers create their own music within the guidelines of the system.

Indian musicians use some instruments: hand drums, bamboo flutes and double-reed instruments, and *sitars*. The *sitar* is a complicated string instrument with five melodic strings, two drones, and 13 more strings that sound in sympathy with the melodic strings. It looks like a large guitar with pegs along the neck of the instrument.

China. China's musical heritage is as old as India's. Although China had no system of writing music, accurate verbal accounts are available about music throughout its history. Like Indian music, Chinese music was closely related to philosophy and religion.

The Chinese developed a system that included the 12 pitches that appear within the octave in Western music. Although they had

more than five pitches, their basic melodic tool was the pentatonic scale.

The Chinese developed several exotic instruments. One was a model of a crouching tiger with a serrated ridge or set of wooden slats along its backbone. It was sounded by dragging a bamboo stick across the bumps or slats. Another instrument was a mouth organ with 17 bamboo pipes.

In some periods of China's history, music thrived; in other eras it hardly survived. Much of the music was created for the official court, often for banquets. A few large orchestras existed in China—a situation that was rare outside of the West. Many theatrical, operalike productions were presented also.

In 1911 the last Chinese dynasty fell, and the country was declared a republic. The ensuing years have been hard ones for Chinese music, largely because of internal strife and repression. Since 1949 the Communist Party has controlled China, and until the late 1970s sophisticated music was discouraged. A rebirth of interest in Western culture has now taken place, and several exchanges with other countries have been arranged. Some of the old Chinese musical tradition is being preserved on Taiwan, but the influence of Western music is strongly felt there.

Arabian music. The Arabian world extends 4,000 miles from the north coast of Africa (just across the Strait of Gibraltar from Spain) eastward to the borders of Pakistan. Although most Arabs share the same religious faith—Islam—their culture and music have never been well unified. Four main groupings of Arabian music can be identified. One is Persian, which centers in Iran. A second is Arab, centering in Egypt and Saudi Arabia. A third is Andalusian; it exists mostly in North Africa. The fourth is Turkish. To further complicate matters, Arabian music has intricate and confusing music theories that vary from country to country. And when performed, the music often differs from the stated musical theories.

Much music from the Arabian world is vocal and is characterized by a tense, nasal quality. Some call-and-response between soloist and chorus is found. Accompaniment often consists of hand claps or tambourines—small hoops with a hide stretched over one side and metal jingles in the hoop. Mohammed, the prophet of Islam, did not approve of music in the mosque, so it is restricted in orthodox Islamic worship. A few restrained prayers and chants are "sung" in the mosque, but they are not officially considered to be music, so they are acceptable.

In Iran the basic feature is a *gushe*, which is similar to the Indian *raga*. Usually playing a flute, the performer improvises a highly decorated line based on the *gushe*. The rhythm is free, allowing performers to follow their musical inclinations.

Important Arabian instruments include the *tombak*—a drum in the shape of an hourglass, which is played with the hand and fingers; the *ud*—a string instrument with a pear-shaped body; and the *rebab*—a direct ancestor of the violin.

Although there are some professional musicians in the Arabian countries, there are few concerts in the Western sense of the word. Cafés are the usual setting for music performances, and people may listen or sip a drink as they wish. As an added attraction the more thoughtful numbers may be interspersed with the gyrating female dancers for which the Arabian world is noted. Artistic musical standards are difficult to maintain against such competition, and they seem often to be abandoned.

Jewish music in Israel. Because the Jews were dispersed throughout the world for so long, their nonreligious music has assimilated many regional characteristics. Even the pre-Christian music of the Jews was influenced by both the East and the West, primarily because Jerusalem was a crossroads for caravans traveling between the two worlds. The Arabian culture, which almost surrounds Israel, has also exerted its influence. Many Jews, however, sing Arabian songs in a style different from the one they use for Jewish music.

Jewish religious music has remained rather consistent in form and content. Judaism was not as evangelistic as Christianity; it tended to keep its faith within the group and seldom in-

corporated local music into its worship. Its religious music consists of sung prayers and invocations, not anthems such as are found in many Protestant churches. The use and type of music varies according to the degree of orthodoxy. The more orthodox congregations permit only unaccompanied chanting by cantors, with a free rhythm and some decorative notes. More liberal congregations often employ non-Jewish instrumentalists and singers to perform adaptations of music written for Christian worship.

Since the establishing of modern Israel in 1948, attempts have been made to create new folk traditions to help unify a multiethnic nation whose bonds are largely religious and political. New popular songs have been composed about economic and political topics. Arabian tambourines and hourglass drums, as well as guitars and accordions, are used for accompaniment. Arabian-type scales are often harmonized with Western chords. Like its people, Israel's music is highly cosmopolitan.

Latin American music. The term *Latin American* includes a wide variety of music. To begin with, the music of Spain itself is immensely varied. It includes the music of the Spanish gypsies and of the Basque people of northern ·Spain; it exhibits Arabian influence resulting from 600 years of occupation by the Moors. With the Spanish conquests in the New World, elements of Spanish music were transplanted to the Americas. Here it was mixed with native Indian music and the music of the blacks, especially in Cuba, Brazil, and the West Indies.

In the centuries since the Spanish entered Latin America, their music has been adapted so extensively that it has become impossible in many cases to identify the source of a particular song. Some Spanish dances have been adapted, also. For example, the *bolero* was originally Spanish, but in Cuba its rhythm became more complex. Elements of Latin American rhythms appear in jazz. Among other features carried over from Spanish music into Latin American music are the frequent use of meters having three notes to the beat, the presence of a line moving in parallel thirds with the melody, and melodies with a rather narrow range.

Mexican music is largely Spanish in character, more so than most other Latin American music. Some Mexican Indians have retained their own music, but the Indian influence is not significant in Mexico's music. Mexicans have a narrative type of song called a *corrido*, which relates an event or tells a story. Instruments play an important role in Mexican music and are sometimes featured in instrumental interludes. The often-heard *mariachi* band consists of from three to twelve people playing violins, guitars, brasses, and other instruments. Some of the band music has a complex rhythmic structure.

Latin American music enjoys considerable favor in the United States. Much of it, however, is commercial music created for nightclubs and cocktail lounges. It is not authentic, and to a musician it is less interesting than the legitimate music of the Latin American peoples. Fortunately, some Latin American folk songs have been incorporated into the musical heritage of the United States, and Latin American people have preserved some of their distinctive songs.

Africa south of the Sahara. The areas north of the vast Sahara desert are largely Arabian in character. To the south are the provinces of the black peoples, and it is their music that will be discussed here. For the sake of brevity, the term will be shortened to Africa.

Music for the African is more important, more an integral part of life, than it is for many of the peoples of the world. Music is called upon to cure illness, appease gods, and celebrate the birth of a baby. Some music is sheerly for entertainment and is performed by men whose livelihood comes from their music making. In some tribes there is a small musical elite, usually drummers, who practice their trade from youth. They spend most of their childhood learning how to drum and do not perform publicly until they are young adults.

The Western idea of a performer and a passive group of listeners is unusual in Africa. An African musical performance is truly a participatory event in which everyone sings, claps, or dances. Furthermore, African musicians want the music to have an impact on the listeners.

They do not particularly care whether they consider the music "beautiful," but they do want them to share their feelings.

Music is even used for signaling. Sometimes the drum rhythms resemble a simplified Morse code, but the signals are also related to the pitch structure of the language. Many African languages are tonal. A sound, *ba* for example, takes on a different meaning depending on the pitch level at which it is spoken. As many as four pitch levels are found in some languages. A drummer then approximates the pitch of the word being signaled by playing different-sized drums or hitting a log drum at different places.

Form in African music is based on a short phrase that is repeated, varied slightly, or alternated with group response. The call-and-response technique between leader and group is central to African music. It assures the participation of which Africans are so fond.

Improvisation is common in African styles. The variations of the short musical unit are improvised. Not only does the leader improvise, in some tribes, the group members improvise simultaneously among themselves, so that several lines of music are being sounded at the same time.

Melodically, African music is not far different from Western music. The underlying scale contains seven different notes—the pattern described in Chapter 3. But more use is made of microtones and the pentatonic scale. Glides and other ornaments are incorporated into the singing, and this sometimes disguises the true pitch of a note.

The main feature of African music is its rhythm. The fact that it does not follow a regular pattern has already been mentioned. A feature of West African music is the musician's ability to maintain a steady tempo for minutes or even hours. Western musicians keep a generally steady tempo, but they make slight fluctuations in it. The exactness of the tempo in African music makes it easier to emphasize the irregular accents and rhythmic patterns.

A more spectacular feature of African rhythm is the sounding of two or more rhythms at the same time—a technique that occurs most often in drumming but also appears in other types of music. Some works contain as many as six different rhythmic parts sounding simultaneously. The effect can be exciting.

African music includes some simple types of harmony and counterpoint. One type is the parallel movement created by a melodic line and its duplicate on a different pitch. There are also some two-part rounds. These rounds may have developed from instances in which either the leader or chorus was overly anxious and began its part before the other had finished. Accompaniment is evident in African music. Instruments such as the xylophone or harp sometimes accompany a melody by persistently repeating a short melodic phrase that contrasts with the melody.

American Folk Music

The English heritage. The main source of American folk music is the British Isles. Many songs were imported intact from Britain, and others have been patterned after British types.

The most significant type of British folk song is the *ballad*, a narrative song ranging from 5 to 20 stanzas in length. Traditionally the ballad had iambic meter and stanzas of four lines, in which a four-foot line alternates with a three-foot line. Here is an American example:

> *When John Henry was a little baby*
> *sitting on his pappy's knee,*
> *He grabbed a hammer and a little piece of*
> *steel,*
> *said, "This hammer'll be the death of me."*

Ballad stories are often tragic. In "John Henry" the hero dies with a hammer in his hand.

In a ballad the narrator-singer is a third person relating a tale, so he or she is not personally involved. The music usually reflects this by a calm and detached attitude.

In older ballads the music often reveals a seven-note modal scale, not the major-minor system of today. Some, such as "John Henry," conform to the pentatonic scale. The rhythm depends primarily on the text, which means

that a regular pattern is followed. Much of the ballad singing in the United States is unaccompanied, although in Kentucky an accompaniment is taken for granted and is provided by a banjo, guitar, or dulcimer. The dulcimer looks like a long, flat violin with three strings. It is laid on the player's lap and plucked with a quill. Two of its strings produce a drone, a common feature of ballad accompaniment.

The ballad style is evident in many American folk songs associated with occupations—seafaring, cattle herding, forestry, mining, farming, railroading, and so on. "John Henry" is such a song. The ballad's influence can also be observed in American religious hymns. It has been estimated that most songs in the English heritage descended from about 55 tunes or "tune families."

Non-British music also came to the United States with various immigrant groups, and a few such songs were incorporated into the culture and stand along with the British-style music. "Du, du liegst mir im Herzen" is a German song that has been adopted into the culture; "Alouette" is a French-Canadian example; and "Chiapanecas" (sometimes called "The Mexican Clapping Song") is a Latin-American contribution that is clapped and stomped at many major league ballparks. Some of these songs have had new words put to the music. Unfortunately, much non-British music was lost in the New World.

American Indian music. The functional nature of American Indian music is apparent in the names given to the ritual procedures. As the titles imply, a sun dance or rabbit dance is created for a specific purpose.

Traditionally, Indian instruments consisted of a variety of drums, usually played with sticks. Sometimes kettledrums were filled with water or the drum head was moistened before playing to achieve the pitch desired by the performer—a practice that indicates some musical sophistication. Many types of rattles were developed. Several types of flutes were played, especially by the men, who performed love music on them to impress their chosen young women.

The Indian population was never large (not more than one or two million in all of North America), and it was spread over a vast land area. As a result, musical styles differed widely among the various tribes, a fact also true in Africa.

Indian music has not had a significant effect on other American music for two reasons. First, most Indians do not live in close proximity to non-Indians. They have been set apart on reservations, and their music tends to remain there. Second, Indian music is quite different from Western music. In some respects it is more oriental than Western. When one culture incorporates music from another, the two styles are likely to be somewhat similar. Some change, but not too much, is accepted in music. In the few instances in which Indian music has been incorporated into art music, it has been changed freely and Westernized.

Occupational songs. An important contribution to America's folk-music heritage can be heard in songs about various occupations. In many cowboy songs the text and music are often tinged with loneliness and melancholy, reflecting life on the frontier—not an easy or particularly happy existence. Some of the cowboy tunes originally had other words before they were adapted by the cowboy. Such adaptations are common in folk music.

The development of the railroad provided another source for occupational songs. Some of these songs are about the men who worked the railroads ("Drill Ye Tarriers, Drill"), some describe famous personalities ("John Henry" and "Casey Jones"), and others tell about trains themselves ("The Wabash Cannonball"). Sailors have also provided songs. But today's computers and assembly lines do not encourage the development of song literature. One doesn't sing to a computer, and the noise of an assembly line drowns out other sounds. So the occupational song may have become a thing of the past.

Afro-American music. It is difficult to determine which aspects of Afro-American music

were transplanted from Africa and which were developed in America. In a complex and pluralistic society, the sources of a cultural merger are hard to assess. In any case, some of the African rhythmic ideas, the call-and-response patterns, the love of instruments, and improvisation are now a part of American music.

The African influence has been felt most in the area of performance; the spiritual is a good example. Actually, the spiritual, which is so widely associated with the American black, is largely borrowed from southern rural whites. In text and melodic ideas, black and white spirituals are almost identical. The difference between the two kinds of spirituals is in the way they are sung. The black spiritual is more rhythmic and stresses call-and-response, with some improvisation; the white version is more lyric and less exuberant. Performance differences are also apparent in other types of black folk music: work songs, love songs, ballads, and lullabies. Some were originated by blacks, but many were simply taken from the American culture. The songs may look similar in notation, but in performance the Afro-American qualities become evident.

Another performance area in which the influence of African music is evident is the variety of singing style. African singers produce more varied sounds when singing. Some tones are purposely harsh and raucous in order to imitate animals; some are tense, and some are throaty, but generally the style is relaxed and warm.

The song that evolved to accompany work is definitely an outgrowth of black culture. Songs sung *while* working (not songs *about* work) are not common in Western music, except in sea chanties. The text of some of these songs is not related directly to the job at hand; often the words supply only a pleasant accompaniment to labor.

As in Africa, instruments play an important role in Afro-American folk music. Some of the instruments are derived from Europe, while others are intended to duplicate sound effects. Included in the latter category are washboards, pans, cowbells, bottles, various clappers, and the gutbucket (an inverted washtub with a rope pulled through it and connected to a stick; the pitch is varied according to the tension of the rope).

The greatest contribution of blacks to American music is jazz. It is so significant that half of a chapter of this book is devoted to it.

Folk and ethnic music is important partly because there is so much of it and so many people find it appealing. It has influenced the de-velopment and content of art music. In some cases folk melodies have been incorporated into operas or symphonies, but more often composers have been influenced by a rhythmic pattern or style of melody that they heard in folk music.

Folk music can stand quite well on its own merits. It has a simple charm and a basic expressiveness that are fascinating.

16

Music of the Ancients and the Not-So-Ancients

No one knows how or where music began, but it seems to be a part of life in every age and place. Pictures on the walls of pyramids and on Mesopotamian vases show people making music. In early Greek civilization poets such as Homer sang their tales as they accompanied themselves on simple stringed instruments. In ancient Israel David soothed King Saul with harp music.

The intellectual Greeks considered music an important part of a citizen's education. Their dramas included a chorus that chanted and sang its lines. The Greeks developed several instruments, including the harplike lyre, which is seen on many music emblems today. Most impressive, however, were Pythagoras' discoveries about the physical laws of sound. Pythagoras (or some of his assistants) discovered that intervals are determined by mathematical ratios, and that there is a correlation between these ratios and the degree of consonance or dissonance suggested by any particular interval.

Our understanding of Greek music is as limited as our knowledge of almost all music until about the twelfth century: We cannot determine how the music sounded. No recognizable system had been devised for writing music; or if one existed, it has been lost. Only a few scraps of music notation have been found, and attempts to reconstruct these fragments have been mostly guesswork.

The Romans had music, too. Probably most of it, along with much of Roman culture, was taken over from Hellenic (Greek) civilization. The Romans emphasized military music more than did the Greeks.

With the fall of the Roman Empire, the Christian church deliberately attempted to root out of society everything that had been associated with pagan Rome. One object of this reform was Roman music, which had often enlivened festivals and orgies. Almost all remnants of Roman music have been lost or destroyed.

Early Christian music assumed much of the heritage of the Jewish temple. Daily prayer hours were adopted, along with the responsive singing of psalms between a soloist and congregation. As the church spread through Asia Minor into Europe and Africa, it accumulated other musical elements. The fact that the early church incorporated singing into its worship activities is recorded in Matthew 26:30 and Mark 14:26 and in non-biblical writings. It is probable that during the first three centuries of the Christian church, there were no uniform musical customs.

Gregorian Chant

From the fourth to the sixth centuries A.D., music in the church became more uniform and evolved along Western lines. Trained singers were given more responsibility for the music. Late in the sixth century Pope Gregory I, with the help of many assistants, began a recodification and compilation of chants. He assigned particular chants to certain services throughout the year. Gregory's work was so highly esteemed that even today this entire body of church music is called *Gregorian chant*. (It is also known as *plainsong* or *plainchant*.) When Gregory's work was done, the church had a *liturgy*—a body of rites prescribed for public worship.

Gregorian chant is different from most music heard in America today. In chant only one line of music is heard, without the enriching sounds of harmony. And even the melodic line is different. In place of beats and regular rhythmic patterns, there is a flexible rhythm. Furthermore, the familiar major-minor scale system is lacking. No attempt is made to appeal to the senses or to involve the listener's emotions. Only men's voices are used, and they sing in a restrained, nonemotional way.

Gregorian chant is very much interwoven with religious practice. It was created for one purpose only: to contribute to the spirit of worship. Heard as concert music, Gregorian chant seems rather dull. When sung by the religious in a seminary or monastery, however, it is strangely moving. Undoubtedly the impression is created partially by the setting and the obvious religious devotion of the participants, and by the knowledge that the music helps to put worshipers in the procession of the faithful stretching back nearly 2,000 years. But much of the effect is due to qualities of the music itself.

Traditionally, the Roman Catholic Church specified the order and content of every service, depending on the type of service and its place in the church year. Since Vatican Council II (1964–1967), much of the former practice has changed, and more freedom is permitted in the amount and type of music that can be incorporated into the service. The most significant change has been the acceptance of *vernacular* languages (non-Latin). Unfortunately, most chants lose much of their effectiveness when translated, so chant is being heard less widely now than in the past.

The liturgy of the Roman Catholic Church can be either spoken or sung. The services for which the liturgy is written fall into two categories. One is the *Offices*, or *Canonical Hours*. These services are celebrated at stated times in the day according to the Church calendar. The other service is the *Mass*, which celebrates the Eucharist or Holy Communion. Mass also consists of two categories: the *Ordinary*—those parts that are ordinarily present in every Mass; and the *Proper*—those parts that are proper to a particular day in the Church calendar.

The musical example on page 154 shows a *Kyrie* (*keer*-ee-ay), which is one of the parts of the Ordinary of the Mass. The words, which are Greek, are translated, "Lord have mercy upon us; Christ have mercy upon us." The first part of the example is the Kyrie in the traditional Roman notation with its four-line staff. Following it is the same music in modern notation.

Even in modern notation the music looks unusual. It has no meter signature. Almost all the notes have the same rhythmic value, but the last note of each phrase is consistently longer. The grouping of notes is irregular; sometimes there are two in a group, sometimes three or more. Except for the places at which the double vertical lines occur, the melody does not move very far from one note to another; its contour is smooth. The entire melody covers a range of only seven notes, and most of its phrases begin and end on the same note. The piece is quite short.

As you listen to a recording of the Kyrie or other examples of Gregorian chant, remind yourself that this is not concert-hall music. It is not going to command your attention through mighty sounds or dramatic changes. Rather, it

seeks to convey a spirit, an attitude. The music strives for a purity and reverence worthy of acceptance by God. Although such an ideal may seem remote from the busy pace of present-day American life, seldom has an ideal come closer to fulfillment in music.

Unlike other early music, Gregorian chant was carefully preserved in the monasteries by oral tradition and written manuscripts. This music has been painstakingly researched by musicologists both within the Church and outside it.

Secular Music

Although Gregorian chant dominated the musical world for many centuries, there also existed music of a *secular* (worldly or nonsacred) nature. Most nonreligious music was not preserved, so less is known about it. Secular music was in the language of a particular country—French, German, English, Italian, Spanish—rather than in the ecclesiastical or church Latin prescribed for worship. At first, secular music was largely the contribution of wandering musicians who traveled from place to place singing songs, reciting poems, and even exhibiting trained animals. They were the entertainers of that time. Later, about the twelfth and thirteenth centuries, troubadours and trouvères dominated secular music in France. They were noblemen who were poets and composers but not performers; they hired minstrels to sing their songs. The music was for solo voice and was often sung with instrumental accompaniment. Most of the poems and songs were about an idealized type of love, not bawdy or physically passionate. Several thousand such poems and songs have been preserved. Unlike Gregorian chant, they display regular rhythmic patterns.

During this time a close relationship existed between secular vocal music and instrumental music. A song could be played or sung, or both.

Some of the instruments of medieval times are pictured in Color Plate 1. The goddess Music holds a portable organ, and other figures are playing instruments common during the fourteenth century. Starting at the top center and moving clockwise the instruments are "pig snout" psaltery, mandola, clappers, long trumpets, kettledrums tied around the waist, bagpipe held by the man and a double-reed instrument called a shawm held by the woman, jingle drum, and vielle.

Many songs appeared in conjunction with dancing. The rhythm for the dances and for other secular pieces followed any of six *rhythmic modes*—patterns similar to those by which poetry meters are classified today. The short-long pattern corresponds to today's iambic meter, while the long-short pattern corresponds to the trochaic. The term rhythmic mode is unrelated to the word *mode* as it is applied to scale patterns.

Until about 1000 A.D., music consisted largely of single melodic lines. Although examples of the simultaneous sounding of tones are found in early Western music, as well as in the music of other civilizations, these examples account for only a small part of the total body of music.

In the eleventh century Western music began to change. It began to feature the sounding of musical pitches at the same time. Medieval composers, many of whom were anonymous monks, accomplished this in the simplest possible way. They merely added another layer of sound to the existing lines of Gregorian chant, something like adding a layer to a cake. At first the added line ran exactly parallel to the original line but four or five notes below it. Since this did not allow much musical freedom, the added line was permitted to break out of its strictly parallel pattern, and little by little it assumed a more independent character. When independent lines of melody were written to be performed at the same time, polyphony was accomplished.

Polyphony (pronounced po-*lif*-o-nee) is an important concept in music. It is the combining of lines of nearly equal melodic interest; no particular line is superior. Listening to polyphony might be compared to watching a three-ring circus. Each act is equally interesting. Although it is not easy to look at all the acts at once, there are no breaks in the action.

An interesting aspect of this early polyphony was that notes of the same pitch, those an octave apart, and those four and five tones apart were considered to be consonant. These are the same intervals Pythagoras had regarded as most consonant. In other words, the interval of a third—the interval upon which our present system of chords is based—was regarded as a dissonance. It would be nearly 500 years before chords containing thirds would be considered consonant enough to appear as the important final chord of a piece.

The Gothic Period and the Motet

The late medieval period from about 1100 to 1450 has come to be known as the *Gothic* period. This was the era during which great cathedrals were built, universities were founded, and the Magna Carta was formulated. It was also the period of the Crusades and the Hundred Years War.

The music that developed during this time is termed Gothic, and it was characterized by an intellectual type of polyphony. One type had the chant melody sung or played in long notes, while the added part sounded several shorter notes within the same duration. Later the chant melody and extra part were designed to match the specified patterns of the rhythmic modes. Sometimes as many as four lines were combined in the music. When words were added, the piece became known as a *motet*, from the French *mot*, meaning word.

The motet was a curious musical animal. First of all, it combined various languages as well as sacred and secular texts. One line might be a French love song, another might be a Latin song praising the Virgin Mary, and still another might be a phrase of Gregorian chant. Second, composers tended to concentrate on working out each line, relatively unconcerned about how it sounded with the other lines. Some strong dissonances resulted. Third, composers

became fascinated, especially in the fourteenth century, by mystical relationships and concealed meanings in the music. They took delight in concealing a chant phrase in the upper lines. Or they set up a complicated scheme of rhythmic and melodic patterns, so that a rhythmic pattern might repeat three times for every two times the melodic pattern repeated. Such intellectual complexities pleased the medieval musician but were generally lost on listeners, since they could be comprehended only by looking at the music and not by hearing it. Such music was a form of intellectual puzzle rather than an art form to be heard.

As the 1450s approached, the Gothic motet rapidly disappeared, although traces of its compositional techniques can be found even today. Gregorian chant was continuing to influence other musical forms. The long stretch of human history called the Middle Ages was drawing to a close. This period had not been dark, as it is sometimes described. Developments had taken place in music and other fields. In fact, the years leading up to 1450 had laid the foundation for a new era—the Renaissance.

Gothic Period, 1100-1450

Historical Events
1200   Crusades; Magna Carta; feudalism
1300   Papal schism
1400   Growth of cities; beginning of banking

Prominent Composers
Machaut, Landini

New Large Form
Mass

New Small Forms
Motet, secular ballads

Prominent Musical Characteristics
Vocal polyphonic sacred music, based on chant;

nonmetrical rhythm; complex compositional devices—canon, diminution. Accompanied solo secular song.

Predominant Musical Effects
Reverent and restrained

Visual Arts
Great cathedrals built, Giotto, Ghiberti, Fra Filippo Lippi, Botticelli, Donatello

Literature
Dante, Petrarch, Boccaccio, Chaucer

Philosophy
Abelard, Thomas Aquinas, R. Bacon

Sculptured figure of Christ on the cathedral at Chartres. (Marburg—Art Reference Bureau.)

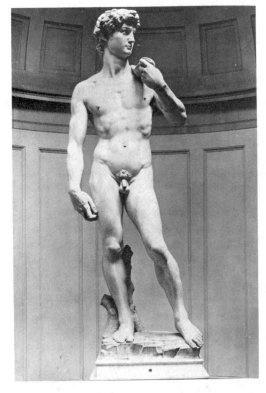

David *by Michelangelo. (Italian Government Travel Office.)*

The Renaissance

The word *renaissance* literally means rebirth. Historically it meant a revival of interest in the philosophy and arts of ancient Greece and Rome. Music, however, had no ancient Greek roots to return to, so the concept of rebirth in regard to music has little direct significance. The term *Renaissance* as applied to music simply refers to the style that predominated from about 1450 until 1600.

The Renaissance reflected an intense interest in ancient Greek civilization. This interest led to a curious union of Greek and Christian belief. Michelangelo combined pagan and Christian elements by decorating the ceiling of the Sistine Chapel with alternating figures of prophets and sibyls. Erasmus, the great philosopher, regarded Socrates as a pre-Christian saint and once wrote, "St. Socrates, pray for us."

Closely allied with the renewal of interest in ancient Greek ideals was the "humanistic" view of mankind. This ideal, still very much alive today, affirmed that human dignity consists of moral and intellectual freedom. Rabelais expressed it in *Gargantua* with the words "fais çe que voudras" ("do what you will"), and Leone Battista Alberti phrased the spirit of the time by writing "men can do all things if they will." As a result of such thinking a new emphasis was placed on people and their lives on earth. People began to delight in the natural world and their place in it.

Leonardo da Vinci was one of the few persons who actually could do nearly all things well. He was a painter, sculptor, mathematician, musician, inventor, writer, anatomist, and athlete. Many people, however, had interests and knowledge in various areas of life.

The results of humanism are well illustrated by the two treatments of the human body shown on page 157. One is a Gothic sculpture found on the cathedral at Chartres, France. Notice that this figure has a spiritual, otherworldly quality. The attitude of the head is serene, and the position of the body is formal. The proportions of the figure are distorted through exaggerated length, thus giving the body an emaciated look. The feet seem to dangle from the robes as though they were merely attached. Michelangelo's *David*, on the other hand, looks like a magnificent Greek god (the figure of David stands more than 13½ feet high). The impression is one of confidence in and admiration of man. David looks natural, almost casual, and free. The human body emerges from the withered state given it by medieval beliefs to the idealized status accorded it by Renaissance attitudes.

With the increasing interest in the value of human existence, there was a corresponding interest in the fine arts. A beautiful painting or piece of music began to have value for its own sake and not merely as a means to religious devotion. As a result of this fortunate change of outlook, the list of great Renaissance sculptors and painters is long—Botticelli, Leonardo, Michelangelo, Dürer, Raphael, Titian, Brueghel, Tintoretto. Botticelli's *The Adoration of the Magi* (Color Plate 2) shows the Renaissance fondness for order and balance. A group of figures at the left of the painting is balanced by a group on the right. The infant Jesus is in the center. The converging lines of the Greek and Roman ruins add perspective to the painting and show the renewed interest in these ancient civilizations.

Not only were works of art being enjoyed in a new climate of acceptance, the increasing level of the economy, especially in the cities of northern Italy and the Netherlands, meant that money to hire artists and musicians was available. The Church sought rich adornment for its buildings—one of several practices that led to the reform movement started by Martin Luther in 1517. The effect of the Reformation on the world of music did not show its full impact until after 1600, but the seeds of change had been planted.

An event that reached into every area of human endeavor—education, religion, commerce—was Gutenberg's invention of printing from movable type. Printing made possible the wide dissemination of music, beginning with the appearance of the first printed music book in 1501.

The spirit of the times was one of optimism and discovery. The voyages of Columbus, Cabot, Balboa, and Magellan took place during the Renaissance. Science advanced, too, but not without opposition from the Church. In anatomy Andreas Vesalius made the main contributions, and in astronomy Copernicus set forth the heliocentric theory of the solar system. Francis Bacon cheered on the new discoveries with the words, "We are not to imagine or suppose, but to discover, what nature does or may be made to do." Rabelais, Machiavelli, Boccaccio, Montaigne, Thomas More, and Erasmus were exploring new ideas in literature and philosophy.

Renaissance Music

The musical Renaissance started in the Netherlands, which then included Holland, Belgium, and parts of France. Composers of the area had reached a level of proficiency that was the envy of Europe. They were lured away from their homeland to better-paying jobs in Spain, Bohemia, Austria, Germany, and especially the cities of northern Italy. The style and technique of the Netherlands became internationally known and imitated. So cosmopolitan did composers become that they thought of themselves as musicians first and as citizens of a particular country second. This outlook is well illustrated by Orlando di Lasso (the name he used in Italy), alias Roland de Lassus (the name he used in Germany), who wrote music in the German, French, and Italian idioms, as well as in the Netherlands style. Versatility was further evidenced by the scope of a musician's duties. A musician was employed not just to compose but also to perform, to train a choir, and to teach.

The two main employers during the Renaissance were the Church and wealthy nobility. Logically, the music tends to divide itself into two types, secular and sacred. Sacred music was often based on chant, although themes from other compositions and secular tunes were woven in. The vocal lines often imitate each other, especially at the beginning of a new phrase of text. By having one voice enter after another, the composer can draw attention to each successive voice part, and the words can be more easily understood.

Secular music was less imitative. It was influenced by dance styles and forms and was intended to be entertaining.

During the Gothic period the chant phrase had been in the middle voice, with other parts added on either side; together they encompassed a rather narrow pitch range. About 1450 the voice parts were spread over a greater range with the addition of a bass part, and this change established the soprano, alto, tenor, and bass structure still used today. All parts were given equal importance.

Renaissance motet. As mentioned earlier, during the Gothic period a motet was a composition based on a line of Gregorian chant to which were added other melodies containing other words, often in various languages. The

motet of the Renaissance is quite different. It is a unified piece with all voices singing the same text. The Gothic motet was always based on Gregorian chant. The Renaissance motet, on the other hand, did not always borrow from chant, but it conveyed that spirit and was suitable for inclusion in worship.

Palestrina's "Sanctus" (Record 2,A) from the Mass *Aeterna Christi Munera* (a portion of it appears on page 161) shows many characteristics of his writing style. The title of the Mass comes not from its words but from the phrase of chant on which portions of this particular mass are based.

What are the significant features of "Sanctus" and other Renaissance motets?

1. The text is in ecclesiastical Latin. It is:

Sanctus, Sanctus, Sanctus,
Dominus Deus Sabaoth.
Pleni sunt coeli et terra gloria tua.
Hosanna in Excelsis.

Holy, Holy, Holy,
Lord God of hosts.
Heaven and earth are full of thy glory.
Hosanna in the highest.

Renaissance, 1450-1600

Historical Events
1450   Gutenberg invents movable type
        Columbus and others make voyages
        Protestant reformation
1500   Copernicus publishes conclusions on
        the universe

Prominent Composers
Morley, Palestrina, di Lasso, Byrd

New Small Forms
Madrigal, motet, chorale melody

Prominent Musical Characteristics
Polyphony, bass voice present, use of modes; mostly small vocal ensemble music; lute and keyboard; gentle rhythmic flow; harmony oc-

curs, a consequence of linear writing

Predominant Musical Effects
Restrained and intimate

Visual Arts
da Vinci, Van Eyck, Durer, St. Peter's built in Rome, Michelangelo, Raphael, Brueghel, Titian, Giorgione, Tintoretto, Veronese

Literature
Ariosto, Rabelais, Spenser, Marlowe, Shakespeare

Philosophy
Machiavelli, More, Luther, Erasmus, Montaigne

2. The music is polyphonic. All the lines are given equal attention, and each has distinct melodic character.

3. Each voice usually enters in imitation of another. Look closely at the notes for the words "Sanctus." First the soprano starts, followed by the alto two beats later, the tenor halfway through measure 3, and finally the bass in measure 7. All voices sing the first eight or nine notes in imitation. But as the music progresses, the voices tend to move on to melodies of their own. At each addition of a new phrase of the text, the process of imitation is repeated. It is through the use of such imitative entrances, sometimes called *staggered entrances* or *points of imitation*, that Palestrina makes the words of the text easier to hear.

4. It does not have a strong feeling of harmonic movement. The sound is pleasing and smooth, but the chords lack the harmonic "drive" found in later styles. This is due partly to the polyphonic nature of the music, with its emphasis on the horizontal line, and to the fact that systematic harmony had not yet been developed.

5. The music lacks a strong feeling of meter or beat. Again, this is similar to Gregorian chant, which has no meter. Although present-day notation for "Sanctus" includes measure bar lines, the original probably had none. The bar lines have been added by editors for the convenience of modern-day singers, so that they can more easily keep their place. Most of the chord changes in Palestrina's music occur at moments of subtle stress, which give the music a gentle rhythmic regularity. Absent, however, is a feeling of definite rhythmic patterns.

6. The motet has no written accompaniment. Most motets are performed today *a cappella* (literally, "for the chapel," meaning without accompaniment), although during the sixteenth century instruments often doubled the voice parts.

7. A small choir is most appropriate for performing the motet. During the Renaissance probably not more than two singers were assigned to each part. Boys, or men singing in falsetto voice, sang the high voice parts since women were not allowed to participate in the Mass.

8. The melodies are very singable. The range of notes in any one part generally does not exceed an octave. Furthermore, the singers do not have to move far from one pitch to the next, although the bass part usually contains more leaps than do the other lines.

9. The form of this motet is derived from the structure of the text. Each verse is treated to its own polyphonic setting. The form, then, is a succession of verses, each with music that is not repeated in other verses. The reappearance of the opening melodic line in this motet is quite unusual.

10. The music has a restrained, unemotional quality. Bombast and emotionalism were considered insincere and not in keeping with the attitude of respect and awe that should prevail in the worship of God. Even though the text speaks of "Hosanna in the highest," the music does not suggest a triumphal procession or a fanfare. When Palestrina does emphasize particular words, he does it so subtly that the modern listener may not notice the emphasis.

11. The melodic lines are fitted together with unexcelled craftsmanship, hard to appreciate unless you are familiar with Renaissance choral music, but this is why Palestrina stands out among composers of his time.

The madrigal. The main type of secular music in the Renaissance was the *madrigal*. It has sometimes been described as a secular version of the motet, but there are significant differences between the two forms. The madrigal is in vernacular language rather than Latin. Its text deals with sentimental and sometimes erotic love. The texts of madrigals written early in the Renaissance generally had little literary merit, but later better texts were selected. Madrigals were very popular, and an enormous number were composed. They were sung at courtly social gatherings and at meetings of learned and artistic societies. In England, madrigal singing—with its requirement of music reading—was expected of an educated person.

A lute or harpsichord was often used to accompany the singing of a madrigal. The instrumentalist simplified the written parts, reducing the complicated polyphony to chords.

Plate 1. *Goddess of Music.* (Scala/EPA.)

Plate 2. *The Adoration of the Magi* by Sandro Botticelli. (Andrew Mellon Collection, National Gallery of Art, Washington, D.C.)

Plate 3. *The Holy Family* by El Greco (Domenikos Theotokopoulos). (Samuel H. Kress Collection, National Gallery of Art, Washington, D.C.)

Plate 4. *The Oath of the Horatii* by Jacques Louis David. (Louvre, Paris. Courtesy of Art Reference Bureau, Inc.)

Sanctus

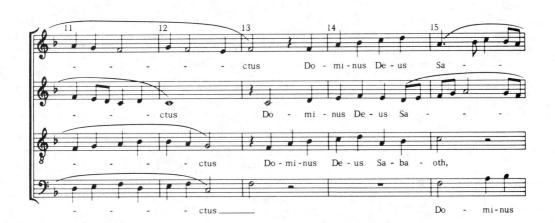

The madrigal was largely an Italian development, associated with composers such as da Rore and Marenzio. By the mid-1500s madrigals had spread to other countries, reaching England late in the century. When the first madrigals with English translation were printed in 1588, the response was a brief but brilliant period of original English secular music. The English madrigal is especially enjoyable for three reasons: (1) Its text is in English, so no translation is necessary; (2) its composers had a knack for making the lines of music tuneful and singable; and (3) the English had the delightful trait of not taking themselves too seriously. No matter how sad the song may be, the listener senses a tongue-in-cheek quality.

One well-known English madrigal is "April Is in My Mistress' Face" by Thomas Morley (Record 4,B). About half of the music appears on pages 163 and 164. The text is a wistful comment on life. In this work *Mistress* does not mean paramour, as it does today; fiancée is closer to the original intent.

The madrigal is similar to the motet in several respects. There are imitative entrances at the beginning of word phrases, and the texture is basically polyphonic. The vocal lines are smooth and singable. The harmony is not firmly established in one particular key. The use of instruments was optional during the Renaissance, but today both madrigal and motet are sung without accompaniment. The form is a phrase-by-phrase setting of the text.

There are significant differences between the two forms, however. The madrigal's rhythm is more metrical, causing the moments of rhythmic stress to fall in a more regular pattern. The tempo is faster. Here Morley tends to set the women's parts in contrast to the men's, which may or may not be an attempt to relate

to the text of "April Is in My Mistress' Face." The language is English not Latin. And in overall spirit this madrigal is vastly different from Palestrina's motet.

Other Renaissance music. Vocal music was not the only type of music composed in the Renaissance, although it predominated. Keyboard instruments included the delicate virginal and the organ. There were string instruments called viols, which came in a variety of sizes.

The lute was the most popular instrument of the Renaissance. It had a pear-shaped body and varying numbers of strings. Its pegbox was slanted back sharply away from the rest of the instrument. The fingerboard had frets—upraised strips placed across the neck, as on a guitar. The lute was played by strumming, and rather intricate music could be executed on it.

Wind instruments included the sackbut, which was a medieval trombone, and the krummhorn, which was similar to an oboe. The trumpet, recorder (a type of flute), and drums were found during that time, too. Composers did not specify what instruments were to play a part unless the piece was clearly for a keyboard instrument.

Renaissance music is not concert music in the usual sense of the term. Madrigals and virginal music were written to be performed at social gatherings in large houses by trained amateurs—usually the educated elite of a society. Motets were written for worship services. Because Renaissance music is not particularly suitable for a concert hall, it is not heard frequently today. Recordings and college concerts are its chief promoters, and many high school choral groups perform a few Renaissance works during the school year.

April Is in My Mistress' Face

Thomas Morley (1557-1603)

Giovanni Palestrina

Giovanni Pierluigi da Palestrina was born in 1525 in the town of Palestrina near Rome. His music education began at Rome's Saint Mary Major, where he was a choirboy. From that time on, Rome was the center of his life. He studied music with two Frenchmen who lived in Rome, and for a short while he studied with a famous Netherlands composer named Jacob Arcadelt. Within five years after the bishop of Palestrina became Pope Julius III, he installed Palestrina as choirmaster at St. Peter's.

The Council of Trent was held intermittently between 1545 and 1563. The Church felt threatened by the impact of the Reformation, so the council met to respond to the situation and to acknowledge the need for some reform within the Church. One phase of the Church's life that came under attack was the music for the Mass. Over the centuries it had acquired a complicated polyphony that made the words unintelligible, and the church fathers did not like the use of noisy instruments and the careless and irreverent attitude of many of the church singers. So Palestrina composed for a Church that wanted to return to the simplicity and purity of its earlier music. To his credit he achieved this ideal *without* discarding the highly developed style of his predecessors. His music is the embodiment of the worshipful ideal of Gregorian chant.

With the election of Paul IV there was a general tightening of rules, and Palestrina was dismissed because he was married. For five years he directed the music at St. John Lateran, and then he was called back to Saint Mary Major. As he grew older, his fame and fortune increased, and included responsibilities such as serving as advisor to a society of professional musicians. At his funeral in 1594 his coffin bore the words *Musicae Princeps*. He was truly the prince of Roman music during the Renaissance.

Thomas Morley

Little is known about Thomas Morley's early life, and there is some doubt about the year of his birth, which was either 1557 or 1558. For a while he was a student of William Byrd, the greatest English composer of his time. Morley held several appointments as a church musician, eventually leading to his appointment as organist at St. Paul's in London. It's likely that he knew Shakespeare and wrote music for some of his plays. In 1591 he undertook some espionage work among the English Catholics living in the Netherlands (these were the times of religious wars), and the assignment nearly cost him his life. Soon after this venture he was sworn in as gentleman of the Chapel Royal.

In addition to writing much church music and some instrumental works, he took advantage of the popularity among the English in the 1590s for Italian madrigals fitted with English texts. He published a number of madrigal collections, and in 1598 Queen Elizabeth's government gave him a monopoly to publish music books. Some of his madrigals are original, while others are plagiarized without acknowledgment, a not uncommon practice in his time. His most famous publication was a textbook, *A Plaine and Easie Introduction to Practicall Musicke*, which was widely read for 200 years.

Morley was in ill health during the last years of his life, and the information available today indicates that he died about 1603.

Other Renaissance Composers

English Composers

William Byrd	(1543–1623)	probably the best English composer of the Renaissance; madrigals, church music, and keyboard music
William Cornyshe	(c. 1465–1523)	songs
John Dowland	(1562–1626)	madrigals
Robert Fayrfax	(1464–1521)	church music
Thomas Tallis	(c. 1505–1585)	church music
John Taverner	(c. 1495–1545)	church music
Thomas Weelkes	(c. 1575–1623)	madrigals
John Wilbye	(1574–1638)	madrigals

Netherlands Composers

Jacob Arcadelt	(c. 1505–c. 1567)	*chansons* (songs), madrigals; influential teacher in Rome
Jacobus Clemens	(c. 1510–c. 1556)	church music
Heinrich Isaac	(c. 1450–1517)	church and secular music; international in use of texts
Jacob Obrecht	(c. 1452–1505)	church music; introduced new technical devices
Johannes Ockeghem	(c. 1430–1495)	church music; introduced new technical devices
Jan Sweelinck	(1562–1621)	*chansons* in old style
Adrian Willaert	(c. 1480–1562)	influential composer and teacher at St. Mark's in Venice

French Composers

Clément Jannequin	(c. 1475–1560)	*chansons*; fond of imitative sounds in music
Claude Le Jeune	(1528–1600)	madrigals, *chansons*
Claudin de Sermisy	(c. 1490–1562)	*chansons*

German Composers

Hans Leo Hassler	(1561–1612)	*lieder* (a *lied* is a German version of the *chanson*), church music
Orlando di Lasso (Roland de Lassus)	(1532–1594)	*lieder* (also wrote in French and Italian styles)

Italian Composers

Costanzo Festa	(c. 1490–1545)	early madrigals
Carlo Gesualdo	(c. 1560–1613)	madrigals with experimental harmonies
Luca Marenzio	(1553–1599)	madrigals
Philippe de Monte	(1521–1603)	madrigals
Claudio Monteverdi	(1567–1643)	madrigals written when a young man; important Baroque composer later
Giovanni Mario Nanino	(c. 1545–1607)	Palestrina's successor at Papal Chapel
Cipriano da Rore	(1516–1565)	probably the best composer of madrigals

Spanish Composers

Antonio de Cabezón	(1510–1566)	keyboard music
Francisco Guerrero	(1527–1599)	church music
Cristóbal de Morales	(c. 1500–1553)	church music
Tomás Luis de Victoria	(c. 1549–1611)	church music in style of Palestrina

17

The Baroque Period and Baroque Music

Even before 1600, the approximate beginning of the Baroque period (Ba-*roke*), a new style and spirit were emerging. The Renaissance was being replaced, not necessarily by better artistic works but by creations in a different style. The result was a vast enrichment of the art of music.

Sometimes in everyday usage *baroque* means extravagant, grotesque, and in bad taste. In discussions of the fine arts, however, *baroque* refers only to the style of artistic expression prevalent roughly from 1600 to 1750. And this expression was by no means grotesque or in bad taste.

The years from 1600 to 1750 saw such turbulence and change that it is impossible to characterize the period fully in a few lines. The following information, however, may provide at least some indication of the times.

Characteristics of the Baroque Style

One of the most striking features of the Baroque was its fondness for the large and grandiose. An architectural example is seen in Lorenzo Bernini's monumental colonnades enclosing the vast piazza in front of St. Peter's Basilica in Rome. The huge columns reach out before St. Peter's like giant pincers seeking to draw everyone into the building. There are four rows of columns running parallel to one another. Measured across, the piazza exceeds the length of two football fields; the colonnades are made up of 284 different columns. Statues of 140 saints sit on top of the columns. Baroque painters, architects, and composers seemed at times to want to overwhelm the viewer or listener.

A second notable characteristic of the Baroque was its interest in the dramatic. In music three major dramatic forms were developed: opera, oratorio, and cantata. Drama can also be seen in the twisted lines and struggling subjects in art works. Rembrandt van Rijn's *Christ in the Storm on Lake Galilee* (page 15), painted about

View of the piazza in front of St. Peter's in Rome from the roof of the Basilica. Note Bernini's huge colonnades. The statues of Christ and the Apostles in the foreground are 19 feet high.

1633, features the play of light to achieve a sense of drama. The light actually seems to be coming from the left side of the picture, and it gives the scene an eerie pall. The mast crosses diagonally through the picture, and the sails are twisted, another popular Baroque effect. All the figures show emotion except Jesus, whose face is illuminated on the right side of the painting.

A third significant trait of the Baroque was the intensity of religious feeling, which tended to be either Protestant or Catholic. Protestant churches established themselves generally in northern Europe and on the British Isles. Prot-

estant worship was devout, simple, and very serious. John Milton's *Paradise Lost* and John Bunyan's *Pilgrim's Progress* are two monumental books that express the Protestant spirit.

The Catholic form of religious intensity was generally found in southern Europe. The Catholic Counter-Reformation developed in response to the Protestant Reformation, and a series of tragic religious wars between Protestants and Catholics ensued. A happier result, however, was the encouragement of some outstanding religious art. El Greco's *The Holy Family* (Color Plate 3) demonstrates the spiritual qualities of the Baroque outlook. The bodies have been elongated, which gives them a more other-worldly appearance. The flickering light and turbulent sky (in contrast to the serene expressions on the faces of the women) also reflect the Baroque character of the work.

Although it was marked by religious fervor, the Baroque era was also a time of significant advances in science. Among the famous scientists of the period were Sir Isaac Newton, who developed the theory of gravity; Kepler and Galileo, who developed Copernicus' theories about the movement of planets; William Gilbert, who introduced the word *electricity* into the language; Robert Boyle, who helped make chemistry a pure science; Robert Hooke, who first described the cellular structure of plants; Sir William Harvey, who described the circulation of the blood; Gottfried Wilhelm von Leibniz, who with Newton developed infinitesimal calculus; and René Descartes, who founded analytical geometry.

The Baroque saw the rise of a sizable middle class that was breaking away from the traditional society based on inherited land, title, and wealth. One result of this change was the inclusion of some everyday scenes in paintings, prose novels, and comic operas.

Governmentally the Baroque was a mixture of petty principalities and absolute monarchies that continually quarreled with one another. The church still patronized the arts, but its role was less important than it had been in the Renaissance. The middle class, made up of merchants and financiers, ran the cities of northern Europe, while the Hapsburg and Bourbon dynasties ruled to the south.

In short, the Baroque era was a time of contrasts. Religious fervor existed side by side with scientific advances, drama, and grandeur. This quality of dualism, at times bordering on cultural schizophrenia, is also evident in Baroque music.

Features of Baroque Music

The Baroque period in music covers about 150 years. Some scholars have divided the period into three sections: early, middle, and mature. Music in the early years tended to be experimental, while the middle and mature periods

represent the style usually associated with the term *Baroque*. The mature Baroque brought forth more sophisticated works, which culminated in the music of Bach and Handel.

Homophony. Homophony (pronounced ho-*mof*-o-nee) is the type of music most familiar to us today. Most pieces we know have melodies that we can whistle or sing. Usually they are accompanied, but we seldom pay much attention to the accompaniment. The main thing is the melody. It may seem illogical that homophony developed after polyphony (music with several equal voice parts). Apparently medieval musicians found it easier to combine melodies than to analyze and rearrange the simultaneous sounds that make up chords.

A little homophonic music existed long before the Baroque, but composers had used it rarely in serious musical works, so it had not developed very far. By 1600 the polyphonic style of Palestrina had reached its fullest potential. Composers began to feel that something new and fresh was needed. The process of change is clearly evident in the books of madrigals by the outstanding, innovative composer Claudio Monteverdi (1567–1643). Between 1587 and 1603 Monteverdi published four books of madrigals in Renaissance style. In 1605 he published a book of pieces that were homophonic, some of which had accompaniments. By the eighth book (1638), Monteverdi's music called for small vocal and string ensembles.

Actually, Baroque musicians did not throw away polyphony. They wrote and performed in both the homophonic and polyphonic styles. They called the homophonic the "new style" and the polyphonic the "old style," and they maintained a rather good balance between the two.

Major-minor system. The Baroque saw the culmination of a process that had been developing slowly for a hundred years or more: the abandonment of all modes except the two that today are called major and minor. This change opened up two possibilities that composers had not explored: (1) A more solid tonal center could be established, and (2) the tonal center could be moved to different pitches during a musical work.

The establishment of a tonal center means that at almost any point in the music the composer can create a feeling of motion or of rest, depending on the harmonies chosen. The effectiveness of a harmonic progression depends in part on the convincing presence of the tonic or key center. Without an established key center there is nothing for the chords to go out from or return to. The "magnetic pull" of the tonic is necessary.

Baroque composers discovered that if it was possible to establish a key, then it was also possible to move that key center—to modulate. It was simply a matter of transposing the chord

patterns to a different key center at a later point in the music.

Sequence. Baroque composers were fond of repeating a melodic figure several times in succession, each time at a different pitch level. The term for this practice is *sequence*. It is easily visible in the subject and countersubject of Bach's C Major Fugue (page 108). The first three phrases of the subject have virtually the same rhythm and pitch relationships; the same is true for the first portion of each of the first three phrases of the countersubject. Sequence provides unity to the music by using the same pattern, and variety is present through the use of differing pitch levels.

Baroque Period, 1600-1750

Historical Events

1600   King James Version of Bible; Pilgrims land in America

Absolute monarchies in many countries

Newton writes about physical laws

Thirty Years War; War of Spanish succession

Encyclopedie published

Watt invents steam engine

1700   Jenner develops smallpox vaccine

Prominent Composers

Monteverdi, Gabrieli, Vivaldi, Purcell, Lully, Telemann, Rameau, Bach, Handel

New Large Forms

Opera, oratorio, cantata, unaccompanied sonata, concerto grosso, suite

New Small Forms

Chorale, fugue, passacaglia, toccata, prelude, overture, chorale variation, chorale prelude, recitative, aria

Prominent Musical Characteristics

Change to major-minor system; systemized

harmony; solo singing important; virtuoso singing; homophony introduced and existing along with polyphony; equal temperament; modulation; organ and harpsichord, plus instrumental music other than keyboard; melodic sequence; much use of strict metrical rhythm; terraced dynamics; basso continuo

Predominant Musical Effects

Expressive solo singing; consistent mood throughout sections of music; some works in large dimensions

Visual Arts

Bernini, Rubens, El Greco, Rembrandt, Velasquez, Van Dyck, Poussin, Watteau, Hogarth, Fragonard, Gainsborough

Literature

Cervantes, Pepys, Milton, Pope, Swift, Defoe, Gray

Philosophy

F. Bacon, Descartes, Grotius, Hobbes, Spinoza, Locke, Voltaire

Tuning. The opportunity to modulate was helped when musicians finally overcame the 2,000-year-old problem of how to tune instruments. Acoustics is a complex topic, and it would take too much space to explain it here. Briefly, nature made a mistake. If some intervals are adjusted so that they are perfectly in tune, other intervals will be out of tune. If keys with one or two sharps are tuned perfectly, keys with many sharps or flats will sound terrible. The solution, finally adopted in the Baroque, was to tune all intervals slightly but equally out of tune, by a standard known as *equal temperament.* It was to promote such tuning that J. S. Bach wrote his *Well-Tempered Clavier,* which included a piece in each of the 12 major and 12 minor keys.

Figured bass. The harmonies in Baroque music became so well standardized that musicians devised a system of shorthand called *figured bass* to notate chords. The composer was responsible for writing out in full the bass and soprano (bottom and top) parts, but he needed to provide only cues in the form of numbers and an occasional sharp, flat, or natural for the inner (alto and tenor) parts. The outer voices became the two important lines in Baroque music, with the melody being the most important. The bass part provided a foundation to the music. Because it sounded nearly all the time, it came to be known as *basso continuo* (continuous bass), for convenience usually shortened to *continuo.*

Metrical rhythm. Although Renaissance music had a steady pulse, this pulse was not organized into patterns. Metrical rhythm with its bar lines and meter signatures was a product of the Baroque period, and Baroque musicians adhered to metrical rhythm slavishly, except when performing recitatives. The patterns came to rule the music to such an extent that later composers complained about "the tyranny of the bar line." Tempos were steady except for a slight slowing down at the end of a piece. The rhythm of Baroque music was so regular that Baroque orchestras, which were small by today's standards, could perform the music

without a conductor. All they needed was a nod from the keyboard player to start.

Terraced dynamics. The gradual increase or decrease of volume, which is so familiar today, was not common in the music of the Baroque period. Renaissance composers had written no dynamic markings at all in the music, and Baroque composers wrote very few. Often composers rehearsed and performed their own music, so extensive markings were unnecessary. The few dynamic markings that are present, however, call for abrupt changes of dynamic level. A *forte,* or loud level, is likely to change suddenly to a *piano,* or soft level. Logically, these changes are called *terraced dynamics.* One can only speculate on the reasons for the abrupt changes. Artists and musicians in the Baroque were interested in dramatic contrast, both visual and aural. Also, the keyboard instruments of the time could not make gradual changes, so variety in dynamic level had to be achieved abruptly or not at all.

Doctrine of affections. The word *affections,* as used in the term *doctrine of affections,* has little to do with love. Instead, it is related to the mental state projected by the music, and often with the union of words and music. For example, if the text says "leap up," the composer might make the pitches "leap up" at that point. Another result of this doctrine was the repeating of words or fragments of the music to allow time for expression. Sometimes long runs were written for particular words or syllables. In instrumental music the doctrine of affections dictated that the composer establish a mood or "affection" at the outset of a piece and then stay with that mood until the end of the movement. The doctrine of affections was of considerable importance during the Baroque, but it is of little concern to the listener today.

Instruments. Two keyboard instruments were important in the Baroque period: the organ and the harpsichord. Both were described in Chapter 6. The organ had existed in rudimentary form for 1,500 years, but it reached its highest development during the Baroque. In fact, many organs built in the twentieth century represent attempts to copy the organs of the eighteenth century. During the late nineteenth and early twentieth centuries several ranks of pipes were added to organs to imitate the sound of trombones and other instruments. These synthetic efforts were nearly always unsuccessful parodies.

The harpsichord was frequently played in the Renaissance, but it became more important in the Baroque period. At about the time the Baroque period ended, the harpsichord faded in prominence and was not heard much again until the twentieth century. In the last several decades there has been a revival of interest in the harpsichord, and new instruments are being manufactured. The harpsichord has even enjoyed some vogue in popular music in recent decades.

Several orchestral instruments are featured in Baroque music. One is the flute, which was then usually constructed to be held straight out from the player's mouth, rather than to the side as it is today. The flute was made of wood and had a lighter, less penetrating tone quality. The trumpet was given important solo roles during the Baroque period. It had no valves, and therefore the pitches were controlled entirely by the player's lips. Many of the Baroque trumpets were small, making it easier for the player to reach the very high notes heard in some Baroque compositions. The violin achieved a major role in Baroque music. It did not look quite the same as it does today. The fingerboard was shorter because players were not required to play very high notes. The bow stick curved slightly away from the hair, its shape resembling the archer's bow, for which it was named. The hair tension was rather loose, and the strings were set on a flatter plane, making it easier for the violinist to play on more than one string at a time.

The performance quality on orchestral instruments was probably not impressive by today's standards. Most players held other jobs, usually not associated with music, and the technical development of their instruments was not advanced. The exceptions to this general situa-

tion were the trumpeters of the time, who were extremely competitive; it is probable that they performed impressively. The level of playing on the organ and probably the harpsichord was also quite good.

Performance of Baroque Music

There were no professional orchestras during the Baroque period. The orchestras that did exist were associated with the court and often involved only part-time musicians. The orchestra was small—about 20 to 25 players. There was no conductor who stood before the group. Usually the harpsichord player began the music by giving the other musicians a nod.

There were no public concerts as we know them today. Performances of music were held in churches or in the courts of the nobility.

The choirs were also small by today's standards. For instance, Bach's choir at Leipzig sometimes numbered fewer than 30 singers. At one time he was down to three altos, and he wrote a letter to the town fathers asking for funds to employ a fourth. (His request was refused.)

Improvisation was an important aspect of Baroque musical performance. The filling in of the figured bass by the keyboard player has already been mentioned. A church organist was expected to improvise intricate and complex music. The improvisational ability of some Baroque composers, including organists Bach and Handel, made them legends in their time. A singer or instrumentalist would frequently add little ornaments and embellishments to the line of music. What we see notated in Baroque music is in some cases only a skeleton of what was actually performed.

Forms

The significant types of Baroque music have been presented earlier in this book. Now it would be wise to summarize them and associate them with characteristics of Baroque writing and performance practices.

Instrumental music. The suite is one of the Baroque's primary contributions to instrumental music. It was discussed in some detail in Chapter 12 in conjunction with keyboard music.

Another prominent instrumental form of the Baroque is the fugue, also discussed in Chapter 12. It is a contrapuntal form especially well suited to keyboard instruments such as the harpsichord and organ, which have different manuals and stops for producing varied tone qualities for each entering voice in the fugue.

A third important instrumental form of the Baroque is the concerto grosso, discussed in Chapter 10. Vivaldi's *The Four Seasons* is an example of this form, which illustrates the Baroque fondness for contrast—in this case, between small and large groups. Several solo sonatas were also written during the Baroque period.

Vocal music. A most important contribution to the Baroque period was opera, which was discussed in Chapter 13. Despite their historical importance, Baroque operas are seldom performed today. Early in the Baroque period opera sank into mere virtuoso display by the singers, to the detriment of the musical quality. The recitative style has remained, however, not only in opera but also in the oratorio and cantata. The aria is another feature of opera that has carried over into other musical forms.

Baroque oratorios and cantatas are still performed widely today. The oratorio was presented in Chapter 8. The cantata is strongly associated with the Baroque period and contains many of the features of Baroque music just presented.

Bach's Cantata No. 147

In many ways a cantata is a "mini" oratorio. It is for soloists, chorus, and orchestra and contains recitatives, arias, and choruses. There are no costumes, scenery, or acting. There are some differences, however. The cantata is shorter, smaller in scope, and less a drama. For example, Handel's *Messiah*, discussed in Chapter 8, has 53 parts and covers the entire mission of Jesus. Bach's Cantata No. 147 has 10 parts.

Another difference is the presence in Baroque cantatas of a *chorale* (coh-*rahl*) melody as a theme for several sections of the work. A chorale is a type of hymn closely associated with Martin Luther and the Reformation. Its melody is solid, stately, and uncomplicated. Luther's "A Mighty Fortress Is Our God" is a good example of a chorale. Chorales were designed for singing by the congregation during worship services, and so the "theme" for the cantata was familiar to the listeners in the Lutheran church service, for which this cantata was composed.

Cantata No. 147 is somewhat longer than most cantatas, but in other respects it is typical. It was written about 1730 for the Feast of the Visitation of the Blessed Virgin Mary, although portions of it had been written by Bach 14 years earlier for another cantata. The text is the product of a man named Franck and is based on Isaiah 11:1–15 and Luke 1:39–56, the prophecy of Elizabeth and Mary concerning Christ.

You already know part of Bach's Cantata No. 147 "Herz und Mund und Tat und Leben" ("Heart and Mouth and All My Being"). The familiar portion is "Jesu, Joy of Man's Desiring," which was mentioned in Chapter 1 and appears on Record 1,A in the *Record Album*. The cantata is divided into two main parts: "Jesu, Joy of Man's Desiring" is the chorale that closes each part.

Part I of the cantata begins with a chorus. It is contrapuntal and contains some sections for orchestra alone, others for chorus without orchestra. The text is:

> *Herz und Mund und Tat und Leben*
> *Muss von Christo Zeugnis geben*
> *Ohne Furcht und Heuchelei,*
> *Dass er Gott und Heiland sei.*

> *Heart and mouth, and all my being*
> *Must show praise to Christ the Savior,*
> *Without false deceit or fear,*
> *Witness that the Lord is here.*

The second section is a recitative in which Mary describes her vision to Elizabeth. The third section is an alto aria. Actually, it is a duet between the singer and the oboe d'amore, a seventeenth-century instrument similar to the

English horn. The section urges the listener not to deny God. The fourth section is another recitative, and it exhorts the listener to give everything to God.

The fifth section is another aria-duet, this time between soprano and violin. Its text is:

Bereite dir, Jesu, noch itzo die Bahn.
Mein Heiland, erwähle
Die glaubende Seele
Und siehe mit Augen der Gnade mich an!

Prepare, O Lord Jesus, thy path from above.
My Savior, receive
The souls who believe,
And look on thy people with mercy and love.

The sixth and closing section of Part I is the chorale, the music to "Jesu, Joy of Man's Desiring."

Part II consists of two more arias—one for tenor and one for bass—a recitative, and the chorale again, with a different set of words.

Jesus bleibet meine Freude,
Meines Herzens Trost und Saft,
Jesus wehret allem Leide,
Er ist meines Lebens Kraft,

Meiner Augen Lust und Sonne,
Meiner Seele Schatz und Wonne;
Darum lass' ich Jesum nicht
Aus dem Herzen und Gesicht.

Jesus, source of ev'ry blessing,
my heart's supreme delight;
Jesus lightens all my troubles
He is my sustaining might,

Joy and sunshine of my vision,
My soul's treasure and delight,

I will not let Jesus go
from my heart and from my sight.

The arias in Part I are in minor keys a fifth apart, and in Part II in major keys a fifth apart, indicating Bach's concern with the overall design of this cantata. The arias and recitatives are varied in style of accompaniment.

Congregational singing was especially significant because of the low educational level of the worshipers. A large proportion of the population in the time of Bach could not read or write. Nor did they receive information via mass-communications media. So pictures, statues, and music in churches were intended to be educational as well as beautiful. The text of a choral work was chosen for purposes of instruction as well as worship.

The cantata and oratorio were not the only types of vocal music written for Protestant worship services. Another type of religious music is the *Passion*, which is like an oratorio except that its topic is the suffering of Christ during His trial and crucifixion. The work that earned posthumous recognition for all of Bach's music is the *St. Matthew Passion*. Like his cantatas, this work gives a prominent place to a chorale: "O Sacred Head Now Wounded."

Another type of Protestant choral music is the *anthem*. It is a composition that has a religious text in English and is intended to be performed during a worship service. It may be either accompanied or unaccompanied.

Another type of choral music is the *Requiem*. The Requiem Mass is a Catholic service for the dead, and its prescribed Latin text has been set to music by several great composers—Mozart, Verdi, and Berlioz, to name three. The Protestant Johannes Brahms also wrote a Requiem, but he selected his own scripture passages from the Bible and kept them in German, not Latin. Accordingly, he called his work *A German Requiem*.

Giovanni Gabrieli

Giovanni Gabrieli (c. 1557–1612) was the nephew and pupil of Andrea Gabrieli (1520–1586), an outstanding Renaissance composer. Giovanni's fame later eclipsed that of his uncle. The church music of Venice, where the Gabrielis spent most of their lives, was written for St. Mark's cathedral, which featured two choirs facing each other from opposite sides of the room. In addition to the choirs Giovanni Gabrieli placed instrumental groups in the galleries. The effect was a sixteenth-century version of stereophonic sound. In its rich sounds and powerful qualities, G. Gabrieli's music is more a forecast of the Baroque style than it is typical of the Renaissance style. He was one of the first composers to indicate dynamic levels in the music and to designate specific instruments for certain parts.

Claudio Monteverdi

Claudio Monteverdi lived from 1567 to 1643. His life seems to parallel the change from the Renaissance to Baroque styles in music. He was schooled in the Renaissance tradition and wrote well in the Palestrina idiom. His books of motets and madrigals, however, paved the way for the coming of the Baroque style and homophonic music.

Monteverdi held two important positions during his lifetime. One was in the court of the Duke of Mantua. Then in 1613 he was appointed choirmaster of St. Mark's in Venice, a post he held until his death 30 years later. Not only did he compose many religious works and madrigals, he was also the most successful opera composer of his time. More than anyone else he promoted the ideals of opera and transformed it into a successful public medium. His contributions to opera include a reduction in the amount of recitative, which had predominated in early opera, and the addition of more beautiful melodic lines. He also infused his operas with more musical expression and encouraged instrumentalists to try effects such as tremolo (an agitated, back-and-forth movement of the bow on the string) to create more drama.

Heinrich Schütz

The life of Heinrich Schütz (1585–1672) spanned the transition from the Renaissance to the Baroque. His music seems to combine the cultures of Germany and Italy. His early life was spent in the service of a prince at Hesse-Cassel. Later he went to study in Venice with Giovanni Gabrieli. He adopted from him the idea of using two choirs in contrast to each other. Schütz had an interest in drama and became the first German composer to write an opera. His best works are church music. He composed several cantatas and Passions, a number of which are still performed today.

Jean-Baptiste Lully

Jean-Baptiste Lully lived from 1632 until 1687. He was a dominating and sometimes exasperating personality. Though Italian by birth, he made his way into the court of the French kings by wit and luck. There he changed his name from Italian to the French version by which he has been known throughout history. Lully was a supreme entertainer in what was then the most sumptuous court in Europe. He staged dance spectaculars that were the favorites of the king of France. His major musical contribution was the development of the French overture, an instrumental form in which the three sections are arranged in a slow-fast-slow pattern. The story of Lully's death is apparently true. To keep the performers together, he would beat time by pounding a stick on the floor. One day he happened to hit his toe with the stick, his foot became infected, and he died.

Henry Purcell

Henry Purcell lived from 1659 to 1695 and holds a special place in the hearts of the English people. He was the foremost composer of his time, and much of his music is still heard today. His brief career as a composer began in the court of Charles II and extended through the rather turbulent reign of James II into the period of William and Mary. Purcell was a successful composer in all forms, including opera, anthems, and instrumental music.

Georg Phillipp Telemann

Telemann was born in 1685 and lived until 1767. He was the most famous composer of the first half of the eighteenth century. Most of his life was spent around Hamburg. He left behind an enormous amount of music—40 operas, 44 Passions, 12 Lutheran services, and well over 3,000 works of other types. He was adept at composing instrumental music, including a number of well-known flute works.

Baroque Composers Presented Earlier

Johann Sebastian Bach, page 116
George Frideric Handel, page 66
Antonio Vivaldi, page 93

18

Classicism and Classical Music

By the time of Bach's death in 1750, the elements of Baroque style in art and music had largely fallen into disuse. In fact, Bach's own sons thought of their father as an out-of-date old man—not an unusual attitude of sons toward their fathers. The world *was* changing. The intensity of religious feeling and the domination of the churches were passing. Gone was the love of the dramatic and grandiose. A new age had arrived—one that would see significant changes in the style of art and music.

The Rococo Subperiod

As with all stylistic periods in music, the Classical period didn't have a clearly marked beginning. Evidence of the gradual departure from the heavy, complex Baroque style was the *Rococo* or *galant style*, which began early in the eighteenth century in the courts of Europe, especially France. It was the art of the nobility, of the lavish courts of Versailles and similar places. Like the aristocracy they served, Rococo music and art were light, elegant, and frivolous. In painting the Rococo was represented by Fragonard, Watteau, and Boucher. Their subject matter was often amoral love, and their pictures were laced with figures of cupids and thinly clad nymphs. Boucher's *Allegory of Music* (opposite) is typical. Rococo furniture and clothing were highly decorated; the lace cuff and the powdered wig were in vogue. Elegant manners were cultivated.

François Couperin (1668–1733) is probably most representative of Rococo composers. He wrote a large amount of music, mostly suites, for the clavecin, the French version of the harpsichord. The titles of some of his pieces include "The Prude," "Tender Nanette," and "The Seductress." Bach later used some of Couperin's music as models when he wrote his *French* and *English Suites*. Couperin's music is highly em-

Allegory of Music
(1764) by François
Boucher. (Samuel H. Kress
Collection, National
Gallery of Art.)

bellished, with many ornaments added to the happy, short melodies.

Another Rococo composer was Jean Phillippe Rameau (1683–1764). He is as much remembered for his writings on music theory as for the music he composed. Some of Bach's sons also contributed to the Rococo style. Carl Phillip Emanuel Bach (1714–1788) was the best known. Domenico Scarlatti (1685–1757), who was mentioned in Chapter 12, and Giovanni Battista Pergolesi (1710–1736) also wrote Rococo works.

Although music and art in the Rococo style were not profound, they served as a pleasant diversion for the aristocracy during much of the eighteenth century. More important, the Rococo represented a break away from the complex counterpoint of the Baroque, and it ushered in a new type of music.

The Classical Attitude

The words *classic* and *classical* have several meanings. They can describe something of high quality that has achieved a degree of permanence, such as a novel that has become "an American classic." They can indicate that something conforms in every way to the standard. The terms are often used to distinguish music of the nonpopular type from the popular. But designating music as "popular" and "classical" is an overworked and inaccurate way of classifying it.

What does the word mean to a student of the fine arts? In the arts and literature, *classical* refers to the works of the ancient Greeks and Romans. At a university the Department of Classical Studies explores the writings, languages, and other cultural contributions of ancient Athens and Rome.

A return to the style of ancient Greece and Rome presents the musician with an impossible task. No one knows how Greek and Roman music sounded because recordings were 2,000 years in the future, and no systems of early notation remain today. For these reasons, the word *classical* when used in music means an attempt to capture the ancient Greek attitude or outlook toward works of art.

In music the classical outlook was predominant from about 1750 to 1825, and these years are called the Classical period. They are also known as the Age of Reason or the Age of Enlightenment. The thinkers of that time believed that truth can be realized only by the process of reason, so there was an emphasis on intellectual activity and learning. They also believed that the universe is a machine governed by inflexible laws that people cannot override. So whatever is true is true throughout the world; it is universal. In addition, they considered emotions an unworthy guide to truth and thought that rational intellect should control behavior. Classical thinkers were not impressed by the unknown because they believed that in time they would come to know it through thought and study. They rejected the mysticism of the Middle Ages because they felt that it had stifled the natural capacities of mankind. Reason, not faith, was to be the new beacon.

Look at a nickel. Thomas Jefferson is on one side, and Monticello, his home, is on the other. Jefferson designed Monticello himself. Notice that it has pillars and a dome; Jefferson adapted his design from Greek and Roman architecture. In his intellectual curiosity and delight in reasoning, Jefferson personifies the Classical man. He was gifted in the arts, appreciated order, and sought truth through logic.

Another man of the Enlightenment was François Arouet (1694–1778), who called himself Voltaire. His brilliance, energy, passion for justice, wit, and hatred of superstition and intolerance made him a feared and respected thinker. Yet Voltaire personified the inconsistencies of the age. His writings shook the established government and religion, and his diatribes led to a year in prison; but several of his most searing writings were published anonymously, and when their authorship was attrib-

uted to him he violently denied them. He reflected the spirit of his age by demonstrating a general optimism about humanity; but this view did not keep him from believing in rule by the elite. Again and again he campaigned against the Church, proclaiming *"Ecrasez l'infame"* ("Crush the infamous thing"); but he also believed in God and wanted "a wise and simple cult with one God." One of his books is even dedicated to Pope Benedict XIV. Voltaire lived comfortably and was a shrewd businessman. "This profane time," he wrote, "is just right for my ways. I love luxury, even a soft life, all the pleasures, the arts and their variety, cleanliness, taste, and ornaments."

David's painting *The Oath of the Horatii* (Color Plate 4) illustrates the formal, restrained qualities of the classical attitude. The three sons of Horatius are swearing to their father that they will come home either with their shields or upon them. Notice how frozen the figures are, like characters in pieces of sculpture. Notice also the symmetry and the balance of design—the staged and planned appearance, the focus of interest (the swords) in the center, the group of figures to the left of Horatius (his sons) and the right (the weeping women). The composition of the painting causes one line to lead to another in a balanced way—the spear on the far left with the legs of the sons, the lines of the two women on the far right, and so on.

Patronage

Although it was beginning to wane, patronage was still a part of the Classical era. Briefly, the patronage system was one in which a composer accepted exclusive employment under the auspices of a patron. Patrons were from either the aristocracy or the Church. The more frivolous taste of the aristocracy gave impetus to the movement away from the heaviness of Baroque style toward the more fanciful style of the Classical period.

When a composer found a good patron, he was assured a comfortable life and a cultured audience for his compositions. The writing of new works was expected. At its best, patronage was a good incubator for creative talent.

There were liabilities, however. Most serious among them was that the composer had to please the patron, or else perhaps end up helping in the stables or looking for a new patron. The result was much trivial music written according to standard formulas. Too, the patronage system regarded the composer not as a unique creative artist but as the source of a product for the privileged classes to exploit and enjoy. Since the relationship between a composer and his work was taken lightly, it was common practice for composers to borrow themes and ideas from one another. In fact, plagiarism was understood to be a form of flattery and commendation. Legal niceties such as copyrights and royalties were unheard of. Not until the arrival of the Romantic philosphy of the nineteenth century did composers feel compelled to create in a way that was uniquely individual.

Music of the Classical Period

It is hard to realize that Mozart and Haydn lived only two generations later than Handel and Bach. Their music is so different. What were the changes that occurred from Bach's generation to Mozart's?

One Baroque feature that was abandoned was the continuo and its figured bass. Classical composers wrote out every note, with the exception of cadenzas. Also dropped was the idea that a single mood or feeling should prevail throughout a movement. Classical composers wanted to achieve a difference between themes.

Homophony. The Classical period saw the balance shift more heavily in favor of homophonic music. Some counterpoint is still heard in Classical music, of course, but it is more as contrast with the prevailing homophonic texture than as an equally prominent style. Symphonies, rondos, and sonatas have themes—predominant melodies that are best shown off when treated singly rather than in combination with other melodies, as in polyphony.

Instrumental music. The balance shifted somewhat more to instrumental music during the Classical era, but vocal music was still impor-

---

Classical Period, 1750–1825

Historical Events
1750   Factory system begins
            American and French revolutions

1800   Napoleon becomes dictator

Prominent Composers
Mozart, Haydn, Gluck, J. C. Bach, C. P. E. Bach

New Large Forms
Symphony, solo concerto, sonata, string quartet

New Small Forms
Sonata form, rondo, theme and variation, minuet and trio, scherzo

Prominent Musical Characteristics
Piano replaces harpsichord; distinction be-

tween orchestral and chamber music; gradual crescendo-decrescendo; cadenza; clearly defined formal schemes; music largely homophonic; melodies often built out of short melodic fragments

Predominant Musical Effects
Balanced, neat, polished, planned, in good taste.

Visual Arts
David, Ingres

Literature
Goldsmith, Fielding, Burns, Goethe, Schiller

Philosophy
Hume, Rousseau, Kant

tant. Mozart, for example, earned most of his meager income from composing operas, not symphonies.

Absolute music. The main output of the Classical period consisted of abstract or *absolute music*—music with no nonmusical associations. Absolute music must stand or fall on its ability to be interesting in and of itself. Much of the instrumental music of the time is known only by number or by key: Symphony No. 40 in G Minor. In some cases, publishers added titles because they are easy to remember. They may or may not have much to do with the content of the music. Haydn's *Sunrise* Quartet was so named because the first edition carried a design that looked like the sun on the front of the music.

Dynamic changes. To make their music more interesting, composers in the Classical period developed the crescendo and decrescendo. Musical performance during the Baroque probably included some gradual changes in dynamic level, in addition to the abrupt changes of terraced dynamics. Performers probably added some dynamic changes that were not written out in the music. But during the Classical period the gradual change of dynamic level was notated and carefully rehearsed.

Key arrangements. Classical composers were also conscious of keys. Most of the forms mentioned earlier—sonata form, minuet and trio, and others—call for a pattern of keys as well as a pattern of themes. The composer's careful attention to key may have had an effect on the eighteenth-century listener; it is hard to say how people heard things almost 200 years ago. Today we are accustomed to music that modulates frequently or has no key at all, so the impact of key change in Classical music is reduced for us.

Melodic style. Many Baroque melodies are broad and overarching, but Classical melodies often seem to be made up of short fragments strung together. The Classical type of melody helped produce clear formal designs. The melody composed of short musical ideas is especially suitable for development—an important feature of sonata form.

Musical Performance

Symphony orchestra. The most important development of the time was the orchestra. Prior to the Classical period there was no clear-cut distinction in music for large and small groups. The music was much the same, and the composer often did not specify what instruments should play the work. But Classical composers realized that music can be composed to exploit the advantages of either a small or a large group. Containing 30 to 40 players, the Classical orchestra was small by today's standard. Its backbone was strings, and the rest of the orchestra consisted of one or two flutes, two oboes, two bassoons, two French horns, two trumpets, and timpani. Clarinets were added before the Classical period ended. This orchestra was not intended for the concert hall. Rather, it played in large rooms, such as in the Schönbrun Palace in Vienna, before private audiences. And the few concerts that were held took place in theaters, not in large halls. There were no permanent orchestras such as the London Philharmonic; those would be organized in the next century.

Chamber groups. Just as the symphony orchestra became somewhat standardized, so did several chamber-music combinations. The most important types of chamber groups were the string quartet and the sonata combination of piano and another instrument.

New Large Forms

Sonata. The sonata became somewhat standardized in the Classical period. Usually it is a work in three or four movements for piano plus another instrument or just for piano alone. The first movement (often the longest) is moderately fast and employs sonata form. The second is melodious and generally utilizes a theme-and-variation form or an *A B A* scheme. The final movement is a lively rondo, or sometimes a theme-and-variation or sonata form. If four movements are used, the third is a dance-like movement. Two sonatas have been discussed earlier in this book: Beethoven's *Pathétique* Sonata, which is for solo piano, and Franck's Violin Sonata.

Trios, quartets, quintets. Many of the chamber-music works of the Classical period adhere to the same forms and follow the same pattern of movements as the sonata. Haydn's Op. 76 No. 3 quartet discussed in Chapter 11 is a good example of this type of ensemble.

Solo concerto. In a sense the solo concerto, which in the Classical period displaced the concerto grosso, is a sonata for solo instrument and orchestra. There are some differences, however. The concerto has two expositions in sonata form, one for the orchestra and another featuring the solo instrument. Then there is the element of virtuosity in the soloist's part. The solo music is more difficult and showy than that given the orchestra. The contrast of the concerto grosso is still there, but it now includes a contrast in the technical proficiency demanded as well as a contrast in the size of sound. In all these characteristics Mozart's Horn Concerto is typical.

Symphony. The symphony was a most significant contribution of the Classical period. This sonata for full orchestra contains four movements; a minuet or scherzo is generally inserted after the second movement. As are most instrumental pieces of the period, symphonies are known by number, and the key is traditionally given along with the title. Chapter 9 presented two examples of Classical symphonies: Mozart's Symphony No. 40 and Beethoven's monumental Symphony No. 5. The "synthesis" example in this book for the Classical period is Haydn's Symphony No. 101 in D Major. It will be presented shortly.

New Musical Forms

The Classical period probably surpassed all others in its promotion of new formal schemes, which is not surprising in view of the interest in rational thought that characterized the time. It would be inaccurate to say that there were no forms prior to the Classical period; there certainly were. But the Classical period introduced a number of new designs and clarified and standardized other forms.

The most important forms are:

Sonata form. The sonata plan presents two contrasting themes in different keys, provides for the developing of those themes, and then presents the themes again. Sonata form is found in the first movement of almost all instrumental works containing more than one movement. It appears in other movements as well. Mozart's Fortieth Symphony has three movements in sonata form.

Rondo. The basic idea of rondo is a theme that recurs, with contrasting material sandwiched between appearances. The idea dates back to medieval times. Composers of the Classical period refined it and placed it as the closing form in multimovement works. The last movement of Mozart's Horn Concerto is a good example of a rondo, as is the last movement of Beethoven's *Pathétique* Sonata.

Theme and variation. Writing a set of variations on a theme was not a new idea, but Classical composers gave it more attention than it had received earlier. The theme-and-variation format is sometimes found as a second movement, and often it is the basis for an entire piece. The second movement of Haydn's Op. 76 No. 3 quartet is a typical adaptation of this principle in a chamber work. The second movement of Beethoven's Symphony No. 5 is a more complex example.

Minuet and trio. The minuet was not a new musical form during the Classical period, but

Haydn and Mozart made it more sophisticated and more appropriate for inclusion in a symphony. The movement as a large three-part form is found in Mozart's Symphony No. 40 and Haydn's Symphony No. 101 (which has a second trio, giving it five parts).

Scherzo. The scherzo is a contribution of Beethoven. He retained the pattern of the minuet but accelerated the tempo, added accents, and in other ways made it more rollicking. His Fifth Symphony contains a scherzo as its third movement.

Classical Vocal Music

The chief vehicle for vocal music activity in the Classical period was opera. Indeed, opera was the most important musical entertainment of the time. Classical operas contain clearly delineated choruses, arias, and recitatives. The singer's part is most important, but the orchestra has some interesting music of its own. Mozart's *Don Giovanni*, discussed in Chapter 13, is typical in its Classical outlook and style.

Because the center of music making had moved from Protestant north Germany to Catholic Bavaria and Austria, Classical composers wrote primarily for Catholic services. Mozart, Haydn, and Beethoven produced church music such as Masses, vespers, and Requiems in the best conservative tradition of the Classical period. Their sacred music represents a rational approach to the faith of the time.

Haydn's Symphony No. 101 ("The Clock")

Haydn's Symphony No. 101 (nicknamed "The Clock") is a good example of music of the Clas-

Listening Guide

Haydn: Symphony No. 101 in D Major ("The Clock"), Fourth Movement   *Record 4,B*

Rondo Form

0:00   First part of main theme (*A*) played by violins.

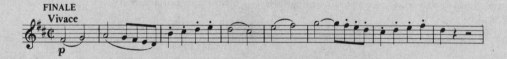

0:06   First part of *A* theme repeated.

0:13   Second part of main theme, followed by a return of the first part of *A* theme.

0:31   Repeat of second part of *A* theme, followed by the first part.

0:48   Transition passage composed of rapidly moving notes.

1:17   *B* theme, which is rather similar to first part of *A* theme, but more chromatic; motive from *A* soon heard in lower instruments while violins play rapidly moving notes.

sical era. It certainly represents the Classical outlook in its well-thought-out, tasteful writing. It seems to contain the "variety, cleanliness, taste, and ornaments" that Voltaire said he liked. It is also "happy" music; its sounds seem to bubble along.

The symphony is homophonic music, with only hints of counterpoint, except in the fourth movement, where there is a brief fugal section. It contains gradual dynamic changes and the expected key arrangements. The melodies are made up of short phrases, which is characteristic of the style. And several of the forms developed in the Classical period are used.

First movement. The first movement is in sonata form; it is preceded by an introduction. Many Classical symphonies include an introduction to the first movement, which usually is not related to the remainder of the symphony except by key. The introduction to the "Clock"

Symphony is in D minor, while the symphony is basically in D major.

The first theme is:

The second theme is:

The development section uses mostly the second theme and a fragment from the first theme. The coda is somewhat longer than usual, a pattern that Beethoven would follow more extensively a few years later.

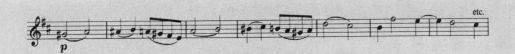

1:53   Return of *A* theme played by full orchestra.

2:24   Contrasting section (C); in minor containing three-note rhythmic motive and other fragments from *A* theme; rapidly moving notes played by violins; sounds somewhat like a development section.

3:11   Return of *A* theme in fuguelike style; much counterpoint.

3:51   Transition section featuring solid chords from three-note motive.

4:06   Coda begins with reappearance of *A* theme, followed by rapidly moving notes for woodwinds and strings.

4:36   Movement concludes with three solid-sounding chords.

Second movement. The name *Clock* probably was the result of the tick-tock pattern heard at the beginning of the movement. It is basically a large three-part form. Of all the movements in the symphony, the second seems to present best the ideal of clear, logical beauty that is a mark of the music and art of that time.

The movement is in *A B A* form. The main theme of the *A* section is shown at the top of the page.

The center section no longer contains the clocklike quality; instead it is louder and has much more "busy" work among the instruments. When the *A* section returns it is about twice as long and complex as it was when it first appeared.

Third movement. The third movement is a minuet and trio with an unusual feature—an extra trio. The effect of this addition is a rondo form consisting of the minuet heard three times with two different contrasting sections.

Fourth movement. The fourth movement is a rondo filled with rapidly moving notes and a little counterpoint. It is presented in a Listening Guide on pages 184–185. The movement exudes energy, clarity, and good cheer, qualities that perhaps best summarize the Classical period.

Classical Composers Presented Earlier

Franz Joseph Haydn, page 99
Wolfgang Amadeus Mozart, page 80

19

The Romantic Outlook and Romantic Music

To most people, the word *romantic* refers to the emotion of love. To scholars, however, romanticism means much more. The word *romantic* comes from *romance*, which originally referred to a medieval poem written in one of the Romance languages and dealing with a heroic person or event. Later the word took on the connotation of something far away and strange or something imaginative and full of wonder. Yes, it also included the idea of romantic love.

Characteristics of Romanticism

Romanticists were fascinated by the unknown and stood in awe of the world. They were impressed by the mystery, not the clarity, of the world and its inhabitants. At times they were almost mystic. Such a quality is revealed in this passage from Wordsworth's "Lines Composed a Few Miles above Tintern Abbey":

> . . . *that blessed mood,*
> *In which the burthen of the mystery,*
> *In which the heavy and the weary weight*
> *Of all this unintelligible world*
> *Is lightened:—that serene and blessed mood,*
> *In which the affections gently lead us on,—*
> *Until, the breath of this corporeal frame*
> *And even the motion of our human blood*
> *Almost suspended, we are laid asleep*
> *In body, and become a living soul:*
> *While with an eye made quiet by the power*
> *Of harmony, and the deep power of joy,*
> *We see into the life of things.*

Romanticists tended to rely on emotion rather than on the intellect that had been central to the Classical outlook. Feelings replaced reason. Truth became what one *felt* to be true, and it was wrong to deny one's feelings. Keats said in one of his letters: "I am certain of nothing but the holiness of the heart's affections, and the truth of the imagination. What the imagination seizes as beauty must be truth." Inevitably, Romanticism became distrustful of reason and science (sometimes called philosophy). To quote Keats again, this time from "Lamia":

> Do not all charms fly
> At the mere touch of cold philosophy?

The Romanticists were intrigued by the long ago and far away. During the Classical period intellectuals had thought of medieval times as the "dark ages"; the Romanticists thought of them as heroic. Literature contains many examples of this attitude, as in Tennyson's *Idylls of the King*, Keats' *Eve of St. Agnes*, Coleridge's *Christabel*, and Scott's *Ivanhoe*. Eugene Delacroix chose Dante's *Inferno*, a writing from early in the fourteenth century, as the subject matter for his painting *The Bark of Dante* (Color Plate 5). It shows the struggling souls of the wicked Florentines trying to escape from Hell by climbing into the boat with Virgil and Dante. Also evident in the painting is the Romantic artist's fondness for the far away and exotic. In music this trait can be found in works such as Rimsky-Korsakov's tone poem *Scheherazade* and Act II of the opera *Parsifal* by Wagner.

Not only were the Romanticists impressed by the unknown forces of the world, they reveled in the struggle against them. Coleridge's ancient mariner was "alone on a wide, wide sea." Delacroix's Florentines struggle helplessly against their fate. In this Romantic painting, the water and clouds swirl in a terrifying way. The twisted, pained bodies are very much involved in the scene. Gone are the even planes and the formal balance that typified Classicism. Dante (in the cloak and hat) stands about two-thirds of the way to the left of the picture. The bodies of the sinners writhe throughout the scene.

The Romanticists resented rules and restraints. They regarded the Classical period as cold and formal, and they were unimpressed by its rational deductions and universal laws. They felt perfectly capable of making their own rules, and they proceeded to do so in their artistic works. They cherished freedom, limitless expression, passion, and the pursuit of the unat-

tainable. After all, what more glorious struggle could there be than the yearning and seeking after the impossible? This search is perhaps best epitomized in the legend of the Holy Grail, which was a favored theme in Romantic literature and operas (particularly Wagner's *Parsifal*).

The Romanticists had a rural orientation instead of the urban outlook of the Classical period. They were attracted by nature because it represented a world unspoiled by people. Sometimes nature was extolled to the point of pantheism—the belief that God and nature are one. The rural interest of the time led to landscape painting and poems on natural phenomena. Beginning with Jean Jacques Rousseau and the Earl of Shaftesbury, and continuing through the American Henry David Thoreau to the present time, a group of philosophers have expounded the idea of natural goodness, in which the "artificialities" of civilization are rejected because they corrupt human beings. Wordsworth summed up the Romanticists' thinking on nature when he wrote, in "The Tables Turned":

> One impulse from a vernal* wood
> May teach you more of man,
> Of moral evil and of good,
> Than all the sages** can.

Because the Romanticists were highly subjective and individualistic, it was almost inevitable that they would become self-centered. Works of art were no longer objective examples of a person's craftsmanship; they were considered instead to be a projection of the person who created them. Romantic artists felt that a bit of their psyche had been given to the world in their poems or preludes. And this personal work was no longer done for a patron. It was now for posterity, for an audience that someday, somewhere would appreciate its true stature. Some Romanticists were nonsocial, if not antisocial. They withdrew into a world of their

---

*spring
**wise men

own, surrounded by a close circle of friends and admirers. And yet the Romantic era saw the establishment of the concert hall with its large audiences, and some Romanticists thoroughly enjoyed the adulation of the public. In any case, the attitude toward musical creativity changed, and with it came the altered position of the musician and composer in society.

Romantic Music

A number of significant changes occurred in music during the nineteenth century. Some of them had a permanent impact on music, while others had a less lasting influence.

Romantic Period, 1825–1900

Historical Events

1820   Louisiana Purchase
        Monroe Doctrine declared
        McCormick invents reaper; Morse telegraph
        Daguerre takes first photographs
        California gold rush
        Darwin writes *Origin of Species*

1850   Civil War in United States
        Germany united under Bismarck
        Edison invents electric light and phonograph
        Roentgen discovers X-rays
        Spanish-American War

Prominent Composers
Beethoven, Schubert, von Weber, Chopin, Liszt, Mendelssohn, Berlioz, Schumann, Franck, Verdi, Brahms, Tchaikovsky, Fauré, Dvořák, Mussorgsky, Borodin, Rimsky-Korsakov, Rachmaninoff, Puccini, Wagner, Grieg, Elgar, R. Strauss, Mahler, Sibelius, Bruckner, Saint-Saens

New Large Forms
Art song, symphonic poem, grand opera and music drama

New Short Forms
Short lyric, instrumental pieces

Prominent Musical Characteristics
Cyclical treatment of themes; theme transfor-

mation; music for virtuoso instrumentalist; largely homophonic; rubato; sudden and dramatic changes of mood and dynamic level; motives; rich harmony with many chromatic alterations; large orchestra; long compositions; new timbres; piano very important

Predominant Musical Effects
Frequent and dramatic changes of mood; large, powerful, rich, luscious quality of sound; highly expressive; often free and unplanned in sound; climaxes of feeling and volume

Visual Arts
Goya, Gericault, Corot, Turner, Delacroix, Millet, Daumier, Manet, Degas, Renoir, Monet, Rodin, Seurat, Cezanne, Van Gogh, Gauguin, Homer

Literature
Coleridge, Wordsworth, Scott, Byron, Austen, Shelley, Keats, Pushkin, Heine, Cooper, Balzac, Hugo, Stendhal, Sand, Lytton, Dickens, Poe, Dumas, Thackeray, Longfellow, Hawthorne, Melville, Stowe, Whitman, Tennyson, Eliot, Tolstoy, Dostoevski, Browning, Twain, Ibsen, Stevenson, Wilde, H. James

Philosophy
Hegel, Mill, Comte, Kierkegaard, Schopenhauer, Marx, Engels, Thoreau, Spencer, T. H. Huxley, Emerson, Haeckel, Nietzsche

Aspects of Performance

Public concerts. One important change was the end of the patronage system and the increasing popularity of the public concert. No longer was music designed to be played in a room for a small audience of rich, well-born people. Now the music had to be louder, so that the sound would project in a large hall. And it catered to the new merchant class that had become significant in society. These changes encouraged a different way of thinking about music.

Virtuoso performers. The demands of the concert hall led to the development of the "personality" performer. People went to hear a certain person play the piano or violin rather than just to hear some music. Often it was the personality of the performer that sold the tickets. He or she was expected to dazzle the audience with skill, and even the performer's appearance contributed to the desired aura. One handsome concert artist of the time enhanced his image by carefully removing his white gloves as he sat down at the piano. These gloves were left on the piano at the conclusion of the program to give the ladies in the audience something to fight over.

The nineteenth century also saw the rise of the conductor and the permanent orchestra. Prior to the Romantic era, a group of musicians had usually been started by the first violinist or by the player seated at the keyboard. In some cases a conductor tapped out a few measures, and the orchestra continued the music by itself. Now the conductor had a more important role to fill. As music became longer and more complex, conducting technique made a greater difference in the quality of the orchestral sound. The conductor's role is to keep the performance together by starting the group precisely, maintaining the tempo, indicating levels of loudness and softness, and giving cues—visual indications that an important passage is to begin at that moment. The conductor also gives the musicians an idea about the interpretation of the music and its style.

Piano. As Chapter 12 pointed out, the nineteenth century was the "Golden Age" of the piano. Both the playing techniques for the instrument and the amount of music written for it expanded greatly. Showy virtuoso works, character pieces, and mighty concertos were composed for the piano by almost all the great composers of the time—Beethoven, Brahms, Chopin, Schumann, Liszt, Mendelssohn, Schubert, and others.

Musical Forms

The character piece. During the Romantic period composers were especially interested in short works containing one predominant mood. These instrumental "character pieces" carry a variety of names: ballade, impromptu, fantasie, étude, prelude, berceuse, scherzo, and nocturne. The *ballade* and *berceuse* are songlike. An *étude* is a piece that illustrates a particular technical problem. Its name is French for study. In the hands of a composer such as Chopin, an étude is far from being a dull exercise, however. It is an attractive melodic study suitable for concert performance. An *impromptu* is supposed to convey the spontaneity its name implies. A *fantasie* is a completely free and imaginative work. Chopin's *Fantasie-Impromptu*, discussed in Chapter 12, contains both of these characteristics. The *scherzos* by Chopin are not the playful works that Beethoven's are. Instead they are longer and more serious. A *nocturne* (meaning night song) usually has a flowing melodic line; Chopin wrote quite a few works under the designation. Other short compositions were derived from dance forms—mazurka, polonaise, and waltz.

Program music. Because of its brevity the short character piece presented no problems of form. But when they wrote longer pieces, Romantic composers were forced to find something to replace the rejected formal schemes of the Classical period. One answer was program music, instrumental music in which the composer specifically intends the sounds to be associated with nonmusical ideas or objects.

The idea of relating nonmusical subjects to music was not new with composers of the nineteenth century. It had been done before, but the Romantic era saw an unprecedented interest in this type of composition. Program music was for Liszt and Berlioz what sonata form had been for Mozart and Haydn. It provided ideas and guidelines for sizable musical compositions. The next chapter is devoted to a more complete discussion of this type of music, which is so closely associated with the Romantic period.

Nationalism. Nationalism, when associated with works of art, refers to a deliberate, conscious attempt to develop a mode of artistic expression that is characteristic of a particular country, region, or ethnic group. Often it involves subject matter that is unique to one country or people, such as a painting of a national event or an opera about a historical character. During the nineteenth century this attempt at native expression reflected a desire to break away from the prevailing German-Austrian style. Bach, Mozart, Beethoven, Schubert, Liszt, Schumann, Brahms, and Wagner had long ruled the musical world. To composers from other areas, it was time for a change. They knew that Russians, French, and Norwegians were as capable of producing good compositions as were Germans, and they set about proving it. Specific examples of nationalistic music are presented in Chapter 21.

Virtuoso music. The rise of virtuoso performers encouraged the writing of technically demanding music for them to perform. Some stunning works were composed for pianists and violinists during the nineteenth century. Many notes were to be played at a dazzling speed over the full range of the instrument. Liszt's *Mephisto Waltz* is an example of virtuoso music.

Art song. The Romantic era witnessed the development of the art song to its highest level. An art song is the musical setting of a poem, with the music specifically designed to enhance and give expression to the words. In Schubert's "Margaret at the Spinning Wheel," which was presented in Chapter 7, the quality of the lines is fitted to the emotions and words of the text. The piano part contributes much to the artistic impact of the art song.

Romantic opera and choral music. Because Romantic composers wrote so many outstanding instrumental works, their success in vocal music is easily overlooked. The art song has already been mentioned. The power and sumptuousness of Romantic music are also evident in Romantic operas. Everything from the tenderness and passion of Puccini's *La Bohème* to the nearly overwhelming sounds and dimensions of Wagner's music dramas is found. The characteristics of the nineteenth century cited at the beginning of this chapter are apparent in operas of that time: a fondness for the exotic and far away; an interest in the long ago (Wagner's primeval German gods); an obsession with mystery (the curse on Wagner's Rhine gold); and a preoccupation with the struggle against fate (in Wagner's *Ring*).

In addition to art songs and operas, some great choral works were written in the Romantic era. Beethoven wrote several religious choral works, and Felix Mendelssohn (1809–1847) composed successful oratorios. Hector Berlioz (1803–1869) wrote a tremendous *Requiem* calling for many tubas, timpani, and a huge chorus. Liszt created some fine choral works, although they are not often heard today. Brahms' *Ein Deutsches Requiem* (*A German Requiem*) is one of the great masterpieces of Western music, and he also composed several other highly successful choral works. Verdi also wrote a *Requiem*, as did Gabriel Fauré (1845–1924).

Musical Characteristics

Homophony. Because nineteenth-century composers were interested in the expressiveness of music, they avoided intricate counterpoint. They generally wrote a flowing melodic line accompanied by rich harmonies. There are instances of counterpoint here and there in Romantic music, and Brahms was skilled in its use, but homophony predominated.

Rich harmonies. Romantic music has a luscious, sensuous quality found in no other style. When compared with earlier styles, its harmonies contain chords with more notes, its pitches are altered to give richer quality, and a greater percentage of its chords seem to move outside the "gravitational pull" of the traditional tonic and dominant. Romantic composers broke away from the strict adherence to key that had been established in the Classical era. Their harmonies are often highly chromatic, resulting in a considerably weakened feeling of key center, as is evident in Wagner's music. But their harmonies are very rich and beautiful. The first movement of Franck's Violin Sonata is a good example of Romantic harmony.

Use of instruments. New instruments were added to the orchestra during the nineteenth century: English horn, bass clarinet, bass trombone, and harp. The size of most sections was increased, and instruments such as the viola were given more prominent parts. The result was a more powerful and colorful sound. Instrumental techniques were more advanced than in the preceding century. Brahms' Second Piano Concerto is a good example of the way Romantic composers drew the maximum of

Listening Guide

Wagner: *Siegfried's Rhine Journey*   *Record 3,B*

Dawn

0:00   Timpani roll played very softly.

0:04   Fate motive played by trombones, soft and slow; followed by cellos playing a melodic line:

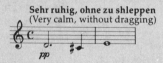

0:42   Siegfried motive played by horns softly; cellos again answer with melodic line at higher pitch than first time:

1:43   Siegfried motive played by French horns more strongly.

1:54   Brünnhilde motive played by clarinet; answered by bass clarinet; music is still soft and slow:

musical passion and brilliance from an instrument.

The increase in the variety of instruments in the orchestra and the desire for a larger, warmer sound caused an increase in the size of the orchestra. The orchestra of 30 or 40 players in Mozart's day grew to 90 to 100 players in the Romantic period.

Length of works. If nineteenth-century composers had a failing, it was a tendency to be long-winded. The length of concertos, symphonies, and other pieces of music tripled in some cases during the hundred years from Mozart to the end of the nineteenth century. Romantic operas are especially long. The high point (or low point, depending on how you look at it) is Wagner's *Ring* cycle of four operas, totaling over 12 hours of music.

Romantic composers were able to develop some magnificent and monumental pieces of music. One of their means for tying together

---

2:21   Violins take up Brünnhilde motive; answered by cellos; music begins to grow in power, and tempo slowly increases.

Parting of Siegfried and Brünnhilde

3:09   Siegfried motive played powerfully by trumpets and woodwinds; portion of Walküre's motive from earlier opera played by trombone.

3:28   Brünnhilde motive returns, played by violins; followed by clarinet and oboe.

3:47   "Desire to travel" motive played by violins:

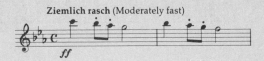

4:11   Music slowly builds, using the travel motive.

4:42   Siegfried motive played more impetuously and loud by trumpets.

5:09   Brünnhilde motive played by violins; followed by French horns as music slowly becomes calmer.

5:55   "Adventure" motive (a transformed version of Siegfried motive) played by solo French horn:

(continued)

6:10   Bass clarinet answers with Brünnhilde motive.

6:25   Motive for Brünnhilde love played by strings:

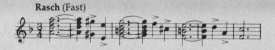

6:42   Motive called "Love's resolve" from earlier opera *Siegfried* is played by strings and woodwinds.

6:56   Adventure motive played quietly by French horn; oboe takes up motive shortly.

Siegfried's Journey to the Rhine

7:16   French horns play a short extension of adventure motive; violins play a decorated version of that motive.

7:37   Orchestra takes up extension of adventure motive; many changes of note by half step are heard.

8:08   Rhine motive played strongly by brasses; later joined by woodwinds and French horns:

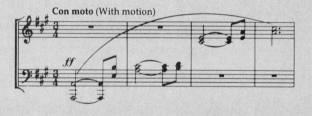

long movements was the use of cyclical writing—the appearance of a theme in more than one movement. Also, Romantic composers wove their compositions in an almost seamless way. Gone are the clear-cut transitions and theme endings that marked the Classical period. Their music seems to roll on in a continuous stream.

Rubato. Rubato (roo-*bah*-toh) is not something that can be seen in the printed score. It exists in the style of performance. The player deviates slightly from the exact execution of the rhythm; a fraction of time is "borrowed" from

one note in order to lengthen another. In fact, the word means robbed in Italian. Rubato gives the performer more opportunity to express feelings.

Undulating dynamics. The Baroque period featured terraced dynamics—abrupt changes from one dynamic level to another. The Romantic period is different in this regard. Instead of level and consistent dynamic planes, Romantic music displays ever-changing nuances of loudness and softness. It reminds one very much of watching a tossing sea. And the extremes at either end of the dynamics spectrum are more pronounced, to exploit the ex-

9:12   Portion of Siegfried motive played rapidly by trombone; later by woodwinds.

9:36   Motive for Rhine maidens and Rhine gold:

10:24   Ring motive is clearly presented; gold motive is passed quietly among the brasses:

11:01   French horns and then trombones play the gold motive.

11:37   Brünnhilde motive and the first portion of Siegfried motive are heard.

12:00   Music closes with full-sounding chords.

pressive potential of softness and loudness. These extremes of dynamics contribute to the great sense of climax that is often achieved in Romantic music.

Expression. The interest in expressing ideas led Romantic composers to write in many clues about the mood of the music. Their notation includes tempo indications and such words as *espressivo* (expressively), *cantabile* (songlike), *dolce* (sweetly), *misterioso* (mysteriously), *maestoso* (majestically), *con fuoco* (with fire), and many more. Also frequent are expressive signs such as accents, sforzandi, and holds or tenuto marks.

Wagner's *Siegfried's Rhine Journey*

The story of Wagner's massive four-opera cycle *Der Ring des Nibelungen* (The Ring of the Nibelung) was briefly described on page 127.

In the Prologue to *Götterdämmerung*, the fourth opera of *The Ring*, the three Fates or Norns (weavers of destiny) are spinning. When their thread breaks, a terrible catastrophe is predicted. The Fates vanish. At this point, a section of the opera called "Siegfried's Rhine Journey" begins. It is often performed as a concert orchestral number without singers. A Listening Guide for *Siegfried's Rhine Journey* begins on page 192.

Hector Berlioz

Hector Berlioz (1803–1869) was born in a small town near Grenoble, France. His father was a well-to-do physician and expected his son to follow in his footsteps. Young Berlioz was even sent off to Paris to go to medical school, but he was much more interested in the musical life of the city, so he decided to give up medicine for music.

While in Paris, he became fascinated with the music of Beethoven and the dramas of Shakespeare. It was while observing one of these dramas in 1827 that he first saw Harriet Smithson and became obsessed with her. Harriet was much too famous an actress to bother with unknown French composers.

In 1830 Berlioz was awarded the coveted Prix de Rome, which gave him an allowance and an opportunity to work in Rome. It was in that year that he turned out his famous *Symphonie fantastique*. When he returned from Rome, after the breakup of an engagement to another woman, a hectic courtship of Harriet Smithson followed. They were finally married, but their marriage turned out to be a stormy one and ended some years later.

Like some other composers of the nineteenth century, Berlioz also wrote reviews and articles. His music achieved success in his lifetime, although some of his compositions have long since been dropped from the standard repertoire. He tried his hand at several operas and wrote a gigantic *Requiem*.

Felix Mendelssohn

Felix Mendelssohn (1809–1847) was born in Germany into a wealthy and cultured family. His grandfather, Moses Mendelssohn, was a famous philosopher and author; the composer's father, Abraham, was a successful banker who was well educated in the arts.

Felix Mendelssohn showed obvious musical talent at an early age and was given every chance to develop it with world travel and the finest education. He was skilled in sports as well as in several of the arts. When he was 17, he wrote the overture to Shakespeare's *Midsummer Night's Dream*, which is regarded as something of a masterpiece even today. (One section is the well-known "Wedding March," often played as the recessional at weddings.)

At the age of 20 Mendelssohn rediscovered Bach's *St. Matthew Passion*, which had been completely neglected since its first performance 100 years before. To promote Bach's forgotten music, Mendelssohn organized a chorus and orchestra and directed them in a public performance of the work.

He himself conducted the first performance of his oratorio *Elijah* in Birmingham, England, in 1846. He had accepted many invitations to visit England and was received with great acclaim each time, especially on this occasion. Mendelssohn died one year later, at the age of 38.

Robert Schumann

Robert Schumann (1810–1856) was born in a small town in Saxony, a part of Germany. His father was a bookseller, and Schumann learned a love of literature at an early age. He undertook the study of law, largely at his mother's urging, but his real interests were piano and literature. Finally he was able to win his parents over to the idea that he should continue in music. He went to study with Friedrich Wieck, one of the leading teachers of his day.

One of the more famous romances of the century occurred when Schumann fell in love with Wieck's daughter Clara. When he first met her, she was a nine-year-old prodigy. She was 16 when Robert realized his love for her. Friedrich Wieck's opposition to the match was extreme. The marriage took place several years later, but only after the couple appealed to the courts against her father. Fortunately, the marriage was a happy one. Clara became the best interpreter and foremost promoter of Robert's music. In 1844 Schumann suffered a severe nervous breakdown. He recovered from it, only to succumb to other illnesses and periods of depression. By 1850 Schumann could neither carry on a public life nor deal with people outside the family. He died at the age of 46.

Schumann's outstanding compositions are for piano, although he did write a number of symphonies, chamber works, and songs.

Camille Saint-Saëns

Camille Saint-Saëns (1835–1921) was a gifted, intelligent man who could converse authoritatively on many subjects other than music. His outlook toward music was more in the Haydn-Mozart Classical tradition than in the Romantic spirit of his time. In this respect he was like Brahms. Unfortunately, in Saint-Saëns' case his attitude led to music that at times seems to lack conviction. He tried little that was unique or innovative.

He did write some interesting works, however. The well-known *Danse Macabre* is one of them. The program that inspired the music is a postmidnight dance of the skeletons and spirits in a graveyard; the event ends with the crow of a rooster. Other quality works are *Introduction and Rondo Capriccioso* for violin, the opera *Samson and Delilah*, and *Carnival of the Animals* for two pianos and orchestra.

Gabriel Fauré

Gabriel Fauré (For-*ay*; 1845–1924) was for many years not fully appreciated outside his native France. Like Franck, he was masterful in his handling of harmony, and his music is subtle and melodious. He wrote many songs and a *Requiem*, which is frequently performed. He also composed for piano, orchestra, and chamber ensembles, especially those including strings.

Anton Bruckner

Anton Bruckner (1824–1896) was born in the small Austrian town of Ansfelden. By nature he was a shy, almost mystical man. He was employed as a church organist, and he did not compose his first major work until he was past 40. A few years later he joined the faculty of the Vienna Conservatory. He wrote Masses, a *Requiem*, and other religious choral music. Like Beethoven, he composed nine symphonies, and all of them are lengthy works. The last was completed just before his death. His body, according to his wishes, is buried under the organ at the monastery of St. Florian, where he had spent much time as a young man.

Gustav Mahler

Gustav Mahler (1860–1911), a pupil of Bruckner, was a successful conductor as well as an excellent composer. He wrote many songs and conceived his instrumental music in a style that is more vocal than instrumental. He followed Beethoven's lead by combining voices and orchestra in several concert works. Mahler believed in the unity of the arts and often combined music, poetry, and philosophical ideas into his compositions. He did not use traditional forms. Instead, his symphonies contain many songlike melodies that are woven together, often contrapuntally, in an intriguing manner. The music sounds so effortless that the listener can easily miss the expertise in his handling of musical ideas.

Jean Sibelius

Jean Sibelius (1865–1957) is noted for his nationalistic compositions, which will be mentioned in the next chapter. His reputation among musicians stems primarily from his symphonies and a violin concerto. He employed vibrant, motivelike themes that seem as sturdy and enduring as the rocks and trees of his native Finland. He treated those themes to extensive development. He was fond of ostinato—those persistent, continuous accompanying figures—and he exploited this device to help build toward climactic moments. He was also a master in writing for the brasses of the orchestra, achieving from them a maximum of brilliance and power.

Sibelius' symphonies are often cyclical. Usually they do not contain traditional forms. The music has a free sound, with many stops and starts and changes of tempo.

Sergei Rachmaninoff

Sergei Rachmaninoff (1873–1943) was famous as a composer and pianist during his lifetime. Like several post-Romantic composers, he tended to be in the shadow of someone else's musical style. In Rachmaninoff's case, it was Tchaikovsky. Rachmaninoff at times equaled his predecessor in the writing of lovely, sentimental melodies, although his composing techniques were perhaps not so imaginative. His best works are for piano; the Second Piano Concerto is the most popular. Like Brahms and Liszt, he drew on a violin caprice by Paganini for his *Rhapsody on a Theme of Paganini*, which was written for piano and orchestra. His solo piano works include two frequently performed preludes, one in C sharp minor and another in G minor.

Romantic Composers Presented Elsewhere

Ludwig van Beethoven, page 81
Johannes Brahms, page 92
Frédéric Chopin, page 117
Antonin Dvořák, page 101
César Franck, page 100
Franz Liszt, page 117
Franz Schubert, page 59
Richard Strauss, page 204
Peter I. Tchaikovsky, page 138
Richard Wagner, page 130

20

Program Music

Program music is instrumental music that the composer associates with some nonmusical idea. The particular associations are often indicated in the title, or in some cases by an explanatory note—the "program." It is the composer who supplies the information about these nonmusical associations. Works that have been named by publishers merely as a means of identification are not really program music. When there is no suggestion of a program, the music is called absolute.

Program music is a special feature of the nineteenth century. It provided composers of that time with a means of organizing a musical work without adhering to the forms that had been so frequently used in the eighteenth century. A nonmusical association provided a stimulus for musical ideas and a "form" of sorts for a musical composition. But the separation between absolute music and program music is not always a clear one. Some program works actually reveal an established form. In other cases music with an absolute title, such as Symphony No. 3, may have been stimulated by nonmusical associations that the composer doesn't care to identify or admit.

Music cannot "tell a story" in and of itself. Only a song with its words can provide a specific message. Music can convey an atmosphere or feeling and can give the listener a general idea. One may hear some massive chords and assume it's the coronation of a king, when in fact the composer had in mind the walking motion of a large animal. The idea of size is there, but a specific association through music alone is impossible. One can make up a story to accompany a program work—or any piece of music. But that story will often bear little resemblance to what the composer had in mind.

Good program music has substance in and of itself and can stand without being associated with a story. Its musical qualities, not its program, determine its success or failure. Sometimes, in fact, programmatic titles are added after the music is completed—certainly a most casual association.

Types of Program Music

Concert overture. An overture to an opera is an instrumental introduction that incorporates programmatic ideas from the story that follows it. A concert overture is similar, but it is not associated with an opera. It is an independent concert piece whose program is self-contained. Several overtures of this type were composed in the nineteenth century. Examples include Mendelssohn's seascape *Hebrides (Fingal's Cave)* and Tchaikovsky's *Festival Overture, "1812."*

Incidental music. Early in the nineteenth century composers were often asked to write music for a drama, not an opera. They would write an overture and five or six other pieces to be performed between acts of the play. Although strictly instrumental music, these works are associated with a particular drama at least by title. Beethoven wrote incidental music, including some of his better known overtures such as *Egmont* and *Coriolan*. Mendelssohn wrote incidental music for Shakespeare's *A Midsummer Night's Dream*. Georges Bizet composed his *L'Arlesienne* for a drama, as did Edvard Grieg for Ibsen's drama *Peer Gynt*.

Tone poem. The most important type of program music is the *tone poem*, also called a *symphonic poem*. The contrasting sections of these long orchestral works are developed along the lines suggested by the nonmusical program being followed. These works are lengthy and complex, almost like symphonies.

Liszt's *Les Préludes*

Les Préludes is undoubtedly Liszt's best known tone poem. It was written first as an overture to a choral work, and it was given a name and program after it had been completed. Liszt chose to associate the work with Alphonse de Lamartine's *Méditations Poétique*. The program that Liszt attached to the score contains this quotation from Lamartine's poem:

> *What is our life but a series of preludes to that unknown song whose first solemn note is tolled by Death? The enchanted dawn of every life is love. But where is the destiny on whose first delicious joys some storm does not break? . . . And what soul thus cruelly bruised, when the tempest rolls away, seeks not to rest its memories in the pleasant calm of pastoral life? Yet man does not long permit himself to taste the kindly quiet that first attracted him to Nature's lap. For when the trumpet sounds he hastens to danger's post, that in the struggle he may once more regain full knowledge of himself and his strength.*

The lines of the poem are pure Romanticism, from the personification of death and its description as "that unknown song" to the exaltation of love and nature, which is also personified.

Les Préludes begins with a three-note germinal idea, one that seems to indicate impending trouble. It is marked with a bracket and X's in the example at the bottom of the page. The full orchestra then takes up the idea and plays a longer melody and accompaniment (top of the next page), both of which expand on the original motive.

The "love" theme that follows also contains the opening motive:

As one would expect, Liszt writes the love music to sound as rich and warm as possible. A second theme is heard in the section depicting love. It too contains the pattern of the motive at the beginning of the measure:

The poem speaks next of a storm and a tempest, so the music suggests upheaval and turbulence. The strings scurry up and down the chromatic scale while the brasses bark out foreboding chords.

The calm of pastoral life is represented in a section embodying some of Liszt's best writing. The motive is now woven into an idyllic theme played by the horn and woodwinds:

A shepherdlike melody is then combined with the theme containing the original motive:

This music evolves into a robust closing section that depicts the final triumph of mankind. Again the motive is incorporated into a theme that suggests a call to battle:

One of the features in *Les Préludes* is Liszt's considerable skill in *theme transformation,* the technique of taking a motive or theme and transforming it into an entirely new melody. The original motive in *Les Préludes* assumed several widely differing characters in the course of the tone poem. Theme transformation should not be confused with theme development or theme and variation, which was discussed in Chapter 16. Variation involves keeping the theme intact to some extent (perhaps only its harmony or rhythm) through a series of musical treatments. Transformation is a freer concept, in which only a few characteristic intervals are preserved, sometimes interspersed with new material.

Theme transformation provides music with some degree of unity, although the listener may not be aware of it. Since tone poems often lack traditional formal structure, the employment of elements of a theme in several guises helps provide a better sense of organization. Composers other than Liszt have exploited this technique; Brahms was a master in its use.

Richard Strauss' *Don Juan*

Strauss wrote *Don Juan* in 1888 when he was 24 years old. The literary work that inspired him was a poem by Nikolaus Lenau. Don Juan is the legendary hero whose life has become a search for one momentary pleasure after another. He jumps from mistress to mistress. In Lenau's version of the story (another version was presented in Mozart's *Don Giovanni* in Chapter 13), Don Juan's escapades are part of his idealistic search for the perfect woman, an explanation that seems hardly credible in light of his conduct. Nevertheless, the harm he has brought to others begins to weigh upon him, and his concern for the pleasure of the moment leaves him increasingly dissatisfied and bored with life. Finally he is challenged to a duel by Don Pedro, the son of a nobleman who Don Juan has killed. Don Juan battles gloriously and has Don Pedro at his mercy. At that moment he realizes that victory is worthless and that defeat would relieve him of the tedium of living. He allows Don Pedro to kill him.

Strauss included only three excerpts from Lenau's poem at the front of the score. Nothing else is indicated about the program, so listeners can fill out the details to suit themselves. This process may in fact make the music more enjoyable. Like all good program music, however, it can stand very well without literary association.

Despite the fact that *Don Juan* is a tone poem, it is in a rather loose sonata form. A simplified score is included in the *Study Guide and Scores* so that this rather complicated work can be comprehended more easily. (The music appears on Record 4,A in the *Record Album*.)

The most important theme, which might be called the Don Juan theme, is a composite of motives that are developed later in the work. The profusion of melodic ideas is in itself a commentary on Don Juan's nature—impatient for adventure, full of vitality and power, lusting for love and life:

Later:

The first amorous episode suggests lighthearted flirtation:

Soon comes the first true love scene. The winds sound a radiant chord, the solo violin plays sweetly, and this lovely theme is heard:

It grows more passionate as the music progresses. The Don Juan theme is heard again as the hero awakens from the oblivion of this love and sets out for new adventures.

His next conquest is less willing. Don Juan pleads with her, and the gasping tones of the flute seem to indicate her halfhearted resistance. She soon weakens, and a second beautiful love theme is heard:

This theme has about it an air of sadness and regret, and there follows the inevitable feeling of boredom. The music reaches a soft, quiet climax, ending with a touch of hopelessness.

Here another Don Juan theme appears, played by the four horns:

Presently Don Juan runs to a carnival (in Lenau's version it is a masked ball). The section juggles a theme of its own with motives from the original Don Juan theme. After a while the music becomes increasingly solemn, reflecting Don Juan's feelings of depression. In this condition he sees the ghosts of his previous mistresses, and their melodies reappear briefly.

Then comes the challenge of the duel. Don Juan responds, and the music grows stronger, reinforced by the second Don Juan theme played again by the horns. The pitch level is three notes higher than it was in its first appearance, and this change adds to the exhilaration of the music. There is a short return of the opening music, which gains in driving force.

Suddenly there is a deathly halt—apparently the moment in which Don Juan decides to give up. The music shifts to minor, and the trumpet jabs out a dissonant note. In shuddering sounds Don Juan's life is ended.

Richard Strauss

Richard Strauss (*Ree*-kard Strouse; 1864–1949) was born of a musical family but was related neither to the Johann Strauss family of waltz fame nor to Oskar Straus, composer of operettas. Richard's father was a horn player in the orchestra at Munich, and his mother was the daughter of a wealthy brewer. His parents' aptitudes may explain his own love of music and good business sense.

From childhood Strauss displayed unusual musical talent. In his early twenties he was already writing his famous tone poems, and he soon established himself as an outstanding musician. In those days he was considered a radical. His works were in the general style of Wagner, who had been dead for five years when Strauss wrote *Don Juan*, his first successful tone poem. Probably it was the colorful quality of his writing, rather than any musical innovations, that earned him his early reputation. His best known works composed before 1900 are tone poems. Six are standard orchestral fare today: *Don Juan, Death and Transfiguration, Till Eulenspiegel's Merry Pranks, Thus Spake Zarathustra, Don Quixote,* and *Ein Heldenleben* (A Hero's Life).

After 1900 Strauss turned to opera. His first successful opera, *Salome* (1906), was a German setting of Oscar Wilde's decadent version of the biblical story. Strauss' next opera, *Elektra*, is based on a version of Sophocles' play. Since the opera dwells on the emotions of hatred and revenge, Strauss seized the opportunity to experiment with bold and innovative harmonic writing. In both *Elektra* and *Salome* the action involved such excesses of blood-letting that the public began to wonder if Strauss could surpass his reputation for producing the macabre. Evidently he couldn't, or he chose not to do so, because for his next opera, *Der Rosenkavalier* (The Knight of the Rose), he switched style completely. The story is humorous, centering on the decadent elegance of the powder-and-wig world of the eighteenth century. The music is beautiful and sensuous.

By the end of the First World War, Strauss' creative career was largely behind him. He continued to live in his villa in the Bavarian Alps and write operas until his death in 1949.

21

Nationalism and Impressionism

Several factors in the nineteenth century encouraged nationalistic movements in music. One was the prevalence of Romanticism, which exalted individual feelings and the inherent goodness of mankind in the natural state. The eighteenth-century intellectual had considered common folk to be untutored and rough; Romanticists idealized them as uncorrupted by civilization. Furthermore, the life of the common people was a source of subject matter that composers and artists had seldom tapped in the past.

There was another reason for the growing tide of nationalistic art. The nineteenth century was a time of rising political nationalism. The countries of Italy and Germany were finally organized. Wars were pathetically frequent, and in such conflicts a nation's efforts involved the citizenry to a degree that was unknown in previous centuries.

To assert their independence from German influence, nationalistic composers often wrote tempo markings and other musical indications in their native language instead of the more internationally accepted Italian. So Debussy wrote *vif* instead of *vivace*, and some Americans even today write *lively* or *fast*. Such manuscript notation does not affect the sound of the music, of course, but it provides some insight into the composer's thinking and the temper of the time.

The Russian Five

Until well into the nineteenth century, Russia had little musical tradition of its own. For entertainment the czars imported French and Italian opera as well as French ballet. Mikhail Glinka (1804–1857) was the first native Russian composer to write an opera on a Russian theme. Today he is generally considered the father of Russian music.

More important to the emergence of Russian music was a group of five composers who lived in the latter half of the Romantic period. Their leader was Mily Balakirev (Bah-*lah*-ke-ref; 1837–1910). He himself was not a talented composer, but his contribution was significant. He persuaded the others—César Cui (1835–1918), Alexander Borodin (*Bor*-oh-deen; 1833–1887), Modest Mussorgsky (1839–1881), and Nikolai Rimsky-Korsakov (1844–1908)—that they need not copy the German style in order to compose great music. He urged them to draw on the musical resources of their native Russia.

Generally the "Five" had little formal training. Balakirev was self-taught, and Cui, an engineer, was not a particularly successful composer. Rimsky-Korsakov was an officer in the navy and he sailed extensively; his travels included a trip to the United States. At the age of 27 he was appointed professor of composition and orchestration at the Conservatory of St. Petersburg. Like Berlioz, he wrote a widely acknowledged treatise on orchestration.

Rimsky-Korsakov represents a phase of Romanticism called *exoticism*. Like many other Romantic composers, he felt drawn by the mystery and splendor of Eastern cultures. For example, his best known work is *Scheherazade*, a tone poem based on the Persian legends in *A Thousand and One Nights*. His "Song of India" from the opera *Sadko*, and "Hymn to the Sun," from the opera *Le Coq d'Or* (The Golden Cockerel), are other familiar works that reveal his interest in the Orient. Rimsky-Korsakov also wrote nationalistic music and worked avidly to advance the cause of Russian music.

Of the "Five" the most original was Mussorgsky. He chose an army career and later became a clerk in the engineering department. He was perhaps the most technically inept of the five composers, but his music best represents the Russian character. His opera *Boris Godunov* (*Goh*-duh-noff) explores the intrigue and tragedy that shaped the reign of Czar Boris. The libretto is derived from a play by Pushkin.

Mussorgsky wrote in other mediums in addition to opera. He was an especially good art-song composer. His tone poem *A Night on Bald Mountain* is descriptive and somewhat eerie. *Pictures at an Exhibition*, originally for solo piano, was orchestrated by Maurice Ravel. It is an exciting work in either form—a musical description of a series of paintings created by Victor Hartmann, an artist friend of Mussorgsky's. The music ranges in mood from the twittering "Ballet of the Chickens in Their Shells" to the massive finale, "The Great Gate of Kiev."

Borodin was a celebrated chemist and an excellent composer. Had he been able to devote more time to composing, his name would be better known than it is today. His Second Symphony is still performed, as are *In the Steppes of Central Asia* and String Quartet No. 2. His greatest work is the opera *Prince Igor*, which was completed after his death by Rimsky-Korsakov and Alexander Glazounov (1865–1936). Excerpts from Borodin's works were once used for most of the music for a Broadway musical.

Borodin's *Polovtzian Dances*

Prince Igor is not so much a drama as it is a series of scenes or tableaux. In Act Two there appears a section called "Polovtzian Dances" (Poh-*loft*-zeon). These dances are available in two versions: One is for orchestra alone; the other, more nearly resembling the original, is for chorus and orchestra. The dances themselves are only distantly related to the story line. After a short introduction a wistful melody is heard in a section called "Dance of the Young Girls." (It is the melody for a popular song called "Stranger in Paradise.")

The haunting quality of this melody is precisely what marks Borodin's music as nationalistic and Russian. It is inconceivable that Liszt or Brahms would have written that melody—it just doesn't sound German. Nor is there anything Italian, Irish, or American about it—it *feels* Russian.

Without pause the music moves to the "Dance of the Men." It features a brilliant clarinet solo, which is soon taken up by other instruments. As the clarinet finishes its solo, the brasses come in strongly with a vigorous theme reminiscent of the music in the slow introduction:

The music has a primitive quality, which is another feature of Russian nationalistic music. To the cultured European musician of that time, this music sounded coarse and crude.

The "General Dance" that comes next is novel, even after a hundred years. The rhythm has a barbaric force that impels the music along. There are pedal tones and chords with their middle notes missing. The contrasting middle section of the dance is named "Dance of the Female Slaves." The three chromatic notes in the melody suggest the enticing movements of the girls as they dance for the Khan.

The "Dance of the Little Boys" is in a brilliant § meter conducted with one beat per measure. Logically, the "Dance of the Little Boys" grows into a repeat of "Dance of the Men." The rapid notes of the boys' dance are combined with a sturdy melody sung by the men (music at the bottom of the page).

All the dances are then repeated and combined. First the young girls' music is heard, then it is enhanced with a flashy line of counterpoint in the violins and flutes. The dances of the boys and men are repeated before a second "General Dance" concludes the work. Even this final number is combined with an earlier dance—the first "Dance of the Men"—with long, sustained notes in the chorus. The music pushes forward to a dazzling conclusion.

Other Nationalistic Music

Hungary-Bohemia. Franz Liszt was affected by the spirit of nationalism. His interest in such music is apparent in 20 *Hungarian Rhapsodies* and several shorter works.

Bohemia, which is today part of Czechoslovakia, produced two nationalistic composers in Antonin Dvořák and Bedřich Smetana (1824–1884). Throughout most of the nineteenth century, Bohemia was part of the Austrian empire. So the style of Dvořák and Smetana does not differ substantially from the prevailing Romantic style of the time. Bohemia was too steeped in the German-Austrian culture to create new styles. But Bohemian nationalism asserted itself in folk melodies and native subject matter. Music from Smetana's opera *The Bartered Bride* and his tone poem *The Moldau* are frequently performed today. Dvořák, whose String Quartet No. 6 is discussed in Chapter 11, also arranged native dances and wrote several operas. His Symphony No. 8 makes skillful and charming use of folklike melodies.

Scandinavia. Edvard Grieg (1843–1907) of Norway was the leading proponent of Scandinavian music. Among his well-known works are the *Peer Gynt Suites.* He also wrote a highly

successful and melodious Piano Concerto, as well as many shorter piano pieces and chamber works.

Finland's Jean Sibelius also exhibited nationalistic tendencies, especially in the early part of his career. One of the themes from his *Finlandia* was made the national anthem of Finland. He also used native themes as the basis for program works such as *The Swan of Tuonela* and *Pohjola's Daughter*.

England. The music of Edward Elgar (1857–1934) enjoys perennial popularity among the English and the musical world at large. His music is not conspicuously different from that of other Romantic composers, nor is it particularly nationalistic, but it is melodious and varied. Elgar is the composer of *Pomp and Circumstance*, the stately march that has become standard fare at graduation exercises. More typical of his writing, and more worthy of attention, is his *"Enigma" Variations* for orchestra. On the score, before each variation, he has inscribed anagrams, initials, and other clues to indicate which family member or friend is being represented in each variation. Guessing the intended identities is the puzzle or "enigma" for which the work is named. This composition would be little more than a clever gimmick if the music were not so listenable and well constructed.

Italy. Nationalism in Italy was evident primarily in its operatic tradition. Italian nationalism in instrumental music did not come to the fore until the twentieth century, with the works of Ottorino Respighi (Res-*peeg*-ee; 1879–1936). His familiar *Pines of Rome* and *Fountains of Rome* are decidedly nationalistic, and his handling of coloristic effects is typically Romantic.

Spain. Nationalism in Spain was evidenced by composers such as Isaac Albéniz (Al-*bay*-neez; 1860–1909), Enrique Granados (1867–1916), and Manuel de Falla (de-*Fy*-ya; 1876–1946), all of whom exploited the rhythm of Spanish dances. Although their careers extended into

the twentieth century, their works are essentially Romantic in character.

Impressionism

The predominant style of French music at the end of the nineteenth century and the beginning of the twentieth was *impressionism*. In one sense it represented French nationalism, because it was a conscious attempt to break away from the influence of German music. French composers also wrote program works based on French stories. But impressionism made more of a mark in the musical world.

Impressionism is an artistic viewpoint. It is based on the belief that experiences in life are largely impressions or sensations rather than detailed observations of artificial experiences. For example, when we enter a room we do not note every imperfection or the placement of each small article. Under normal circumstances we are content to gain a general impression of the room and to disregard the unnecessary details within it.

Impressions are not stationary. A cloud may reveal an interesting and distinctive shape, but within a minute or two it has changed somewhat. People move about, too. They do not normally pose in the manner traditionally required by portrait painters. So impressionistic painters caught people at a particular moment in a casual, unposed situation.

Impressionist painters also experimented boldly in the treatment of light, since lighting conditions markedly affect the visual impression of a scene. Realizing that a view changes as the light conditions change, impressionist artists tried to capture a scene quickly. They would make several rough sketches of a landscape. Perhaps they would make one early in the morning, another at noon, and another at sunset, and then they would finish the scenes in the studio. Their most frequent subjects were landscapes and casual views of people. Claude Monet's *Rouen Cathedral, West Façade, Sunlight* (Color Plate 6) demonstrates the impressionistic style of painting.

Writers and poets worked along similar lines. Some, including Mallarmé and Verlaine,

Plate 5. *The Bark of Dante* by Eugene Delacroix. (Louvre, Paris. Courtesy of Art Reference Bureau, Inc.)

Plate 6. *Rouen Cathedral, West Façade, Sunlight* by Claude Monet.
(Chester Dale Collection, National Galley of Art, Washington, D.C.)

Plate 7. *Snowing* by Marc Chagall. (The St. Louis Art Museum.)

Plate 8. *Three Musicians* by Pablo Picasso. (Collection, The Museum of Modern Art, New York. Mrs. Simon Guggenheim Fund.)

were known as symbolists because they were more interested in mystery and broad truths than in reality. Symbolism appealed to these writers because a symbol hints at a truth without actually stating it. Here again is the characteristic vagueness of impressionism. Lines in a poem were intended to convey an impression through the sounds and rhythms of the words. Definite meaning was avoided. According to Mallarmé, "To name an object is to destroy three-quarters of the pleasure in it."

The impressionistic movement was unusual in the extent to which writers, artists, and musicians were united by common attitudes. Many of them knew and admired one another's work. Perhaps the impressionist view of the time was the common denominator among the arts: The painter wanted to capture a fleeting moment on canvas, the author in the printed and spoken word, and the composer in the transitory world of sound. And so they shared in common the subtle nuances of light and shadow, the vague contours, and the veiled thoughts that mark the impressionist. The compositions of Claude Debussy are the epitome of impressionism in music.

Debussy's "Clair de Lune"

"Clair de Lune" ("Moonlight") is one of Debussy's best known compositions. It is a portion of the *Suite Bergamasque* for piano, but it is usually heard today as a separate piece, often transcribed for instruments other than piano. It is full of impressionistic writing. To help you study it, a simple one-line score of this work is provided on pages 210–211, and it appears on Record 4,B.

First of all, notice that the opening melody consumes the first 14 measures of the piece. Many times the last note of a measure is tied to the first note of the next measure. (In music a *tie*

is a curved line connecting two notes of the same pitch so that they sound as one long note.) The effect is to blur the metrical pattern of the music. In measures 3, 13, and 14, Debussy borrows the pattern of two subdivisions per beat, while during the rest of the piece he has established a pattern of three subdivisions per beat. This alteration also tends to blur the rhythm. Similar effects are evident throughout the piece. At measure 15 the music is marked *tempo rubato*, meaning that the music should be played with a flexible tempo. All of these techniques convey a feeling of rhythmic fluidity that is characteristic of impressionistic music.

The melody is exceedingly simple. Actually, it is nothing but the major scale of the piece: D flat major. To this simple melody Debussy merely adds a few alternating notes, more or less as ornamentation. In any case, the melody is not the kind of solid tune that one might find in a Bach chorale or an operatic aria. It is more delicate and decorative.

One characteristic that a line score does not show well is the general effect of the music. At measure 25 a wiggly line has been placed to the left of each chord. This indicates that the pianist should not strike all the notes simultaneously but rather should roll out the chord, which gives the music a harplike effect. The harmonies, not shown here, add richness to the sound. Then there are frequent doublings and even triplings of various notes, so that the same note is repeated in one or more octaves. The spacing of the chords and melodic notes creates a certain haunting effect that can soon be recognized as characteristic of impressionistic music.

The opening melody returns in measure 51, giving the piece a three-part form. Impressionistic writers, along with other Romantic composers, tended to reject the forms of the Classical era, but there is something so basic about many of the structures that composers found themselves using them whether they favored them or not.

Clair de Lune
(Moonlight) 1890

Claude Debussy

Claude Debussy

(New York Public Library.)

Claude Debussy (Deb-you-*see*; 1862–1918) was born in a small town near Paris, and at the age of eleven he entered the Paris Conservatory. He often revolted against the rules of composition his professors tried to teach him—a trait that lasted throughout his life. When he was 22 he won the Prix de Rome, a coveted award that included a period of study in Rome.

Debussy loved the gaiety and bustle of Paris, and he also valued the company of painters and writers such as Mallarmé, in whose home they often gathered. His early admiration for Wagner faded after a second visit to Bayreuth in 1889, and he developed a strong dislike for German Romantic music and philosophy. He was a writer of articles on music, and he articulated his sentiments well. He regarded sonata form as "a legacy of clumsy, falsely imposed traditions," and he considered thematic development to be a type of dull "musical mathematics." He offered another observation to the French who were tempted to imitate Wagner: "The French forget too easily the qualities of clarity and elegance peculiar to themselves and allow themselves to be influenced by the tedious and ponderous Teuton."

Predictably, Debussy cast his own opera, *Pelléas et Mélisande*, from a completely different mold. Built on a story by Maeterlinck, it is dreamlike and restrained. In one scene with her lover Pelléas, Mélisande unbinds her hair while doves fly about. The text is elusive; nothing is stated clearly. Mélisande's words exemplify the effect: "Neither do I understand each thing that I say, do you see? . . . I do not know what I have said. . . . I do not know what I know. . . . I say no longer what I want to." This opera is not a favorite of the opera-going public, but many critics consider it a masterpiece.

World War I profoundly affected Debussy. For a while it caused him to lose all interest in music. The war was not his only torment, however, for he was slowly dying of cancer. In March 1918, during the bombardment of Paris, he died.

Debussy was a careful workman, and his piano works are held in high regard, perhaps because they reveal a free and sensitive style reminiscent of Chopin. Debussy added much that was his own, however: parallel chord movement (forbidden in conventional harmonic writing), chords with added notes, and new colors. He wanted the sound of his piano works to suggest a "sonorous halo"—an apt description of impressionism. Representative of his piano works are *La Cathédrale Engloutie* (The Sunken Cathedral), *Reflects dans l'Eau* (Reflections in the Water), and several preludes.

His orchestral works, too, are typically impressionistic. There are three nocturnes, each conveying a distinctive mood: *Nuages* (Clouds), *Fêtes* (Festivals), and *Sirènes* (Sirens). In *La Mer* (The Sea), Debussy writes his impressions of the sea as it might be observed on three different occasions. Also frequently performed are *Ibéria* and the perennial favorite *Prélude à l'après-midi d'un Faune* (Prelude to the Afternoon of a Faun).

Maurice Ravel

Because Maurice Ravel (1875–1937) followed Debussy both chronologically and stylistically, he has tended to be in the background despite his many fine compositions. He did have the good fortune to be born into the family of a mining engineer who had once aspired to be a musician himself; so the father encouraged his talented son's musical education. Like Debussy, Ravel studied at the Paris Conservatory. Although he was a composer of some merit, the professors at the conservatory four times denied him the coveted Prix de Rome, an award for which he was highly qualified. The arbitrary nature of these decisions caused a public furor that eventually led to the resignation of the conservatory's director.

A French patriot, Ravel drove an ambulance along the front lines during the First World War. After the war he was recognized as France's leading composer, and he toured the United States in 1928. Eventually his polished post-impressionistic compositions became dated in a world whose tastes had changed. At about the age of 60 he developed a rare disease of the brain and slowly lost his speech and motor coordination. In desperation he agreed to a dangerous operation, from which he never regained consciousness.

One of Ravel's best known orchestral works is *Bolero*, which draws its rhythm and spirit from the Spanish dance of the same name. Other compositions include the Concerto in G Major for Piano and *Concerto for the Left Hand*, as well as works for orchestra: *Daphnis et Chloé*, *La Valse*, *Rapsodie Espagnole* (Spanish Rhapsody), and *Ma Mère l'Oye* (Mother Goose)—a ballet from which he compiled music for a suite.

Originally created for Diaghilev's Ballet Russe, *Daphnis et Chloé* was rewritten by Ravel into two suites. The second of these is an enormously exciting work that presents music from three scenes in the ballet. "Daybreak" offers a musical impression of rippling brooks, bird songs, and shepherd's tunes. "Pantomime" portrays a mythical meeting of a shepherd with Pan and the nymph Syrinx. The invention of a simple musical instrument, the Pan's pipe, is represented by a long flute solo. The final scene of the suite is the "General Dance," which suggests a fiery pagan ritual and features the unusual meter of $\frac{5}{4}$.

22

What's Different About Twentieth-Century Music

Living in the twentieth century, we are so close to the events going on around us that it is hard to see them in perspective. Furthermore, most of us seldom consider how the changes in society affect the creative artist. For these reasons, it is wise to take a closer look at the character of our time and assess the ways in which it is influencing the fine arts.

Modern Society and the Creative Artist

The modern world is increasingly shaped by technology and machines. Just about every civilized human activity is involved in some way with technology. Not only does this have vast economic implications, it affects people's values and thinking as well. The vast array of goods made possible by technology and mass production in an affluent society has encouraged a materialistic attitude—placing primary value on material goods. As someone has said of the average American: "He buys things he doesn't need, with money he doesn't have, to impress people he doesn't like." Whether this is true or not, the description indicates that nonmaterial pursuits such as learning, truth, and beauty usually come out second to a Florida vacation and a shiny sports car.

Twentieth-century society is becoming increasingly urban in its orientation. More and more people live in metropolitan areas, and the urban way of life is being imitated by those living in the country. Nature no longer seems central to existence or to the enjoyment of that existence. Rather, nature is manipulated to achieve other ends, most of which are beneficial to society, as when rivers are dammed to produce electric power and water for irrigation.

Technology has made any place in the world accessible in a few hours by jet, and instant communication via radio and television has been a reality for years. These advances have made human beings think and act in international terms. Except in newly emerging nations, the ardor of nationalism has decreased somewhat. The nations of Europe, which were at war with one another so frequently during the nineteenth century, have now joined into the European Common Market.

Despite the many factors that might be expected to draw the peoples of the world together, international relations have been chaotic in the twentieth century, erupting into two world wars and numerous lesser conflicts. Society has been further shaken by the changes and problems arising from the vast increases in population, the pollution of water and air, the burgeoning and decay of large cities, technology, the new status of women—and the list could be lengthened considerably.

The intellectual climate of the twentieth century differs from that of the nineteenth. Generally, contemporary thought is far more objective and concerned with scientific inquiry. Sometimes, in fact, it is charged that the modern outlook is objective to the point of being cold and calculating, like a machine. Many intellectuals feel that they have outgrown the slushy sentimentality of the Romantic period. They no longer stand in awe of mystery and the unknown. On the contrary, they are exploring the outermost reaches of space and the innermost realms of the mind.

In spite of their material comforts and intellectual achievements, people today seem to be less clear about the meaning of life than were their predecessors; consequently they seem no happier. Many old beliefs have been rejected, but new understandings and beliefs have not appeared. The result is a feeling of confusion, a desire to escape from reality, or a sense of being hopelessly trapped in the tangle of life. Modern drama illustrates these points well. In Jean-Paul Sartre's *No Exit* the three characters are trapped in their private hell, which is largely of their own making. In Samuel Beckett's *Waiting for Godot*, two characters symbolizing mankind wait for Godot, who will take care of their problems. Godot never shows up.

There is a fear that people are becoming dehumanized and depersonalized; people and feelings seem to be lost in the hectic activity of life. This fact has encouraged several counterintellectual movements—faddish interests in oriental philosophies and religions, astrology, and quasi-psychological theories of self-fulfillment, for example.

Coupled with the difficulty of finding meaning in life is the constant change that people see all about them. But change to what, and for what reason? Sometimes change seems to be valued for its own sake. Yet a few of the older values persist. Some nineteenth-century ideas, specifically those of Thoreau (who in turn drew upon the ideas of Jean Jacques Rousseau), have received renewed attention in recent years.

Creative artists are especially sensitive to what they see about them. They often mirror the feelings of the times in which they live. They react to circumstances and give expression to prevailing attitudes. Creative artists do not, of course, all react alike. Some become cynical and discouraged; others withdraw along an escapist route that ignores society. Still others become "commercial," bowing to mass taste in order to get a fair share of society's material comforts.

One of the several trends in twentieth-century art—fantasy—can be seen in Chagall's *Snowing* (Color Plate 7). A number of painters have become concerned with "the inner eye," the introspective look at imagination and feeling. Such a view seems to be an artistic counterpart to Freudian psychology and its interest in dreams. Marc Chagall appears never to lose the memories and dreams of his childhood in a Jewish community in Russia. *Snowing* depicts some of that personal mystery and fantasy.

With advances in transportation and communication, creative artists are usually internationally minded. They know the work of other writers, painters, and composers, and this exchange encourages international styles in architecture, art, and music.

Twentieth-Century Musical Characteristics

Virtually every aspect of music has been altered in the twentieth century, but not by everyone and not in the same way. One characteristic of twentieth-century music is its diversity, its pluralism. (Subsequent chapters look at the more significant types of music this century has brought forth.) There is, however, a sizable carry-over into the twentieth century from the music of preceding centuries. Although there are some composers who have created music that bears little relationship to previous music, most composers have been evolutionaries, not revolutionaries. The twentieth century has retained some of the old, while adding much that is new to music.

Rhythm. The twentieth century has seen a move away from metrical patterns based on the regular recurrence of an accented beat. Composers in this century have preferred freer concepts of rhythm such as the use of mixed meters. The composer shifts the metrical pattern to suit the music rather than making the music conform to a regular meter. For example, the frequent meter changes in Stravinsky's *The Rite of Spring* were pointed out in Chapter 4. The effect, when done with the right type of music, can be quite exhilarating.

Another feature of rhythm in this century is the presence of polyrhythm and polymeter, also discussed in Chapter 4. These words imply the use of more than one rhythmic or metric pattern simultaneously. As you may recall from the discussion of ethnic music (Chapter 15), polyrhythms are frequent in African and Latin American music. Small amounts of polyrhythm can also be found in compositions of Western composers in the nineteenth century, but the twentieth century has exploited these devices as never before in art music. A similar feature of contemporary music is the rhythmic

ostinato—the persistent repetition of a rhythmic pattern. When used properly, the effect of rhythmic ostinato is almost hypnotic.

Rhythm itself has become more prominent in twentieth-century music. Although melody and harmony are certainly significant in this century's music, they are less important than they were in the nineteenth century. Composers have become much more interested in rhythmic effects.

The percussion section is now featured more prominently. In music of previous centuries, timpani rolls and an occasional cymbal crash were heard but not the variety of sounds that characterize more recent music.

Melody. The twentieth century has witnessed a return to the medieval modes that flourished before 1600. Modal scales reappeared in art music early in the century and began to surpass major and minor keys in popular music in the 1960s.

Twentieth-century composers have broken away from the idea of balanced phrase design. In the Baroque and Classical eras phrases seemed to run in multiples of four. Four measures were answered by another four, and these eight measures added up to a logical unit of musical thought. It was all very symmetrical. But with increasing frequency nineteenth-century composers began to favor phrases of irregular length, and this trend continued extensively into the twentieth century. Gone is the idea of statement and answer, the balanced design so basic in music of previous centuries.

Many twentieth-century melodies have moved away from the idea of the song melody—a beautiful, singable series of tones. Instead, melodies have become far more angular and instrumental in concept. Their range is wider, their intervals are greater and more awkward to sing, and some of the patterns must be executed too rapidly to be singable.

Harmony. By the end of the nineteenth century, composers had "stacked" more pitches onto the triad and the seventh chord. Such procedures weaken the feeling of a root or fundamental tone in the chord because the total sound contains the notes of two or more triads:

In the example the ninth chord contains three complete triads: C E G, E G B♭, and G B♭ D. Depending on how the composer treats this chord and how the listener hears it, the sound can be interpreted in several different ways. The logical consequence of an increase in chord size is *polychordal* and *polytonal* music, in which two or more key centers occur simultaneously. The effect is almost always more dissonant, but it can also be quite interesting.

Some twentieth-century composers, beginning with Arnold Schoenberg (see Chapter 25), felt that the tonal system of the eighteenth and nineteenth centuries had been pumped dry of its possibilities. So they discarded it entirely, including the idea of a tonal center, and replaced it with atonal music—music with no feeling of key. Such music still contains harmony, but it is not related to any tonal system.

A third development of twentieth-century harmony is the practice of *pandiatonicism*. Instead of adhering to a particular tonal system, with its implication of a key and particular chords to go with that key, the composer is free to harmonize according to intuitive instincts. Tones appear in a chord merely because the composer likes the particular sound at that point in the music.

A fourth development affecting harmony in the twentieth century is the exploration of different chord structures as an alternative to the "every-other" pattern of thirds that has prevailed from about 1650 until the present. Composers have experimented with chords built in fourths (C F B♭), in fifths (C G D), and in seconds (C D E F). Seldom do composers rely on an unusual chord structure for an entire piece, but they do intersperse the new chords among the more traditional ones based on the every-other pattern.

A fifth influence on contemporary harmony is the return of modes. If two similar chord progressions are played, one major and one modal, the listener hears two different musical effects.

Sixth, composers began more and more to use progressions of chords that differed from what was common in the eighteenth and nineteenth centuries.

Dissonance. The history of music shows a steady trend toward increasing dissonance. It is as though the temperature were creeping up from 0 degrees to 100 degrees on the thermometer. Of course, the amount of dissonance is a relative matter. There is little that is purely dissonant, except perhaps a chord in which every note on the keyboard is sounding, and little that is purely consonant, except possibly the octave. In any case, the twentieth century has moved about as close to complete dissonance as possible. One composer calls for the pianist to take a stick that is 14⅔ inches long and push it down on the keyboard. Obviously all notes under the stick will sound. Another composer asks the performer to push an elbow down on the keyboard. Although most composers do not go to this extreme, it is clear that dissonance is a more important factor in twentieth-century music than it has been in any other century.

Some current dissonances do not create tension, which was their usual purpose in previous centuries, but rather offer a certain color or tonal effect. Whether the dissonant chord is perceived as tension or as a coloristic effect depends on the listener's inclination and the structure of the music.

Counterpoint. After the Baroque period counterpoint was less common than homophony. This situation has changed in the twentieth century. The line-against-line writing of the Renaissance and the Baroque has interested composers again, and today counterpoint and homophony exist as equals. Contemporary counterpoint differs, of course, from that of the sixteenth century. Now the notes and intervals can be as free as any found in lines of melody, so counterpoint is often quite dissonant.

Orchestration. The orchestra reached its maximum size at the beginning of the twentieth century. A few post-Romantic composers wrote gigantic works. (One calls for a thousand performers. Most of them are singers, but the orchestra does include such uncommon instruments as chains and euphoniums.) Stravinsky's *Rite of Spring* requires a large orchestra. Around 1920, however, there was a trend away from the large orchestra and the monumental composition toward a renewed interest in the smaller orchestra and chamber music. Composers, instead of striving for an impressive mass of sound, tried to achieve greater clarity in their writing. Even when a full-sized orchestra is present, many of the players do not play much of the time. Gone are the rich sounds of the nineteenth century. There is new interest in the concerted style that characterized the con-

certo grosso, and new effects are achieved by balancing different timbres and sections of the orchestra.

Timbre. A most significant development in twentieth-century music is the interest musicians have taken in sounds and tonal effects. Every conceivable sound has been milked from conventional instruments and the human voice—shrieks, babbling, teeth-clicking, tongue-clacking, banging, rasping, squeaking, buzzing, and noises of every type. In addition, composers have moved on to unconventional sounds created by synthesizers and recorded on

Twentieth Century

Historical Events

1900	Automobiles begin to appear on roads
	First airplane flight by Wright brothers
	Freud founds psychoanalysis
	World War I
	Einstein writes theory of relativity
	Great Depression in U.S.
	World War II
	Atomic energy harnessed
1950	United Nations founded
	Korean War
	"Sputnik" launched
	Humans walk on moon
1975	Vietnam War ends

Prominent Composers
Stravinsky, Schoenberg, Bartók, Berg, Ives, Copland, Shostakovich, Prokofiev, Britten, Menotti, Vaughan Williams, Hindemith, Poulenc, Milhaud, Villa-Lobos, Webern, Penderecki, Cage

New Forms
Jazz, electronic music, aleatory music, tone row

Prominent Musical Characteristics
Counterpoint again significant; new chord pat-

terns; polytonality; atonality; tone-row technique; polyrhythms; mixed meters; increased dissonance; some return to modes; interest in nonconventional timbres; dissonance often unresolved; chamber music again significant

Predominant Musical Effects
Restrained, balanced, concise; some music primitive-sounding; use of tonal "effects"

Visual Arts
Duchamp, F. L. Wright, Matisse, Kandinsky, Braque, Picasso, Klee, Rivera, Orozco, Rouault, Mondrian, Miró, Chagall, Lipchitz, Moore; Pop art; Op art; chance painting

Literature
Maeterlinck, Zola, Kipling, G. B. Shaw, Masefield, Mann, Lawrence, Frost, Maugham, Lewis, T. S. Eliot, Joyce, Dreiser, Fitzgerald, France, Malraux, Hemingway, O'Neill, A. Huxley, Benét, Faulkner, Sandburg, Stein, Steinbeck, Thomas, Williams, Miller, Orwell, Cummings, Auden

Philosophy
Bergson, Dewey, Pierce, W. James, Spengler, Russell, Santayana, Sartre, Camus

tape. The timbres heard in the twentieth century are more varied than those occurring in any other century.

Cosmopolitanism

Twentieth-century musicians have been influenced by music from every geographical and historical source. Although nationalism is still alive, with evidences of ethnocentrism (the belief in the superiority of one's own culture), composers display a wide-ranging musical interest. Twentieth-century music is pancultural and panhistorical as no other music has been.

Composers also feel free to change styles, as Stravinsky did, and to seek out new directions for their compositions. For example, Karlheinz Stockhausen changed his orientation from highly controlled, intellectual electronic music to a farcical stage work in which the performers do partly what they want to.

In fact, styles in the twentieth century seem to "burn themselves out" much more rapidly than in the past. The throbbing style associated with Primitivism was favored for about a dozen years. It was replaced by Neo-Classicism, which lasted for about 20 years. During these same 30 years works in other styles were also being composed.

The music of this century has undergone enormous changes and has moved in several different directions at the same time. That fact, among many others, makes this a fascinating century.

23

Twentieth-Century Music: The Mainstream

As the preceding chapter pointed out, twentieth-century music is highly diversified. Some of it is new and experimental, deliberately rejecting the influence of other times and places. Some of it is subjective, or what is called *expressionistic*; this type of music is presented in Chapter 24. Some twentieth-century music is cerebral, intellectual, and academic; it is covered in Chapter 25. If the experimental, expressionistic, and intellectual music were somehow to be removed from the body of music composed in this century, probably more than half of all twentieth-century music would still be left. Much of it is a logical evolution of trends observable in the nineteenth century, and some of it utilizes ideas and practices from folk-ethnic music.

It is hard to know what to call this body of "conventional" music. Some writers have coined the word *folkloric* because the music is partly derived from folk or ethnic sources. But folk influences are found in only a portion of this music, so folkloric is not an adequate term. *Traditional* is not an accurate word because most twentieth-century composers broke with nineteenth-century traditions to some extent. *Cosmopolitan* or *eclectic* are not ideal descriptions because many composers did not attempt to integrate a variety of musical styles in their music. *Mainstream* seems to say it best; it refers to music that is neither experimental nor committed to a particular compositional outlook.

One feature of twentieth-century music is its lack of a clearly dominant style. Although the music of the past 80 years is quite pluralistic, these works exhibit enough similarities so that they can be grouped logically in the same chapter.

Bartók's Concerto for Orchestra

No single work can adequately display all the traits of "mainstream" twentieth-century music. Béla Bartók's Concerto for Orchestra is as representative an example as any. It contains most of the twentieth-century features described in Chapter 22: polymeters, disjointed melodies, dissonance, counterpoint, coloristic writing, an interest in timbres, and aspects of folk music and eighteenth-century art music.

Bartók wrote his Concerto for Orchestra in the summer of 1943 for a $1,000 commission from the Boston Symphony Orchestra. "The general mood of the work," he wrote, "represents, apart from the jesting second movement, a gradual transition from the sternness of the first movement and the lugubrious death-song of the third to the life-assertion of the last." The work is called a concerto because single instruments and sections are treated in a concerted manner, as in the Baroque. There is also an element of virtuoso musicianship in the concerto.

First movement. The first movement opens with a spacious and quiet introduction. The theme is based on the interval of a fourth (indicated by brackets):

The phrases of this theme are separated by shimmering chords played by muted strings—an indication of Bartók's interest in tonal effects.

The first theme of the main part of the movement, which moves at a rapid tempo, consists of a syncopated figure that ascends and descends rapidly. The second half is a nearly exact inversion of the first half:

Again the interval of a fourth is prominent. There is a contrasting idea that is somewhat folklike in style. The development section of the movement is highly imitative, and there is a shortened recapitulation. The movement contains many elements of sonata form.

Second movement. This movement is entitled "Games of Pairs" because the wind instruments are paired off at specific pitch intervals: the bassoons in sixths, the oboes in thirds, the clarinets in sevenths, the flutes in fifths, and the muted trumpets in seconds. This is the "jesting" movement that Bartók mentioned in his synopsis. The whole thing seems to be a tease.

After five short sections in which each pair of instruments is featured, there is a chorale for the brass, accompanied by a snare drum with the snares disengaged. Following this there is a restatement with more elaborate instrumentation, giving the movement a large three-part form.

Third movement. This movement is the "lugubrious death-song." It features a long oboe solo. The music is rhapsodic and seems to rise to a peak moment of tragedy.

Listening Guide

Bartók: Concerto for Orchestra, Fifth Movement   *Record 5,B*

Three-Part Form

A

0:00   Introductory theme played forcefully by French horns:

0:05   Tempo becomes very fast and dynamic levels very soft; violins play "perpetual motion" type of theme of continuous fast notes; basses and timpani add interesting rhythmic pattern.

0:34   Fast notes break off; orchestra plays several times a figure with two faster notes and a longer note:

0:46   Fast notes and "perpetual motion" idea begin again; rhythmic interest added by chords played by French horns.

0:57   Pattern with two fast notes and longer note appears again.

1:14   Woodwinds take up "perpetual motion" theme, answered by strings and syncopated chords.

1:53   Bassoon plays theme from opening measures of movement; is followed by other woodwinds, sometimes playing theme in inversion (upside down).

2:04   Tranquil section featuring woodwinds; is based on opening theme.

2:19   Strings answer quietly with notes moving slowly.

B

2:35   Woodwinds begin an ostinato; violins soon begin fast notes, while syncopated rhythmic patterns are heard in low strings.

2:45   Trumpet plays new theme at loud dynamic level:

2:54   Theme played in inversion by another trumpet.

3:02   Theme played by French horn; followed one measure later by trumpet playing theme in inversion; pedal note in low strings changes.

3:10   Trumpet begins developing theme; pedal note changes; music leads to short timpani solo.

3:31   Harp and violins quietly play very high notes as introduction to strings playing a short fugue based on theme; music has an oriental quality.

3:42   Theme played by second violins.

3:53   Theme played by first violins; second violins begin counterpoint.

4:07   Cellos play theme.

4:30   Theme enters quickly in basses, cellos, violas, and violins as woodwinds continue moving notes and then play portion of theme containing repeated notes.

4:38   Same entrance procedure for theme repeated, with theme in inversion.

4:53   Woodwinds play slightly varied version of theme in rapid order—first flute, second flute, first oboe, second oboe, clarinet, French horn.

5:04   Rapid entrances of varied and inverted theme—second bassoon, bass clarinet, first bassoon, clarinets; fragments of theme passed among strings.

5:19   Repeated notes giving "chattering" effect played by strings; lead to timpani solo.

A'

5:28   Strings begin "perpetual motion" idea; soft dynamic level; timpani also has important part; syncopated pattern played by French horn and low strings.

5:45   Loud pairs of chords by orchestra alternated with runs by strings.

5:53   Two fast notes and longer note pattern featured; very loud and complex.

6:18   Tranquil section; slower and softer; violins play melodic line similar to tranquil portion found in *A* portion of movement.

6:38   Transition containing many changes of notes by half step played by woodwinds.

6:53   "Perpetual motion" theme starts very quietly again in strings; opening theme played in imitation by bassoons, bass clarinet; the opening interval and other fragments of theme played by other woodwinds; music builds slowly in loudness and intensity.

7:42   Coda begins as brasses play fugue theme in long notes, similar to chorale; woodwinds and strings play continuous running notes; very loud.

7:59   Strings play portion of opening theme very loudly in repeated pattern; woodwinds continue rapidly moving notes in contrary direction to strings.

8:19   Music slows down and speeds up again over snare drum roll; woodwinds and strings exchange measures of rapidly moving notes.

8:27   Brasses play portion of fugue theme in long notes.

8:36   Closes with kaleidoscopic rush of sound.

Fourth movement. Bartók calls this movement "Interrupted Intermezzo." The melody is folk-like; it is introduced by the oboe and continued by the flute. Notice that the first six complete measures all begin on the same note, A#:

The melody that follows sounds almost like a waltz, but not quite. Its meter changes repeatedly, usually adding or subtracting half a beat.

Fifth movement. The final movement of this monument of twentieth-century music is presented in a Listening Guide on pages 222–223. In the movement Bartók engages in a great deal of contrapuntal writing. He also employs a theme of continuously running notes, much like the "perpetual motion" pieces by Paganini and others.

Latin America

The Brazilian Heitor Villa-Lobos (1887–1959) was encouraged by Milhaud in 1915 while the latter composer was with the embassy. Villa-Lobos was a man of tremendous energy who adopted ideas from many sources. His greatest inspiration was the music of the Brazilian people. Although his 2,000 works are of uneven quality, many are fascinating and unique. His *Bachianas Brasileiras* and *Choros* are filled with rich sound that alternates between being romantic and blatant.

Villa-Lobos composed nine *Bachianas Brasileiras*, in which he tried to combine Bach with Brazilian music. Villa-Lobos wrote: "This is a special kind of musical composition based on an intimate knowledge of J. S. Bach and also on the composer's affinity with the harmonic, contrapuntal, and melodic atmosphere of the folklore of the northern region of Brazil." The "Aria" of *Bachianas Brasileiras No. 5* was composed in 1938. In 1945 a second movement was added.

The "Aria" is for soprano and eight cellos—hardly a typical scoring. The music is not typical either. During much of the work the singer just vocalizes an *ah*. The melody is luscious:

The middle section is somewhat like a Brazilian popular song, with syncopation and frequent changes of tempo. The soloist's line sounds improvised. The text is a poem praising the beauties of nature. When the opening theme returns, the singer hums it.

Carlos Chávez (1899–1978) was Mexico's leading composer. His *Symphonie Indea* is based on genuine Inca music, and his *Toccata for Percussion* is an exciting, rhythmic work.

Alberto Ginastera (Hee-nah-*stair*-ah; 1916–1983) is an Argentinian composer who has achieved fame for his instrumental and vocal works. His music sparkles with Latin American color. Two of his operas are *Bomarzo* and *Don Rodrigo*.

Other Twentieth-Century Music

England. The twentieth century has produced several first-rate English composers. The foremost is Ralph Vaughan Williams (1872–1958). Vaughan Williams helped revive interest in English folk music and contributed to the improvement of music in the Church of England. For vocal texts he drew on the works of England's finest poets. He also incorporated themes from Elizabethan composers into such works as *Fantasia on a Theme by Thomas Tallis*, for double string orchestra. As he grew older—he composed until he was 80—his music became more modern and complex. His Sixth Symphony, an important work, is far different in style from his early folklike compositions such as *Fantasia on "Greensleeves."*

Another outstanding contemporary English composer is a man with the wonderfully appropriate name of Benjamin Britten (1913–1976). His natural musical ability has been compared to Mozart's. Britten began composing at an early age and was remarkably facile at working out music in his mind. He wrote for every medium and for varied levels of musical sophistication. His *The Young Person's Guide to the Orchestra* was presented in Chapter 6. Britten toured the United States frequently and at one time considered living here.

Britten's forte was the composition of vocal works, especially operas. Among his successful operas are *Peter Grimes* (1945), *The Rape of Lucretia* (1946), *Let's Make an Opera* (1948), *Billy Budd* (1951), *The Turn of the Screw* (1954), *Noye's Fludde* (Noah's Flood, 1957), and *A Midsummer Night's Dream* (1960). He also wrote for voices and instruments: *Serenade for Tenor, Horn, and Strings* (1943); *Nocturne*, for tenor and small orchestra (1958); *The Ceremony of Carols*, for boys' voices and harp (1942); and the *War Requiem* (1962).

William Walton (1902–1983) seemed to inherit the great choral tradition of his English predecessors. Perhaps his most famous work is the oratorio *Belshazzar's Feast*, which was presented in Chapter 8. He also composed several film scores, including the music for Sir Laurence Olivier's *Henry V* (1944) and *Hamlet* (1947).

France. Following World War I, France went through a violently anti-Romantic reaction. The informal spokesmen for the new music were a poet, Jean Cocteau, and an eccentric musician, Erik Satie (1866–1925). Satie reacted to past music in his own inimitable way by writing little compositions entitled *Three Pieces in the Shape of a Pear, Three Flabby Preludes for a Dog*, and *Dried Embryos*. He filled his scores with sly directions: "Play like a nightingale with a toothache" and "With astonishment." The purpose of such titles and directions was to ridicule the seriousness with which Romantic and impressionistic composers had approached their craft.

From this stream of irreverent thought came a group of French composers known as "The Six," so named by a critic who likened them to the Russian Five. The most important of these composers were Darius Milhaud (Mee-*yo*; 1892–1974), Arthur Honegger (On-eh-*gair*; 1892–1955), and Francis Poulenc (Poo-*lank*; 1899–1963). These men progressed beyond the Cocteau-Satie phase into mature composers in their own right.

In 1914 Milhaud went to Brazil to serve as secretary to the French ambassador. Latin American music made a lasting impression on him, as did the jazz he heard in the United States. Although hindered by arthritis, he toured extensively. During World War II he fled France for the United States, where he taught for several years at Mills College in California.

Milhaud was a prolific composer. He wrote in every medium. Most of his music is characterized by a French lightness and charm. He was fond of bitonality. Some of his works show the influence of the jazz he heard in Harlem, especially his ballet *La Création du Monde* (The Creation of the World), written in 1923. Its plot is similar to Stravinsky's *The Rite of Spring*. The similarities stop there, however. Milhaud specifies a 17-piece jazz band instead of a huge orchestra.

Honegger was more conservative than Milhaud. While Milhaud was writing his early irreverent works, Honegger was writing the tone poem *Pacific 231*, a description of a steam-powered locomotive. By that time, 1922, tone poems had become strictly passé. Throughout his life he proceeded to write as he wished, without being unduly influenced by changing compositional fashions. His most successful works are of large scope, involving chorus, soloists, and orchestra. *Le Roi David* (King David, 1921) is the best known of these. Later he wrote more purely instrumental numbers, including symphonies and chamber works.

Poulenc's music most nearly expresses the Cocteau-Satie attitude. Most of his works are intended to be charming and pleasant, even gauche in a well-mannered way. He wrote nothing for full orchestra, preferring instead to write songs, vocal works, and some chamber music. He also wrote two operas: *Mamelles de Tirésias* (1947) and *Les Dialogues des Carmélites* (1953). The two operas are entirely different. *Mamelles* is a surrealistic farce in which people change sex, and babies are born in incubators. It also spoofs some well-known composers and old-fashioned music. *Les Dialogues* is serious and devout—the story of a Carmelite nun who chooses death rather than return to the outside world.

Germany. Carl Orff (1895–1982) is best known for the dramatic cantata *Carmina Burana*, which he wrote in 1936. It is based on a famous thirteenth-century collection of student songs and poems that were discovered in an old Bavarian monastery. Orff inserts spoken lines of Latin into the work and makes extensive use of ostinati. The music has a driving rhythm and a primitive feel.

Hebrew music. Ernest Bloch (1880–1959) was international in his musical outlook. He was Jewish, and his music shows the strong influence of that culture. He wrote a number of works, such as the Hebrew rhapsody *Schelomo* (Solomon) for cello and orchestra, *Baal Shem* for violin, and *Avodath Hakodesh* (Sacred Service) for baritone, chorus, and orchestra. Born in Geneva, Bloch lived in Switzerland and France before settling in the United States.

Italy. Ottorino Respighi (1879–1936) wrote in the romantic tradition and is one of the few Italian composers to be known for his symphonic music rather than his operas. His most famous works are three nationalistic symphonic poems: the *Fountains of Rome*, the *Pines of Rome*, and *Roman Festivals*. *Fountains* recalls historic sites, *Pines* is impressions of nature, and *Festivals* describes various moods of the Roman people. *Pines* includes the song of a nightingale played from a recording.

Central Europe. Zoltán Kodály (Ko-*die*-ee; 1882–1967) was a Hungarian composer, a collaborator and friend of Béla Bartók. Both men spent years collecting and editing Hungarian folk music. Kodály was not an experimental composer but rather chose to update idioms that would be understandable and appreciated by the people. At times his style is strongly romantic. He is well known among music teachers in America for his contributions to teaching children to sing accurately and listen carefully.

Leoš Janáček (*Ya*-na-check; 1854–1928) is a Czechoslovakian composer who has been compared to the nationalistic Russian Mussorgsky because of his rather untrained, rough-hewn style. He never lost his love of folk music and its style. Many scholars consider him an underrated composer, and his music is much better known in Europe than in America. His most famous work is an opera, *Jenufa*. He also composed a *Slavonic Mass, Sinfonietta* (for orchestra, with heavy brass scoring), and a number of chamber works.

Russia

Since the revolution in 1917, the philosophy of Social Realism has dominated in Russia. It demands that composers write music that is useful and understandable to the general public, so composers in communist countries are required to be acutely aware of the musical traditions of the people. *Avant garde* compositions are frowned upon by the government because of its desire to prevent cultural elitism.

One of the most important Russian composers of this century, Dimitri Shostakovich, is discussed in Chapter 9. Another important composer is Sergei Prokofiev (Pro-*ko*-fee-eff; 1891–1953). His Second Violin Concerto serves as the concluding work in this discussion of mainstream twentieth-century music.

Prokofiev's Second Violin Concerto

Prokofiev composed his Second Violin Concerto in 1935 for the French violinist Soëtans. The work, like much of Prokofiev's music, seems to be a mixture of nineteenth-century lyricism and twentieth-century dissonance and hardness. The result is some truly beautiful and interesting music.

First movement.   The first movement is in traditional sonata form, except without the double exposition. A Listening Guide for the movement appears on pages 228–229.

Second movement.   The slow movement is testimony to the romantic side of Prokofiev's writing. As the strings delicately pluck out accompanying chords, the solo violin plays this expressive melody:

Later a second theme appears; it contrasts with the earlier lyric melody. The first theme, somewhat varied, returns to close out the movement.

Third movement.   In contrast to the second movement, the third is aggressive, rhythmic, and dissonant, thereby showing the other side of Prokofiev's musical personality. The movement has several themes; the main one is:

Although the movement contains some moments of lyrical melody, the overall quality is one of brashness.

Listening Guide

Prokofiev: Violin Concerto No. 2, First Movement   *Record 5,B*

Sonata Form

Exposition

0:00   First theme, outlining minor triad, played softly by solo violin:

0:24   First theme in violas and cellos; free material in solo violin.

0:46   First theme in imitation between low strings and solo violin, rather soft.

1:11   Transition theme, marchlike, played in little faster by woodwinds; free material for solo violin:

1:40   Descending pairs of chords played somewhat softly by woodwinds, with solo violin playing free material.

2:04   Second theme, in major key, played by solo violin; slower tempo:

2:29   Horn plays part of second theme, followed by solo violin.

2:44   Oboe plays part of second theme in high notes.

3:12   Codetta begins a climax of sound at rapid tempo; music slowly becomes calmer.

3:44   Pause.

Development

3:46   Solo violin and strings outline chords, quietly and slowly, linking exposition and development.

4:13   First theme plucked in low strings; decorated first theme played by solo violin; off-beat chords plucked by upper strings.

4:34   First theme appears in the first note of the pairs of eighth notes played by solo violin; faster tempo:

4:50   First theme plucked by low strings; solo violin plays decorative material in triplets based on the first theme; afterbeats in strings.

5:03   Second theme in long note values played by winds at rather full dynamic level.

5:16   Second theme in long note values played by violins; free material for the solo violin; music is quieter and slower.

6:03   First theme plucked by low strings; afterbeat chords plucked by violins; free material for solo violin.

6:19   First theme fragment passed among woodwinds, with solo violin and low strings playing material based on scales.

6:38   Three consecutive sets of four chords playing in pulsating way.

Recapitulation

6:48   First theme in low strings; soft dynamic level.

7:28   Transition theme in woodwinds; free material in solo violin; faster tempo.

8:13   Second theme played in high notes by solo violin; slower tempo.

8:43   Second theme, with rhythmic changes, played in imitation by solo violin and low strings.

9:14   Coda begins softly at fast tempo, with chords outlined by solo violin; chords in long note values in woodwinds.

9:46   Fragment of first theme in low strings and horn and violin in imitation; rather soft dynamic level.

10:24   Closes quietly with plucked chords by strings and solo violin.

Béla Bartók

(Library of Congress.)

Béla Bartók (1881–1945) was born in a small town in Hungary. His father was director of an agricultural school, and his mother was his first music teacher. After she was widowed, she became a schoolteacher, and they moved frequently. Finally they settled in Pressburg, where Bartók began serious study of piano and composition. In 1899 he enrolled in the Royal Conservatory in Budapest. He became an excellent pianist and gave concerts throughout Europe. During much of his life, piano teaching was Bartók's main source of income.

Bartók first became noted, however, not as a pianist or composer but as a collector of Hungarian folk songs. He made a significant contribution to scholarship in this area.

In 1907 he became a professor of piano at the Royal Conservatory and spent most of the next 30 years in Budapest. He received little recognition until the late 1920s, when his works began to earn attention outside of Hungary.

After the rise of Hitler and the subsequent collaboration of Hungary with Nazi Germany, Bartók felt impelled to leave his homeland. In 1940 he came to the United States. He had to leave most of his worldly goods behind, and his health was failing. He was appointed to a position at Columbia University, primarily to continue his folk-music research. He received a few commissions for compositions. ASCAP (the American Society of Composers, Authors, and Publishers) provided him with medical care, and jazz musician Benny Goodman also aided him. In 1945 he died of leukemia, with his true stature as a composer still not appreciated.

Bartók's early works display an admiration for Richard Strauss and Debussy, but in 1911 he changed to more barbaric, heavily dissonant works. He is best remembered for his six string quartets, *Music for Strings, Percussion, and Celesta*, three piano concertos, and the Concerto for Orchestra. His *Mikrokosmos* is a set of 153 piano pieces in six volumes, arranged so that the music progresses from simple pieces for the beginner to works of awesome difficulty. His later works are more consonant and mellow.

Sergei Prokofiev

Sergei Prokofiev (1891–1953) was born in a village in southern Russia. His mother taught him to play the piano and encouraged him to compose. By the age of nine he had written a three-act opera. After his family moved to Moscow, Prokofiev studied with outstanding teacher-composers, including Rimsky-Korsakov, there and at the Conservatory in St. Petersburg. In his early years his music was more dissonant and the melodies unpredictable; his teacher considered him somewhat of a musical revolutionary. Before the revolution in 1917 he had composed his First Piano Concerto and his well-known *Classical Symphony*.

After the revolution he left his native country and lived in Paris. He continued to compose and give concerts. In 1933 he decided to return to the Soviet Union, where he was greeted warmly by both the public and the government. As he grew older, his music became more mellow. During these years he composed the popular *Peter and the Wolf, Lieutenant Kijé, Alexander Nevsky,* and other works. Following World War II he, along with Shostakovich, was accused of being "formalistic," but he did not allow government pressure to interfere with his work or musical style. By the time he died Prokofiev had composed eight operas, seven ballets, seven symphonies, five piano concertos, two violin concertos, two cello concertos, music for films and chamber groups, ten piano sonatas, and many songs. Prokofiev is one of the giants of twentieth-century music in terms of both quantity and quality of composition.

24

Expressionism and Primitivism

Although dissatisfaction with Romanticism began to appear late in the nineteenth century—in the music of Debussy, for example—the real break came just before World War I. Two somewhat similar courses were taken: *expressionism* and *primitivism*. The two movements largely spent themselves by the end of the first quarter of this century.

Expressionism

The center of expressionism was Vienna, the home of Sigmund Freud—a circumstance that may or may not be related. Vienna was also the home of the painters Wassily Kandinsky (1866–1944), Paul Klee (1879–1940), Oskar Kokoschka (1886–1980) and Franz Marc (1880–1916). These painters distorted images on their canvases and probed into the realm of the subconscious. They depicted hallucinations that defied conventional ideas of beauty in an effort to achieve maximum expression. Their colors are often blatant and unreal, with emphasis on intensity of experience and grotesque subjects. Expressionism takes special interest in the demonic forces hidden within the human personality. *The Cry*, the painting by Edvard Munch on the opposite page, indicates the nature of art during this time. Many paintings are completely abstract, especially those by Kandinsky. Elements of expressionism found their way to America in the writings of Franz Kafka (1883–1924). In a sense, the writers James Joyce, William Faulkner, and Tennessee Williams are descendants of this tradition.

The musical leader of expressionism was Arnold Schoenberg. Beginning with his Op. 11 (*Three Pieces for Piano*), written in 1909, he began composing atonal music—music with no tonal center. To musicians of the time, eliminating the tonal center was almost as traumatic as eliminating gravity from our universe would be to us. It was just that unimaginable. To fill

The Cry *by Munch. (Vaerihg—Art Reference Bureau.)*

the void left by the lack of tonality, Schoenberg concentrated on changes in orchestral color. Instead of changing key center, he altered the timbre.

Schoenberg's one-character opera *Erwartung* is typical of the expressionists' preoccupation with the macabre. The opera portrays the actions and thoughts of a woman who goes at night in search of her lover in the forest. In her overemotional state, her moods range from joy to fear to anguish and hysteria. She can't find

him. Exhausted, she sits down on a bench. She feels something at her foot, and discovers that it is the body of her lover. She lies down beside it and kisses it. Her mood changes as she reviles her dead lover for having been unfaithful to her (Death being the "other woman"). She kicks the body. Later she caresses it again, and as the sun rises, she sings her irrational goodbyes.

In 1912 Schoenberg wrote *Pierrot Lunaire*, a setting of 21 short poems by Albert Giraud. The poems are sophisticated and expressionistic. One verse of the poem "The Sick Moon" is:

You die of unappeasable sorrow,
Of longing, deep within,
You nocturnal, deathly-sick moon,
There on the dark pillow of the sky.

To add to the expression of the music, Schoenberg calls for a singsong vocal style called *sprechstimme*, which is a combination of speaking and singing. Audiences found the work eerie. One critic said, "If this is the music of the future, I pray that my creator may spare me from it."

Closely associated with Schoenberg were Alban Berg and Anton Webern. Although both men moved on in their mature years to individual styles, they followed the expressionistic tendency to some extent. Berg's opera *Wozzeck* (*Vot*-zek) is an important work of the twentieth century. The plot is about a soldier, Wozzeck,

who offers himself to a doctor for medical experiments in an effort to support his mistress and her child. She is unfaithful despite Wozzeck's devotion, and he slits her throat. He throws the knife into a pond, then, afraid that it might be found, he wades into the water after it and drowns.

Primitivism

A second main trend in the early twentieth century was an interest in the art and music of non-Western civilization. African sculpture and masks began to interest the artistic world, as did Gauguin's paintings of Polynesian culture. Although it was written in the nineteenth century, James Fenimore Cooper's phrase "the magnificent savage" didn't catch on until the twentieth century.

The high point of primitivism was probably reached in 1913 with the premiere of Igor Stra-

Listening Guide

Stravinsky: *The Rite of Spring*, Act I   *Record 5,A*

0:00	"Introduction" begins with bassoon solo played in high register; the music is slow and rhythmically free.

0:33	Opening melody returns in bassoon.
0:44	English horn plays a contrasting figure.
1:14	Oboe and clarinet sound melodic figure that descends by half steps; other woodwinds enter as music gradually increases in activity.
2:30	Clarinet plays melodic figure loudly in high range that ascends by wide intervals.
2:49	Muted trumpet plays the clarinet figure in inversion.
3:03	Opening melody played again by the bassoon.

vinsky's ballet *Le Sacre du Printemps* (The Rite of Spring). The music was written for a production conceived by Sergei Diaghilev, impresario of the Ballet Russe. Each year he brought a new and stunning ballet production to Paris. With keen artistic judgment and calculated showmanship, he decided to capitalize on the Parisians' interest in primitive art. He chose to depict prehistoric rites culminating in the sacrifice of a human being—hardly typical of the stories usually associated with classical ballet.

On opening night the ballet and its music literally caused a riot. The audience was split between those who cheered and those who jeered at the new production. Objects were hurled into the orchestra pit and onto the stage. Pandemonium reigned. No one, not even the dancers, could hear the music. The choreographer stood in the wings yelling out the rhythmic pattern so that the dancers could stay together.

How could any serious work, written in good faith, cause such violence among a fashionable audience? Probably no one on that famous evening in 1913 thought about it at the time, but the disagreement involved the purpose of the fine arts. The audience was accustomed to ballets that presented pleasant music amid beautiful scenery. Their main expectation of art, music, or ballet was that it be lovely. In *The Rite of Spring*, the dancers were clothed in dark brown burlap; their gestures were rough and angular. The music seemed brutal to the point of vulgarity. The very basis of artistic belief was being assaulted.

A Listening Guide for *The Rite of Spring* begins below, and the work is included on Record 5,A in the *Record Album*. The music opens with a section labeled "Introduction." The scene is a primitive forest in which strange and eerie sounds are heard, buzzing and bubbling. Most of this section is played by the woodwinds.

3:14   Violins pluck repeated accompanying figure.

3:36   "The Dance of the Adolescents" begins with orchestra playing persistent, driving chords with irregular accents that continue intermittently for the next several minutes.

3:56   Trumpet plays short melodic figure that descends by half steps.

4:24   Bassoon plays simple melody derived from rhythmic pattern.

(continued)

4:56   Persistent rhythm is broken by some held notes in brasses, but the "Dance of the Adolescents" soon starts again.

5:19   French horns sound short melodic figure that is gradually taken up by the other instruments.

5:55   Trumpets play the third short melody heard in the "Dance of the Adolescents"; music grows more active.

6:56   "Dance of Abduction" begins with brasses holding long note that soon gives way to music with rapid tempo and irregular meters.

7:10   French horns sound primitive-sounding figure that is heard often in this dance.

7:55   Passage containing solo notes for timpani is played; other instruments respond to timpani in irregular metrical patterns.

8:21   Following a long trilled note played by the flute, the "Round Dances of Spring" begins tranquilly and slowly with high and low clarinets playing together.

8:47   Mood of music changes with sustained heavy downbeats from the low strings followed by three slow notes played by the violins.

In the "Dance of the Adolescents" that follows, Stravinsky unleashes the potent power of rhythm. The effect resembles the wild beating of savage drums. Much of the music is quite dissonant and the rhythmic patterns irregular. Gone is the underlying regular beat that had prevailed for 300 years.

The "Dance of Abduction" is even wilder. A scampering tune is played by the woodwinds and answered by a horn call. The meter signatures change with much frequency. Polyrhythm—the superimposing of two or more rhythms—is also evident.

"Round Dances of Spring" brings some relief from the frenzy that precedes it. The tempo is slow, and the flutes and other woodwinds

Sostenuto e pesante (Sustained and heavy)

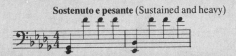

Woodwinds sound free-sounding lines between the sections for the strings; last portion of "Round Dances" becomes dissonant and loud.

11:29 Following a loud, long chord, the music becomes lively with rapidly moving notes interspersed among accented chords.

11:50 Music returns to tranquil melody that opened "Round Dances of Spring."

12:16 "Games of Rival Tribes" begins at fast tempo with several timpani solos.

12:50 Flowing melody is first played by the oboe and clarinet.

Molto allegro

This melody is repeated over and over and alternates with scampering music that began "Games of Rival Tribes."

13:52 New countermelody is introduced in the tuba part; is used for "Entrance of the Sage"; and gradually takes over, with bass drum and cymbals heard clearly.

15:00 "Dance of the Earth" begins very quietly after a pause.

15:21 Music takes off at extremely fast tempo; chords punched out through thick fabric of sound containing many repeated notes.

16:38 Music closes in crescendo of sound.

play a melody that resembles an American Indian tune in its simplicity.

The music becomes energetic again in "Games of Rival Tribes." The idea of competition is expressed by pitting one section of the orchestra against another, each with its own distinctive music. The music is often *bitonal*—being in two keys at the same time.

The "Entrance of the Sage" brings back the main thematic material with a thick orchestration.

Act 1 ends with "Dance of the Earth." It, too, suggests violence and upheaval. The low-pitched instruments play an ostinato line, but, because of the dense quality of the music, the individual lines tend to become lost. The ballet must be seen with this portion of the music if the music is to be fully appreciated.

The second and final act of the ballet depicts the sacrifice of a young maiden to the Chosen One so that the God of Spring may be satisfied. It is similar in style to the first act.

To the listener hearing it for the first time, *The Rite of Spring* may sound like a jumble of random notes. It may even seem that the instrumentalists can play anything they want and no one will know the difference. Such an idea is not correct. Stravinsky carefully planned everything in the score, and he wrote detailed directions for the playing of each part. He even

went so far as to tell the timpani player when to change from hard to soft sticks, the French horn players when to tilt the bells of their instruments in an upward direction, and the cellists when to retune a string so that a chord could be played on open strings to achieve a more raucous effect.

Primitivism appealed to other composers during this time. Béla Bartók wrote *Allegro Barbaro* in 1911, and several of his other works are wild and rhapsodic. Some of Sergei Prokofiev's early works have driving rhythms and blatant melodies. Ernest Bloch's Violin Sonata, written in the 1920s, has a violent character.

Igor Stravinsky

Stravinsky at the age of 84. (Louis Ouzer, Rochester, N.Y.)

Igor Stravinsky was born in 1882. His father was the leading bass at the Imperial Opera in St. Petersburg (Leningrad). The boy studied piano but not intensively, because his parents wanted him to become a lawyer. He studied law at the University of St. Petersburg and simultaneously studied music with Rimsky-Korsakov.

Stravinsky soon became associated with Sergei Diaghilev, manager of the Ballet Russe. Once a year for several years, Diaghilev brought Russian music and ballet to Paris with great financial and artistic success. In 1910, after hearing only one of Stravinsky's compositions, he assigned the 25-year-old composer to write a new ballet. It was *The Firebird*, which is usually heard today in a suite that Stravinsky himself arranged. *The Firebird* was so successful that it earned for the young composer the chance to write a second new ballet, *Petrouchka*, for the next season. Like *The Firebird*, *Petrouchka* is based on a Russian legend. Stravinsky was given another commission, and this time his creation was the startling *The Rite of Spring*.

The year 1913 was the last before World War I, which seriously curtailed artistic activity in Europe. During the war Stravinsky moved to neutral Switzerland. The Revolution in Russia cut off his income, and the ballet company had disbanded. He lived quietly in Switzerland for five years, recovering from a serious illness.

After the armistice, he settled in France. At that time Paris was rich with artists and writers—Picasso, Valéry, Gide—who expressed Neo-Classical sentiments in their works. Stravinsky became a French citizen and traveled widely as a conductor and pianist. In 1931 he came to the United States to lecture at Harvard University. When World War II prevented his return to Europe, he settled in Hollywood, and became an American citizen in 1945. Although none of Stravinsky's later compositions caused riotous premieres, he is considered one of the greatest composers of this century. On his eightieth birthday he was the honored guest of President Kennedy at the White House, and on another occasion he was the subject of a special one-hour program presented on national television. He died in 1971.

Despite superficial changes of style, Stravinsky remained true to his objective conception of music: Since a piece of music is something a composer makes, it is essentially an object rather than a representation of his psyche. Therefore a person's compositions need not be in a consistent personal style. The skill of composition is paramount; the composer's personality is irrelevant.

Alban Berg

Alban Berg, the son of a shopkeeper, was born in 1885 in Vienna. At the age of 14 he took up composing, an interest that kept him occupied when he was confined by asthma and poor health. After graduation from school he took a position as an accountant for the government. He met Schoenberg when he answered Schoenberg's newspaper advertisement for composition students. He was Schoenberg's student for about seven years.

Berg's early compositions were in the Wagnerian, nineteenth-century tradition. But by 1911, the last year he studied with Schoenberg, Berg had changed to atonal, expressionistic works. Most of his instrumental music is for chamber-music groups, except for *Three Orchestral Pieces*. Later works in the tone-row idiom (see Chapter 25) include a *Chamber Concerto* and his esteemed Violin Concerto.

Berg's place in music history is largely the result of his opera *Wozzeck*, which he composed in 1921. The plot, described on page 234, is pure expressionistic theater. The opera is carefully planned in terms of its musical forms. Its three acts each contain five scenes, and each scene uses a form: passacaglia, fugue, suite, sonata, scherzo, and so on.

He died in 1935 of blood poisoning that resulted from a bee sting and a subsequent infection.

25

Intellectualism: Mind over Music

Musical styles seem to move in either of two directions: toward emotional and subjective expression or toward intellectual objectivity. The Baroque period was more emotional than the Renaissance, and it was followed by the objectivity of the Classical period. Then came the most subjective style of all, the Romantic. The inevitable direction of music after Wagner and Debussy was toward more objectivity. And so there evolved an attitude called *Neo-Classicism*. It sought to duplicate the restraint of the Classical period and viewed artistic endeavor in a less passionate light. Neo-Classicism is exemplified in the sensitive painting *The Lovers* by Picasso (page 141). In a number of respects Picasso's *Three Musicians* (Color Plate 8) also represents an intellectual approach to painting.

On this matter Igor Stravinsky's position was straightforward and consistent: "What is important for the clear ordering of the work . . . is that all the . . . elements . . . should be properly subjugated and finally subjected to the rule of law before they intoxicate us." For him, writing a musical composition was like solving a problem; it was a task to be done by applying the intellect. Therefore, music is meant to express nothing except the composer's ability to contrive interesting tonal and rhythmic patterns.

This Neo-Classical position earned Stravinsky a reputation as leader of a trend euphoniously named the "Back-to-Bach" movement. Baroque forms such as the concerto grosso were revived during this time, and there was a renewed emphasis on counterpoint and the linear aspect of music.

Stravinsky's *Symphony of Psalms*

The Neo-Classical, intellectual frame of mind was dominant throughout much of Stravinsky's life. He wrote stage works on such Classical subjects as *Oedipus Rex, Orpheus,* and *Apollon*

Musagete, in addition to Neo-Classical instrumental works. His *Symphony of Psalms* was commissioned by the Boston Symphony Orchestra and completed in 1930. According to his *Autobiography,* Stravinsky went about the assignment very rationally. He decided to write a work of "great contrapuntal development" and chose a choral and instrumental ensemble in which "the two elements should be on an equal footing." He then decided on verses from the Psalms. The orchestra is unique: no violins, violas, or clarinets; twice the number of oboes and flutes, two extra trumpets, and two pianos. A choir of only men and boys is preferred.

First movement. The text for the first movement is taken from Psalm 39, verses 12–13. It is, "Hear my prayer, O Lord, and give ear to my cry." This movement can best be studied while following the Listening Guide that appears on pages 242—243.

Second movement. The text of the second movement is an affirmation of the power of God: "I waited patiently for the Lord: and He inclined to me, and heard my cry." The form of the movement is a double fugue. The opening subject is played by the oboes and is another angular melody:

After the first subject is played by the cellos and basses, the second subject is sung by the choral group. This melody is less angular than the instrumental subject.

The orchestra and chorus develop their subjects. The first four notes of the orchestral subject are repeated in an ostinato manner as the chorus reaches a climax of sound. The movement ends with a sudden hush.

Third movement. The third movement is a song of praise, beginning with the word "Alleluia," followed by "Laudate Dominum" ("Praise ye the Lord"). These words are heard frequently during the movement.

The movement is divided into three clearly defined sections. The first and last are slow, while the middle section is rhythmic and faster. The first section is built on the Alleluia figure sung by the choir (shown in the previous musical example), which is developed later against an ostinato in the orchestra. The second section features rapidly repeated chords in the brasses played against an ostinato in the piano and low strings:

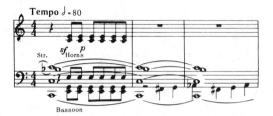

In the third section the original tempo returns, and the chorus sings a melodic figure against a sustained background. A canon is heard, and the music works toward a mighty climax of sound, which subsides with a repetition of the words "Alleluia, Laudate Dominum."

Hindemith's *Kleine Kammermusik für fünf Bläser, Op. 24, No. 2*

Paul Hindemith was a German composer who lived from 1895 to 1963. He was strongly Neo-Classical in his approach to composing. Much of his music sounds like an updated version of the eighteenth-century counterpoint of Bach. Translated, the title of this piece means "Little chamber music for five winds." The work is for woodwind quintet: oboe, flute, clarinet, bassoon, and French horn. It was composed in 1922 and represents Hindemith at his exuberant best. Like Stravinsky's mature works, it shows strong Neo-Classical tendencies in its sparse scoring and the short, concise format of its movements. There is no attempt to impress the listener with lush sonorities.

Listening Guide

Stravinsky: *Symphony of Psalms*, First Movement   *Record 5,A*

0:00	Begins with short, accented chord, followed by oboes and bassoons outlining chords in free-sounding manner; same idea repeated two more times.
0:23	French horn and cellos play fragment of first theme (*A*):

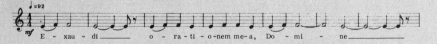

0:34	Altos enter singing first theme (*A*): accompanying woodwinds change to outlining chords at half the speed of previous outlining; some persistently repeated figures also heard.
0:53	Full chorus sings *A* theme.
1:10	*A* theme performed again by altos and oboes; cellos and string basses play a steady pattern of very short notes.
1:30	Short, accented chords followed by chord outlines, as in opening of movement; tenors sing a line containing only one pitch.

ful). Its chromatic first theme is clearly presented by the clarinet and then the oboe:

The accompanying rhythmic figure is taken from the first four notes of the theme. The second theme in the movement is more songlike and is first played by the oboe.

The second movement is a waltz. The sections are rather short, and their pattern is *A A B C B A*.

The third movement is marked *Ruhig und einfach* (Quiet and simple). It's an elegant slow movement with long melodic lines. There are several ostinato accompanying patterns. One feature of the movement is the imaginative manner in which Hindemith writes for the instruments. In one place the flute plays notes lower than those of the clarinet and horn, an unusual arrangement that gives an interesting tonal effect.

The fourth movement is quite fast. It is built around a short pounding theme that alternates periodically with short solos for each instrument:

1:40   Second theme (*B*) sung by altos and basses; trombones and bassoons play steady line of very short notes:

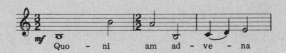

2:24   Music reaches climactic point; chord outlining played again by orchestra; chorus all in same rhythmic pattern.

2:32   *A* theme sung by tenors; very short "dry" notes played by low strings and oboes; music gradually increases in intensity as fragments of *A* theme are heard again.

3:02   Brasses enter as music moves gradually to final climactic chord.

3:19   Closes at loud dynamic level.

The fifth movement is very fast, with an "arch" form that is *A B C B A*. The differences among the themes are as much rhythmic as melodic. It is presented in the Listening Guide below.

Tone-Row Music

Arnold Schoenberg (whose expressionistic compositions were mentioned in Chapter 24) experimented with different principles of composition until 1923, when he settled on a type of atonality variously called *twelve-tone, tone-row, dodecaphonic,* or *serial music.* The principle is relatively simple. The composer arranges the 12 tones of the chromatic scale in any order. This is the "row"—a series of intervals that forms a unique melody. It is not a chromatic scale, because the notes do not progress by half steps. The pitches in the row need not all appear within the range of a single octave, either, so wide interval leaps are sometimes encountered. No tone in the row can be repeated until all 12 tones have been heard, because such repetition would emphasize one particular note.

Listening Guide

Hindemith: *Kleine Kammermusik Für Fünf Bläser, Op. 24, No. 2,* Fifth Movement   *Record 3,A*

0:00   Flute, oboe, and clarinet solidly play *A* theme:

0:12   Oboe softly plays the off-the-beat *B* theme, while bassoon sounds accompanying line moving in contrary motion.

0:18   Flute joins oboe on *B* theme as music gets louder; theme is extended and grows quieter with clarinet passage.

0:35   All except French horn play a varied version that develops first three notes of the *B* theme; music is rather soft.

No special importance is attached to any tone in the row; all are equally significant. So there can be no tonic or tonal center.

While the tone-row technique may appear limited at first glance, it has been calculated that there are 479,001,600 different tone rows available. And each row can be treated in countless ways. It can appear in chords as well as in melodies. The row can be transposed, or it can be moved to a different octave. It can be subdivided into phrases of different lengths.

Tone-row music is *not* a set of variations on a theme. Schoenberg saw it as an entirely new approach to music, not a vehicle for more examples of theme and variations. In some works the row can seldom be detected by ear. It is more a framework for musical ideas than a recognizable theme.

Schoenberg's "Unentrinnbar"

In the late 1920s Schoenberg wrote several choral works, including *Four Pieces for Mixed Chorus*. One of these is "Unentrinnbar" ("Inevitable"), which is on Record 5,B. In this work

0:47   Short, concluding melodic idea (C) begins in the oboe.

1:02   Flute introduces *D* theme, which is more lyric and smooth than preceding themes.

1:21   *D* is repeated by flute, while more rhythmic interest is added to accompaniment.

1:35   *B* theme returns, played rather softly.

1:41   Flute joins oboe in repeating of *B*, music increases in intensity.

1:55   *A* theme returns, played forcefully as in beginning by flute, oboe, and clarinet.

2:07   *C* melodic idea returns, played by oboe.

2:17   Coda begins with clarinet playing melodic fragment from *A*.

2:25   *B* played loudly with much dissonance.

2:46   Closes with three low chords.

the sopranos begin the row, which is easily recognizable in its various forms as the piece progresses:

Strong and brave are those who ac-com-
Tap-fe-re sind sol-che, die Ta-

-plish the deeds which___ their cour-age does
-ten voll-brin-gen___ an die ihr Mut

The tenor part enters exactly four measures later, in strict imitation. The alto part starts in measure 3 and presents the inversion, or upside-down version, of the row. The example includes the original row for purposes of comparison:

The bass then enters in strict imitation of the alto.

The soprano part begins something different after it has completed the row. The two versions are:

The second line is the reverse of the first. The musical term for this relationship is *retrograde*. In this piece the rhythm of the retrograde version differs from the rhythm of the original row.

Finally the fourth version of the row is heard, the *retrograde-inversion*, shown at the top of the next page.

The four versions of the row—the original row, the inversion, the retrograde, and the retrograde-inversion—represent the basic techniques of the tone-row system. The scheme for the entire 31 measures of Schoenberg's "Inevitable" is given at the bottom of the next page.

The rules of tone-row composition as applied in pieces of music display some flexibility. "Inevitable" adheres to the rules closely, probably because it's a short piece. But the tone-row composer can move notes from one octave to another in a technique called *octave displacement*. The composer can also spell a note differently, as long as it sounds the same. The notes F# and Gb, for example, are the same pitch and can be seen in the excerpt showing the original and the retrograde. Notice the first note of the original and the last note of the retrograde. Some repetition of notes is allowed in the row, as long as it does not give dominance to a particular tone. A few short interruptions of the row are permissible.

Serialism

Since 1950 a number of composers have turned to the tone-row principles developed by Schoenberg. This trend can be attributed primarily to the influence of a quiet student of his: Anton Webern (*Vay*-burn; 1883–1945). He wrote in the same compositional idiom as Schoenberg, but his music is even more austere and economical. Of his 31 compositions the longest is ten minutes, and his complete works can be performed in less than three hours. His dynamics are usually the softest imaginable, and his frail tone-row melodies are passed note by note from one instrument to another in the subtlest kind of interplay. The principle of economy in composing was carried to its limit by Webern. If he had written more sparsely, one feels, the music would disappear.

A parallel to Webern's music can be found in the art of a twentieth-century Russian painter named Kasimir Malevich. In 1918 he painted *White on White*, which appears on page 248. Malevich's painting may be an idea carried to an extreme point, but the principle of a calm, objective, abstract art form holds some artistic appeal.

On first hearing, Webern's music sounds like muted chaos. Little blobs of sound appear and disappear at apparent random between gaps of silence. But intensive listening discloses that what at first seems disorganized is actually organization of an intense and compact nature. The musical ideas are trimmed mercilessly to exclude every bit of waste or decoration. Only the absolute essentials remain.

Webern's Concerto for Nine Instruments

Among Webern's most interesting works is a composition that is only nine minutes long: Concerto for Nine Instruments. It carries the

Measure	1	2	3	4	5	6	7	8	9	10	11	12
Soprano	row ———————————————┤ retrograde ——————————┤ retrograde - inversion ———
Alto			inversion ————————┤ retrograde - inversion ———————————┤ row ——→
Tenor					row ————————————┤ retrograde —————————————
Bass							inversion ————————————┤ retrograde -

Measure	13	14	15	16	17	18	19	20	21	22	23	24
Soprano	retrograde - inversion ————————┤
Alto	————————┤ retrograde ————————————┤
Tenor	inversion ————————————┤ retrograde - inversion ———┤
Bass	inversion ——┤ row —————————————————————————

Measure	25	26	27	28	29	30	31
Soprano	row in long note values ———————————
Alto	inversion in long note values ———————— second half first, then first half
Tenor	row in long note values —————————— second half first, then first half
Bass	inversion in long note values ———————

Suprematist Composition: White on White
(1918) by Kasimir Malevich. (Collection, The
Museum of Modern Art, New York.)

idea of tone row to a further level of development. The concerto is based on this row:

The brackets over the row indicate that it can be
divided into three-note segments, each consisting of two adjacent notes and one that is either
a line or space farther away. The first three
notes can be considered a miniature row, followed by its retrograde-inversion, retrograde,
and inversion. So the row itself is highly
organized.

The composition starts:

If you analyze the example, you can see that the
groups of three notes are retained, although

with octave displacement. The first group is
played by the oboe, the second by the flute, the
third by the trumpet, and the fourth by the
clarinet. Notice also that a different rhythm is
associated with each three-note group, and that
different articulations (slurring and tonguing)
are specified.

The original three-note groups appear again
in the concerto, but the order of their appearance is varied, as are the time values and timbres. In the following excerpt notice that the
three-note figures have the interval sequence
varied, the time values and articulations reversed, and the timbre changed.

Webern's composition has no actual themes.
It is held together by the row and the three-
note motives. The composition is generated
from a principle of composing that presents the

same ingredients continuously but in ever-changing ways. "It is always something different and yet always the same," Webern said of his music. In any case, his intellectual control over the music seems to be complete.

Anti-Intellectualism

Following World War I French artists, musicians, and writers grew increasingly anti-Romantic in their reaction against the seriousness of recent styles in art and music. The informal spokesmen for the new music were the poet Jean Cocteau and the musician Erik Satie, both mentioned in Chapter 23. On one occasion Satie created some music that he asked the audience *not* to notice. He instructed them to talk or wander about the room as it was being played. When the audience did not follow his suggestion, he became extremely irritated and walked around urging individuals to talk and otherwise ignore his music.

Elements of this irreverent approach found their way into the music of other composers, especially Francis Poulenc and Darius Milhaud. When balanced with a skilled composing technique, anti-intellectualism was in some ways a refreshing change from the heaviness of nineteenth-century music.

Aleatory Music: The "Uncomposition"

While Satie and Cocteau were anti-intellectual, the American John Cage (b. 1912) is purposely nonintellectual. He has been a prime promoter of chance or *aleatory* music. In such music the sounds are determined partly by chance and are therefore unpredictable. A clarinet player, for example, may be instructed to play anything he or she wishes for six beats, or to rest during that time. Or the selection of notes may depend on throwing dice. One of Cage's piano pieces is written on several disconnected sheets of paper. The player is told to drop the sheets, pick them up at random, and then play the pages in the new order. The resulting sounds are clearly a product of chance.

To understand what Cage is trying to achieve, you need to know his underlying phi-

losophy, even if you don't agree with it. For centuries Western civilization held to the idea of progress, the idea of working toward goals. Through increases in knowledge, which in turn led to such practical outcomes as improved medical care, more food, a shorter work week, etc., it was held that the human race was progressing. But the idea of progress has come under attack in the twentieth century from existential philosophy and from advocates of oriental religious beliefs. The idea of progress is false, they claim; there is only change, not progress. The implications of the only-change, no-goal-toward-which-to-progress position are enormous. It's a little like removing the goal lines and uprights on the football field and ceasing to keep score or time; the game just happens. About the only assumption that one can make is that the players will eventually tire and stop playing.

This view rejects the idea that art must have meaning. As the poet Archibald MacLeish says:

> *A poem should not mean*
> *But be.*

Depicting a Campbell's soup can or comic strip character in a painting is not, as some people believe, a comment on the vulgarity of modern civilization. The content of such works is so blatant that it no longer invites interpretation, which is the way the artist wants it. A picture is a picture, and that's all. In his book *Silence*, Cage urges the composer to "give up the desire to control sound, clear his mind of music [in the usual sense] and set about discovering means to let sounds be themselves rather than vehicles for man-made theories or expression of human sentiments." Relying on chance devices is one way in which Cage and others encourage the listener to listen to sound rather than to seek relationships in the sounds. While at first glance it may seem foolish to determine musical sequence by dropping the pages of music on the floor, such a procedure comes from the consistent application of a philosophical position.

It is difficult to predict much of a future for chance music. Although any object can be contemplated for what it is, the trouble with Pop art and chance music is that they lack the evidence of skillful invention and elegance necessary to make the works artistically interesting. Very little talent or devotion is usually exhibited in a painting of a soup can or in a musical work calling on the performer to manipulate a dial on a radio. Things that nearly everyone can do are not valued highly.

Arnold Schoenberg

(New York Public Library.)

Arnold Schoenberg (*Shu(r)n*-bairg; 1874–1951) was born in Vienna. He began studying violin at the age of eight and was an avid participant in amateur chamber-music performances. After his father's early death he went to work as a bank clerk. He had little formal advanced music training, but for many years had exhibited an interest in composing. This interest grew increasingly stronger, and so he decided to make music his lifework. First he spent two years in Berlin as music director in a cabaret; then he returned to Vienna as a teacher, theorist, and composer. His career was interrupted for two years while he served in the Austrian army in World War I.

In 1925 he was appointed professor of composition at the Berlin Academy of Arts. His stay in Berlin ended when Hitler came to power. Although Schoenberg had been converted from Judaism to Catholicism, he left Germany and came to the United States, becoming an American citizen in 1940. He taught at the University of California at Los Angeles until his retirement. His musical activities continued until his death in 1951.

Prior to 1908 his music stood firmly in the tradition of Wagner and Mahler. His best known composition of the period is *Verklärte Nacht* (Transfigured Night), a tone poem for string orchestra. The literary work that inspired the music is pure Romanticism. As a couple walks through the woods, the woman confesses that she has been unfaithful. The man assures her that he still loves her, and her gratitude transfigures the night.

Around 1908 Schoenberg began to turn toward smaller groups of instruments. He started to write more contrapuntally and to employ much more chromaticism. Slowly he developed an atonal style.

About 1923 he devised the tone-row system that was described earlier in this chapter. He followed tone-row principles for most of his works from that time on until the end of his life, departing from them occasionally in some of his later works. Schoenberg is as much remembered for his influence on twentieth-century music as he is for his compositions. His best known compositions are *Pierrot Lunaire,* Variations for Orchestra, and several chamber works.

Paul Hindemith

Paul Hindemith was born in Hanau, Germany in 1895. When he was 11 and his father objected to a musical career for him, he ran away from home. He earned his living by playing violin in dance orchestras and movie theaters. (Those were the days of silent pictures.) He later enrolled in the Conservatory at Frankfurt. There he won a prize for one of his compositions, a string quartet. After another successful string quartet he became interested in jazz, and this interest resulted in his Concerto for Piano and Twelve Instruments.

In 1927 Hindemith was appointed professor at the Hochschule in Berlin. He encouraged his students to learn several different instruments and to participate in a variety of musical activities. At that time he was much interested in practical, "usable" music; the term *Gebrauchsmusik*, which means literally use-music, was applied to it. This music was not technically difficult and was meant for everyday use. Between 1936 and 1955 he composed a sonata for almost every orchestral instrument, including the tuba.

When the Nazis came to power, German culture was purged of anything more modern than the music of Wagner. Shortly before the outbreak of World War II, Hindemith escaped and emigrated to the United States, where he later became a citizen. He accepted an appointment to the faculty at Yale University and continued to teach there until 1953. He retired to live in Zurich, Switzerland, although he did make many trips back to the United States. He died in 1963.

Hindemith's best known works are two operas: *Mathis der Maler* (Matthias the Painter), based on the life of Matthias Grünewald, the *Die Harmonie der Welt* (The Harmony of the World), based on the life of the sixteenth-century astronomer Johannes Kepler. Hindemith arranged symphonic poems that bear the same names as the operas.

Hindemith was influential not only for his compositions, but also for his writings on music theory and harmony. He was also a leader in the "Back-to-Bach" movement.

Anton Webern

Webern was born Anton von Webern, but he dropped the royal *von* from his name after the 1918 revolution in Austria. He was born in 1883, the son of a mining engineer in southern Austria. While in school young Webern took lessons in cello, piano, and music theory. When he completed school at the age of 18, his family gave him a trip to the Wagner Festival at Bayreuth as a graduation present. This trip inspired a youthful effort at a large-scale work entitled *Young Siegfried*. Webern's style soon began to change after he met Arnold Schoenberg in 1904. He studied with him for a little over two years, but they maintained a lifelong friendship even after Schoenberg had moved to Berlin and then on to the United States.

Webern began his professional career in 1908 as a conductor. Except for a tour of military service during World War I, he conducted orchestras in various Austrian cities. In 1920 his attention shifted to private music teaching. He also came in contact with the activities of the Social Democratic Party and took up duties as conductor of a workers' chorus. He was very active in the Socialist movement.

Webern's atonal style began to emerge shortly before World War I, but his better known works were written after that time, especially during the 1920s. In 1927 he was appointed conductor and advisor for Radio Austria, a job he held until his political party went out of power. He continued to compose throughout World War II, during which his son was killed in battle and his home was destroyed by bombing. As the last days of the war approached, his future looked brighter. He had received official letters from Vienna asking him to play a leadership role in reconstructing the cultural life of his country. He was shot in 1945 in an unfortunate accident as he lit a cigarette during a time of strict curfew. He died widely esteemed by a few other composers, including Stravinsky, but largely unknown to the general public.

26

Music Now

With the end of World War II in 1945, the world moved into a new era. In a faltering manner the nations and peoples of the world started to rebuild in both a physical and emotional sense. Webern also died in 1945, but his influence was soon felt on the world of art music. Partly because of him composers such as Stravinsky began writing in a different style. Also, a new generation of composers was soon to appear, and with them an interest in the new ways of producing and reproducing sound electronically.

From about 1945 to 1960 the struggle for musical predominance was between those who favored strict controls on music in terms of tone-row principles and those who favored few controls—chance music and improvisation. The most prominent person promoting controlled composition was the Frenchman Pierre Boulez (Boo-lez, b. 1925), who was for several years musical director of the New York Philharmonic. In addition to a row of pitches, one of his compositions contains a rhythmic row (A at the bottom of page 253), a row of articulations (B), and a row of dynamics (C).

So rows control four aspects of the music: pitch, rhythm, articulation, and dynamics. Other composers also control timbre. Such compositions are usually frighteningly difficult to perform.

When tone-row principles are applied more broadly, the music is generally called *serial*. Other serial composers in addition to Boulez are: Karlheinz Stockhausen in Germany and Luigi Berio and Luigi Nono in Italy. An earlier version of controlled music was created by the Frenchman Olivier Messiaen (Mess-yun, b. 1908). In some of his music he uses one series for melody, another for dynamics, another for timbre, and another for rhythm. Each of his four series is of a different length.

Chance music and its leading proponent, John Cage, were discussed in Chapter 25. Other types of music allowing for some chance or unplanned elements include the "third stream" music of Gunther Schuller, in which some jazz improvisation is designated, and the "stochastic" music of Yannis Xenakis (Zeh-*nock*-iss, b. 1922). Xenakis was born in Athens and later studied architecture and composition in Paris. He believes that musical compositions should be based on the calculus of probabilities. In his music it does not matter if a particular note is played or not, since the ear cannot perceive every individual sound. *Metastasis*, written in 1955, used 63 instruments (mostly strings); but it consists of *glissandi* (slides) with only the upper and lower pitch limits specified. The effect is one of a "haze" or rain of sounds.

Electronic Music

As music moved into the 1960s, both the serial and chance types began to give way to a third type: electronic music. Today it is equally prominent in the art music being created. Even some advocates of other types of composition—

John Cage, for example—have moved toward electronic music.

There are two types of electronic music. *Musique concrète* is one. Recordings are made of natural sounds and voices—parts of human speech, a fly buzzing, the wind, a motor roaring, water dripping. Then the tape is manipulated according to the desires of the composer. It can be speeded up or slowed down. It can be spliced. It can be recorded through a second or third recorder and thus the sounds combined. The composition in *musique concrète* is a segment of tape that contains selected and manipulated sounds in a planned sequence.

An American advocate of *musique concrète* is Vladimir Ussachevsky. He combines natural sounds and sounds from musical instruments, usually percussion, on tape. For instance, from the ring of a gong he may salvage only the last portion or "afterglow" of the sound. Then he may treat the taped portion in any of the ways previously described.

Musique concrète has functioned successfully as background for movies, plays, and ballet

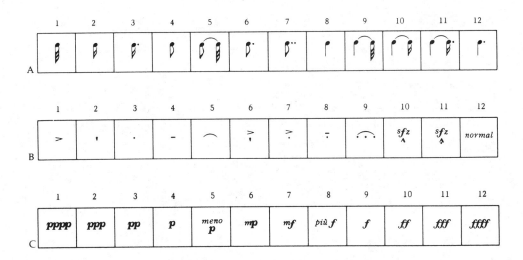

scenes, especially when eerie and unearthly music is required.

The other type of electronic music consists of sounds produced on electronic equipment (synthesizers and oscillators) and then recorded on tape. This music had its beginnings in the Studio for Electronic Music of the West German Radio in the 1950s. All sounds within the limits of human hearing are possible, even those too high or low to be identifiable as musical pitches. This range is considerably larger than the customary 88 pitches available on the piano keyboard. Furthermore, every level of volume and timbre can be reproduced. Also possible are machine rhythms, which are more complex and more accurately executed than those produced by humans.

Electronic music is not performed in the usual sense of the word. A button is pushed to start the machine. If the technician who prepared the tape has followed the directions accurately, the listener hears *exactly* the sounds the composer intended. The need for a performer is completely eliminated. The idea seems revolu-

tionary at first. And yet in the visual arts no one expects to watch a painting being repainted by a "performing" artist; we see just what the original artist painted. The same principle prevails in electronic music.

The *Record Album* (Record 4,B) contains a portion of an electronic work, *Until Spring*, by the contemporary American Morton Subotnick. A Listening Guide for the opening portion of this work appears below. Subotnick considers creating such music with the synthesizer "like sculpting sound." *Until Spring* deals with three gestural qualities: thrusting out, becoming, and being. The opening minutes of the work are contained in the album.

A computer is not essential for electronic music, although it is often involved. The computer can "create" a musical composition from a prescribed program. The computer program can produce whatever type of music is desired—Mozart-like compositions, popular songs, or psychedelic synthesized sounds. Also, the music the computer specifies can, depending on the program, be played on a convention-

Listening Guide

Subotnick: *Until Spring*   *Record 4,B*

0:00	Opening section containing rather soft but long, eerie, howling sounds that are modified slowly by slight changes of timbre, pitch, and amount of dissonance.
0:39	New section begins containing glissandos (rapid sprays of sounds) of high, rapidly repeated notes interspersed among low, plucked sounds in an irregular pattern; little dynamic change; patterns are alternated between the two tracks available on the recording.
1:09	Rapid changes of loudness are introduced to the glissandos.
1:25	Return to opening quieter material, but this time containing rapidly repeated vibrator-like pulses; somewhat less dissonant and eerie than the opening section.
2:18	Return to glissandos; more rapidly repeated notes sounded; many quick changes of dynamic level and alternation of tracks on the recording.
2:29	The excerpt fades to a conclusion.

al instrument or sounded on a sophisticated synthesizer.

Creating electronic compositions is a highly specialized skill. To do it, one almost needs to study electrical engineering as well as music. Instruction in electronic composition is now being offered in many European and American music schools.

The potential of electronic music has barely been tapped. There is a vast world of sound-manipulation possibilities to be investigated.

Eclecticism-Consolidation

Although contemporary art music is pluralistic, with composers writing in widely divergent styles, there are some composers who use what they believe is the best of each style. They owe allegiance to no musical system or philosophy, and their compositions cannot be classified in any of the categories previously mentioned.

In the opinion of many musicians, the leading composer today is Krzysztof Penderecki (Pen-der-*et*-ski), who was born in 1933 near Cracow, Poland, but now lives in the United States. He is most interested in timbre and tonal effect, but he also uses the tape recorder in some compositions. His best known works are *The Passion According to St. Luke* and *Threnody to the Victims of Hiroshima*.

Other eclectic, experimental composers include the Italian Luigi Dallapiccola (b. 1904), the Pole Witold Lutoslawski (b. 1913), and the German Hans Werner Henze (b. 1926).

Crumb's *Night of the Four Moons*

In the discussion of each style period and type, one or more works has been selected to exemplify that kind of music. Deciding on the most representative works is difficult, especially so in the case of very recent music. However, George Crumb's series of four songs entitled *Night of the Four Moons* (Record 5,A) appears to demonstrate well a number of the trends in art music today. It was composed during the Apol-

lo 11 moon flight July 16–24, 1969. Crumb writes of the work:

> *I suppose that* Night of the Four Moons *is really an "occasional" work, since its inception was an artistic response to an external event. The texts—extracts drawn from the poems of Federico García Lorca—symbolize my own rather ambivalent feelings vis-à-vis Apollo 11.*

It was commissioned by the Philadelphia Chamber Players and involves a chamber ensemble consisting of an alto singer, alto flute (doubling on piccolo), banjo, "electric" cello (that is, amplified through a speaker), and one percussion player playing a number of instruments: a large drum, crotales (metal shells struck together), cymbals, tambourine, Japanese Kabuki blocks, bongo drums, Chinese gong, Tibetan prayer stones, vibraphone, and African thumb piano (mbira). The singer's part requires *sprechstimme*, unvoiced singing, and whispering, in addition to normal singing.

The score is preceded by two pages of lengthy instructions to the performers. These directions include specifications regarding placement on stage, stage lighting, the dress of the singer (a Spanish cabaret costume), and stage entrance and exit ("should be solemn and suggest a somnambulistic, trancelike quality").

The text of the work consists of fragments of poems by Federico García Lorca, which are in Spanish. The text for the first song is:

> *La luna está muerta, muerta;*
> *pero resucita en la primavera.*
>
> *The moon is dead, dead;*
> *but it is reborn in the springtime.*

The other three songs are: "*Cuando sale la luna* . . . " (When the moon rises . . .), "*Otro Adán oscura está soñando* . . . " (Another obscure Adam dreams . . .), and "*Huje luna, luna, luna!* . . . " (Run away moon, moon, moon! . . .).

The music has some of the sparse quality developed by Webern, some of the aleatory

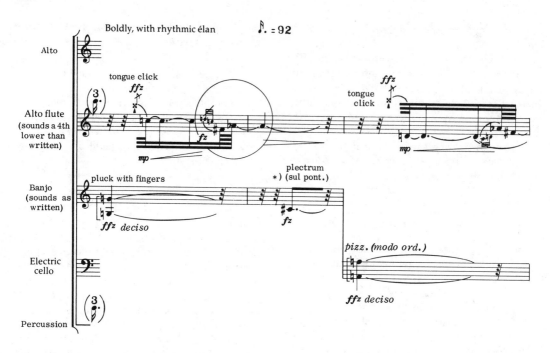

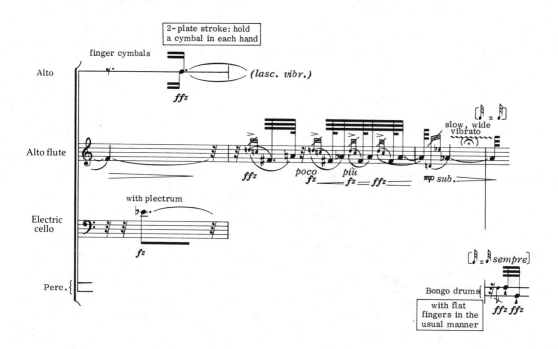

techniques promoted by Cage, some elements of theater, and quite a bit of interest in timbres. The first line of the first song appears on page 256. The unifying element in these lines is the figure circled in the example. The figure is also inverted. Crumb writes of this song:

> "The moon is dead, dead . . . " is primarily an instrumental piece in a primitive rhythmical style, with the Spanish words stated almost parenthetically by the singer. The conclusion of the text is whispered by the flutist over the mouthpiece of his instrument.

The music has notated rhythm, but no metrical, steady beat. Dynamic markings and varied timbres add much to its effect, which seems to be a combination of intellectualism and mysticism.

The Future of Music

Where does music go from here? No one knows, of course. Electronic music may turn out to be merely a passing experiment, al-though that does not seem likely. There may be a rebirth of interest in an earlier type of music, or some new type that is unknown today may emerge.

Only two predictions can be made with confidence about music in the future. First, there will be music. People have found sound and its manipulation too fascinating, too satisfying, to abandon it completely. In fact, the indications are that music and other fine arts will mean more, not less, in the years to come. Second, music of the future will differ from music of the past. The creative mind is restless and forever unsatisfied with previous accomplishments. It wants to experiment with new ways and new materials. The truly creative artist is constitutionally unable to make imitations or be content with the efforts of others.

By definition, creativity involves the bringing forth of something new and unique. And in the art of music, as in any creative endeavor, there will always be something new under the sun. The product of an imaginative and skilled composer will always be a fascination to hear and a joy to understand.

27

American Music

Music in America had a slow start, for several reasons. The nation began as a loose confederation of small, struggling settlements, isolated from the mainstream of European life by 3,000 miles of ocean. Physical survival was the uppermost concern. There was no stimulating contact with recent artistic creations. Furthermore, in those early days there could be no truly American music, since the settlers came from other lands and were steeped in the traditions of English, Dutch, or German music.

The Puritan influence, too, was strong in the Colonies. These devout people thought that art and theater were morally wrong. At best, art and music were mere diversions; at worst, they were products of the devil. The only music permitted was the unaccompanied singing of psalms and hymns. The first book published in America was the *Bay Psalm Book,* in 1640. The first edition had no music, and none was added until the ninth edition in 1698.

The most sophisticated music written in America before the Revolutionary War was the product of the Moravian communities around Bethlehem, Pennsylvania, and Winston-Salem, North Carolina. These people had come from the Moravian area of present-day Czechoslovakia, bringing with them a rich musical heritage. Besides music for church services, they also wrote chamber works. Musicologists are still discovering some of this fine music. There were several active composers in the Moravian community, but John Frederick Peter (1746–1813) was the most skilled. He came to America in 1770.

The first native-born American composer was an amateur, Francis Hopkinson (1737–1791), who was a friend of George Washington and a signer of the Declaration of Independence. His most famous song was "My Days Have Been So Wondrous Free." In 1788 he published some songs for which he also wrote the words. He dedicated the book to Washington.

If Francis Hopkinson's compositions did not sound particularly different from English music at that time, the works of William Billings (1746–1800) did. Billings was a tanner by trade, but he had an insatiable drive to write music. And he was a firm believer in American music for Americans. He explained in his first collection, *The New England Psalm Singer* (1770), that he would follow his own rules for composition. One of the techniques he used in his hymns was "fuguing," which was a high-class name for imitation. Billings was not modest in making claims:

> [Fuguing] is twenty times as powerful as the old slow tunes. Each part striving for mastery and victory. The audience entertained and delighted. Now the solemn bass demands their attention; next the manly tenor. Now here, now there, now here again! O ecstatic! Rush on, you sons of harmony.

Whatever Billings lacked in training was offset by his native musical ability. Despite some crudities, his music has a quality that has attracted many musicians and lay people, especially in this century. The tune "Chester" is one of his best known. A version of it from Billings' *Singing Master's Assistant* is shown below. The melody is in the tenor part, the third line from the top. The music is plain and unadorned. "Chester" has reappeared in the annals of American music, specifically in the twentieth-century music of William Schuman.

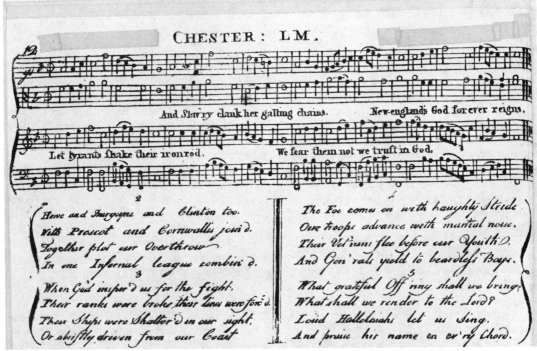

"Chester" by William Billings, as it appears in his Singing Master's Assistant. The initials L. M. in the title mean "long meter" and indicate that there are eight syllables in every phrase of the text.

Prior to the twentieth century, Billings wrote the only music that could be considered completely American. Even our national songs had their roots in Europe. The origin of "Yankee Doodle" is unknown, but it was first printed in Glasgow, Scotland, in 1782. The British sang it to ridicule the Yankees, who promptly took it over as their own song by adding new verses. The melody of "The Star-Spangled Banner" was adapted from a popular English drinking song, "To Anacreon in Heaven," composed by John Stafford Smith (1750–1836). The words were written as a poem by the American Francis Scott Key as he watched the British bombard Fort McHenry in 1814. It was not officially made the national anthem until 1931. "America" is sung to the same tune as the British national anthem "God Save the King," which was written by the English composer Henry Carey (1685–1743). The words as sung in this country were contributed by the American Samuel Francis Smith (1808–1895) at the suggestion of Lowell Mason.

The Nineteenth Century

The name Mason is important in American music. Lowell Mason (1792–1872) wrote many hymns, including "Nearer, My God, to Thee," and conducted the Handel and Haydn Society in Boston. His most significant achievement was the establishment of music in the curriculum of the public schools in 1838. He also spread the idea of music for the masses by organizing "conventions" for the training of music teachers. He made several lengthy trips to Europe to study. Two of his sons founded the piano-manufacturing company of Mason and Hamlin, and a third son became a well-known music teacher.

America imported not only much of its music but many of its musicians as well. Many European virtuosos found it profitable to tour the United States. The most sensational of these was the singer Jenny Lind, who was advertised by her brilliant promoter, P. T. Barnum, as "the Swedish Nightingale."

An American piano virtuoso was Louis Moreau Gottschalk (1829–1869). He was a handsome man who cultivated some of the mannerisms of Liszt. He wrote sentimental works with such tear-jerking titles as *The Last Hope* and *The Dying Poet*.

Louis A. Jullien (1812–1860) conducted with a jeweled baton. He played some good music, including works by American composers. But his biggest success was a number entitled *Fireman's Quadrille*, during which, as flames burst from the ceiling, he brought the local fire department into the hall to quench the blaze dramatically.

For sheer spectacle Jullien was matched only by Patrick Gilmore (1829–1892), a bandmaster who organized colossal extravaganzas. One was the Great National Peace Jubilee in Boston in 1869. The performance included a chorus of 10,000, an orchestra of 1,000 cannons, and 100 firemen pounding anvils in the "Anvil Chorus" from Verdi's *Il Trovatore*. The only way for Gilmore to top that was to organize a World Peace Jubilee. For this he brought Johann Strauss from Europe to lead his *Blue Danube Waltz*. Although the orchestra was held down to 1,000 players, the chorus was increased to 20,000 singers.

From Jullien's orchestra emerged a young German violinist named Theodore Thomas (1835–1905). In 1862 he organized his own orchestra. He maintained high standards of performance and sought to educate the audience; in so doing he laid the foundation for the symphony orchestras of today. He traveled throughout the United States and for a while conducted the New York Philharmonic. Later he organized the Chicago Symphony and served as conductor for many years.

The revolutions in Europe, especially Germany, in the mid-1800s brought thousands of immigrants to America. Many were musicians who soon became affiliated with orchestras and opera companies throughout the country. The European immigrants constituted an interested audience for the German symphonic music that Thomas performed for them.

Stephen Collins Foster (1826–1864) was a native American composer both by birth and by compositional style. He was not a Southerner, as many people believe. He was born in Lawrenceville, Pennsylvania, of a middle-class family. His parents did not consider music a suitable career for a man, so they did nothing to encourage him. He was a dreamer and a failure at almost everything he undertook—work, marriage, and serious musical compositions. But he was a genius at writing popular songs. He wrote about two hundred of them, many for minstrel shows. "Beautiful Dreamer," "My Old Kentucky Home," "Old Folks at Home," "Camptown Races," "O Susanna," and others are still heard today.

Late in the nineteenth century a few capable American composers began to write longer and more sophisticated works. Most of these composers lived around Boston, and almost all of them had studied in Germany at one time or another. Consequently, much of their music sounded like works of the European masters with whom they had studied. The "Boston" or "New England" group included George W. Chadwick (1854–1931), Horatio Parker (1863–1919), Arthur Foote (1853–1937), and John Knowles Paine (1839–1906), who taught Foote. Little of their music is heard today.

Edward MacDowell (1861–1908) had excellent musical training. He studied at the Paris Conservatory when he was 11, and was a classmate of Debussy. He also played for Liszt at Weimar in 1882. After his return to America, he was professor of music at Columbia University for eight years. Most of his works are for piano; *Woodland Sketches* and "To a Wild Rose" are representative of his style. He also wrote four piano sonatas and two piano concertos. His Suite No. 2 (*Indian Suite*) was a landmark because it was one of the first American works to use music from native sources.

The Twentieth Century

Soon after the turn of the century, the popularity of German Romanticism began to wane in America, only to be replaced by attempts to imitate impressionism. The best known "American impressionist" was Charles Tomlinson Griffes (1884–1920). At first he wrote in the German tradition, but he later switched to the Debussy-Ravel style. "The White Peacock" from *Roman Sketches* is still frequently performed. Charles Martin Loeffler (1861–1935), who immigrated to America from Alsace at the

age of 20, also wrote music of a somewhat impressionistic nature.

Thus, as the twentieth century began, American music was in a dormant state. All around was a rich heritage of folk music in the songs of the blacks, the lumberjacks, the sailors, the cowboys, the Indians, and the mountaineers, as well as the ballads and folklore brought to America by its myriad immigrants. But except for MacDowell, no American composer had chosen to draw on the musical resources of this country. They apparently felt that the music of their own culture was inferior. Not only did it seem necessary for all serious musicians to study in Europe, it was considered advisable to pattern new compositions on European models.

One composer, however, was writing modern, innovative American music prior to World War I. At the time, however, virtually no one had heard of Charles Ives.

Charles Ives

Ives (1874–1954) was born in Danbury, Connecticut, the son of a bandmaster. His father was no ordinary town band leader. He encouraged his son to listen carefully and try to write different tonal effects. "Stretch your ears," was his advice. And so young Ives experimented with various acoustical effects, such as new tunings for the piano or two bands playing different music while marching toward and away from each other. He attended Yale as a music student and upon graduation went to New York, where he literally made a fortune in the insurance business. He had a country home in Connecticut. In the evenings he sat at his desk and composed for relaxation. As he finished a page of music, he stacked it on the floor near him. When the stacks became too high, he carried them out to the barn for storage. Because he had no need for money, he did not bother to have his works published and sold. For years no one knew about them.

Shortly after the turn of the century, Ives was writing novel harmonies and rhythms that did not appear in Europe until a decade or more later. He experimented with such ideas as polytonality, dissonant counterpoint, atonality, polyrhythm, chords with added tones, unusual melodic intervals, and *sprechstimme*, the kind of singsong speech that Schoenberg used in several of his works. Ives' song "Autumn," presented in Chapter 7, is rather traditional compared to much of his other music.

Ives' Symphony No. 3, written between 1901 and 1904, won him the Pulitzer Prize in 1947. Another work that is often played is the Piano Sonata No. 2 (*Concord*), which contains fragments of several well-known tunes heard in Concord, Massachusetts, between 1840 and 1860. The fragments Ives selected, the manner in which he employed devices such as polytonality, the character of his melodies, and his use of instruments produced music that was in no sense a copy of Stravinsky or Bartók. It was American music. At long last the seed planted by Billings, the tanner, was flourishing in Ives, the insurance man. But until the 1930s no one knew it.

Mainstream Nationalists

Most of the music that is considered "American" is somewhat nationalistic or Neo-Romantic in character. This type of music can be represented by two specific works: George Gershwin's *Porgy and Bess* and William Schuman's *New England Triptych*.

Gershwin's *Porgy and Bess*

Gershwin was impressed by DuBose Heyward's novel *Porgy*. The story deals with the poor blacks who lived on Catfish Row in Charleston, South Carolina. Gershwin saw the dramatic possibilities in the story and decided to write an opera based on it. To make his opera more authentic, he spent the summer of 1934 in Charleston observing the ways of the people. He heard the street cries of the vendors and listened to the songs the children sang as they played. Then he returned to New York and spent another nine months writing *Porgy and Bess*.

Porgy and Bess concerns itself with the common people. For realism, Gershwin has the characters speak most of their lines instead of singing in recitative style. And he incorporates the music of these people—the blues and other features of jazz—into the opera. Although he does not include actual folk songs, he does maintain a folklike quality in the music. The jazz elements are written down rather than improvised.

The story of *Porgy and Bess* is filled with tragedy. Porgy is a crippled beggar who leads a lonely life. Bess, a loose-living woman, comes to town with her lover, Crown. Neither Bess nor Crown is accepted by the people of Catfish Row. Crown kills one of the local men in a fight, and Bess takes refuge from the police in Porgy's shanty. Their relationship grows to one of genuine love.

One day a big picnic is held on a nearby island. Because he's crippled, Porgy can't attend, but he encourages Bess to go. As she's about to catch the boat back to Catfish Row, she is abducted by Crown, who has escaped from jail and is hiding on the island. When Crown learns of Bess's love for Porgy, he sets out to kill his rival. In the fight between the two men, Crown is stabbed and dies. Porgy is taken off to jail on suspicion of murder.

Now is the moment Sporting Life has been waiting for. He represents the easy, evil life that Bess left behind when she moved in with Porgy. Because it's doubtful that Porgy will ever be freed from jail, Sporting Life is able to persuade Bess to go back to New York with him. But Porgy is released, and when he returns home he finds Bess gone. "Where is she?" he asks. "New York," answer his neighbors. The opera closes with the pathetic scene of Porgy climbing into his goat cart to go after Bess.

Porgy and Bess opens with the lullaby "Summertime." The mood is lazy and relaxed, and the accompaniment suggests a gently rocking motion. Short notes introduce each new idea, and the last syllable of each phrase is sustained. The effect suggests snatches of thought spoken at random. Later in the song Gershwin adds some vocal devices he heard that summer in Charleston such as a slide, or *glissando*, and a little catch on the word "cry." The rhythm on the word "jumpin'" increases the feeling of bounciness. The word "hush" is given a place of prominence so that the "sh" sound can be easily heard. Jazz harmonies are evident.

In "I've Got Plenty of Nothin'," Porgy displays a carefree spirit, telling everyone that he has everything he wants, so he doesn't have to worry about material goods.

"Bess, You Is My Woman Now" (Record 5,B) is a glorious duet between Porgy and Bess. It sounds more like opera than folk music. As is typical in such duets, the man sings first to initiate the exchange of feelings, the woman answers, and then they sing together. The two parts are quite different. Porgy's part is a countermelody to what Bess is singing. This duet also contains some jazz elements.

In "It Ain't Necessarily So" Sporting Life tries to con the people over to his way of life. His words are not those of an honest skeptic but of a sly salesman. The pitches of the melody seem to slink about in a manner that is just right for Sporting Life's personality. The song is in an *A B A* form. The main portion is heard twice; then there is a contrasting section, which is followed by return of the main portion. The contrasting section features nonsense syllables rather than regular words.

Throughout *Porgy and Bess*, there is an attempt to duplicate black dialect by making some changes in grammar and pronunciation. The linguistic result is seldom accurate or realistic. But the content of the opera—its music, story line, and characterizations—is strong enough to make it an artistic success.

Schuman's *New England Triptych*

In 1956 William Schuman turned to the music of the early Boston tanner William Billings. He chose three of Billings' songs to serve as the basis for this orchestral work. The word *triptych* (*trip*-tic) comes from a Greek word meaning three layers or parts.

In the program notes—Schuman requested that they be included whenever possible—he pays this tribute to Billings:

> *The works of this dynamic composer capture the spirit of sinewy ruggedness, deep religiosity, and patriotic fervor that we associate with the Revolutionary Period.*

> *Despite the undeniable crudities and technical shortcomings of his music, its appeal, even today, is forceful and moving. I am not alone among American composers who feel an identity with Billings and it is this sense of identity which accounts for my use of his music as a point of departure. These pieces do not constitute a "fantasy" on themes of Billings, nor "variations" on his themes, but rather a fusion of styles and musical language.*

The first movement of the triptych is built from the anthem "Be Glad Then, America." The opening timpani solo is developed further in the strings:

Trombones and trumpets start the main section, which is a free and varied setting of the words "Be glad then, America, shout and rejoice":

The timpani lead into a fugal section based on the theme for the words "And ye shall be satisfied":

The music gains momentum and combines themes as it continues to a climax.

Playing melodic themes on the timpani became possible late in the Romantic period through the addition of pedals, which enabled the player to regulate the tension of the drumheads more quickly and thereby change pitch.

The excitement that can be created by exploitation of rhythm is illustrated in the fugal section of the music. In the following example, the regular beats have a number above them, and the syncopated notes are marked by an X:

The meter changes from $\frac{2}{4}$ to $\frac{3}{4}$ and back to $\frac{2}{4}$.

The second movement is based on Billings' anthem "When Jesus Wept." The text of the original anthem is:

> *When Jesus wept, the falling tear*
> *In mercy flowed beyond all bound;*
> *When Jesus groaned, a trembling fear*
> *Seized all the guilty world around.*

The tenor drum with snares loosened opens the section. With its hollow sound, it imparts the feel of a funeral procession. The bassoon begins Billings' melody, followed by the oboe:

The melody is a moderately long round. Schuman probably chose these two instruments because their timbres suggest melancholy. The tune would not sound nearly as plaintive if played by a flute or clarinet.

After the oboe-bassoon duet, the strings play in the same mournful mood. The duet returns again to complete the three-part form. The funeral cadence of the drum closes the movement.

The final movement is based on Billings' marching song "Chester," and it is dazzling. A simplified score for it is included in the *Study Guide and Scores* book, and it appears on Record 5,A in the *Record Album*. The tune is played by the woodwinds in a straightforward hymn style. But suddenly the tempo doubles. Flashy runs are heard, and fragments of the theme appear from time to time. There is even a "fife and drum" duet between the piccolo and snare drum. The percussion instruments add conspicuously to the fireworks that conclude the triptych.

Mainstream Composers

Walter Piston (1894–1976) was somewhat classical in his writing. The music for his ballet *The Incredible Flutist* is often performed as an orchestral suite. Most of his works are instrumental and include several symphonies. For many years he taught at Harvard, and he wrote several textbooks on music theory.

William Grant Still (1895–1978) was the first black American composer to receive international recognition. He had varied experiences as a jazz musician and as a director in music publishing and recording. He studied with the composer Edgard Varèse. During his 50 years as a composer Still produced a variety of works, including popular songs and some experimental pieces as well as motion picture scores and religious music. Probably his best known work is *Afro-American Symphony*, composed in 1930.

Howard Hanson (1896–1981) is one of the outstanding names in American music. He is noted both as composer and teacher, and he served for many years as director of the Eastman School of Music. He promoted American music in many capacities. His works are romantic and rather heavy in nature. Hanson's Symphony No. 2 (*Romantic*) is a moving work. His opera *Merry Mount* is based on an early American story.

Virgil Thomson (b. 1896) was for many years the music critic for the New York *Herald Tribune*. He was not a prolific composer, but his works tend to be witty, sophisticated, and objective. He cooperated with Gertrude Stein on two operas: *Four Saints in Three Acts* and *The Mother of Us All*. Some of his film scores are played often, particularly *The Plow That Broke the Plains* and *The River*. He has also written some abstract instrumental works.

Roger Sessions (b. 1896) generally writes in a complicated manner. He maintains that instrumental music is a medium for expressing highly serious thoughts (not verbal ones, however). His music takes on the characteristics of depth and complexity. His not-lengthy list of compositions includes two operas as well as orchestral and chamber music. Like Piston, he was a university professor.

George Gershwin (1898–1937) had little musical training. His early efforts were confined to popular songs and musical comedies. In 1924, when he wrote *Rhapsody in Blue*, he did not feel competent to write for instruments other than the piano, so he had Ferde Grofé do the orchestration. Gershwin's writing style matured rapidly, only to be cut short when he died from a brain tumor. Other well-known works include *An American in Paris*, for orchestra; Concerto in F, for piano and orchestra; and *Porgy and Bess*, which was presented in this chapter.

Roy Harris (1898–1979) was a westerner in education and outlook. His interesting ideas about music contributed to some outstanding compositions. He believed that music should be emotional but not romantic and that emotion is best achieved when the tempo is kept close to that of the normal heartbeat (72 to 80 beats per minute). His most successful work is Symphony No. 3. It was written in 1937–1938 and is in one movement.

Samuel Barber (1910–1981) was a highly regarded American composer, as evidenced by his commission to compose an opera for the opening of the Metropolitan Opera House in Lincoln Center. His music frequently shows evidence of Neo-Romanticism, as in the lush *Adagio for Strings*. He was equally successful in vocal or instrumental mediums. Besides writing several symphonies and concertos, Barber combined vocalist and orchestra well in *Knoxville: Summer of 1915*. His opera *Vanessa* is considered one of the best written in the twentieth century.

Elliott Carter (b. 1908) developed slowly as a recognized composer. Since 1950, however, his work has assumed more importance and has received high praise from the critics. Most of his compositions are for instrumental groups. His style is complex and appears to be influenced by the music of Schoenberg and Stravinsky.

William Schuman was born in New York City in 1910 and entered the music world as a Tin Pan Alley songwriter and song plugger. At the same time, he was enrolled in a business curriculum at New York University. He heard his first symphony concert when he was about 20 years old. It had such an impact on him that the next day he withdrew from his business course and quit his job with an advertising agency. He switched his major to music. By the late 1930s Schuman's music was being performed by major orchestras at home and abroad. In 1945 he became president of the Juilliard School of Music, a position he held until 1961.

Schuman is equally successful in writing for vocal and for instrumental groups. Most of his vocal works date from the early 1940s and include *Pioneers*, based on Walt Whitman's poetry; a "secular cantata" titled *A Free Song*; and the short, vivacious "Holiday Song." His instrumental works are better known. They include a number of symphonies and chamber works. Some, such as *New England Triptych*, are based on nationalistic themes.

Alan Hovhaness Chakmakjian was born in 1911 in Somerville, Massachusetts, of Armenian-Scottish parents. Early in his career he dropped his long and complicated last name. From the beginning he seemed destined to bring together the best of two worlds, the old and the new, the Occident and the Orient. His musical training in his younger years was largely confined to Boston and the New England Conservatory of Music. He did, however, study astronomy and Eastern music and religions.

Hovhaness began to receive public attention in the late 1940s. Thereafter he received several awards and grants to study music and compose. These grants took him to India, Japan, and Korea. His creative work seems to have increased with these journeys. His opus numbers are well past 200.

Norman Dello Joio (b. 1913) combines old and new elements in his music. His *Ricercari, Variations, Chaconne and Finale,* and Concerto for Harp and Orchestra all employ old forms. He also reaches back in music history and selects portions of Gregorian chant for thematic material.

Vincent Persichetti (b. 1915) draws from any source and utilizes any technique that he thinks will contribute to his music. He is especially successful in writing for piano. His seven symphonies are worthy of careful listening, as is his Quintet for Piano and Strings.

Ulysses Kay (b. 1917) writes both instrumental and choral works. Probably his best known works in each areas are *Sinfonia in E,* written in 1950, and *Choral Triptych,* written in 1962.

Ned Rorem (b. 1912) is one of this century's most talented art-song composers. He studied for five years in France, and much of his music shows the French influence. *Poems of Love and the Rain* (1963) is a cycle of 17 songs, of which each text except one is set twice. Other groups of songs include *Two Poems of Plato* (1964, in Greek), *Hearing* (1966), and *Some Trees* (1968).

Gunther Schuller (b. 1925) is the leading advocate of what he calls the "third stream" movement, which combines contemporary art music and jazz. Unlike the planned jazz writing of Milhaud and others, actual improvisation by jazz musicians is called for in Schuller's music. Among his works in this vein are *12 by 11, Concertino for Jazz Quartet and Orchestra, Densities I,* and *Night Music.* These four works were written between 1955 and 1962. Prior to that time Schuller wrote abstract instrumental compositions using tone-row techniques, and since 1962 he has turned to opera. The "third stream" concept is an idea that seems logical but in fact is not easy to accomplish. So far it has not caught on in a big way, and Schuller himself has moved to other types of music.

Lukas Foss was born in Berlin in 1922 and came to America in 1937. His early works were in the style of Hindemith, but later he became interested in improvisation. *Time Cycle* was written for soprano and orchestra with improvised interludes.

Intellectualism

Not many American composers have been attracted to the tone-row techniques of Schoenberg as their dominant type of composition. Many of them have experimented with the idea, and some have used the principles of tone-row compositions for a few works. Only two names are rather generally associated with such compositions: Wallingford Riegger and Ernst Krenek.

Wallingford Riegger (1885–1961) began composing in the tone-row idiom soon after Schoenberg developed the style. He was essentially a conservative tone-row composer in that his rows often resembled traditional tonal music. Several of his best compositions are written for modern dance companies and for dancers such as Martha Graham and Charles Weidman. He also used Latin-American rhythms in some of his works. His best known orchestral work is Symphony No. 3.

Ernst Krenek (b. 1900) was born in Vienna and immigrated to the United States as a young man. His style is much more severe and stark than Riegger's. He was much influenced by primitive music, and he has maintained some of this tradition while writing in the serial or tone-row idiom. He has written a wide variety of works, including some for the stage, ballet, incidental music, film music, orchestral works, electronic music, and vocal and choral music.

Experimental Music

Since World War II American composers have turned increasingly to experimental and electronic music. It appears that some of the fires of nationalism that flamed in the music by American composers in the 1920s, '30s, and early '40s have given way to more international and experimental styles. The techniques of these composers are discussed more thoroughly in Chapter 26, which devotes its attention to experimental and electronic music.

George Antheil was born in 1900 in Trenton, New Jersey. He was one of the pioneers in breaking away from conventional music and advocating "an anti-expressive, anti-romantic, coldly mechanistic aesthetic." This belief led him to create the famous (or infamous) *Ballet mechanique* in 1924. The score specified eight pianos, a player piano, and an airplane propeller, but he later revised this score to include more pianos as well as anvils, bells, automobile horns, and buzz saws. Such compositions earned him a reputation as "the bad boy of music." Antheil had a variety of nonmusical interests also. He wrote several books, including one in which he predicted (and missed by one month) the bombing of Pearl Harbor by the Japanese in 1941. He also authored a book on criminology, advised police departments in criminal endocrinology, and with movie star Hedy Lamarr invented and patented a radio torpedo. Somehow in his busy life he found time to write six symphonies and a number of other stage works. He died in 1959.

Like Ernst Krenek, Edgard Varèse (1883-1965) was born and trained in Europe but spent most of his creative life in the United States. He is remembered as much for his influence on other American composers as for his own compositions. He was very much interested in tone colors and unusual rhythms, and he built strange and perplexing compositions by adding one layer of sound to another. Some of his better known works are *Octandre* (1923), *Hyperprism* (1923), *Ionisation* (1931), and *Density 21.5* (1936). Varèse was dreaming of electronic machines before they became a reality. His culminating work was written for the Brussels Worlds Fair in 1958—*Poème électronique*, an eight-hour work played stereophonically through 425 loudspeakers and accompanied by a series of images projected on a screen.

Henry Cowell (1897-1965) set about creating new sounds with the conventional piano. In some numbers he requires the pianist to play clusters of tones over two octaves with the left forearm. In another work he instructs the piano player to reach into the piano and strum the open strings. On other occasions he has a second person hold down some of the dampers on the keys throughout the performance of the composition.

Otto Luening and Vladimir Ussachevsky are considered here together because they have created a number of works jointly. Together they explored new avenues in electronic music in America.

Otto Luening was born in Milwaukee in 1900. He was a talented musician who studied flute and composition and later went to study music in Munich and Zurich. He returned to the United States in 1920 to become one of the cofounders of an opera company in Chicago.

Ussachevsky was born in Manchuria in 1911 of Russian parents. He came to the United States in 1930. He attended the Eastman School of Music, where he studied composition with Howard Hanson. He had written a number of compositions for conventional instruments and voices prior to moving into the field of electronic music.

Together Luening and Ussachevsky presented the first public concert of tape-recorded music in the United States. The year was 1952. Since that time they have explored this area extensively and have contributed much to the development of this type of music in America.

Milton Babbitt (b. 1916) was a trained mathematician. After World War II he started working with the tone-row system. Later, however, he became director of the Electronic Music Center operated jointly by Columbia and Princeton Universities. Since about 1960 almost all of his compositions have included electronic sound.

Charles Wuorinen (b. 1938) was born in New York City. His father was a history professor and his mother was an amateur musician. His interest in music began early, and at the age of 16 he won the Philharmonic Young Composer's Award. Since that time he has enjoyed a steady succession of awards, fellowships, and commissions. He has written some compositions in the tone-row system, but most have been in the electronic music area. Many of these works involve synthesized music coupled with conventional instruments.

John Cage (b. 1912) is undoubtedly the most experimental and controversial American composer. He was born in Los Angeles and received much of his early musical training from an aunt. Cage flirted with painting, literature, and architecture before deciding on a career in music. He studied for a while with Arnold Schoenberg, but he felt constrained by the rules of Schoenberg's type of composition. By the 1930s Cage was working with the "prepared piano"—tacks, bolts, and other foreign objects had been placed on the hammers and strings of the piano to produce different timbres when the keys were struck. About 1940 he became fascinated with oriental music and philosophy. This interest led to his chance or aleatory works discussed in the preceding chapter. His most famous work is 4'33", in which not a single sound is made! (The sounds will come, Cage claims, from our environment and our minds.)

From chance and indeterminacy Cage has more recently tried his hand at computer music with a work entitled *HPSCHD*, which employs a complicated mathematical computer program that is broken into 59 channels of sound.

George Crumb was born in Charleston, West Virginia, in 1929. Among the awards he has won are the Pulitzer Prize in 1968 for *Echoes of Time and the River: Four Processionals for Orchestra*, and the International Rostrum of Composers Award (UNESCO) and the Koussevitzky International Recording Award, both for his 1971 composition *Ancient Voices of Children*. His *Night of the Four Moons* was presented in Chapter 26. He currently teaches at the University of Pennsylvania.

Morton Subotnick (b. 1933) is an imaginative electronic composer. He teaches at the California Institute of the Arts at Valencia, established by the Walt Disney estate.

American music has had a rags-to-riches history. From weak imitations of European styles, American music has progressed to a place of equal prominence in the world. America has developed a body of music uniquely its own. With the tremendous vitality of its cultural life and the increasing attention being paid the arts, music in America should continue to change and expand.

28

Jazz, Rock, Country, Etc.

Jazz and rock are both American types of music. They are among our nation's most recognized contributions to the world of music. Both types have their promoters and detractors, and both developed under a cloud of doubt about their musical quality. Regardless of their artistic merits, or lack of them, no presentation of American music can be adequate without some discussion of jazz and rock.

Traditional Jazz

The roots of jazz reach back to black Americans' African heritage. But other elements have also influenced jazz: minstrel show music, work songs, field hollers, funeral marching bands, blues, French-Creole and Spanish-American music, and more recently, West Indian music. Jazz did not develop as a musical form until about the beginning of the twentieth century. Basin Street in New Orleans is traditionally considered its birthplace, and it was brought to public attention by the funeral procession. On the way back from the cemetery the band played its tunes in a way quite different from the somber sounds that accompanied the march to the gravesite. They shifted the emphasis from the strong to the weak beat, and the players launched into a decorated version of the melody. When Storyville, New Orleans' red-light district, was closed down in 1917, many jazz musicians lost their jobs and sought work in other cities. Jazz moved up the Mississippi River through Memphis and St. Louis to Chicago and the rest of the United States.

Two types of Afro-American folk music existed with early jazz and later merged with it. One of these was *ragtime.* It featured the piano, occasionally in combination with other instruments. The music sounds like a lively march with a decorated right-hand part. Early musicians associated with ragtime are Scott Joplin in

Sedalia, Missouri, and Ben Harvey, who published his *Ragtime Instructor* in 1897.

The other type of music involved with early jazz was the folk *blues*. Its musical characteristics will be discussed shortly. Some of the most famous names associated with blues are Leadbelly, a Texas convict whose real name was Huddie Ledbetter; W. C. Handy, who was known for his "Memphis Blues" and "St. Louis Blues"; and Ferdinand "Jelly Roll" Morton, whose first published blues appeared in 1905—the "Jelly Roll Blues."

Like folk music, jazz was created by mostly untutored musicians who could not have written down what they had played and sung if they had wanted to. But jazz is different in two respects. It has sprung from the cities rather than the fields and forests; it is an urban form of music. And for most people it is a spectator experience. Usually only a few people perform, although listeners may contribute a little hand clapping and foot stomping.

But what is jazz? It has several elements.

Melody. The most significant feature of jazz melodies is the *blue note*. These notes are derived from an altered version of the major scale. The blues scale merely lowers the third, fifth, and seventh steps. Many times performers shift between the regular note and its lower counterpart as if they were searching for a sound. And in truth they may be. The blue-note interval is an approximation of a microtone, roughly half of a half step in this case. The African heritage is the influence behind its use in jazz. Blue notes are a source of subtle color. Their effect in jazz is further enhanced by the fact that the chord in the harmony usually contains the particular note at its conventional pitch, while the lowered blue note appears simultaneously in the melody. This combination creates an interesting and characteristic dissonance.

Harmony. Early jazz harmony was as conservative as any church hymn. The typical chords were the same three that form the backbone of traditional tonal harmony: tonic (I), dominant (V), and subdominant (IV). More recently,

more modern versions of jazz have employed the advanced harmonic idioms of Debussy, Bartók, and Stravinsky. The appeal of jazz, however, does not lie primarily in its harmony.

Rhythm. Here is one of the most important features of jazz. Although its meter is nearly always two beats per measure, with irregular meters occurring only rarely, the jazz musician employs an endless variety of syncopated patterns and rhythmic figures over this regular pulse. Syncopation—the redistribution of accents so that the rhythmic patterns do not conform to the meter as the listener expects—is the lifeblood of jazz.

Jazz rhythms do not fit well into the traditional divisions of time according to sixteenths, eighths, and quarters. Jazz musicians perform rhythm with small deviations of timing and accent that cannot be adequately conveyed through notation. They even make slight alterations of conventional notation patterns when they read them. These deviations in rhythm are one reason that conservatory-trained musicians often do not achieve a true jazz sound.

Timbre. The basic tone color sought by jazz instrumentalists is perhaps an unconscious imitation of the black singing voice: a bit breathy, with a little vibrato (rapid and slight variance of pitch on a single tone). Certain instruments, therefore, have become associated with this idiom. The saxophone was intended to be a concert instrument, but it was taken up by jazz musicians because it can produce the desired quality. Besides, it is not so difficult to play, and it has a loud tone. Mutes—metal or fiber devices inserted in or over the bell to change the tone quality—are often used on brass instruments, and their names are as distinctive as the sounds they produce: *cup, wah-wah,* and *plunger,* the last of which can be duplicated by the end of a rubber sink plunger. Many jazz trumpeters use a particular type of mouthpiece that helps them produce a more shrill sound and makes high notes easier to play. In jazz style the clarinet is played in a manner that produces a saxophonelike quality. It differs from the orchestral clarinet's tone. The tone qualities of other instruments also vary according to whether they are playing orchestral music or jazz.

Some jazz timbres, like the bongo and conga drums and the Cuban cowbell, are from Afro-Cuban sources; others, such as the Chinese woodblock, cymbals, and vibraphone, have an oriental flavor.

Repetition of material. Jazz has no form that is applicable to all its styles. Generally it is a series of stanzas based on the chords to a popular tune. The form of the blues is more definite. A line is sung and immediately repeated, and then a third line concludes the stanza. Sometimes the singer does not sing all the way through a section, and an instrumentalist fills in with a short solo called a *break.*

Text. The metrical scheme of the text is often one of the standard poetic meters. It is not uncommon to find iambic pentameter in verses of the blues. The texts seldom have literary significance, but some are quite moving.

Improvisation. Improvisation is a fundamental component of jazz. Traditionally jazz is not written down because it is made up on the spot. This improvisation gives it its ever-fresh quality. Sometimes people confuse a lively popular song with jazz. A popular song does not become jazz until it is improvised upon.

What happens is this. The musicians agree that they will play a certain popular song in a certain key. They also agree generally on the order of each player's featured section. Then the first player, while keeping in mind the harmonies and melody of the song, improvises a part that reflects the rhythmic and melodic characteristics of the jazz style being played. This procedure is followed as each player takes a turn. On the final chorus all play together in simultaneous, semi-accidental counterpoint. It is like an improvised musical conversation. Throughout the number no player knows exactly what the others will do, but each follows

his musical instinct and fits his part in with the others. Nor is he entirely certain what he himself will do, because each time he takes a "ride" on the number, he will play it somewhat differently.

In several types of jazz a number of players improvise at the same time. This results in a type of "accidental" counterpoint that is held together only by the song's basic harmony and the musical instincts of the players. The presence of simultaneous improvisations in both African music and jazz can hardly be a coincidence. Sometimes there seems to be so much improvisation that the melody is no longer identifiable. Why? Because the player improvises on the basic harmony as well as on the melody. For example, if the song starts on the tonic chord, as it usually does, and if the piece is in the key of C, then the notes of the tonic chord will be C E G. The improviser may play any or all of these three notes and can play tones that are nonharmonic in relation to that chord. In other words, the player can weave other tones around the notes of the chord. That is why the melody of the popular song may no longer be recognizable in the new embroidery of sound.

The particular song may get lost for another reason. Many popular songs have simple chord patterns, so there is often little difference between the chords of one popular song and another. When the melody is being improvised upon, the harmony is often not distinguishable from that of other songs. And the rhapsodic nature of jazz improvisation also leads to a sameness of mood that makes it more difficult to distinguish the basic song.

The Development of Jazz

The 1920s saw the real emergence of jazz, which was given impetus in 1918 by Joe "King" Oliver's famous Creole Jazz Band in Chicago. Other musicians soon became prominent: Paul Whiteman, whose band presented the first jazz concert in 1924, featuring the premiere of George Gershwin's *Rhapsody in Blue;* Bessie Smith, the famous blues singer; Fletcher Henderson and his band; Bix Beiderbecke, who

Duke Ellington in 1943. (Library of Congress.)

started "white" jazz with his cornet and the band called the "Wolverines"; and the notable Louis Armstrong, who began his music making as a boy in a New Orleans waif band. Through his trumpet playing and vocal renditions, Armstrong had much influence on the basic sound and style of jazz.

The prevailing style in the 1920s was *Dixieland*. It is characterized by a strong upbeat, a meter of two beats to the measure, and certain tonal and stylistic qualities that are impossible to notate. It has a "busy" sound, since there is simultaneous improvisation by perhaps four to seven players. Dixieland style used to be described as "hot"; it is fast, furious, and usually loud.

During the depression of the 1930s, the hiring of bands became prohibitively expensive. So pianists enjoyed increasing popularity, especially as they developed a jazz piano style called *boogie-woogie*. It features a persistently repeated melodic figure in the bass, or, in musical terms, an ostinato. Usually the boogie-woogie ostinato consists of eight notes per measure, which explains why this type of music is some-

times called "eight to the bar." Over the continuous bass the pianist plays trills, octave tremolos (the rapid alternation of pitches an octave apart), and other melodic figures.

The *swing era* in jazz lasted from 1935 to about 1950. It featured intricate arrangements and big bands of about 17 players, under the leadership of such musicians as Benny Goodman, Count Basie, and Duke Ellington. It was also the era of the featured soloist—Gene Krupa, Fats Waller, and Tommy Dorsey, to name a few. Other notable figures from the period include Artie Shaw, Harry James, Glenn Miller, Coleman Hawkins, and Fletcher Henderson. Musically, swing has four beats to the measure and rhythm with a "bounce." The swing era was one in which the audience danced. Its "concert halls" were such places as the Roseland Ballroom in New York and California's Hollywood Palladium.

Following World War II there emerged a style called *bebop*, or, more commonly, *bop*. It was developed chiefly by Charlie "Bird" Parker and Dizzy Gillespie, who once defined the term by saying that in bop you go *Ba-oo Ba-oo Ba-oo* instead of *Oo-ba Oo-ba Oo-ba*. What he was describing was the nearly continuous syncopation that occurs in bop. It also features dissonant chords and freely developed melodies. Often the performers play in unison at the octave instead of presenting the traditional improvised counterpoint. In bop the fifth degree of the scale is lowered, which is a carry-over of the blue notes discussed earlier. The bass drum does not sound all the time—a change from earlier styles. Instead, the bass viol is given the responsibility for keeping the beat. Bop bands were much smaller than the bands of the swing era.

Stan Kenton was the leader of *progressive* jazz, which is characterized by big bands and highly dissonant chords. In a sense, the progressive style is an updated, intellectual version of the swing style that prevailed about 15 years earlier.

With Miles Davis and Dave Brubeck, jazz turned toward a "cool" style, still intellectual and well ordered but performed by much smaller groups. Charlie Mingus, Ornette Coleman, and John Coltrane led a movement to-

The Grateful Dead (Steve Renick.)

ward *free form* jazz, in which all restraints were removed. No longer was improvisation held together by the harmony.

Over the years jazz has become more a "listener's" type of music, in contrast to its early history. Gone is much of jazz's image as a "music of the people." It has "grown up" in the sense that it is not always played just for fun, at least not by many jazz musicians. It is now serious business, performed by musicians who have studied Stravinsky and Bartók. Jazz represents the rediscovery of the art of improvising, which was largely neglected after the time of Bach and Mozart. Perhaps it was a better counterbalance to the deadly seriousness of nineteenth-century music than were the arty, chic attempts promoted by Satie and his followers.

Rock

Rock is generally considered to be a combination of the rhythm-and-blues music of America's blacks and the country-western style associated with Nashville, Tennessee. The people most associated with early rock (then called rock 'n' roll) in the 1950s are Elvis Presley, Jerry Lee Lewis, Little Richard, Chubby Checker, and Bill Haley and His Comets. The music was as forceful and untamed as the image Presley projected with his leather jacket and swaying body (earning him the title "Elvis the Pelvis"). The pounding beat of rock led one critic to define it as "Music in which the bass drum carries the melody."

As rock developed in the 1960s, it became somewhat more complex. The twist and discotheques came in about 1960, followed two years later by the "surfing" music of the Beach Boys and Jan and Dean. The "English invasion," as some writers refer to it, took place about 1964 with the appearance of the Beatles and the Rolling Stones. That was also the year that the "Motown sound" was born with the Supremes and other groups. Folk rock appeared about 1965 with Bob Dylan, the Byrds, and the Mamas and the Papas. Psychedelic or "acid" rock appeared in 1966 with such groups as the Jefferson Airplane (now known as Jefferson Starship) and the Grateful Dead. By the early 1970s there were many types of rock, including combinations of rock with religious, theatrical, blues, jazz, and other styles. The Beatles were representative of the changes that took place in rock during the 1960s. They moved from the early "funky" sound to music that contained elements of electronic music, Baroque style, oriental music, and nineteenth-century art songs. However, the group's final recording, before they broke up in the late 1960s, was a return to the early rock sound.

How does rock differ from jazz? One characteristic of rock has already been mentioned: the heavy beat.

A second characteristic is frequent use of the modal harmonies that had fallen into disuse after the Renaissance. By 1970 more popular songs and rock pieces were in modes than were in the traditional major-minor system.

A third characteristic of rock is the departure from the standard formal schemes of the popular songs of previous decades. Most popular songs had been in an $a\ a\ b\ a$ form, with eight measures for each portion. Rock phrases are more irregular, perhaps to fit the blank verse of many of the texts.

A fourth and very significant feature of rock involves the different timbre of the music. The dance band of the preceding decades, with its saxes and trumpets, was replaced by the small group, with its electric guitars and electronic organ or piano. Rock is often played through amplifiers turned up to a loud level. The singing is generally a little higher in pitch and lighter in quality than the singing in earlier pop music.

A fifth change in rock is the use of different chordal progressions. The traditional dominant-to-tonic progression is less favored than adjacent or parallel chord movement (e.g., I-II-I-VII-I). Other somewhat nontraditional patterns are also found. The use of the modes gives the chords a different quality.

A sixth feature of rock is the dominance of small groups (many times composed only of males) instead of the individual "idol" of the preceding decades. The appearance of the groups is different too. From the dinner jacket of the 1930s and '40s and the leather jacket of the late 1950s, the style of performers' clothes

has changed to highly individual attire that ranges from denim to very bizarre outfits.

A seventh characteristic is the dependence on recordings. Rock music exists primarily on records and tapes. "Live" performances are limited, and some performers never perform in person. The sound of a recording is affected significantly by recording engineers.

An eighth feature of rock is its folk qualities. Some actual folk melodies have been revived, and much folklike music has been created. Like folk music, rock is often learned by imitation and is not written down.

A ninth characteristic of rock is its great diversity. For many people rock has become synonymous with popular music, so the word *rock* has lost some accuracy in definition. Some rock is in a quite conventional ballad style and is hardly rock at all; some borrows freely from art music; some is known as "new wave," some as "punk" rock; some is a form of social protest against injustices in society; some involves the dubbing in of electronic sounds; some is in a folk style; some is surrealistic or intentionally absurd; some is barbaric and psychedelic and is performed to flashing lights; some involves exaggerated emotions on the part of the performers; some is violent and animal-like in its primitive sounds; some is strongly oriental in character. There is also "bubble-gum" rock for early adolescents.

Like jazz, rock has now been around long enough for nostalgic revivals of earlier rock styles and stars.

Rock is as much a social as a musical phenomenon. It is often identified as the music of youth. The large number of people between the ages of 10 and 25, the affluence that allows them to buy records and clothes of their choice, the youth orientation of American culture, the rapid rate of technological and social change that has increased the differences in viewpoint and orientation between young and old, the advent of mass communication, television, and especially the prevalence of recorded music—all of these factors and more have contributed to a musical situation that is unlike anything ever encountered before.

Another difference from previous times is the current importance of the recording sound engineer. Most popular music, especially rock, is nearly as much the technician's creation as it is the performer's. The development of the multiple-track tape recorder allows for the easy addition of accompanying parts and additional sounds. Also, a great deal of music judgment is required in reducing or "mixing down" the 16 or more tracks to the final stereo, or 2-track, version. In addition to adjusting the loudness of the various tracks, the sound engineer can add or subtract reverberation, control the sense of presence in the sound, and alter the timbre of instruments and voices. Errors can be spliced out and corrections inserted. The final record is usually quite different from the original sound—the record is likely to be far more impressive.

Other Types of Popular Music

Country. The country music associated with Nashville, Tennessee, has been popular for many years. The musical qualities of the country style reveal an ancestry in the southern mountain folk songs, which in turn grew out of English folk songs. The texts are sometimes narrative in form, and they often express sadness. The harmony, rhythm, and phrase patterns are simple and direct. The songs are often accompanied by electric guitars and fiddle, except in the bluegrass style, in which only acoustic (nonelectric) instruments are acceptable. The singing quality contains little vibrato or dynamic range, and there is a tinge of melancholy in the tone. Notes are seldom sustained.

As with any popular style, the sociological factors are as significant as the musical factors. The increased interest in country music correlates to the renewed interest in "nostalgia"—the looking back with favor on the past when life seemed simpler and happier. The primary audience for country music is the white working-class population. The enthusiasm and loyalty to its stars, such as Johnny Cash, the late Hank Williams, Buck Owens, Mel Tillis, Dolly Parton, Loretta Lynn, and others, are great. In country music soloists are more significant than groups.

Soul. Soul is the popular music associated with America's black population. Its musical qualities reveal some aspects of African music, especially in the style of singing. It is emotional and forceful, with calls and exclaimed words. Open chords and parallel chord movement are characteristic of its harmony. The dynamic levels are often loud.

Some writers include rhythm-and-blues and gospel music in the soul category, and the relationships are close among these styles. Prominent names in soul music include James Brown, Smokey Robinson, Wilson Pickett, and the groups associated with the Motown sound.

Sometimes the same song will reach the top of popularity charts in the soul, country, and general popular music listings, but only occasionally. For example, the Beatles were never particularly popular with blacks. The ethnic associations of popular music influence its acceptance with various segments of the population. The preference is based on the style and timbre of the music rather than on the message of the words, although the background of the performer makes some difference. A few songs with a message about war, poverty, or ecology achieved limited popularity in the late 1960s and early 1970s, but the trend then returned to the overwhelmingly favorite topic of popular songs: love and its pain and joy.

Broadway musicals. The Broadway musical is an American tradition extending back well into the nineteenth century, although it has distant ancestors in the *vaudevilles* of France and the *Beggar's Opera* of Handel's London. An immediate predecessor was the operetta, which was usually based on long-ago-and-far-away subjects, such as those in Sigmund Romberg's *The Desert Song* and Victor Herbert's *The Red Mill* (which takes place in Holland). By today's standards the operetta seems stilted. In the past 50 years musicals have become more contemporary and substantive.

West Side Story, the musical by Leonard Bernstein and Stephen Sondheim, is an example of this change. It is about the gang fights and prejudice between ethnic groups on the

West Side of Manhattan. The plot is an updated version of the Romeo and Juliet story. It features Tony, a young man of Polish descent, and Maria, a Puerto Rican girl. Instead of a balcony, as in Shakespeare's version, they meet on a fire escape. Before the story concludes, Tony unintentionally kills Maria's brother in a gang fight, and Tony is killed in an act of revenge by the Puerto Rican gang. He dies in Maria's arms.

The setting allows Bernstein, who was for over a decade Musical Director of the New York Philharmonic and a recognized composer and pianist, to write in the varied styles of his cosmopolitan musical interests. Latin American music is represented by the song "America," a number in the style of a *huapango* with alternating meters, and by portions of "The Dance at the Gym," which was mentioned in Chapter 4. Jazz is especially evident in the "Jet Song" and "Cool." Popular ballad style is well represented by "Tonight" and "Maria." Operatic influences can be heard in "I Have a Love" and "One Hand, One Heart." Humor has its moment in "Gee, Officer Krupke!" The musical opens typically with an overture, which is a potpourri of the songs in the show. *West Side Story* also contains dances woven naturally into the action.

Because it is live theater, the Broadway musical is tailored for its audience. A musical is normally tried out in Philadelphia, New Haven, or another "out-of-town" city prior to opening in New York. Portions of the musical that appear not to please the audience are deleted or rewritten. No one worries about being faithful to an artistic goal or theory because the main concern is: Is it good box office? Such a situation would appear to be harmful to creative artists and writers. Interestingly, this has not usually been the case. Composers, writers, and stage directors have worked around the limitations of audience preferences and often produced imaginative and worthy productions. The Broadway musical is thriving.

By no means have all the types of popular music been covered. In addition to jazz, rock, country, soul, and Broadway musicals, there are the songs of Burt Bacharach and other music for films, the big band sounds of Buddy Rich and Doc Severinsen, the staid music of Lawrence Welk, and many more. The world of music is larger and more interesting because of the many types of popular music.

Appendix A

Attending Musical Performances

It is possible, of course, to hear music by listening to a recording. However, recordings do not provide the sense of involvement that attending a performance does. Listening to a recording is like watching a movie or television version of a play; it is more detached and less immediate.

You should be aware that the opportunity to attend musical performances will never be so convenient or inexpensive (that's right) again after you finish college. Colleges offer performances of students and faculty, and often bring in outstanding professional performers in a concert series. Most on-campus performances are free, especially those presented by students. The professional performers (with the exception of popular music performers) who appear on campus can usually be heard by students at reduced ticket prices.

Assuming that you (or your instructor) have decided that you will attend a performance or two, what performance should you go to? Some, such as symphony orchestra concerts and chamber-music performances, are quite formal; others, such as jazz performances, are less formal. Usually only one type of music is performed at a performance. Rarely is a symphony orchestra followed by a rock band.

Performances also differ in length. Usually a recital (which implies that it is for a soloist or small group) lasts about an hour and a half, probably with an intermission. An orchestra concert is somewhat longer, and rock and jazz performances can be quite a bit longer. Longest of all, usually, are operas and oratorios, which can last for three hours or more.

Concerts of instrumental music usually don't have a great deal of visual interest. The players sit and play, and that's it. Opera has the visual elements of scenery, costumes, and actions. Popular music concerts are often "choreographed" with motions and dancelike routines.

When attending a musical performance, keep in mind that the main reason for being there is to listen to the music. You will then be in the proper frame of mind to gain the psychological satisfaction and enjoyment described in Chapter 1. It is easy to be distracted at a performance by such things as what to wear, when to applaud, how to act, and so on. These are secondary matters, but if they become primary concerns, the performance will probably not be enjoyable.

Let's take a look at some of these secondary matters. What are some of the traditions associated with audience behavior? At performances of art music, do *NOT* talk, whisper, rustle a program, or cough while the music is being performed. (Experienced concert-goers seem to have trained themselves to hold back all coughing and related activity until the end of a movement or work.) If the main point of attending a performance is to listen to music, then nothing should intrude on anyone's concentration.

As for applause, *never* (well, almost never) applaud between the movements of an instrumental work. Save it until the entire work is completed. In an opera there is applause after duets, solos, and choruses. Sometimes the verbal cheering of "Bravo" is in order. There is much applauding in jazz and rock concerts at the ends of songs and after individual solos. If you are in doubt about when to applaud, just hold back and imitate what others at the concert do.

The conductor is given special treatment at a performance of art music. He or she is the last to enter and is applauded by the audience (but not the performers unless it is a guest conductor). The conductor also bows after the performance and acknowledges the orchestra members by shaking the hand of the first violinist, who is referred to as the *concertmaster*. Individual members of the group are acknowledged by standing and being applauded if the performers have had an especially important part that was performed well. Quite often the entire group is asked to stand.

Soloists rate even higher on the "recognition order" than the conductors. They enter last and leave first, and usually take some bows alone.

Most performances have a printed program listing the music to be performed, usually given to you when you enter the hall. Seldom are the works to be performed announced from the stage, except at popular music programs. Even the traditional extra number, or *encore*, played or sung at the end of the performance is often not announced.

The opposite page shows a program containing a minimum amount of information. It lists the names of the group or the individuals if there are only a few of them. On one side of the page are the names of the compositions, and on the other side are the composers and/or arrangers, sometimes giving the years that the persons lived. For works with several movements, each movement is listed by its main tempo marking. Song recitals have programs listing each song by title and composer, and oratorios list each recitative, aria, and chorus. An opera program looks like the program for a play, with a listing of acts and scenes and a short phrase about the time and place. Opera programs often contain a synopsis of the story. Some programs for professional performances contain notes interspersed among the advertisements. These remarks may be helpful, and then again they may not; it depends on how well the writer communicates with nonmusicians.

The dress of both the audience and the performers is somewhat dictated by tradition. Instrumentalists wear a conservative suit or dress for afternoon performances and black for evening performances. Thus, they keep their attire from drawing attention from the music. Choirs often wear robes for the same reason. In popular music there is an emphasis on the personality of the performer; so much variety of dress is almost expected.

The tradition that the audience wears tuxedos and long dresses to performances of music has long since passed in most places. Usually you will be wearing the right thing if you put on a coat and tie or dressy outfit for Sunday and evening concerts. Other performances are less formal and almost anything clean is appropriate.

Yes, traditions or no traditions, musical performances can be enjoyable.

1982/1983

INDIANAPOLIS SYMPHONY ORCHESTRA

JOHN NELSON, Music Director
Raymond Harvey, Exxon/Arts Endowment Conductor
Kenneth Kiesler, Assistant Conductor
Erich Kunzel, Sunday Night Pops Music Director

Great Classics Series/Second Concert
Thursday Morning, October 21, at 11:00
Friday Evening, October 22, at 8:30
Saturday Evening, October 23, at 5:30

KAREL HUSA   *Music for Prague 1968**
Introduction and Fanfare
Aria
Interlude
Toccata and Chorale

HAYDN   Concerto for Cello and Orchestra in
D Major, VIIb:2
Allegro moderato
Adagio
Rondo: Allegro

LYNN HARRELL, Cello

Intermission

SCHUMANN   Symphony No. 3 in E-flat, ("Rhenish"),
Op. 97
Lebhaft
Scherzo: Sehr Massig
Nicht schnell
Feierlich
Lebhaft

JOHN NELSON, Conductor

Notes for this program begin on page 41.

*First ISO performance.

Appendix B

How Music Is Written Down

The ability to read or at least follow written music is not necessary for understanding what is heard, but it certainly helps. Like getting across town—you *can* walk, but it is easier and faster on a bicycle or in a car.

How does reading notation help you learn more about music? Mainly by reinforcing visually what you hear. What you see *and* hear is usually remembered better than what you only see *or* hear. The relative values of seeing and hearing differ for each person. Some people find a visual image (including written words) to be of limited value, while others rely strongly on sight.

Notation is educationally useful because you can look at the symbols and gain some idea of how the music will sound. You can tell if the notes go up or down or stay at the same level. And many people have a general notion about how rhythmic values are represented in the notes. So you can often follow a line of music, even if you can't read it in the sense of singing or playing it.

Importance of Notation to Music

Music is an art that depends on re-creation. When you look at a painting, a piece of sculpture, or a building, you experience exactly what the artist created without involving an intervening person. Not so with music. Someone must bring it to life; it requires an intermediary. A few compositions exist only on discs or tape, and in such cases there is no performing intermediary. In some types of music, such as jazz, the performer is the creator of the music because, to a degree, it is made up as the performer goes along. However, in most cases even composers can't remember or render their own music completely. They can't play several instruments at once, and they can't perform their music if they are not physically present. So other performers are needed.

Until notation was developed, all music had to be remembered, and human memories are only partially accurate. Furthermore, works that exist only in people's minds are generally short. It is very difficult to remember extended compositions without the aid of notation. Some folk pieces are long, especially the music in African and Indian ceremonies, but these usually repeat basically the same music over and over with slight variations.

Until the twentieth century, notation was the only means of preserving music accurately. Even today with the means to record music, notation is almost always necessary if a performer is to render what someone else has written. Learning a piece by listening to a recording is only moderately successful, and it is usually limited to short works.

Limitations of Notation

People have found it difficult to devise a system of musical notation. Systems of writing existed at least 2,000 years before the present system was developed. The earliest attempts at indicating music were "cue cards" that reminded the performer what to do. They were about as useful as telling someone how to find a particular place in a city by saying, "Go south for a while, then turn east for a short distance, then go further south, then a little more to the east—you can't miss it."

A more specific system was developed in the eleventh century by a monk named Guido

d'Arezzo, who came up with the idea of establishing relationships between pitches. With only minor changes his ideas appear today as the *solfa* syllables—*do, re, mi, fa, sol, la,* and *ti.* These syllables imply a fixed relationship between any two notes. *Do* to *re* is a standard distance, *re* to *fa* is another, and so on for all combinations of pitches in a given key.

Guido's idea is effective in learning to read music, but it is inadequate as a system of notation, for two reasons. One, it doesn't specify exact pitches; it indicates only relationships. Two, it fails to account for rhythm.

Notation of pitch. Modern notation specifies pitch by placing marks on horizontal lines, somewhat like a graph. Each line and space represents a specific pitch. Only five lines are grouped together because more than that would make it harder for the eye to locate notes. The exact pitch is indicated by a *clef* that tells the musician what note names are assigned to each line and space. The five lines in the clef are called a *staff*. Three types of clefs are used in America: 𝄢 called the F, or *bass*, clef (pronounced base); 𝄞 called the G, or *treble*, clef; and 𝄡 called the C clef, which serves as both the *alto* and the *tenor* clef. The clefs indicate definite pitches, all named for letters of the alphabet from A to G. The note names indicated by the treble and bass clefs are shown in Figure 1.

The pitch G is indicated by the treble clef at the point where the curl goes around the sec-

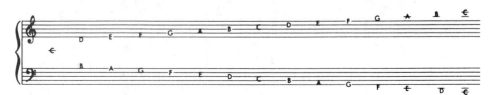

Figure 1.

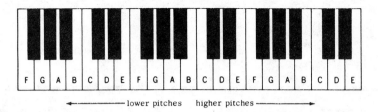

F G A B C D E F G A B C D E F G A B C D E

←——————— lower pitches   higher pitches ———————→

Figure 2.

ond line. The two dots of the bass clef appear on either side of the fourth line, which is F; the large dot of the bass clef begins on the same F line. In the alto and tenor clefs the line on which the two bows meet is the pitch C.

Small changes of pitch are indicated by the *sharp* sign (♯) or the *flat* sign (♭). The general term for these signs is *accidentals*. The sharp placed before a note raises the pitch one half step, while the flat placed before a note lowers the pitch one half step. Sometimes the *natural* sign (♮) is seen. It cancels a sharp or flat previously applied to the note.

When certain notes in a piece are flatted or sharped consistently the composer writes the appropriate sharps or flats at the beginning of each staff of music, to save writing the sign each time that particular note appears in the music. These clusters of sharps or flats at the beginning of each line are called the *key signature*.

The pitch range of a staff can be extended upward or downward by adding short horizontal lines called *leger lines*. Some leger lines appear in Figure 1.

Pitches on the keyboard. Most instruments are constructed in such a way that the pitch rela-

tionships of the notes are not visible to the eye. Keyboard instruments such as the piano and organ are different because the pattern of pitches is visible. The black keys on the piano are found in groups of twos and threes. All white keys are identified in relation to these groups of black keys. For example, every C on the piano is a white key immediately to the left of a two-black-key group; every F is a white key immediately to the left of a three-black-key group. The white keys are named consecutively from left to right, using the letters A to G (Figure 2).

To find the sharp of any white key on the piano, find the black key touching it on the *right*. To find the flat of any white key, find the black key touching it on the *left*. If there is no black key on the side where you are looking, the nearest white key in that direction is the sharp or flat.

On the keyboard in Figure 3, notice that each black key has two names. For instance, the key can be called G sharp (because it is to the right of G) or A flat (because it is to the left of A).

Middle C, the note midway between the treble and bass staffs, is also the C nearest the middle of the piano keyboard. Using this as a guide, you can look at any note on the staff and find the exact tone it represents (see Figure 4).

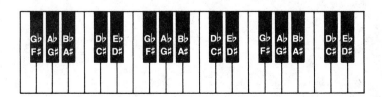

Figure 3.

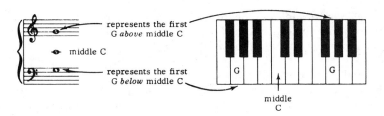

Figure 4.

Rhythm. In addition to indicating pitch according to its placement on the staff, each note indicates a duration. Basic to the notational system for rhythm is the 2:1 ratio that shows comparative durations. For example, a whole note (o) lasts twice as long as a half note (♩), which lasts twice as long as a quarter note (♩). An eighth note (♪) is half as long as a quarter note, and a sixteenth note (♪) is half as long as an eighth note. In the following chart of note values, the dotted arrows represent the passing of time; they do not appear in actual music.

Consecutive notes may share flags (wavy lines on the stems) for ease in writing and reading:

The notes represent sound; *rests* indicate silence. The 2:1 ratio also applies to rests. The symbol for the whole rest is ▬ (hanging from the fourth line of the staff). The symbol for the half rest is ▬ (sitting on top of the third line).

Notes are sometimes seen with a dot to the right of the note head. A dot on the right (*not* over or under the note head) adds *one-half* of the note's value to the note. If a half note receives two beats, a dotted half note lasts for two beats *plus* half again as much (one beat), for a total of three beats.

$$♩. = ♩ + ♪ = 1½ \text{ beats}$$

$$♩. = 2 + 1 = 3 \text{ beats}$$

$$♪. = ♪ + ♪ = ¾ \text{ of a beat}$$

$$o. = 4 + 2 = 6 \text{ beats}$$

Measures are set apart by vertical bar lines on the staff. (In fact, measures are sometimes called *bars*.) Each measure contains all the notes to be sounded over the span of time designated by the meter.

Two-beat meter:

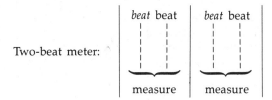

Any type of note can equal one beat. The type of note is indicated in the *meter signature* (also called *time signature*). The meter signature appears at the beginning of nearly every piece of music. Most meter signatures aren't hard to figure out. The *top* number indicates the number of beats in each measure: A 4 means four beats, a 3 means three beats, and so on—usually.

The *bottom* number in the meter signature tells which note value lasts for one beat: 4 means a quarter note, 8 means an eighth note, and so on—usually. The 2:1 ratio mentioned earlier is maintained no matter what note value represents the beat. Therefore, it is possible to write music by choosing any one of two or three different note values for the beat; each version will sound exactly the same but the notation will look different.

The meter signature is *not a fraction;* $\frac{3}{4}$ does *not* mean three-fourths because it does not represent a portion of anything. Two abbreviated meter signatures are seen frequently: C (common time) means $\frac{4}{4}$, and ₵ (cut time, sometimes called *alla breve*) means $\frac{2}{2}$.

Meters are of two types. One has beats that are subdivided into a background of twos, and it is called *simple* time. The other, called *compound* time, subdivides the beat into threes. The meter signature for compound time is more complex. Since the common note values subdivide in multiples of *two*, some type of *dotted* note must represent multiples of *three*. (Since a dot adds half the preceding value—or one-third of the note's total duration—a dotted beat note creates the 3:1 ratio necessary for notating compound meter.) Furthermore, the meter signature must somehow indicate to the performer that the meter is compound. A signature such as is $\frac{2}{1\frac{1}{2}}$ impracticable, so the number of beat *subdivisions* is indicated in the top number, and the note value of each of these subdivisions is indicated in the bottom number. A meter signature of $\frac{6}{8}$ usually means that there are two beats per measure, and a dotted quarter note lasts for one beat:

Tempo. The meter signature says nothing about the tempo of the music—the speed at which the beats recur. Tempo is indicated in two ways. One way is to specify the number of beats per minute. Some pieces display a marking like this at the beginning: $\bullet$ = M.M. 120. The initials M.M. stand for Maelzel's Metronome. (Maelzel patented the work of another man and had the device named for himself.) The number refers to the number of ticks that are to be produced per minute. The quarter note means that in this particular piece each quarter note should last for one tick, with other note values in proportion to this norm.

The other way to indicate tempo is to provide verbal directions, such as fast or slow. These provide only a general idea of the speed of the music. The words are traditionally written in Italian, although in the last 100 years some composers with strong feelings of nationalism have chosen to use their native tongue. These words are significant for the listener because they are often listed in concert programs to identify the large sections of a piece of music. Here are some of the most common terms.

Italian Term	*Meaning*
Largo	Very slow, broad
Grave	Very slow, heavy
Adagio	Slow, leisurely
Andante	"Walking," moderate tempo, unhurried
Moderato	Moderate speed
Allegretto	"Little allegro," moving easily
Allegro	Moderately fast, moving briskly
Allegro molto	"Much allegro," very brisk
Vivace	Lively
Presto	Very fast
Prestissimo	As fast as possible

Composers often couple other directives with the tempo marking. Usually the additions have more to do with style than with speed (such as *con fuoco,* with fire or force; *sostenuto,* smooth, sustained). Within the broad framework of a specified tempo there may be indications of lesser tempo changes: *meno,* less (as in *meno allegro*); *piu,* more; *poco,* a little; *rit.* or *ritard,* gradually slower; *accel.* or *accelerando,* gradually faster.

Dynamics. The notes themselves provide no indication of the dynamic level at which they should be sounded. To inform the performer about this, the composer places small letters at appropriate places in the music. Two Italian words are basic: *p,* or *piano,* which means soft; and *f,* or *forte,* which means loud. (The instrument known today as the piano was originally called the *pianoforte* because it was able to make gradual changes from loud to soft.) The descriptive words can be even more extreme: *ff,* or *fortissimo,* means very loud; and *pp,* or *pianissimo,* means very soft. Or they can be made more moderate by adding the prefix *mezzo* (pronounced *met*-zo), meaning medium; *mf,* or *mezzo forte,* means moderately loud; and *mp,* or *mezzo piano,* means moderately soft.

Gradual changes of volume are indicated by *cresc.* or *crescendo,* meaning get louder; and *decresc.* or *decrescendo,* meaning get softer. The latter term can be indicated equally well by *dim.* or *diminuendo.* Frequently the *crescendo* is represented by the sign ◁ and the *decrescendo* by the sign ▷.

Indications about dynamics are not the only marks telling the performer how to interpret a certain passage in the music. Some markings tell the performer to "punch out" a note, some direct holding a note longer than normal, and some call for a particular style in sounding a passage. Occasionally words describing the desired expression are written on the music.

Our present system of music notation is a significant accomplishment, but it is inadequate in many ways. It is rather specific about pitch and rhythm, but it can't show the subtle deviations that make a performance musically satisfying. A performance that adheres slavishly to just what the printed music specifies will sound mechanical and dull. Also, some styles are especially difficult to put into notation. The limitations of printed symbols place quite a bit of responsibility on the performer, for whom the page of music is about as complete as the script of a play is for an actor. It provides the bare essentials. It is the performer who must bring the notes on the page to life as music.

Glossary

The number at the end of each definition indicates the page on which the term is defined in context.

Absolute music Music that is free of extramusical associations. 182

A cappella Unaccompanied choral music. 160

Accidental A sharp, flat, or natural sign written in the music to show a departure from the prevailing key signature. 282

Aleatory music Music in which the sounds are partly or entirely the result of chance. 249

Anthem A religious choral work in English performed in a Protestant worship service. 175

Aria A long and complex vocal solo with instrumental accompaniment. 61

Arpeggio In "harp" style; a broken chord in which the notes are played one after another instead of simultaneously. 22

Art music Music that exists only for the intellectual and psychological satisfaction it provides. 4

Art song A musical setting of a text by a trained composer. 56

Atonality Music not in any key or tonality. 22

Ballad An English narrative folk song told in simple verse. 149

Beat A recurrent pulse in music. 24

Bel canto Literally, "beautiful singing" in Italian; a style of opera in the first part of the nineteenth century that featured much vocal technique. 127

Binary form Two-part form, *A B*. 55

Bitonality Two or more different keys occurring simultaneously. 237

Blues A forerunner of jazz containing certain lowered pitches in the melody and organized into 12-measure phrases. 270

Boogie-woogie A jazz piano style featuring a repeated figure in the bass part and highly decorated melody line. 272

Bop (bebop) An advanced jazz style for a small group involving nearly continuous syncopation and flowing melodic line. 272

Cadence A melodic or harmonic formula that gives a sense of phrase ending. In poetic usage it sometimes refers to "beat" or "tempo." 22

Cadenza A section of free material that sounds improvised, played by the soloist in a concerto. 86

Canon Music in which one or more lines imitate one another for an entire work. 30

Cantata A short oratorio, often developed around a chorale melody. 174

Chaconne A work featuring variations on a pattern of chords that are repeated throughout the work. 30

Chamber music Instrumental music in which each part is performed by only one player. 94

Character piece A short keyboard work expressing a mood or idea composed during the Romantic period. 111

Chorale A stately hymn tune used in the German Lutheran Church. 174

Chord The simultaneous sounding of three or more pitches. 21

Choreographer The person who plans the movements of dancers. 133

Chorus (1) A sizable group of singers that sings choral music; (2) a section of an opera or oratorio sung by a chorus. 62

Chromatic Melodic or harmonic movement by half steps. 17

Clavier A general term indicating any keyboard instrument. 104

Coda, codetta The concluding portion of a section or movement, usually giving an impression of an ending. 71

Concertmaster The first chair player in the first violin section of an orchestra. 278

Concerto A multi-movement work contrasting music for a solo instrumentalist and an orchestra. 84

Concerto grosso A multi-movement work contrasting a small instrumental group with a large group, generally associated with the Baroque period. 84

Concert overture An overture not associated with an opera or drama. 201

Consonance A group of simultaneous sounds that seems agreeable or restful. 21

Continuo (basso continuo) A bass line for keyboard in which the player is given only a succession of single notes and other symbols from which to fill out the remainder of the harmony. Also the instruments that play that part. 172

Contour The shape or outline of a melody. 19

Corrido A narrative song of Mexico. 148

Counterpoint Two or more melodic lines occurring at the same time. 20

Countersubject The contrasting theme in a fugue. 106

Cyclical form The appearance of a theme from one movement in another movement of a multi-movement work. 75

Development (1) The manipulation of themes; (2) the section in sonata form devoted to the development of themes. 70

Dissonance A group of simultaneous sounds that seems to be disagreeable or unpleasant. 21

Dixieland A jazz style for a small group of players and containing two beats per measure and a rather fast tempo. 272

Doctrine of affections The Baroque practice of attempting to project states of feeling and ideas in music. 172

Dominant chord A chord built on the fifth degree of a major or minor scale. 22

Double (1) A variation of a stylized dance; (2) the addition of a different instrument or voice on a part. 105

Double exposition A version of sonata form used in concertos in which the first exposition features the orchestra and the second the soloist. 86

Double stops The sounding of two different pitches simultaneously on a string instrument. 35

Drone A low, continuous sound that lasts throughout a piece. 144

Dynamics The quality of loudness in music. 27

Embellishment The addition of melodic figures and ornaments to a melody. 19

Equal temperament A system of tuning in which all intervals are adjusted to divide the octave into 12 equal parts. 172

Ethnic music Music that is characteristic of a particular group of people. 142

Exoticism A phase of romanticism that draws on scenes from the Orient and Middle East. 206

Exposition (1) The opening section in sonata form 70; (2) the opening section of a fugue. 107

Fantasia A short, free-sounding instrumental work. 98, 107

Figured bass A shorthand system of numerals and accidentals used in the Baroque for indicating chords. 172

Finale (1) The concluding movement of some musical works; (2) the last piece in an act of an opera. 73

Fine arts Art areas in which objects are created only for the psychological satisfaction that people find in them. 4

Folk music The music of the common people of an area. 142

Form The pattern or plan of a musical work. 29

Free form jazz A sophisticated type of jazz containing few stylistic guidelines. 273

Frets Metal strips on the fingerboard of guitars and similar instruments that help the player in finger placement. 47

Fugue A composition in which the main theme (subject) is presented in imitation in several parts. 106

Gregorian chant The liturgical chant of the Roman Catholic Church. 153

Harmony The simultaneous sounding of several pitches. 21

Homophony A texture consisting of a line of melody and accompaniment. 23, 170

Improvisation Music that is made up on the spot, usually according to guidelines. 144

Incidental music Music composed to be performed in conjunction with a drama. 201

Interval The distance between two pitches. 17

Invention A short contrapuntal piece for keyboard. 107

Inversion (1) Turning a melody upside down, so that an ascending interval descends and vice versa 246; (2) rearranging the notes in a chord so that its basic note is no longer on the bottom. 74

K. Designation for Ludwig Köchel, the man who assigned numbers to Mozart's compositions. 104

Key (1) See **Tonality;** (2) the portion of an instrument that is manipulated by the player's fingers. 36

Kyrie The first standard portion of all Masses. 153

Leitmotiv A motive or theme that is associated with a particular character or idea, especially in the music of Wagner. 127

Libretto The text of an opera or oratorio. 121

Lied The German term for art song. 56

Liturgy A prescribed text for worship. 153

Madrigal A free, secular, imitative work for voices. 160

Major chord A three-note chord in which the distance from the lowest note to the middle note is two whole steps, and from the middle to the highest is one and a half steps. 21

Mass The celebration of Holy Communion in the Roman Catholic Church. 153

Melody A series of consecutive pitches that form a unified and coherent musical entity. 16

Meter The pattern created by stressed and unstressed beats. 25

Microtone An interval of less than a half step. 144

Minor chord A three-note chord in which distance from the lowest note to the middle note is a step and a half, and from the middle to the highest is two whole steps. 21

Minuet and trio A three-part form in the three-beat meter and style of a minuet. 72

Modes The non-major/minor scale patterns that can be played on the white keys of the piano. 18

Modulation Changing the tonal center as the music progresses, usually without a break. 22

Monophony A single unaccompanied melodic line. 23

Motet (1) The Gothic motet combined phrases from Gregorian chant with complex melodic and rhythmic relationships 156; (2) the Renaissance motet was a polyphonic, sacred composition for voices. 159

Motive A short melodic or rhythmic fragment that achieves structural importance through its frequent recurrence. 19

Movement A large, independent section of an instrumental composition. 18, 68

Musique concrète Natural sounds that are recorded on tape and modified by a composer. 49, 253

Mute A device for muffling or dampening the sound of an instrument. 35

Octave A pitch that has twice or half the frequency of vibration of another; usually the two pitches carry the same letter designation. 17

Octave displacement Using a note with the same letter name as the original but in another octave. 246

Op. (Opus) "Work," usually with a number to show the order in which the composer's works were written. 41

Opera A drama set to music, with its lines sung with orchestral accompaniment. 119

Oral tradition The process in which music is preserved by people hearing some music, remembering it, and then performing it for someone else. 142

Oratorio A sizable work for chorus, soloists, and orchestra, usually on a religious topic, that is performed without scenery, costumes, or acting. 60

Ostinato A short, persistently repeated melodic or rhythmic figure. 29

Pandiatonicism Selection of chords without regard for traditional harmonic functions. 217

Passacaglia A melodic ostinato in the lowest-pitched part that is repeated throughout an entire work. 30

Passion An oratorio based on Jesus' Good Friday suffering according to one of the four Gospels. 175

Pentatonic scale A five-note scale, usually in the pattern of the black keys on the piano. 144

Phrase A rather short, logical segment of music, comparable to a clause or language. 27

Pitch The perceived highness or lowness of a musical sound, largely determined by the frequency of its sound vibrations. 16

Polymeter The presence of two different meters at the same time. 26

Polyphony Music in which two or more melodies of approximately equal importance occur at the same time. 23, 155

Polyrhythm Several different rhythmic patterns occurring simultaneously. 26

Polytonality Several tonal centers existing at the same time. 217

Prelude (1) A short instrumental work; (2) a piece to be played as an introduction. 107

Program music Instrumental works associated by the composer with some extramusical idea or object. 31, 200

Progressive jazz A sophisticated form of jazz involving dissonant chords, usually for a big band. 272

Raga A melodic formula found in the music of India. 145

Ragtime A forerunner of jazz, usually in a march-like style for piano and containing a decorated righthand part and many syncopated rhythms. 269

Range The upper and lower pitch limits of a voice or instrument. 18

Recapitulation The section of sonata form in which the themes from the exposition are heard again. 71

Recitative A style of singing that covers its text in an economical and direct way and is designed to be similar to the natural inflections of speech. 55

Register The general level of pitch in a melody. 18

Requiem The funeral Mass of the Roman Catholic Church. 175

Retrograde The reverse version of a melody or tone row—what is first is now last, etc. 246

Rhythm The sensation of motion in music; a factor regulated by the duration and strength of the various sounds. 24

Rhythmic modes The constant repeating of certain rhythmic patterns similar to the poetic meters of today. 155

Rococo The decorative, light style of eighteenth-century European courts. 178

Rondo The appearance of the theme three or more times with contrasting portions between its appearances. 87

Round The same melody sounded in strict imitation at two slightly different times in a short song. 20

Rubato A performer's slight deviation from strict interpretation of rhythm. 194

Scale A series of pitches that proceeds upward or downward according to a prescribed pattern. 17

Scherzo The third movement of some symphonies and other such works, usually in a playful style. 75

Sectional forms Musical forms built around somewhat distinct portions or sections. 29

Secular music Music that is worldly or non-sacred. 155

Sequence Repetition of a phrase or figure at another pitch level from the original. 171

Serialism The application of the principles of tone-row music to other aspects of music such as dynamic levels and articulations. 252

Sforzando A loud, accented note or chord. 74

Sinfonia An introductory movement to a longer work such as cantata or opera. 107

Sonata (1) A multi-movement work for piano and another instrument, or for piano alone 96; (2) a form consisting of an exposition section, followed by a development and a recapitulation. 30, 69

Strophic song Song in which several verses of words are sung to the same melody. 54

Subject The main theme of a fugue. 106

Suite (1) A collection or group of stylized dance music 104; (2) a collection of portions of a larger work such as a ballet or opera. 134

Swing Jazz arranged for bands of 18 or so players; usually created to be danced to, thus the type of rhythm called "swing." 272

Symphony A sizable multi-movement work for orchestra. 68

Syncopation The displacement of an accent so that it occurs where it is not normally expected or it is lacking where it is expected. 26

Tala A rhythmic cycle of beats found in the music of India. 146

Tempo The speed of the beats in a piece of music. 24

Ternary form Three-part form, *A B A*. 55

Terraced dynamics Levels of loudness that change abruptly from one level to another. 172

Texture The basic setting of the music: monophonic, homophonic, or polyphonic. 23

Theme A central melody in a composition. 17

Theme and variations A work consisting of a theme and altered versions of that theme. 29

Through-composed song Song that contains no repetition of lines of music. 56

Timbre Tone quality or tone color. 27

Toccata A flashy work, usually for a keyboard instrument. 107

Tonality Centering pitches around a particular pitch. 22

Tone poem (symphonic poem) A sizable orchestral work of program music. 201

Tone-row music (also *twelve-tone* or *dodecaphonic*) A composition based on a formula that uses each of the 12 tones of a scale including all the half steps before a tone can be used again in the row. 244

Tonic chord A chord built on the first degree of a major or minor scale. 22

Transposition Rewriting a piece of music at a different level of pitch but retaining the same intervals among the pitches. 18

Trill An ornament with a rapid alternation between the written note and the note immediately above it. 112

Vibrato Slight, rapid fluctuations of pitch. 35

Virtuoso A technically skilled performer. 61

Wind ensemble A wind band that employs sparser instrumentation than the traditional band. 45

Index

Homophony, 23, 170
Honegger, Arthur, 225–226
Hopkinson, Francis, 258
Hovhaness, Alan, 265
Humanism, 157–158

Imitation, 160
Impressionism, 208–209
Impromptu, 190
Improvisation, 144
    in Baroque music, 173
    in jazz, 271
    in non-Western music, 144
Incidental music, 201
Indian music, 145–146
Instruments, musical:
    African, 148–149
    Afro-American, 150–151
    band, 41
    Baroque, 172–173
    brasses, 37–39
    folk, 46–47
    in future, 248–249
    Indian, 146
    keyboard, 45–46
    orchestral, 34–41
    percussion, 39–40
    popular, 47–48
    in Renaissance, 162
    in Romantic music, 192–193
    strings, 34–36
    suggested works, 44
    in twentieth-century music,
        217–218
    woodwinds, 36–37
Intervals, 17
Invention, 107
Inversion, 74, 246
Isaac, Heinrich, 166
Ives, Charles, 261–262
    "Autumn," 22, 23, 58

James, Harry, 272
Janáček, Leoš, 226
Jannequin, Clément, 166
Jazz, traditional, 269–273
    development of, 271–273
    variations in, 30
Jefferson, Thomas, 180
Jefferson Starship, 273
Jewish music, 147
"John Henry," 149

Joplin, Scott, 269–270
"Joy," 5–6
Joyce, James, 232
Jullien, Louis A., 268

Kafka, Franz, 232
Kandinsky, Wassily, 232
Kay, Ulysses, 266
Keats, John, 187–188
Kenton, Stan, 272
Key. *See* Tonality
Key, Francis Scott, 260
Key, on instrument, 36
Keyboard, pitches on, 282–283
Key signature, 282
Klee, Paul, 232
Köchel, Ludwig, 80
Kodály, Zoltán, 226
Kokoschka, Oskar, 232
Krenek, Ernst, 266
Krummhorn, 162
Krupa, Gene, 272
Kyrie, 153–154

Lamartine, Alphonse de,
    "Méditations Poétique," 201
Lasso, Orlando di, 158, 166
Leadbelly (Hudie Ledbetter), 270
Leger lines, 282
Leitmotiv, 127
LeJeune, Claude, 166
Lenau, Nikolaus, 113, 202–203
Leonardo da Vinci, 157
Leutgeb, Ignaz, 85
Lewis, Jerry Lee, 273
Libretto, 121
Lied, lieder, 56
Lind, Jenny, 260
Listening:
    attitude for, 7–8
    Guides for, 9, 12–13
    habits in, 12–13
    improvement in, 9–13
    memory in, 9
    reactions during, 11–12
    Study Guide and Scores, 13
    tests of, 13
    types of, 8–9
Liszt, Franz, 117, 191, 207
    Les Préludes, 201–202
    Mephisto Waltz, 113–116
Liturgy, 153

Loeffler, Charles Martin, 261
Lorca, Federico García, 255
Luening, Otto, 267
Lully, Jean-Baptiste, 177
Lute, 161, 162
Luther, Martin, 174
Lutoslawski, Witold, 255
Lynn, Loretta, 275

MacDowell, Edward, 261
MacLeish, Archibald, 249
Madrigal, 65, 160, 162–164
Mahler, Gustav, 198
Major/minor system, 170–171
Major scale, 18
Malevich, Kasimir, 247
    White on White, 248
Mallarmé, Stéphane, 209
Mamas and the Papas, The, 273
Manuals, 46
Marc, Franz, 232
Marenzio, Luca, 162, 167
Mariachi, 148
Mason, Lowell, 260
Mass, 153–154
Mazurka, 190
Measure, 25, 283
Meck, Nadezhda von, 138
Melody, 16–20
    chord outlines in, 19
    in Classical music, 182
    contour of, 19
    embellishment of, 19
    in impressionistic music, 209
    in jazz, 270
    in non-Western music, 143–
        144
    in Renaissance motet, 160
    in twentieth-century music,
        216
Mendelssohn, Felix, 191, 196
    and Bach's music, 117, 196
Menotti, Gian-Carlo,
    The Medium, 128–130
Messiaen, Olivier, 252
Meter, 25
Meter signatures, 283
Metronome, 284
Michelangelo:
    David, 157–158
Microtones, 144
Milhaud, Darius, 225, 249
Miller, Glenn, 272

To the owner of this book:

I hope that you have enjoyed *A Concise Introduction to Music Listening*, Third Edition. I would like to know as much about your experience as you would care to offer. Only through your comments and those of others can I learn how to make this a better text for future readers.

School _____ Your Instructor's Name _____

1. What did you like the most about the book? _____

_____

_____

2. What did you like least about the book? _____

_____

_____

3. Were any chapters assigned in part or not at all? If so, which ones weren't? _____

_____

4. How useful were the Listening Guides? _____

_____

5. How useful did you find the glossary for understanding new terms? Do you recommend its expansion? _____

_____

_____

6. In the space below or in a separate letter, please let me know what other comments about the book you'd like to make. (For example, were any chapters *or* concepts particularly difficult?) I'd be delighted to hear from you!

Optional:

Your Name _____ Date _____

May Wadsworth quote you, either in promotion for *A Concise Introduction to Music Listening* or in future publishing ventures?

Yes _____ No _____

Thanks!

Charles R. Hoffer

FOLD HERE

CUT PAGE OUT

FOLD HERE

FIRST CLASS
PERMIT NO. 34
BELMONT, CA

BUSINESS REPLY MAIL
No Postage Necessary if Mailed in United States

Charles R. Hoffer
Wadsworth Publishing Company
10 Davis Drive
Belmont, CA 94002